Available Now: The Testament of the Ages

Volume 1

THE SHADOWS OF DRAGONSWAKE

In a time when the universe was old, a lone world was born, free from the cosmic struggles of the Amaranthi. Holding domain over these lands were magnificent creatures who called themselves *Dragons*. But even here, upon this isolated world, the *Dark* crept into the hearts of some, and the seeds of tyranny were sown.

War came to the Children of Dragons, and through it all one man stood as witness to the first age of the world—the First Awakened Son, Alak'kiin. As conflict erupts across the once perfect lands of Sylveria, Alak'kiin will be awakened to his own place amongst the divided people—those who align with the *Light*, and those who dwell darkly in *The Shadows of Dragonswake*.

Volume 2

THE EXILES OF GOAB'LIN

Alak'kiin awakens at the end of the 2nd Age of Sylveria and he finds that a new conflict is about to erupt—a war of liberation for the good people of Sylveria. With striking success over the enemy, a new struggle soon ensues, for the people of Sylveria and the Dragons have very different ideas on how the Dark should be contained. But with little recourse, the people are subjected to the Dragons' will, and the enemy is allowed to persist.

Through another age still, Alak'kiin endures, learning through his transcendent journeys what it means to become a Child of the Light, and what it means to have faith beyond the apparent. In this, he will seek to find out how the people might finally overcome *The Exiles of Goab'lin*.

Volume 3

THE LAST WORDS OF ALAK'KIIN

Awakening during the end of the 4th Age, Alak'kiin finds that his purpose is about to be revealed as ancient prophecies begin to be fulfilled. Now, Alak'kiin and the heroes of the 4th Age must strive to overcome the ruinous seeds planted long ago and to bring all things of the past unto their final consummation.

Together they will pass through the frozen wastes of this dying world to make a final stand against the legions born in the fires of darkness.

And in the end, Alak'kiin will confront his greatest enemy—a rogue goddess written into existence by the very words of the Numen himself. And in that moment will be spoken *The Last Words of Alak'kiin*.

Learn more at ***power-in-words.net***

THE TESTAMENT OF THE AGES
VOLUME 1

THE SHADOWS OF DRAGONSWAKE

BY

CHAD J BLANCHARD

THE TESTAMENT OF THE AGES
VOLUME 1

THE SHADOWS OF DRAGONSWAKE

BY

CHAD J BLANCHARD

Copyright © 2024
Chad J Blanchard
All Rights Reserved

ISBN:
978-0-9759717-2-7

There is Power in Words!

Power-in-Words.net

TABLE OF CONTENTS

PREFACE

TO THE TESTAMENT OF THE AGES

SALUTATIONS

Greetings:

I am a child of the Light, awakened long ago to record the events of the ages of the world. I have sometimes been called the Thirteenth *Naiad*, for reasons that will soon be understood.

Since the drawing of my first breath I have been filled with the love of the Numen, who is the god of all things good. For this, I have chosen to follow the path of the Light, and it has been given unto me to write the pages of these books so that the things still fresh in the collective memory of the people will not be forgotten as time carries on and new ages emerge.

Many of the words I have recorded in these volumes are accounts of the things I have witnessed throughout the ages, while others are truths shown to me in dreams and visions. Others still are compilations of events as revealed to me by the blessed *Keepers*, things that I have verified through prayer and supplication to be the truth. I have compiled these books at the conclusion of the *Fourth Age,* for it has been through these eons that I have served as a messenger of the Light, seeking always the arrangement of faith, hope, and love within the hearts of all good people. I have written these books so that it may always be understood that just as time devours all things, so too can it heal all transgressions.

As you read the pages of these books you will see that I have witnessed much throughout my life—both the triumphs of the Light, and its failures. My position as a watcher of the ages has been both a great benediction and the profession of my faith, for my time has been filled with great trials. Nevertheless, I regret nothing, for the fires I have passed through have made me alike to an unbreakable sword refined in the forges of tribulation.

But just as my position has been a blessing, so too has it been a curse; for to have witnessed all things has been to see the cumulative pain and suffering of all times, to see the passing of countless people whom I once adored, and to witness as a land so enchanting as to be called *Sylveria* fell to ruin under the dark onslaught of war. Still, I have accepted all of this as the price of my gift.

Now, so that you might understand all things of these latter times, and all things that might come to be, you must first understand what came before—that which has led the world into its present condition. For this, I have divided my writings into three separate volumes.

The first of these—*The Shadows of Dragonswake*—is my recollection of the ancient history of not only the world of Sylveria but also of the entirety of the cosmos, for it is in those high places that all things truly began. The things that are revealed in this account are the essential foundation of the remaining volumes. Time is weaved together such that all things that have been will make their mark upon all things that will be. The past foretells the future, at least to the measure afforded by fate.

The second volume first recounts the events of the 2nd Age of Sylveria, encompassing the respective circumstances of those times. Following this is a record of the indomitable events of the 3rd Age of Sylveria as witnessed by myself. I have titled these two accounts as *The Exiles of Goab'lin*.

And lastly, the third volume details the culmination of all things as foretold in the first two volumes. Here are the chronicles of not only my own experiences, but also the accounts of those whom I came to love in the times when this reckoned age was consummating. Here, in this book, you will find the stories of the greatest heroes who have ever lived, and the legacies they will undoubtedly leave behind when their own lives pass away, new ages dawn, darkness rises again, and when the good people of the world are tested once more.

These are the first of my words—the first words of Alak'kiin. All that I have written is the truth; there is no deceit within these pages, and my words are not subject to misinterpretation. Although time does indeed change all things and history is written by men with narrow vision, these passages will remain true for all time. Any who read these words will be blessed with knowledge, and any who seek to pervert the truth will not prevail.

Glory and praise to the Numen, to righteousness, and to the Light.

THE SHADOWS OF
DRAGONSWAKE

"For straight ahead did the green moon Imrakul shine as fiercely upon Nefaria as did Aros shine upon Sylveria. But all things were reversed, for whereas Aros gave light to the darkness, Imrakul here gave darkness to the light, shining in a bleak and vacant obscurity that drove the light away, leaving only a trace of radiance upon the dark lands."

THE BOOK OF

AWAKENING

THE AWAKENING OF ALUNEN

When Alunen came into being, both language and a certain understanding were already awakened within her mind. Through no experience had she gained this understanding, so far as she could recall, but all of the elementary perceptions came into her as she took her first breath of air, which was the breath of life and the gift of existence.

Her eyes opened and she saw for the first time a world of beauty, with shades of every color, of landscapes and skies, hills and valleys, plants and clouds, and earth and the heavens above. Although in the very first moments of her awakening Alunen thought that these things seemed familiar, this sense quickly faded away and she was left wondering what was happening, for she had no recollection of what had brought her here to this moment, and to this place.

Yet even without the knowledge of what had come before there was a fundamental understanding of the facts of her existence and how she could perceive it. For she knew that *sky* was the word given to describe the blueness that covered the endless range above; she knew that the glistening blades of *grass* beneath her feet were the softness of the growth of a kind of life that was different. She knew that it was a *hill* that she stood upon; she discerned a difference between this hill and others, and she knew that to the north and south these hills gave way to something larger—great masses of stone that towered above.

Alunen knew that these huge protruding stones that cut the skyline to both the north and south were called *mountains*, and she knew that she stood in the foothills of these mountains overlooking a great *valley*. She knew many things, but not all things did she really understand.

Alunen knew that she existed, but did not know why; she knew that there must be a reason for her being, that she was surely the product of some intent; but just what that purpose might be was truly beyond her comprehension.

The world around her seemed inconceivably huge, the heavens above unfathomable, and great spheres of light shown down upon the land from the sky above. She knew that these great and glowing orbs were called *suns*, but she did not know why it was that they should shine their light down upon all things.

She could not explain this, for she did not comprehend any but the simplest castings of the world around her. But Alunen did understand beauty; and with all that her eyes beheld she was in awe. And she knew that everything before her was not a simple creation of either accident or insignificance, but surely of some divine intent, for every cut of the land and mountains and skies was shaped to appeal to her every sense.

Alunen stood upon a hill that overlooked a valley, near to the southern range of mountains, and a soft breeze blew past, cooling her golden skin, flittering through her shining hair, and drying her hazel eyes ever so slightly. She was naked, but she did not know it, for the thought that a woman might want to cover herself had not yet been realized.

She held up her hands and gazed at them, wondering what they were and why she had them, and then she wondered what all she might be able to accomplish with them. She moved her fingers all together, then one by one, and then traced the shape of her arms and body with the tips. Her sense of feeling was fully dawned in those moments, and she knew that she was a being who could interact with the world around. She looked over her own body, from her breasts to her thighs and torso, to hips, legs and feet, and she knew that she too—like the world around her—was a creation of beauty.

Then Alunen took her hands and moved them to her face and felt the softness of her skin, the shape of her lips and nose, ears and eyes, and she could imagine what she looked like. When her fingers passed through her hair she thought it was alike to the grass of the fields, a golden covering for her own beautification.

Alunen was alone, and though she understood what this meant, it did not trouble her. She knew that she was the only one of her kind here on this hill, and anywhere within sight. But she wondered if there might be others like her somewhere else in the vast world, too far away for her eyes to see, perhaps beyond the hills, perhaps hidden in the valleys between them or the tall grasses upon other rises.

Soon after having examined herself and her surroundings, rising utmost in Alunen's mind was a desire to explore, for she longed to learn of the many things that were before her. She knew she could not reach the skies above, or the heavens or the shining suns—for some force kept her bound to the earth—but she knew that she could move across the land…

So Alunen took her first step, to the north, down the gentle hillside. The grass pricked at her feet, but it did not hurt. It was soft like the hair upon her head, and the pleasure it gave brought the first smile to her face. Step after step, her smile endured, and the pleasure of this existence greatly increased. Soon she was no longer walking, but running, the wind teasing her skin; small flowers and petals and pollens sundered and stirred about as she bound across the glorious landscape.

Her dash disturbed other things too, small creatures that dwelled there in the grasses and shrubs of the hillside—things that must surely be alive like her, though not of the same appearance. Insects and small furry things that were the animals of this great creation all scurried or flittered about, startled, though not frightened, by her rapid descent down the slope. Rabbits and Mice and Squirrels and Weasels darted about, some in front of the woman, some behind, and some ran alongside, themselves excited over this newly awakened being. Beetles and Bees and Butterflies buzzed about, Birds fluttered overhead, and nature was alive in the moments when Alunen took the first run.

She was like the wind, only faster; she was like these other creatures, only made greater; and she was of the same creation as all of the beautiful things around, yet she knew that she was lord over them all.

Alunen laughed with joy, and it was pleasing to her ears. Still she ran, down the verdant slope, the other elements of nature gliding and fluttering, drifting and scattering about as she ran without any intent other than to make this great pleasure endure.

By the time she reached the bottom of the hill, Alunen was short on breath and an aching seized her breast, yet even this was pleasurable, for it was a new experience of her existence. There at the base of the hill that later became known as *Alunen's Run,* amongst a small myriad of colorful flowers, she dropped to the ground, resting her arms on her bent knees, breathing deeply to restore her constitution, for she instinctually knew that when her breath became so strained, she had but to rest a while to recover.

Slowly her breath returned, and when she was certain that she had recovered enough to rise and run again, Alunen instead threw her body back and lay upon the soft field, staring now up at the cerulean and crimson sky as the great spheres that were the suns hovered freely in the heavens.

To stare at these suns burned her eyes, but she could see that they consumed only a small part of the great expanse of the sky, and there was much there in the firmament for her to ponder; for now she realized, as she considered the suns, that each of them was of a different color and that one of them seemed to have moved ever so slightly in relation to the world around. One of them cast a golden glow, while the other was blue, and she could distinguish the warmth and light of each of them upon her bare skin. They were both hung in the eastern sky, the gold was nearer and by far brighter. Together they cast a purplish hue upon the world below.

And then, looking westward, she saw—though it had gone unnoticed before—that a third great sphere was suspended in the heavens as well, this one a deep green, but its light was not nearly as intense as the others. This she knew to be a moon, for it seemed to cast no light of its own. While the suns seemed occupied in the east, the moon sat lonely in the west. Although these heavenly bodies were magnificent and powerful—casting their light upon the world—she knew that these were just other elements of nature, parts of this great creation.

White clouds drifted across the skyline, west to east, moved perhaps by an unseen hand, perhaps by the wind. Far above her, yet below the clouds, great Birds moved in formations, and though they were too distant to see clearly, Alunen supposed that they must be at least as large as was she and that they were watchers of the world and seers of many things that she could not, for their domain was in the high places.

Then something profound and magnificent came into view: out of the east it came, soaring near to the ground... a great and glorious thing... a creature larger than anything she had seen thus far... drifting swiftly through the air was a beast so large that she was made humble by its greatness, for as she herself was lord over the small animals of the world, so too must this creature be lord over the whole of the creation.

It was golden in color, like her own hair, with great legs that dangled as it flew upon giant wings, a tail that trailed behind and a giant neck that extended out before it. Scales covered its entire body, reflecting the light of the suns, glistening nearly as bright, but never stinging Alunen's eyes. She arose from the ground then, her mouth draped open in awe, her eyes wide to take in the wonder.

The golden creature soared closer still, moving even more swiftly than she had run, and a great gust of wind surged as it passed by, stirred by those great wings that flapped along both sides of the giant body, waving through the air with commanding ferocity that told Alunen that this magnificent being must surely be the one who had intended all of creation, so great was its benevolent might.

And as it soared past she was so overcome with the creature's beauty, so intensely awestruck, that she actually felt a surge of absolute peace at the sight, for while the great creature seemed oblivious to her presence, Alunen could clearly see that at the forefront of the great neck of the beast was a head so tremendous and eyes so big and serene that she fell to her knees, not in distress, but because she felt not worthy to even stand in its presence.

It was like a great reptile with two muscular legs at the back of its body with gigantic taloned feet, and two massive arms at the front, each with enormous clawed hands. Each of the talons was at least the size of her entire body, or so she supposed. Upon its face was a stout jaw with giant teeth, sharp and fearsome and divine. Its eyes were great green spheres that might as well have been suns in themselves, so great was their size, and each of them was split by a black slit.

As the creature set itself westward, soaring past Alunen, its tail waved behind, nearly as long as the rest of its body, and she noticed that all along its spine and tail were great ridges of bone that appeared stronger than the mountains that lined the valley. In all that Alunen could see of this magnificent creature she was mesmerized by its glory.

As the giant beast moved onward, Alunen remained on her knees, staring, until it eventually reached the vanishing point of her sight, far to the west. And there, towering high above distant plains, there was an immense lone mountain that had before gone unnoticed, and it tore up through the earth, reaching for the sky.

And when the creature was entirely out of sight and its mesmerizing presence had faded away, Alunen uttered her first spoken word upon this world, and it was *"Dragon"*, for she somehow knew that this was what it was called.

As she heard herself speak her first word, there was excitement in her heart, a beaming delight that she felt in all aspects of her being, and all of her perceptions were intensified, for now she was not entirely alone in the world, and she knew that she must learn more about this creature.

With the Dragon now out of site and her mind still filled with wonder, Alunen looked about, for here she had a whole new perspective of the world, a reason to explore, for she very much wanted to see what other fantastic things there might be.

At the base of Alunen's Run, where she had fallen to her knees and had witnessed the passing of the Dragon, just to the east, there rose another hill that was even larger than hers. A ledge crowned this hill and went around the south face, around the western edge, then back to the east across the northern side. She considered climbing to this ledge so as to see what might be farther to the east, hidden by this tall mound. But there she thought she saw something... perhaps a creature that might not be unlike her, for it moved not on four legs like all of the animals she had seen thus far, but upon two. Yet as soon as she glimpsed it, it disappeared to the north and east side of the hill. And she wondered then if this person, whoever it might be, might have seen the Dragon as well.

Alunen thought of following this stranger, to find out who it might be and what it might know, but she instead reasoned that surely time would reveal all things and that there was no hurry in finding them. So she turned her attention elsewhere, to the valley floor on which she now stood, for since the sighting of the Dragon she had paid it little mind. And so she looked around her once again, to take in all that was before her.

Coursing through the great valley, from east to west, cutting the landscape, was a great river that traced the rises and falls of the terrain.

Other smaller rivers drained from the mountains and fed the great river from both the north and the south. Directly ahead, close to the northern mountain range, was a gathering of green trees so dense that from this distance she could neither see within it, nor even distinguish one tree from another. And upon the lower face of the mountains, where the stone met with the hills, she could see dark holes within the rock that were surely caves. Her eyes fixed on them for a short time, though she did not know why, but soon she turned her attention to the west.

To the west, the great river continued on for a distance before finally turning southward and disappearing around the mountains. On the north side of the river the valley fell down onto the great plains, and further still was the lone mountain that she had seen earlier when watching the Dragon disappear. Alunen was very curious about this mountain and wondered if it might be where the magnificent creature had gone.

To the north and east was the greater extent of the valley. Great rolling hills lined the landscape, more of them to the north of the river than to the south. The two ranges of mountains traversed the edges of the valley until meeting in the east, at a place that was beyond the river's course and the extent of her vision.

Unsure what she desired to do next, Alunen turned her wonder-sparked eyes skyward once again, and as before, she noticed that the gold sun seemed to have moved a bit farther through the sky. The blue sun was stationary, and she could not perceive any change. The green moon appeared to have moved as well, just a bit further to the west.

Alunen did not know why it was that these heavenly bodies should move at all, but she shrugged rather than concern herself and decided that she would now climb to the eastern ledge of the other hill, and then to its top, for from there she might indeed see more than she could from atop the hill of her own awakening.

From where she stood there was a ravine that passed between the two hills that ran north to south and she began walking toward it, looking for a path to mount the ledged hill, for as she drew nearer to it, it seemed too steep for her to climb. After a short time, a third hill came into view, to the south of her, much smaller and with a gentle slope. She could see that this hill connected to her destination by way of a ridge between them, and that by going up there she could likely get to the ledge.

The deeper she traversed the ravine the darker it seemed to get, for the light-giving celestial bodies had left her view, blocked by the hills, and she was covered in shadow. The day had grown warmer and the shade was a comfort that she delighted in. The ground was damp and muddy as she passed through this gorge, for here the grass was thinner, and more of the earth shown through. And in the mud there were uncountable footprints pressed into the earth. Some were small, alike to the animals she had seen in the fields, while others were large, the product of the traipsing of some larger beasts that she had not yet seen. This filled her with excitement, for there must be some new creature still to discover.

But there was one set of footprints that was distinguishably different than all the rest, for when she saw it she noticed that it was nearly identical to her own. Herein Alunen became convinced that she was not alone in these hills, that there must at least be one other that was like her... but where had this stranger gone?

The footprints seemed to have come from the east, from the side of the ravine under which was the high ledge, moved forward to the place where Alunen examined them, then onward to the south, toward the gently sloped hill. Surely, she determined, this person had come this way, up the hill, across the ridge and onto the ledge where she had seen them. Eagerly then, she moved at a fast pace toward the hill, keeping her eyes on the tracks.

When she came to the end of the ravine, which was the convergence of the hills, she mounted the smaller hill swiftly, for it was not too steep at all. As she approached the top, she could see the ridge that would connect her to her destination. She followed the tracks across the ridge until she found her way onto the path. From there, Alunen could see to the west, where the pathway bent around to the north. And she could also see that the ledge continued on to the east, though it was much narrower and was covered with grass rather than plain soil. This path, she thought, would lead her to a higher point upon the hill, for it rose quickly as it bent around to the northeast. She decided that it was this path she would take, for before, this hill had blocked her view to the east, and she wanted to see that which was before hidden from her.

And when she reached the easternmost point of the hill, she saw even more beauty than she had imagined, for to the east, down below, there was a flatland that was traversed by a small river, which flowed into the greater river that divided the valley. Passing over this river was a wide land bridge, and upon the flatlands was a great herd of grazing beasts that were much larger than herself, though still nowhere even close to the size of the Dragon. Peaceful and gentle in appearance were these creatures, and Alunen decided that she would call them *Bison*, for in her mind the name seemed fitting. Standing upon four legs, the Bison were covered in dark hair and they seemed to be consuming the grass of the vast field below. They were thick-bodied animals with small tails and strong legs. Upon their foreheads protruded two small horns.

The Bison were numerous; Alunen guessed there to be several thousand at least, and they grazed upon the fields on both sides of the river, to the east and west of the land bridge. And she decided that she would call this river by the same name as the creatures.

From atop the hill upon which she stood, at the end of the path,

Alunen's gaze followed the Bison River as it cut through the landscape to the north where it drained into the great river; and as her attention flowed from there, back to the north and west, she could again see the small forest to the north and the caves upon the lower face of the mountains, three of them near to each other and a fourth further to the east. And though it seemed unlikely, Alunen thought that she might be able to see something curious—perhaps others like herself—emerging from these caves. But surely, she thought, it was too far away to really see.

And with that thought she was reminded of the one whom she might have seen upon the ledge that encircled the hill to the east, and of the footprints she had seen in the ravine. Alunen looked down the slope of the hill but could not see any sign of another person. And so she decided to climb up the steeper slope of the hill that was above the pathway, for from there, from that high point, surely she would be able to see everything that was happening in the valley.

Worn by an arduous climb, Alunen was again out of breath by the time she reached the peak of the hill. She lay down upon her back, and for a long time she gazed up at the sky, squinting when her eyes wandered too near the suns. All the while that she stared heavenward she noticed that the gold sun continued on its path across the sky, as did the moon, moving ever westward. But the blue sun held its place. And she wondered then if it might never move.

But that tranquil moment was broken by a great and thunderous roar that sounded from far away, from the west. Alunen rose, now sitting. It was a sound that she had not heard before, for thus far she had perceived only the gentle sounds of nature. It was not terrifying, but was a mighty resonance, and when it ceased several moments later, all of nature had been silenced. Alunen had not noticed beforehand how many sounds there were in nature—the breeze blowing past her, the insects buzzing in the air, animals scurrying about, the Bison grunting and moving heavily upon the ground. But now all these noises were vanquished, for they were quieted in reverence of the great and mighty roar.

Alunen leaped to her feet and turned to the west so that she might see what had let loose such an immense bellow. And there, in the valley below, not far from where she had first come to rest after running down the hill of her awakening, near to the point where two rivers met with the greater, she saw something marvelous; for there stood the great Dragon, its wings at its side, and with it were two others that were much alike in all ways, save for the glistening color of their scales. One of them was of a copper color, every bit as magnificent as the gold. The other was silver, as glorious as his companions. Each of the Dragons was splendid in every way, and Alunen was certain that if she were to come down from the hills and come face to face with these great creatures, she would surely learn much.

Without even first thinking to do so, Alunen ran again, for she knew the way back to that spot. When she came back to the south, where the ridge connected the two hills, she hurried across and then down the slopes that she had climbed before. From there, she traversed the ravine as quickly as she could, fearing that she might miss the Dragons if they decided to fly away. Her excitement was manifest in her appearance as she soared through the gorge, her feet barely touching the ground. The wind whipped her, so fast did she move, and her heart leaped; when she came further out of the ravine she could again see the Dragons and her focus remained intent upon them, for she simply had to get near, had to see them up close. Then she would know more, for within her was awakening a great sense of wonderment and mystery about the world around her.

Just what am I, exactly? And why am I here? Why have I been given the gift of life? And who brought me here, out of the darkness? These were but a few of the questions that parsed her thoughts as she moved onward, out of the ravine and into the valley.

Her heart throbbed and her skin became sticky with sweat as she came out of the ravine. A gentle breeze flared up and cooled her skin and dried the perspiration. By the time she had come fully into the valley her breath had expired once again and she could run no more. She could see that the Dragons were still perched upon the ground near the river junction, and though her sense of urgency was no less, Alunen knew that she had to rest.

She fell to the ground there amongst the sparse grass that grew in large patches, tall and vibrant in the fertile valley. There, lying amongst the lush growth, she worried at first that she might not recover soon enough to meet with the Dragons. So tired was her body that her vision grew faint, and she could only stare upward, breathing heavily. She could see neither the river nor the valley, neither the hills nor the mountains, but only a deepening blue sky.

When the faintest of her breath returned, she expended it not in trying to rise to resume her jaunt but instead upon laughing, for though the discomfort in her breast was nearly painful she found great humor in her own impatience; she also knew that this was unlikely to be the only opportunity that she would find to meet with the Dragons. For twice now she had seen them and it seemed that this valley must be a place they frequented.

Laughing still, Alunen tried to rise onto her elbows so that she might be able to see beyond the tall grass, but she could not, for too exhausted was her body still. She did not try to fight it but instead allowed herself to sink back into the grass. And then she lay still, waiting patiently for her strength to regenerate, her eyes closed.

With the images of the world now blocked by her eyelids, Alunen cleared her mind and listened; she could hear only her own breathing, heavy and harsh. But as the moments passed, she noticed that the sounds of nature were returning. And then Alunen could hear something new... voices, deep and powerful, not too distant and bellowing. She could not understand the words that were spoken, for they drifted from afar, carried perhaps upon the wind and muffled; or perhaps they were words incomprehensible, for they were those spoken by Dragons. Nevertheless, Alunen listened, for she found great authority simply in the thundering melody of their voices.

Her eyes were still closed, and her face was lit by the smile that had yet to fade since the moments after her awakening. She lifted her hands to her face and with her fingers felt the curve of her lips and she said, "*Dragon.*" She could feel the changes in the shape of her mouth as she spoke. "*Dragon,*" she said again. And then other words came to her; those she had only thought before, she now spoke. "*Sky*" and "*Mountain*" and "*Hill*" and "*Valley*"; these were those parts of language that were alive within her but which had before been words only in the confines of her mind. Now she could speak, and she felt certain that when she came face to face with the Dragons, she would be able to talk to them.

Alunen's breath had not fully returned, and so she continued listening to the distant voices rumbling in the valley and she traced the lines of her face—chin and cheeks, her eyes and ears. When she felt the shape of her ears, she wondered why it was that they should be pointed rather than rounded, or square, or some other shape. And she wondered aloud, "*Just what am I? And why is it that I am the way I am?*" Still she wondered at so many things but she felt certain that she would only find answers when she at last came face to face with the Dragons.

She moved her hands back to her sides, resting them on the ground, stretched out her legs and her entire body, and then was still. She smiled no longer, though not for lack of delight in these present moments, but only to relax the muscles of her face. Now she was at ease, in no great hurry, but instead content to enjoy the moment as she was in the last stage of her recuperation.

Alunen felt a sudden chill and she opened her eyes. She wasn't sure if it was a trick of her perception or if the lighting upon the world had shifted. She sat up and looked again at the sky. And once more she saw that the gold sun had continued its journey across the celestial sphere and was now closer. The blue sun retained its place in the far east. But the moon had changed...

Far to the west it was no longer a full sphere but seemed cut in half or obscured by something unseen in the distant sky. She wondered what in all of nature could cause something such as this. It was as if it were being swallowed up. And she was fascinated.

She did not know how long she sat there staring at the moon, but it was a sight that she thought most peculiar. And as she watched, the green moon grew smaller and smaller until it was only a tiny point in the far western sky. And then it vanished completely.

Alunen considered then that both the gold sun and the moon had been moving in the same direction—from east to west. Would the sun also be swallowed by the westward sky? And what might happen if it were to be vanquished as well? For it seemed to her that while the blue sun had its purpose and gave its fainter glow, the golden sun was the dominant bearer of light.

It was then that Alunen first realized a concept of time, for in the passing of the moments there was change before her. That which had been was not so anymore. And what would occur later, when more time still had passed? She could remember how the suns and moon had been before, in different places in the sky. This she understood to be the past—the way things had once been. Now, she dwelled in the present, where things were happening, and she understood that following the past and present there must be a future—a time when things would be more different still. She considered all of this, and although she knew these were simple concepts of her reality, and although she did not fully comprehend what it meant, she knew that time was simply a measurement of change.

Then Alunen was distracted by a tickle on her hand, pulling her out of her deep thoughts. Curious, she raised her hand to see what might be the cause of this new sensation. A small thing, an Insect, had come to rest on her skin. It was tiny and bright with a purple and red shell that separated into flittering wings, and she knew that the creature was here only for its own curiosity. Perhaps, she thought, it had seen her from a distance and thought to go to her, just as she was seeking the Dragons. Surely she must be as mysterious to this tiny creature as the Dragons were to her.

The Insect spread its wings wide and then flittered so fast that Alunen's eyes could no longer perceive them, save for the myriad of purple and red, now blended by the swift motion. Then the wings ceased in their buzzing, and then started again… in succession, the wings would hum and whirr, flitter and hiss as if the bug were trying to speak with the woman in some strange language. Again she smiled, for though there surely was some reason for this creature to behave this way, she could not begin to understand it, and she was fascinated. Then, as if frustrated, the tiny creature made a final whizz of its wings and took flight, and was then out of sight. Alunen laughed and said aloud, "Goodbye, little Flitterbug," giving the creature of her first close encounter a name that seemed fitting.

Her breath was nearly rejuvenated, but now Alunen was not quite ready to rise. Her thoughts were deep within the knowledge that was, moment by moment, accumulating inside of her. And she put her hand back to her side and closed her eyes once again. Now she just listened, motionless, alone, and content. She could no longer hear the deep and distant voices of the Dragons and she thought that they might have departed. But she did not concern herself with this, for she felt certain that just as the Flitterbug had found her, so too would she find the Dragons when the time was right.

Now she heard nothing save for the whispering wind through the tall grass and around the hills that were south of the great river. She could feel when clouds moved in front of the two suns, for the intenseness of their warmth lessened, and when they moved onward again, for the light cast from the heavens became warmer upon her bare skin once more. On occasion she could hear a nearby scurrying as some other curious creature moved through the vegetation, perhaps investigating her. She could smell a fragrance, pleasing and pure, that must surely come from the beautiful flowers that were scattered about the fields. Alunen's senses were fully awakened, and though she did not yet understand the reason for her existence, she felt an intuitive gratitude for the life she possessed.

Though her eyes remained closed, she could see the brilliant light of the gold sun through her eyelids, so bright did it shine, and as she considered so many things, she could see images of the past flashing through her mind's eye, projected there, upon the inside of her eyelids. This she understood to be her memory, her recollection of things that had been before. But so too did images come to be there that were of things she had not seen, that had not happened.

She saw as she approached the Dragons, even though she suspected they had already gone away, and she saw as the great creatures looked her over, and she felt excitement of what it would be like if these visions ever came to be. This experience, Alunen understood to be her imagination, and she wondered at this ability to perceive a future that was no longer possible into the visions of her mind.

Suddenly then, a shadow moved quickly over her... The light beyond her eyelids was no longer so bright and the imaginary images, both of things seen and those that had not happened, vanished, for something new was occurring. The shadow had covered her too quickly for it to have been clouds blocking the sun. Alunen's eyes burst open in excitement and she saw that someone stood above, someone much like her!

Blue eyes peered down from a being who was the same likeness as she, and Alunen looked not in alarm, but in wonder, for she immediately felt certain that this was someone of the same creation, for there was hair upon her head and the same pointed ears flanked the sides, poking out of long and curled deep brown strands of hair that were as beautiful as her own golden tresses.

Alunen rolled over, raising up on her arms and turning her head upward; the other woman moved back and lowered herself to the ground, crossing her legs as she sat, a pleasant smile upon her features. This other woman was indeed like her, for her skin was also a golden tint; there were curves upon her breast and she held the same shapes as Alunen herself. Moreso, her blue eyes revealed that she too was filled with intelligence and understanding. For this, Alunen surmised that if this were true, then she must also possess the ability to speak. And so she said, "I wondered if I was alone, here in this wonderful world."

"I wondered so too," the other said. "But then I saw you a while ago, running down the side of this hill and I knew I must find you."

"I went in search of you as well," Alunen replied. "If that was you who was upon the higher ledge of this other hill."

"It was me," the other woman said. "I was exploring, for it was upon that great rise that I awakened, some time ago, before the moon vanished in the west."

Alunen nodded and said, "Who are you?"

"I know only that I have a name, which is Sarak'den. But I do not know who or what I am, or *why* I am. I awoke some time ago. I have no memory of a time before that."

"Nor do I," Alunen said. "But I have a name as well, and it is Alunen. You are like me, are you not, Sarak'den?"

"I surely am. We are the same, save for the hair upon your head is golden and mine is like the earth beneath our feet. We are both beautiful, and I find your form and essence to be astonishing. It was this that drew me to you when I saw you from a distance. This and my curiosity, for I wondered why you were running so swiftly."

Alunen smiled at Sarak'den, taking her words as compliment and feeling the same way in regard to the other woman, for she was of the most appealing nature. She reached out slowly and touched Sarak'den's hand, tracing the lines of it until their fingers felt the others'. Then she said, "I was running because I saw a Dragon! One soared overhead a while ago. And then there were three standing and talking, not far from here. Did you see them?"

"I did not," Sarak'den said. "For I do not even know what a *Dragon* is. I have been spending my time admiring this valley and the rivers and wondering what else there might be beyond. Are these Dragons some great creature that might harm us, and that is why you ran... to escape?"

"No. I was not running from the Dragons, but toward them, for they are something much more magnificent than anything else in the valley. Surely you heard the mighty roar some time ago, for it echoed through the entire valley."

"I heard something, but I did not know what it was, for there was a little bug buzzing in my ear and by the time I got it out, I wondered if I had really heard it or if it was just the annoying little creature that had invaded my head!"

Alunen laughed at Sarak'den's description of the bug in her ear, for her frustration was evident. But she said, "You will understand when you see the Dragons. One of them was golden in color, like my hair, one was copper, like yours, and one was silver. Each of them was beautiful, and they were talking to one another down by the river as surely as you and I are now speaking."

Sarak'den nodded and turned her gaze northward. "Have you taken notice of the caves that are far to the north, at the base of those mountains?"

"I have, and I do not know why, but there is something that draws my attention to them, though I do not know what it is."

"Perhaps we are meant to journey there," Sarak'den suggested.

"Maybe. But I feel most compelled to find the Dragons, for I feel that if we find them they might just tell us what our purpose is and why we were awakened."

"I would very much like to see these Dragons," Sarak'den said, her eyes lighting up. "For when you said the word itself I felt as if there was greatness in it, and I can see that you hold these creatures in high esteem."

"They are beyond my ability to explain. I do not know if it is they who have awakened us or if they are just another great creature of this land. But I do know there is no reason to fear them."

"Where are they now?"

"As I said, they were by the river last I saw them, but I am certain that they have departed, for their voices have been silent and I do not feel their presence any longer. Earlier, when the golden Dragon flew overhead, it disappeared far to the west, near to that lone mountain upon the distant plains. Perhaps they have gone there."

"What should we do now?" Sarak'den asked. "And how should we find these Dragons?"

Alunen considered this for a long moment before saying, "We could go to the river and see what traces of them might remain. Perhaps we can discover more about them, maybe even where they went."

"Or perhaps they will return!"

Elated, the two women rose to their feet together and side by side they held one another's hand and began walking toward the river, where the Dragons had been. They walked without swiftness in their steps, for now neither of them was alone and they felt less urgency in discovering new things, for they had each found a companion in the other.

"Do you think there are others like us?" Sarak'den asked as they trekked through the grass-laden field of the southern valley.

To their perception, much time had passed since they had first met and begun their slow stroll northward; the remaining gold sun had continued its journey across the sky and was now nearly overhead. Still, the blue sun had not moved. And now, the purple hue that had been upon the land had brightened and was more of a golden shade. It was warmer now than it had been before. Although it was not an unpleasant feeling, it made both of the women uneasy, not for the heat, but in that the world was changing and they did not understand why.

"I do not know if there are others," Alunen said, ignoring a strange and unsettling feeling that was rising from her belly. "I awoke upon one hill and you upon another. Look around..." she stopped and turned back to the south and east and raised her free hand, pointing out over the region that was upon their side of the river. "There is a third hill between yours and mine. Perhaps another has awakened upon it, or elsewhere, and is now searching for us, or for the Dragons. Perhaps we will meet with them sometime soon."

Sarak'den frowned, the first such expression that Alunen had seen, and she had compassion, for she knew that it was sadness. She put her free hand upon Sarak'den's cheek, a soothing expression, and said, "There is an uneasy look upon your face. What is wrong? Is it the changing of the sun that makes you feel so? Is it the way that the moon has vanished from our sight?"

"I feel unsettled," Sarak'den said. "I do not know why. I have imagined that this vast world we inhabit was perhaps laid out for us—just you and me. But if there are others, this will not always be so. If there are others it might take away from us, for in you I have found a companion and I do not want others to take your affections. Even as we walk along in joy and wonder, I worry."

"But it was you and I who found each other first," Alunen said. "And I think it certain that there is a special bond between us, for we have been together now for more time than we were apart. Even if there are others, and even if they are as appealing as you, I will not find favor with them, for you are my first friend, and I love you."

Now Sarak'den's frown vanished, but it was not replaced with a smile as before. She said, "There are so many things that I do not understand, Alunen. Who or what are we? What is this beautiful land that is spread out as far as our eyes can see? Why do we not remember anything from before the time when we were awakened?"

"There is much I do not know as well. For I have wondered of late, as I think about how the moon was swallowed by the sky, what will happen if the golden sun is vanquished as well."

"There is a fear in my heart," Sarak'den said. "For there is so much more that is unknown than is known, and just as I long to understand, I worry that we might never have answers. As you said, what will happen if the gold sun leaves us as well? Surely this will happen. We were awakened some time ago, when we took our first breaths, and when the end of this day comes, what will replace it? Will we take our last breaths without ever knowing why we even were here?"

"Then let us find the Dragons before the day ends," Alunen said, now feeling concerned as well. "So that we will not fade away without at least knowing them. They can answer our questions, I am sure."

Sarak'den nodded and gripped Alunen's hand more tightly in her own. "Then let us continue on but hasten our pace through this valley so that we can learn what we may."

Together they walked onward toward the meeting of the rivers that traversed the valley.

When at last they reached the river, the golden sun had strayed further and now appeared overhead. It was the hottest part of this day thus far. Seeing that the Dragons were not there present amongst the brush and grass that grew upon the banks of the river, they sat down, now releasing the others' hand and wondering what to do next.

It was then, there upon the banks of the great river, that something new came into the view of the two women, something they had not seen before. For far to the north, rising high above and beyond the mountains, a darker line was traced across the sky, jagged and uneven, with great peaks and falls. It seemed as if there was a crack in the sky.

"What could that be?" Alunen wondered.

"I do not know," Sarak'den said. "But it fills me with perplexity, for what could such a thing be that it would cut the sky in two? It was not there before, I am certain. It is not alike to the clouds, even distant, but it is like something darkening from far away."

"It is like some dark landscape has appeared out of nowhere," Alunen added.

Sarak'den stared onward toward the north and said, "Look! The longer I stare the more pronounced the sight becomes. It is like mountains, far distant, beyond the edge of this world that can be seen. If indeed they are mountains they are steep and much different than these that line the valley."

Alunen agreed and wondered at just how big the world might be, for in her mind, the vastness of this creation extended only to all that her eyes could see. She had not considered before what might be on the other side of either of the ranges of mountains, or beyond the lone mountain that jutted up from the plains far to the west.

For long moments the women stared, speechless and in deep consideration. Neither of them could comprehend just how far the world might extend and it filled them with both wonder and disappointment, for they were not certain that they would ever get to see just how wholly magnificent this world might be.

Then, as the gold sun moved further, just past the center point of their position, a darkness fell upon them. It was not a darkness caused by a loss of light, but rather it was a darkening of their spirits. Whereas before they had felt a beaming hope and love for the world, they now sensed that there was something more, something distant, and something unpleasant. It seemed to draw the joy out of them, and they could not understand it.

Then, as they stared on in dismay, the distant anomaly began to fade, first to a dull line cutting the skyline, then into obscurity as it vanished completely. It seemed that either the sun had enabled them to see a massive and distant land covered in mountains, or that the faraway lands themselves had existed only for a short period of time.

The women stood and looked away from the north, for now that this mysterious sight had vanished, they were intent once again upon finding the Dragons. They both felt a greater urgency in this now, for the appearance and vanishing of this distant land reminded them that this was an ever-changing world, and they did not know how long they had left to find their purpose.

Together they looked around the bank of the river, and as they walked in different directions, searching for clues, Sarak'den suddenly stumbled and fell into a cleft in the ground. It was not deep, nor did she fall hard, for the soft grass caught her, and she giggled as she bounced on the thick growth. Alunen moved over to the edge, and stood looking down at Sarak'den, then around at the scene, her brow raised in a manner that her friend found curious.

"Be careful," Sarak'den warned. "For there is a ridge around the land right here where the ground is uneven." She was looking around as she talked, still lying on the ground. "What a strange way for the land to be shaped."

Alunen too was looking around and her eyes suddenly brightened, and she said, "It is not so strange, for this small dip in the ground is nothing natural. You are inside the footprint of a Dragon!"

Sarak'den rose quickly to look around. Alunen stepped easily into the giant imprint and together they walked along, tracing the shape of the great mark that was left by a Dragon.

"How big are these Dragons you saw?" Sarak'den said elatedly. "For this footprint must be four times the height of either one of us!"

"They appeared magnificently huge, but even I could not have imagined them to be so big as they must be. But this does not help us, for it gives us no indication of where they might have gone."

And so the women continued to look around. Near to the river, not far from the giant footprint, were patches of sagebrush and shrubs that stood taller than the women, and suddenly Alunen and Sarak'den were alarmed, for there came from within the shrubs a sudden rustling.

"Is someone there?" Sarak'den said loudly, but no one answered.

Alunen started toward the bushes, but Sarak'den did not move and grabbed her friend's hand, holding fast, even pulling her back, whispering, "Wait!"

Alunen looked from Sarak'den back to the bushes and said, "Whoever is there, you can come out, for we are here but for one reason, and that is to find a clue as to where the Dragons might have gone."

The bushes rustled again, and a soft voice sounded out from them, saying, "The Dragons have gone away, and I do not know to where."

"Will you come out?" Alunen asked. "For we would very much like to see you."

The vegetation parted a moment later and from within the thick foliage stepped another who was very much like Alunen and Sarak'den. Her skin was the same golden hue, her body was shaped like theirs, but her hair was the deepest black, and beautiful. There was a look of apprehension in her eyes.

"I am Alunen, and my dear friend is Sarak'den. These are the names that we have awakened with. Can you tell us yours?"

The other one kept her distance, for there was something that had overcome her some time ago that made her hesitant, fearful for a reason Alunen and Sarak'den could not discern. Still, she managed to say, "My name is Sveraden."

"Where do you come from?" Sarak'den asked. Sveraden shrugged, not understanding. "Where were you awakened? Have you come far since you came into being?"

Sveraden pointed eastward and said, "From the hill near the plains that are to the other side of those rises, where large beasts snort and snarl and try to eat your hair!"

Alunen suppressed a smile, for it seemed that Sveraden held within her a greater uncertainty of things unknown, for while she herself had been curious about the Dragons and awed by the Bison, this newcomer seemed uneasy.

"I saw those creatures as well, from a distance," Alunen said. "I call them *Bison*, but I did not go near them. You were close to them?"

Sveraden shivered, though the air about them was warm. She looked away and said, "I did... I awakened not far from them, and they took notice of me. One of them came to me, and I wanted to touch it, because I was curious. Then..." She paused, looking at the ground, and did not finish.

"What is it, Sveraden?" Alunen urged. "What happened? Did the beast hurt you?"

She shook her head, still hesitating, but finally spat out the words, "No! The dirty beast stuck out its tongue and licked my face. Then its tongue got *entangled* in my hair!"

Both Sarak'den and Alunen laughed. Seeing the delight that they took in her misfortune, Sveraden tittered as well, and now felt easy enough with them to draw closer. She said, "Just in case you get licked by a *Bison*, the water of the rivers will wash the slime away. Have you bathed in the waters yet?"

"No," both Alunen and Sarak'den said, raising their eyebrows, for it had not occurred to either of them that they might enter into it.

"It is cool and cleansing. It will wash the dirt off our skin. It is good to drink it, for it has a sweet taste. It is as pleasing to the tongue as the flowers are pleasing to the nose."

"Let us go into the river!" Sarak'den said excitedly, pulling on Alunen's hand, who did not protest. They went first to Sveraden, who did not move away, for she had grown to trust these women, and as they approached, Sarak'den took Sveraden's hand in her own, and the three women moved to the shore and into the water. Filled with new pleasure, the women were enlightened once more by the beauty of the world around them.

After bathing in the pure water, Alunen said to Sveraden, "I am wondering how long you were hiding... Were you in the brush when the Dragons were there?"

Sveraden replied, "I was. I came here after escaping from the Bison's lick. Soon I saw the giant creatures coming from the west, and I hid in the brush because I was scared they would try to lick me too. They were magnificent. Terrifying but magnificent! They appear huge from afar, but up close they are enormous beyond imagining. And when they speak, their words are not like ours, their voices make the air tremble, and everything about them exudes power and authority. The Dragons are wondrous creatures!"

"And *did* they try to lick you, as you feared?" Sarak'den wondered.

"No. I do not think they knew I was there, for to them I might have seemed as nothing more than one of these tiny Insects, small and insignificant.

"And you could not comprehend anything they were saying?"

"I could not, for I suppose it was a language of *gods*. But the tone of their voices held great beauty and passion."

Alunen explained, "We came here to the river to find the Dragons, for if you have not noticed, this is a world that is ever-changing. The moon vanished some time ago, far to the west. And we wonder what will happen if the gold sun leaves us as well, for what might we have if there is no light except that of the blue sun, which seems of a darker and cooler light? And so it is our thought to find the Dragons so that they might tell us what we are and why we are here. Can you tell us where they might have gone?"

"I do not know how you would talk to them, for as I said, their words are strange and are not like ours. But they took flight to the west, toward that distant pinnacle, that mountain that rises out of the plains."

Alunen looked westward and there her eyes remained, for though she had considered this mountain as the possible destination of the Dragons, she had in actuality paid it little mind. From this perspective, where she stood in the valley, she surmised that it must be the tallest of any mountain in the lands of this world. She explained to the others, "I have thought before that perhaps that is the home of the Dragons, and I think this is confirmed by your words, Sveraden, since twice now one of us has seen them going that way."

"But still, how will we talk with them?" Sarak'den asked. "If their words are so strange to us, then won't ours be strange to them?"

"Maybe," Alunen said. "But if they are as mighty and as grand as they seem, perhaps they can speak more than one way. Maybe what was heard before is just the words they use to each other."

"Indeed," Sveraden said. "Maybe they speak to the Birds as the Birds speak, and the Bison as the Bison speaks, and to us they will speak as we speak."

"Then there is only one way to find out," Sarak'den said. "And if they are at that mountain then that is surely where we are to go!"

And so the three women agreed that they would travel westward toward the great and mysterious mountain that must surely be the home of Dragons. But they could see that a small river blocked their way to the west; it drained into the great river that cut the valley, but all throughout it there were jagged stones that they could not walk upon, and the only path that they could think to take was to the south, along the bank of the river, which would take them in the wrong direction. They called this small river *Wayward*, for it caused them to lose too much time and to go out of their way. Furthermore, Alunen knew that even if they were to find a way around this river, the greater river might also block their path, for she had seen that it bent to the south from atop the hills of the southern valley.

They traveled onward, filled with a confidence that Alunen hoped was not false. And all the while the gold sun continued its path through the sky, moving ever westward. Although the women did find a way around the Wayward River, for it was fed by a spring at the base of the mountains, much time had been lost, and they were certain that the day was drawing to its end. Weariness was overcoming them, and they did not notice at all that far to the east the green moon had reemerged in the sky, opposite where it had vanished before.

Their moods were dampening, for there was a sense about them that the day was nearly over, and they did not know what would happen thereafter.

"I am so very tired," Sveraden said.

"I too am weakening," Alunen replied.

"And I do not know if I can keep walking much longer," Sarak'den said.

"Maybe if we rest just for a few moments," Alunen suggested. "Then we can reach the mountain before the end, before the light fades away."

But they were too weary, and before they could even reach the western end of the valley, the gold sun had begun to shrink, just as had the moon before. The light was fading upon the lands. Everything was darkening. Soon, only the blue sun remained, and it seemed dimmer now, not even able to overcome the darkness that was taking the world. And when the last vestige of the golden sun vanished, consumed by the distant darkness, Alunen, Sarak'den and Sveraden fell down into the fields, disheartened, mournful, exhausted, and certain they had failed. The world was just too big...

They found themselves embracing one another upon the cooling ground. They did not talk, but each of them only lay in regret that they had not lived up to whatever purpose there must have been in their existence, for they now felt sleep falling upon them and they could keep their eyes open no longer. Just as they had awakened, now they would fade away.

Their bodies became weak, their minds clouded, their breathing shallow, and as they drifted into slumber, each of them was filled with sorrow, for they were certain their lives were over and they had not found either the Dragons or their purpose.

Sarak'den's final thoughts were on her dear friends Alunen and Sveraden, whom she loved, and she was thankful that she had at least been blessed with the opportunity to spend time with her beautiful companions.

Sveraden's final imaginings found her wishing she had more time in which to uncover the mysteries of her existence, and perhaps to get revenge upon the Bison.

And Alunen's last considerations were upon the Dragons, and though she had not found them, she was thankful that she had been given what time she had in this glorious and beautiful world.

The Awakening of Alak'kiin

When *I* came into being, both language and a certain understanding were already awakened within my mind. Through no experience that I held within my memory had I achieved either this understanding or the knowledge of language.

There was nothingness around me, only coldness and darkness. The coldness was of hard stone beneath my lying body, the darkness was all-encompassing. But I was not afraid. My mind was clouded, but it was clearing moment by moment.

Words... there were spoken words still fresh in my mind, in my memory, but I could not quite recall what they meant. *"Adusius ahava layvakesh..."* They were words not of anything recent, but words of a different time, and their remnant was quickly passing away, their meaning was lost, and I was left alone in the silent dark.

I comprehended what the darkness was—the absence of light, an opposing force of reality—but this was not the darkness of things unnatural. No, I was simply in a place devoid of light; I did not, in those first moments, consider what else there should be rather than darkness, and so I was left only to think upon what I could conceive of in the conscious state I was in.

I knew that I was more than just a cluster of thoughts dwelling in dark suspense, without shape or form. There was a weight upon me, gently pressing me into the unseen stone that lay beneath. There was empty space about me; this was the air, and I perceived that I was breathing.

There were appendages about the core of my body, arms and legs, and I knew that I could move them, and so with my hands I felt around in the space that was above the stone and within the darkness. Above I felt nothing but the cold air pushing ever so gently against my skin. With my arms I pushed myself upward, defying, ever so slightly, the force that held me to the ground below. So I sat up for the first time, having just awakened in a mysterious place of which I could not really conceive.

It was then, as I sat up, that I noticed a faint opposition to the darkness, for ahead of me was a tiny point of light piercing through the darkness, and I knew then that I had the ability to perceive things around me with more than just feeling. I knew that I possessed a sense of sight.

I moved the rest of my body, legs and hands and feet and head, and I began to develop a sense of what my own form was. Still feeling about, I rose upon my legs to stand, and from a higher position I could feel that there was stone above me as well as below. Here, I was in a kind of enclosure of stone, surrounded on all sides save one—the prick of light far ahead that seemed to be a guide urging me toward it.

And so I found that I could move through the darkness upon my legs and toward the light. I passed through the darkness slowly, step by step, filled with curiosity, desire and excitement, for whatever was happening, and for whatever reason, I knew I had been awakened for a purpose, and I knew I was being led by that beacon of light that grew larger with every step forward.

Through this tunnel of stone I progressed, and as I drew nearer to its end, colors filled the light as a landscape appeared through the opening in the stone—greens and reds, yellows and oranges—beautiful images that I had no words to describe, because I could not yet understand them.

The greens were the grasses of the land beyond the cave, the other colors were flowers of the fields, and the more I saw of them, the more I was filled with an intense longing to get closer, so that I might see these spectacles more clearly, might touch them as I had touched the cold stone. I quickened my pace through the cave, and within a short time I had emerged from within.

And when I stepped into the light, I knew I had arrived at a place that I would gladly spend all of the time given to me, for the glory of the sights before me was nothing short of a gift given by whatever had purposed me into existence. All things were given form and beauty for me to perceive by the light of three great spheres that shown through the great blue expanse that was above. These were the suns and moon.

Great stone mountains rose to the south, and when I turned around I saw that more were raised behind me, high over the cave from which I had emerged, to the north, much nearer to me than those of the south. Between these two ranges of mountains were vast fields, seemingly endless, and I could not even suppose how long it might take to cross.

This land was split by one great river and several that were smaller, each cutting the terrain into fragments of beautiful plains and rolling hills. I looked to the east, and there the two mountain ranges converged; to the west they opened up into a great expanse that reached the very edge of my vision. And it was there, to the west, piercing the expanse, that I saw something profound, for it inspired within me a feeling of greatness. It was a mountain, a single crag that tore through the flowing plains, reaching skyward. It was distant, but it was obvious that it was far taller than the mountains on the edges of the valley. This, I was certain, was a monument for whoever had brought me into existence.

Now, uncertain what I was to do, I turned my sight to myself, so that I might fully see my own form, now that I was bathed in the light. I was a man; my arms and legs and hands and feet were attached to my body. My skin was a light golden tone. Serving as the vessel to hold my consciousness, my head rested on my shoulders, my eyes and ears and nose and mouth were mounted impeccably in place upon it. I traced my features with my fingertips so that I might fully imagine what my appearance might be. There was hair upon my head, long tresses that I could see when I pulled them to the front, before my eyes; it was a silvery shade meant to cover my head and shield me from the intensity of the suns.

I knew I was a man, though I did not know what else I might be. I knew I had intelligence, for I could witness and interact with the things around me. I knew I had purpose in existing, though I did not yet know what it might be. And I knew I had a name.

My name was Alak'kiin, and I knew somehow that I was not alone in this wondrous place. There were surely others out there like me, somewhere hidden from my sight, and I knew I had to find them.

I looked to the west along the foothills of the northern mountains and there, a fair distance away, was a dark and thick forest. Behind that woodland I could see other large openings into the stone, alike to the cave from which I had come. Through a certain wisdom that I possessed at the time of my awakening I surmised that if there were others like me they too might come from the caves. I turned that direction, toward the caves, and began walking.

But it was not long before I was set upon by a pack of strange, though beautiful, creatures. From behind, previously hidden in the grasses or the rises and falls of the landscape they came, six of them of various colors and patterns. They were silent at first as they trotted toward me, but when they barked and growled playfully, I turned swiftly to see what new wonder was approaching. These were creatures of this world, large and wild, free and endearing, and I soon came to call them the *Dains*, though in later times they would be called *Dogs*.

They ran and galloped and clambered and jumped each upon four legs that were as long as my own. Their bodies were shaped awkwardly, their chests so thick my arms could not have encompassed them. They had long snouts upon their faces and two flopping ears that bounced and landed out of place as they moved. They had tails longer than my arms, and as a whole they stood as tall as did I. They were far from gentle with one another, but were without malice, for they were simply trifling and frolicking about in this world that was their own. They growled and barked zestfully, but when they looked and saw me, this all stopped, for their eyes were filled with as much wonder at the sight of me as I held for them. And they galloped toward me.

I was not frightened of these great creatures, for there was no animosity in this world, yet I wondered if they might knock me over in their enthusiasm as they approached. But they did not; each of them moved around me, encircling me, poking at me with their cold and wet noses, licking with giant tongues, and I laughed my first laugh, for these playful creatures were surely of the most divine creation. And amongst those first moments of my existence, I fell in love with the Dains.

When the Dains had their fill of the taste of my skin, they spread out, sniffing at the ground, biting at the grass of the fields, now not so absorbed in their interest of me. But when I started moving again, westward, they followed along, some of them running ahead, others behind, and one by my side. It was this one in particular that I soon came to have the most affinity, for he seemed now more interested in walking with me than with his own kind. Frequently he nudged my shoulder, as if making sure that I didn't forget he was there, and his eyes held a deep kind of affection for me. The hair of his body was entirely black, though it shined with a silvery sheen under the light of the suns.

As we walked along, the mountains were to our side, and they were magnificent, giants of nature, spanning so far above that I could not see their tops. Along the base of the mountains were streams of silver rising up from springs beneath the earth and flowing into a nearby river, which itself drained to the south, into the greatest of the rivers in the valley. To the south, though north of the great river, were vast fields of rolling hills covered in growth—grasses of every shade of green, flowers of every tinge of every color, and wandering about these fields were other creatures of many kinds, but none of them were so great—at least in my eyes—as the Dains.

Rabbits bounced about, Squirrels scurried to and fro, Birds fluttered around, going from ground to air and back again. Small Marmots bounced across the fields, Deer nibbled at the flowers and greenery, and countless Insects buzzed around. In all of this I beheld what was most certainly a great creation.

As I continued to the west I was in no hurry, for there was no sense of urgency about me or any thought of what I should be doing with my time. I only thought of admiring nature and of finding others like myself. Yet as I revered the world around me, not knowing what or who I was and why I might be here, my thoughts were deep, for within my mind I was beginning to contemplate something that I considered to be profound...

For it was known to me for reasons unknown that I was part of this existence, and that it must be for a reason, a purpose, the certain intent of something beyond my grasp. Yet it was I who decided to rise in the depths of the cave just after awakening. It was I who decided that I should move toward the light. And it was I who thought to seek out others like myself. These things I did of my own accord, my own will, and my own purpose.

And it was this I considered; for although I was surely designed by the intent of some force or being inconceivable, I acted of my own *free will* in those first and continuing moments of my life.

Buried in these thoughts and filled with admiration of this creation, I moved on, eyes attentive, ears open to the sounds of nature. And with a great and spirited Dain at my side. Looking now at this creature, as I walked along, I spoke my first words, saying, "What should I call you, dear friend? My name is Alak'kiin."

The Dain looked at me and then tilted his head quizzically, as if bewildered by the sounds that came out of my mouth. He, of course, said nothing in response. A smile lit my face and I said to him, "I will call you... *Saxon*, for this somehow seems fitting." He looked at me with approval, woofed, and then turned his attention back to the path ahead.

Then it came, a great disturbance, first to my hearing, then appealing to my other senses; then my eyes fell upon it... The sounds of nature became silent. The Dains ceased their snorting and growling, the Birds of the air quieted their songs, and a great *whooshing* sound filled the skies and stirred the grasses below. I turned quickly in wonder of what might be happening, and there, in the sky, I beheld something most splendid.

A great golden creature that seemed as mighty as a mountain was coursing the sky from east to west. It was neither a Bird nor any other type of animal I had yet to see, but it commanded the winds and soared upon giant wings that waved gracefully up and down, seeming empyreal as it soared the heavens, in the places where the celestial bodies dwelled. So great was its size... and it was followed by a giant tail and led by a great head that was mounted upon a long neck. It was something so gracious that there was but one word that came to my mind... *Dragon!* And this was what I knew this creature must be called.

It flew swiftly to the west and I stood motionless, unable to move for the awe that filled me, until finally it passed from my vision across the horizon, near to that great and jutting crag that was upon the distant plains. In this I was convinced that the Dragon must surely have played some part in my existence, for I had already determined that the mountain was a marker to some god, some higher power.

When at last I looked away from the mountain, Saxon was nowhere to be seen, nor were the other Dains. I supposed that the great Dragon had stricken them with disquieted trepidation, and that they had taken their leave. But moments later, Saxon appeared again, charging as playfully as before to my side.

"What is a Dragon?" I asked the Dain, but he only responded with a pant.

As we continued westward, I dreamed that I would at some time get to see the Dragon up close, for it was something so magnificent that I thought it must be the very one who had purposed my existence and caused me to awaken here in this enchanting world.

As the day moved onward, the gold sun shifted in its position; from east to west it progressed, slowly it seemed, for its movement was only discerned by its position in relation to the blue sun and the land itself. The moon too traced a path through the sky. And all the while the natural world continued on; the animals lived their lives as though the changes in the world affected them not at all. They seemed to have no concerns, for the world provided them with all they needed. They had not, I concluded, awakened at the same time as did I, but rather at a time much earlier, for they seemed familiar with the lay of the land.

I continued on my path to the west, Saxon by my side. On occasion, the other Dains would reappear, popping up out of the tall grass, playful and careless, and though my companion gazed at them with interest, he seemed more content to stay with me.

"You can go," I said to him on one such occasion. "You can go and be with your own kind." At first the Dain looked at me as though considering it, but then his eyes drooped and he appeared sad. But this was fleeting, and a moment later he was nudging my shoulder, biting gently at it, and seeming to try to pull me forward. Then he stopped and darted on ahead a short way, stopped again, looked at me and then ran a bit farther. It seemed that he wanted me to follow.

And so I started faster toward him, and again he stopped, and then waited for me to get near, then he ran a bit more. He was leading me somewhere, I thought, and with nothing else of any importance to do I decided I would see where he might take me.

Once he was convinced that I was following his guidance he trotted along just ahead of me. He led me closer to the mountains, and closer to the dark forest I had seen earlier. All the way to the wooded land Saxon ushered me, and when we arrived, he lay down upon a soft patch of grass to rest. I fell down beside him, not for weariness, but because it seemed as if it would be pleasing.

The Dain rolled onto his side and let out a soft and pleasurable grunt. I leaned back and rested my shoulders and head on his side; he did not object and seemed content in the companionship he had found with me.

I was facing the forest and in these moments I studied the trees, for I had yet to really consider them. I had been close to some of the shrubbery that speckled the hillsides, but the trees were something much greater and much larger. They rose perhaps ten times the height that I stood, and were massive in their girth. Leaves as large as my head grew from many strong branches, and I found it all to be fascinating, though I did not know what other way a forest should be.

I closed my eyes and listened, and I found that the sounds of nature were more prominent without my sight as a distraction. My other senses were keener when I could not see. I felt the rise and fall of my head and shoulders as Saxon breathed deeply and contentedly. I could smell the fragrances of many flowers and plants and things unknown. I could hear the distant growls and grunts of the other Dains, as well as Birds nearby, and other animals scurrying about. And I could feel blades of grass swaying in the soft breeze and brushing up against my skin. The world was a beautiful place, even when my eyes were closed and I could not behold it.

I had nearly fallen asleep in that blissful moment when I suddenly felt a thump upon my chest. I sat up quickly, surprised though not startled. Saxon too lifted his head, for even he had not expected such a disturbance, or perhaps his alarm was only for my sake.

I looked about, and there on the ground not far away was a spherical fruit that I thought should be called an apple. This surely was what had struck me. I looked up at the tall branches of the trees to see if there were others, if this apple had fallen from one of them, but I did not see any.

Then a voice spoke from just a short distance away, saying, "You should eat. It will give you strength."

When I looked, I saw another man, much like myself, leaning against one of the trees, another of the fruits in his hand, half eaten. He was grinning; the man was like me, with a golden-hued skin, and long hair, though his was brown in color, and he had a firm physique. Like me, he was unclothed, for it had not yet occurred to either of us that we might want to wear a covering.

I stood up, took the apple with me, and started walking toward the man. Saxon stood as well and trotted alongside. I said, "My name is Alak'kiin, and I was hoping to meet someone like me."

"And now you have," the other man said. "Now eat! It will make you feel better."

"I do not feel poorly," I said, but I took a bite of the apple nevertheless. It was sweet and cool in my mouth, and I was glad that I had indulged, and now eating seemed to be a natural thing.

"Just wait," the man said. And indeed, as I swallowed the apple, a surge of strength came over me, and though I had not felt poorly before, I did now feel even better.

The pleasure this brought me must have been alight upon my face, for the stranger smiled widely and said, "I am Alim'dar, and it is with great pleasure that I have found you, for I, as well, was hoping there were others like me."

"Where did you come from, Alim'dar?" I asked.

"From a cave, just to the north of this woodland." He took another bite of his apple.

"And I awoke in a cave just a way to the east of here. What do you know of where we are… or what we are? For there is cloudiness in my mind and I do not remember anything that might have come before my awakening."

"Nor do I," Alim'dar said. "I too awoke in the darkness and made my way out into the light. I could see little of the landscape, for this forest extends far to the west. I tried peering inside, between the trees, but it was so shadowy that I could not see far. And so I went to the west and around the woods and there I found a small orchard with another kind of tree that grew these fruits, and I ate."

As we talked, Saxon's attention was divided between Alim'dar and me, for his interest was alight as well. Then, the Dain slowly walked over to the other man and nudged him with his nose. Alim'dar pulled away, only surprised, I supposed by the coldness, and he was not so delighted as I had been at the affection of this animal. And so Saxon moved away as well, back to my side. But Alim'dar followed, and now not surprised he lay his hand upon the Dain's flank, saying, "What an interesting animal."

I nodded in agreement and took another bite. "The apple is well received by my body," I said. "What else did you see to the west of the woods?"

"The rolling hills continue onward for a time, and then they drop off, down to the plains below. There, a distance away, is a great mountain that does not look the same as these." He gestured to the mountains that were just beside us.

"Did you see the Dragon?" I asked.

"I do not know what a Dragon is."

"It was a great and giant creature that flew through the air, from the east to the west, and it seemed to be moving toward that mountain. When it came, all of nature was silenced."

"I did not see this Dragon, but I did notice as all of nature became quiet, and I wondered what had caused it."

"The Dragon was magnificent and it was as if all of the creatures of this world were subservient to it, for they stopped all that they were doing at its passing."

Alim'dar considered this and said, "I would much like to see this Dragon, for it sounds incredible."

Saxon lay back down. I said, "Do you think there are others like us, somewhere in this valley?"

"Perhaps. There are other caves in the mountains, further to the west. I was going to investigate them when I came across the apple trees. Then I was distracted again by the yowling Dains who had drawn near, one of the likes of which seems to have become your companion." He looked down at Saxon. "It was then that I came around the bend of the forest north of here and saw you."

"Would you accompany Saxon and me to these caves?" I asked. "For if there are others maybe they have more knowledge of what we are, and why we have awakened in this land."

Alim'dar nodded, himself curious, and he said, "I will lead you to the caves."

Together the three of us moved northward, then around the edge of the forest and when we came to within sight of Alim'dar's cave of awakening, he pointed at it, saying, "That is the place of my emergence. For it was there that I came into this world." We continued on, talking and wondering at the many mysteries of the world around us.

"The first of the caves that I saw is just ahead, around the protruding edge of that mountain," Alim'dar explained, pointing. When I nodded, he added, "Would you like to race there, to see who might be faster?"

"I do not know why it would matter who arrives first, for do we not want to explore together?"

"Of course," he said, smiling. "I simply propose a feat of skill."

Although I did not understand why it was that my friend, Alim'dar, might want to discover which of us was faster—for I saw not the importance of it—I nevertheless agreed, simply for the reason that it would be a new experience.

As soon as I nodded we began running and as soon as we started, so too did Saxon, for he was filled with excitement by this game. Alim'dar took the lead in our jaunt, and I was exhilarated, not just at the prospect of catching up with him, but with the whole experience, for soon there was not just one Dain running alongside us, but the entire pack had seen us from a short distance and had come to join in.

Over the hills and along the edge of the mountains we ran, Alim'dar in the lead all the while, until finally we came to the edge of the stone mountain and moved around it; we were both startled, when just around that bend, we came face to face with two other men, who were just alike to us. Though he tried to stop himself, Alim'dar slated right into one of them, both of them fell to the ground, and I would have joined them had Saxon not taken my arm in his giant jaws and pulled me gently back, stabilizing me so that I too did not tumble into the others.

The men were like us, golden in skin, heads covered in long hair—one of them with flaxen, the other with black—and both of them with well-defined muscles in their arms, legs and torsos.

The man who had not been struck helped the others to stand; he was the one with the flaxen hair.

"Thank you," Alim'dar said, and to the other whom he had struck he said, "My apologies for running into you, for my companion and I were racing to our destination and we did not know we would encounter you here."

"It is fine," the man with black hair said. "We were up by that cave when we heard the ruckus of these animals that are with you and we came to investigate."

"It is a pleasure to meet you," I said. "For we were going to that very cave, wondering if others like us might have emerged from within. My name is Alak'kiin, and my friend is Alim'dar."

The man with the black hair said, "I am Adaashar, and indeed I did emerge from that cave. I do not know why, nor do I have any memory of what came before my awakening within."

"And I," the other man said. "Am Norandar, and I came from a cave that is farther west. I too have no memory of anything. When I awoke and came into the world it was not long before I met with Adaashar and we became companions, much like you two have."

"Why is it that none of us knows from where we came, or why we are here at all?" Alim'dar wondered. "For we hold no memory of a time before, and it would seem that each of us likely awakened at the same moment."

Adaashar and Norandar were silent, considering this. Then it was Alim'dar who spoke again, saying, "Perhaps we have no memory of a time before we awoke, because we did not exist before then. Maybe the moment of our awakening was the moment of our creation."

"And what would have created us?" Norandar asked. "The Dragon, perhaps?"

"You have seen the Dragon?" I asked excitedly.

"Yes," Adaashar said. "We were not far from here when we saw it soaring through the sky, from the east to the west. It was a marvelous creature that exuded power and authority over all of creation. Indeed, it may be he who is our creator."

"I have wondered the same," I said. "Yet I recall that as I was awakening, there were voices, clouded and seemingly distant, speaking somewhere in my mind or my memory. I do not know what they said, but it makes me think that perhaps there was something before."

The others looked to one another hoping for some more insight, but none of them had anything to add. Finally, Alim'dar said, "Then perhaps our intent should be to find this Dragon."

"It disappeared to the west, beyond the scope of our vision. We do not know where it might have gone, or if it will return."

Just then, a mighty roar pierced the natural resonances of the world around us, commanding and intense. Again, nature was silenced, and all of our eyes grew wide in wonder. We looked first to the direction of the sound, which was to the south, and then to one another. And then, without speaking a word amongst ourselves, we all began to run again, this time southward, toward the shriek, for we were certain that it must be the Dragon.

The Dains—save for Saxon—remained behind.

When we came to the great river that divided the entire valley we stopped, first because we had reached the point where we could go no farther, and secondly because by then our breath was expired. Through our blurred vision we could see that standing just on the other side of the river was not only the great golden Dragon, but also two others, one covered in copper scales and the other with shining silver.

The four of us fell to the ground to watch in wonder. Saxon followed. The great beasts seemed to be conversing with one another, but they were too far distant for us to hear any words. This went on for some time, long enough for us to recover our breaths and regain our strength.

"Let us swim across this river and meet with these Dragons!" Norandar said.

"How do we even know we can swim?" Adaashar asked.

"How do we know we can do anything at all?" Alim'dar wondered. "How do we know how to speak a language, when we never were taught such a thing?"

"Indeed," I agreed. "There are a great many things that we know, but that we do not understand. Perhaps the Dragons can tell us. I agree; let us swim across to the other side."

Then I remembered Saxon; I somehow knew that I could swim, but did not know if a Dain possessed the same ability. So I said to him, "We are going across the river, my friend. You may stay here and I will find you again." He turned his head sideways and watched as my three companions and I leaped into the cool water of the great river and began to swim. But to my surprise, Saxon did not hesitate to follow us into the water, and together we began swimming southward, across the river, the Dain's head bobbing up and down as he paddled through the gentle rapids.

But when we had covered only a fraction of the distance, the currents of the water began to pull us off course to the west. Although we could change the direction of our swim the currents were too strong, and we could not compensate enough. And so slowly, as we tried to reach the Dragons, we were taken further to the west, farther away than we had intended.

When we came ashore on the southern bank of the river we could not even see the Dragons any longer, for we had drifted too far. Resting again now, for the swim had been strenuous, we collapsed onto the sandy shoreline to catch our breaths.

41

After a time Alim'dar spoke, saying, "Where has the moon gone?" I looked to the sky, and indeed, it had vanished from sight, just as the gold sun had moved farther in its own path.

Adaashar said, "The westward sky has taken it."

"What do you mean?" I asked him, looking to the heavens, as were the others.

"Did you not notice that it moved through the heavens from the east to the west? Its course has been laid out as part of this creation, surely. And though it may appear that it has gone away, perhaps it is more likely that it is simply obscured by some other phenomenon that we cannot yet comprehend."

"And what will happen when the gold sun moves westward?" Norandar asked. "Will it too be swallowed by the sky? And if so, what will be left here, in the wake of the light? For can you not see that the hue of the landscape has changed since we first awoke? The blue sun is not so bright, and I feel that it is the gold sun that gives us light and life. What is to come?"

"I do not know," Adaashar admitted. "But let us finish what we started and find the Dragons. They should be to the east of here, a fair walk, for we were drawn away from our course by the fierceness of the river."

"Agreed," Alim'dar said. "And let us make haste."

"Why?" I asked. "What is the hurry?"

"Because," Alim'dar grinned at me, then at the others. "I want to see who can get there first!" And he began running.

The others, feeling challenged, followed. And lastly, Saxon and I took off again at running speed in search of the Dragons.

The hills in this region proved to be difficult to traverse, for they wound about awkwardly; the small ravines between through which we moved would go one direction one moment and another the next. This labyrinth of mounds and gulches led us astray until each of us was once again too tired to continue, so again we rested, drinking from one of the many streams that ran through the lowlands of these hills.

"Alak'kiin," Alim'dar said as he leaned back against a large boulder. "Have you considered at all the strangeness of our names?"

"How do you mean?" I asked, not having before considered this.

"Well, I was awakened with my name, simply knowing it. No one gave this name to me, so far as I know. I would presume the same is true for each of you." The others nodded, as did I. "How came we to have these names, and of what meaning are they?"

I did not have an answer, but I added, "And it is also true that the creatures of this land, the Dains and the Dragons and even the features of the land itself all have names. It is the nuance of our language, and it is strange indeed, for how is it that we have even come to speak a language at all, much less all of us the same?"

"Is it possible, "Adaashar asked. "That we were not simply awakened, or created, but that we existed before this day? Yet we don't remember a life from before?"

"I think it is possible," I said. "When I first awoke, in those first moments, I thought I heard voices, as of someone speaking. I felt like some of the words were my own. But not all of them."

"What did these voices say? For I had a similar sense when I awoke."

"I don't recall. They were muffled, or blurred beyond understanding. Maybe it was just the effect of coming into being—I don't know."

"I experienced the same thing," Alim'dar said. "They were harsh words, I think. I awoke to feel as though... like I was tense, or angry. Yet it very soon thereafter disappeared and faded away. I didn't even recall it until just now, when you mentioned it."

"Norandar, did you experience anything like this?"

"Maybe. I am not certain. Yes, it seems like in my first few moments I held a consciousness that was from before."

"If it is true that we existed before, then this would make sense of our names, perhaps... I hope the Dragons can tell us more about everything."

Even as we spoke of these mysteries, a new one appeared, coming through the maze of channels that ran between the numerous hills. A new type of creature we had not yet seen before came into view, twenty in number. They were larger than the Dains, with large bodies resting on four large legs, with small tails dangling behind. Upon an enlarged head were giant broad and flat antlers. All as one, the four of us spoke the name of this creature, saying, "*Moose.*" And it was obvious to us in that moment that whatever our origin, whatever we were, we were all of the same kind, the same intent and purpose, and we were determined to understand.

The herd of Moose looked at us curiously as they passed by, but otherwise paid us little mind. They were intent on their own destination, and though I thought it might be interesting to see where they would go, I felt more compelled than ever to keep searching for the Dragons.

But the gold sun had moved farther away to the west, and its light upon the land seemed to be dimming. The blue sun did not cast so much light as to ward off the coming darkness. As our constitution was once again depleted, the gold sun had begun its own departure, for it too was vanishing, being swallowed up by the western sky. And we decided then that surely darkness was about to befall the world. We were tired, for it had been a long day, and we longed only to rest.

Before long, each of my companions had fallen into unconsciousness; I could see that they breathed, their chests rising and falling, but they were unresponsive. This I knew to be sleep, and I longed for it myself. I spread out on the ground, and Saxon curled up beside me, resting his large head upon my chest, and we too fell into slumber.

My final thoughts of that first day found me considering what glorious future might await us all when a new day dawned, for what great adventures might the world have in store?

MEETINGS

THE FIRST MEETING

I slept through the night undisturbed and awoke in the morning to the sound of barking; it was a deep woofing, not of alarm but of excitement. Saxon, I knew, had awakened ahead of me, and probably the others would soon follow.

When I sat up I could see that Alim'dar, Norandar and Adaashar were also rising from their slumber, stretching their arms and legs, then standing. I too rose and looked around. To the east stood Saxon, facing the same direction, barking and snarling in his playful way as he excitedly leaped with his front paws into the air.

"What is it, Saxon?" I hollered to him, but then I saw it myself. Standing upon the nearest hill were three others, who were not quite like us. And as I had known upon my own awakening that I was a man, I now knew these three to be women, beautiful and graceful, lovely in every way. One of them had hair of gold, one of the deepest black, and one with an earthen brown shade. The features of their faces were different, but each of them enticing in their own manner.

Now that he had my attention, Saxon quieted and returned to my side. The other men had taken notice as well. The women stood close to one another, a bit apprehensive, perhaps, of who we might be. I raised a hand in the air as a greeting to them, but as I did so, Norandar and Adaashar began moving up the hillside toward them. Alim'dar held back only to observe. The women started down the hill.

Alim'dar looked to me and said, "Are you not going to go to them, like our brothers?"

"Do you not think I should?" I said.

"Let them come to us, Alak'kiin."

"Why?"

"Because it occurs to me that these women must be of the same awakening as us. They look the same in every way, save for their feminine forms... Their skin is the same hue, and their hair the same shades. Yes, they are beautiful, all of them. But at first I felt compelled to go to them, for there is an attraction. Yet there are but three of them, and four of us."

"Why does this matter?" I asked.

"Because, it is presumable that our attraction is to bring us together. But how can we pair three of them with four of us, without one of us being left out? For are you not drawn to their perfect forms of beauty?" I nodded and he added, "I do not wish to cause a disturbance between us, for might we argue over one of them?"

I didn't fully understand what he was talking about, but the others approached now, with the women beside them, and it seemed obvious that the men had not even yet spoken to them, but had only accompanied them down the remainder of the hillside.

"Hello," I said, looking each of the women in the eye. "I am Alak'kiin, and my brothers who escorted you are Adaashar and Norandar. And this is Alim'dar."

Only somewhat shyly then, the gold-haired woman spoke, "Hello to you all. I am Alunen. My sisters are Sarak'den and Sveraden."

"Are there more of you?" Alim'dar asked with an eagerness in his tone.

"Not that we have seen," Sarak'den said. "We found each other yesterday, in the hills and by the river. It was the first day that any of us could recall, the first day of our awakening, and we have seen no others."

"Where did you come from?" Alunen asked.

"We came from across the great river," Norandar said. "We awoke there yesterday as well, in the caves along the face of the mountains."

"In the caves?" Sveraden wondered. "For *we* did not awaken within the depths of the world, but on the surface."

"Why does it matter where we awoke?" Alim'dar asked. "It only matters that we are all here."

"How did you come to be here, on this side of the river?" Alunen wondered.

"We were in the hills to the north," I said. "We heard a great and thunderous roar and we knew it had to be the Dragons that we had seen... Did you see them here, since it is here that you have been since your awakening?"

"We saw them," Alunen said. "But we did not get near to them. Well, Sveraden did, but she was too frightened to speak with them."

"Frightened?" Adaashar asked. "Of the Dragons? Did they seek to harm you?"

Sveraden said nothing, but only shook her head and offered no more.

I continued, explaining, "When we saw the Dragons we ran southward until we came to the river, and then we swam across, hoping to get to them. But the currents of the water dragged us downstream, and we never did. We wandered in these hills for much of the day, until we slept. We never saw the Dragons again."

"They all flew away, to the west," Sarak'den said. "We too wanted to find them, for maybe they can unravel this great mystery."

"What mystery?" Norandar asked.

"The mystery of our awakening... who we are... what we are... and why we are here. There are so many questions, but no answers."

"We too are at a loss, and seek the Dragons for understanding," I said.

"And so what are we to do now?" Alunen asked. "For each of us seeks the same thing, and none of us know where to look."

"You said the Dragons flew to the west?" I asked, and Alunen nodded. "Then I propose that we go that way, across the rest of this valley, and maybe onto the plains that are beyond."

"That great mountain may hold the answers we seek," Alim'dar said. "As well as the Dragons."

"Then let us go westward, together, now that we have found one another."

We moved westward that morning, back through the hills through which my brothers and I had gone the evening before, and we came to a wide river that flowed northward out of the mountains, which was west from the place where we had come ashore; we later called this the *Scaling River*, for just on the other side of it we saw a new landscape unlike any we had seen before.

The hills leveled off there, past the river, and a flatland was covered with a tall kind of grass with blades as thick as our hands and higher than our heads. It had a bluish tint to it, and most curiously there seemed not to be any animals around, scurrying or scampering about, for the blades were still; only Saxon was there, bounding about, but not going into the bizarre meadow. Stranger still was what we did see scattered about this range, for there were huge pieces of broken husks of various colors, flat and weathered.

We all examined the strange grass, but when first Alim'dar reached out and touched one of the giant blades, he pulled his hand quickly back, letting out a slight cry of pain.

"What is it?" Sveraden asked, going to him. The rest of us followed.

"It cut my flesh," he said, with as much curiosity as with pain, and he held out his hand. Upon it was a wound—not deep—but covered now in red blood that was slowly dripping out. But before our eyes, the wound in his skin sealed itself, and he healed of this minor laceration almost immediately. Shrugging, he wiped the remaining blood from his hand onto the softer grass that was nearby. "I would not recommend that we pass through here."

The others began to look around, moving along the grass line, while I still considered the blades themselves. It was fascinating to me that such a thing should exist here, something that was harmful, for until now I had seen nothing in this world that was of any detriment to its inhabitants. So far as I knew, the wound given to Alim'dar was the first any of us had received, the first pain given.

Soon, Norandar came to me, holding one of the large pieces of the husks I had noticed before, but had not considered.

"What are these, Alak'kiin?" he asked. "They are hard and solid, but easy to lift." He made a fist and struck the outer shining face of the strange object. His hand bounced off and the plate was left undamaged.

"Look at them," Sveraden said in her soft and gentle voice, coming up to us and placing her own hand on the large object. "This one is silver, but look at the others... there is a myriad of colors. Silver and gold, green and copper, blue and black, white and even crimson like Alim'dar's blood. And they look familiar, do they not?"

I considered this, and said, "Yes, they look familiar, some like the colors of the Dragons we have seen. Others not..."

"Yes!" Sveraden elated. "Look, these are the scales of the Dragons, fallen or placed here!"

The others heard the exchange and gathered around, each of them reaching out to touch the silver scale, nearly in reverence. The scale was smooth on its outer edge, and solid, but on its outer side there were many scratch marks, as if it had been scraped along sharp edges like those of the razor grass. In the inner, concave surface—for the scales were not wholly flat, but curved ever so slightly—was a softer material, coarse and bumpy.

"If these are indeed Dragon scales," Sarak'den said. "Then does this mean that there are more of them than just the three... the gold, the silver and the copper?"

"That would stand to reason," Alunen said.

"Let us find them as soon as we can then," Adaashar said. "For they become more intriguing with each passing moment."

And so we set out again, now trying to find a path around the thick Razorgrass that we had encountered. But even as we reached the southern end of the field, we also met with the mountainside, and the grass grew so close to it that we could not safely pass. So we turned back northward, hoping to find a way through. As we walked along we gathered various scales of all colors, for we thought in those early moments of our lives that the Dragons—should we find them—might like to have them back.

Even by the time we reached the riverbank we had still not found a way through the thick grass. Irritated at this hindrance, Alim'dar said, "We will have to swim again. Maybe let the currents of the water carry us to our destination."

"The river bends to the south, once it leaves the valley," Alunen informed. "For I could see it from atop the high hill yesterday."

"And look," Adaashar said, staring downriver. "There are many rocks there protruding from the water. And the currents look even stronger. Those rocks will cut us just like the Razorgrass."

"Then what do we do?" Sveraden wondered. "For our progress is blocked. Do we go back the way we came, past the hills to where the... Bison roam?"

"Maybe there is a way around, farther to the east," Alunen added.

But Norandar had other ideas, and while the rest of us had been discussing our options he had been sitting upon a mound of earth studying one of the copper Dragon scales he had been carrying. "It seems to me," he said. "That this world is full of obstacles. Who knows what dangers might be ahead of us, whichever path we take? We can resist them, looking for alternative paths, or we can adapt."

And as he said this, he pulled from the inner side of the scale a great layer of the inner matter; it came off in a sheet as long as his arm and wide as his body. And he set the scale aside, stood up, and wrapped a segment of the sheet around his right hand. Then, standing up, he moved over to the nearest blade of the Razorgrass, and reached out and grasped the sharp edge of the blade, and he broke it off. His hand was uninjured, and the remainder of us marveled at his ingenuity.

And so we did not go into the river that day, nor did we turn back, but instead we harvested the inside of the Dragon scales, and we made for ourselves a covering of this material, which we called *barathea*. By weaving strands of it together we were able to make rudimentary clothing to protect ourselves from the elements—gloves for our hands, boots for our feet, tunics with sleeves and breeches—all to be coverings for our bodies. Not only did we use the barathea from the innards of the scales, but also did we find broken segments of the hard outer scale that we were able to affix to the more sensitive parts of our bodies that might need extra protection.

Even for Saxon, much to his protest, was protective armor made to cover his entire body, and though he allowed us to affix it to him, he whined the entire time, for Dains, it seemed, were not meant to be clothed.

Thus, it was then, on our second day of existence, that we learned to wear clothing, adapting to this beautiful, though sometimes dangerous, world.

Although our progress was slowed by the thick growth, we passed through the Razorgrass and through a shallow river that divided the field in half. When we came through to the other side and passed over a beautiful plain, we were upon the top of a large cliff that looked down over the southern bend of the great river and the great plains to the west. Though the cliff was high, there was a land bridge that spanned the distance between us and those plains, arcing downward.

Here, now through the lacerating field, I removed the protective clothing from Saxon, for the danger was now behind us, and he let loose a growling sigh of happiness. The rest of us left ours on, for now that we were clothed, we felt more comfortable being covered.

As we mounted this land passage, Alunen stopped and looked skyward, then said. "The time approaches as it did yesterday when the gold sun was overhead. For then, the moon had already been swallowed by the west, just as it has today." We all gathered to her and listened, for her words seemed solemn. "I do not know if you saw it yesterday, but when this time approached, something disturbing appeared in the north, beyond those mountains where you men awakened."

I presumed that only the women had seen this, for none others had mentioned it, and I wondered, "What was it, Alunen? What did you see?"

"I don't know what it was, but it disturbed us... Let us wait and see if it shows again."

So we waited for the time that Alunen reckoned, standing there upon the land bridge, and indeed it did come. When the hour approached, a dark and jagged line appeared across the sky, far in the distance, beyond the northern reaches of the mountains of the valley. As it came more into focus with the passing moments, it looked more and more like a dark landscape, perhaps a world that was far away, obscured by clouds or perhaps distant. But it wasn't the simple appearance of this landscape that was disturbing, but rather it was like a shadow was falling upon the entire world—not a shadow cast by the suns, but rather a shadow upon our beings, our spirits. Something was happening in those moments that we could not explain, a disheartening gloom fell upon us that could not be comprehended. Only Saxon was unaffected, perhaps because he was accustomed to it.

But as the moments passed, the darkened, distant region faded away into the sky, and the dispiriting feeling left us. We did not further talk about it then, because none of us could really understand what had happened. I had not, on the previous day, been affected by such an event, whereas the women had. Therefore I could only surmise that to be affected, one must have to be within view of the far away region, or whatever it was.

We continued on down the slope of the land bridge that we later called *Alunen's Reckoning*.

The Company of Dragons

Now upon the far eastern edge of the plains that were to the west of the valley of our awakening, we could see that there was still a great distance to go before we would reach that great and giant mountain that was our destination. And though it was difficult to gauge how far away it was, from this perspective we could see how truly massive it must be. Also, as we moved closer to it, we saw it from a different angle and could only then see how truly magnificent it was.

For it was not alike to any other mountain; it was taller than it was wide, and it curved as it rose toward the sky, its tip pointing to the east. It appeared as if a great claw was tearing up through the plains, a talon much like those of the Dragons. Strewn about the whole of the plains, growing denser as we moved westward toward it, were boulders and stone that made me think that perhaps the initial impression was correct—that this mountain had been raised through some great power from the depths of the earth, quickly and with intent, scarring the plains for all time. And we were more convinced than ever that this must be the home of the Dragons.

The grass of these plains was different than that of the valley. It was tall like the Razorgrass, but soft and not at all harmful; it was thin, with soft blades, sparsely scattered about with large patches of bare soil throughout. It was more of a brown shade rather than green, yet it was incredibly beautiful in its own way, for as the wind blew it moved in waves across the expanse of the plains.

There was different wildlife here as well; Birds of different colors, Mice of a much smaller variety, Rabbits that had small horns upon their heads, and legless Snakes that slithered easily across the flat ground.

Adaashar was most fascinated with the Snakes, and he held an affinity for them; upon our first encounter he lifted one of them up and held gently onto it as it curled around his arm and shoulder, then came to stare him in the eyes. There seemed then to be a bonding between them, much like there was between me and Saxon. As we continued on toward the mountain the snake stayed with him for a time, then it climbed back down his body and legs and slithered into the tall grass and vanished.

We were perhaps halfway across the plains and to the great mountain when Alunen was the first to notice... She started yelling excitedly, "Look! There!" She pointed toward the mountain and we all turned our attention there. "Dragons!"

And indeed, though still far away, it was unmistakable that neither one nor three Dragons were flying eastward, but seven! We were filled with the same awe as when we had seen them before. Long we had waited and sought out these great creatures, and now at last we could see them again.

But, I wondered, would they even see us or simply pass us by, flying onward to whatever was their destination?

First Alunen, then our other sisters, and finally all of us were running in their direction, filled with excitement and anticipation, for not only was it within our reach to see the Dragons once again but also to perhaps have answers to our many questions. It was not long before the Dragons had covered half the distance to us, and it was just as the western sky began its swallowing of the gold sun when they were upon us.

We were screaming so loudly, waving our arms and causing such a disturbance in nature that there was no possible way the Dragons could not have noticed us, for they were flying not far above. And take notice of us they did, for each of the seven drew back in the air just as their attention was captured by the sight of us. They twisted their giant heads about, looking to one another and then back at us, appearing astonished and wondering.

The seven Dragons were colored each differently, just like the scales we had found in the Razorgrass Fields; gold and silver, copper and blue, green, crimson and black. In my own excitement I noticed not that there was one shade of Dragon missing, for there had also been scales of white.

We stopped running, stopped yelling, for we had the Dragons' attention, and each of us dropped to the ground, both from our exertion and for the reverence inspired by these great creatures as they landed upon the plains, together forming a circle about us such that even if we had wanted to get away, we would have had great difficulty. Even Saxon was silent now, and he lay down, curious but also in veneration.

I was astonished by their size, for from a distance they had seemed huge, but up close, as they were, they were enormous. Any one of them could have taken all of us into its giant mouth together, so massive were their heads, so gaping were their mighty jaws. They towered above us, easily fifteen times our own height, and this was without them even fully extended, for after they had landed, they sat upon their hind legs, not unlike Saxon often sat.

Their clawed hands were unbelievably colossal; each of their claws was extended and longer than I was tall, and they dug deep into the earth as they began to speak, their voices deep and commanding.

"maura kitetai''sai karan˘" the Gold Dragon said; its tone suggested that it was a question.

"unborath'daiku'sai naumhemar er˘" exclaimed the Silver.

"maura kitetvai'sai assori˘" the Black Dragon wondered. Another question, perhaps, if one could suppose the nuances of their language was anything like ours.

And then The Copper Dragon replied, *"iimthiringorn'daiku'sai kitetria'torpah'vaino˘ kintuk iimborath'daiku sai naum kitetai' ant˘"*

"ersylve'sai˘" said the Blue Dragon.

The Gold Dragon spoke again, saying, *"unfyffil'nawar karas egowthu karan' masograth harish amal etkoume˘ uingorograin'sai loranor kitetai˘"*

"iimkarleth'kaila norgrakon kronaggas˘" said the Green Dragon, his first words so far.

"horoa sar˘" the Crimson Dragon seemed to ask.

The Silver Dragon replied, *"maura iimnevain'sai ink˘"*

"kintuk osnevain'sai rassesetak˘" the Black Dragon wondered.

"so ' kintuk˘" another agreed.

"etselen iimmorathay'nawar akos tenebus' ant keled˘" explained another. I was losing track of which of the great beasts was talking…

"maura selin rassesetak aril'pait eryanai'˘" The Black Dragon said. *"paiat jorka kun kronaggas kaidoron'sai eryan˘"*

The language was complex; this much I knew. Although it was spoken in the deep and harsh tones of the Dragons, it held a beauty as it flowed; it was this I concentrated upon since there was little chance of comprehending their words.

"arkarleth'nawar aggas selinpenissel'sai gol iimaggas˘" The Blue Dragon said, then added, *"maura selin osmorothay'paiat gol morie˘"*

"iimmorothay'paiat gol aril'nawar etkort˘"

"horoa sar˘"

"mori iimmaswan'nawar˘"

"kitetai''sai init urtheeth'paiat kort˘"

"ku sertak ersylve'sai ' eraggas˘"

They seemed to be speaking faster now, and it was more and more difficult to distinguish between them according to their voices.

"What are they saying?" Alunen wondered.

"They speak with a different tongue," I said. "But can they understand *us*, I wonder."

Then Alim'dar was the first to speak to a Dragon, and he called out to the great Gold Dragon, saying, "We have many questions for you!"

The Dragons each looked down at all of us; they looked surprised, momentarily stunned, perhaps, but then continued their own conversation, their words a mystery to us, and ours, apparently, to them.

"ink kited'sai etmothreon omaselin ' kited'sai omanelf˘" the Gold Dragon wondered.

"nelf˘" the Black Dragon said starkly. *"iim'sai init henar etvai' nonriagroam fauk iimkolus'paiat oreb˘"*

"ku nelf ' elina naigollak' omakulorn' aril'nawar ad selin˘"

"Can you not understand us?" Alunen said loudly so that her voice would carry high enough to reach the Dragons' ears.

They looked at us again but said nothing comprehensible.

"aisau˘ borva osgarimin'nawar init omanelf aldrun'paiat˘" the Silver

Dragon said. *"er'sai inithenar etvai' etriagroam˘"*

"so ' maura sertak eraldrun'paiat˘" the Green Dragon replied.

"uin'sai kun etempa' vai'˘" the Black Dragon said.

"ku ' eraldrun'paiat gol iim˘"

The Copper Dragon then wondered and asked, *"maura sertak iim'sai gol elagain'kaila˘ erkiin'paiat jorka init iim ' mogalet jorka iim kiin'paiat er˘"*

The Black Dragon said, *"uneskarii'paiat sai init kitetai' rassesetak osnelf'sai ' mori ink sai ' kintukrassesetak oskiin'paiat init er˘"*

"We *must* know what they are saying!" Norandar said, as frustrated as the rest of us.

"We can only hope that they will come to understand our words," I said, not knowing what else to do.

"Their words are gibberish!" Alim'dar spat, unsatisfied as well.

"horoa sai init osaril'kaila osnelf ivero es lorvano˘" the Gold Dragon said, and it seemed that he was speaking in a sterner tone.

"iimdurthor'kaila es iimkaila˘" the Crimson Dragon exclaimed.

"so˘" the Blue Dragon said. *"loashen aril'kaila omanelf ivero˘"*

"tener iimkronaggas norgrakon ismaustin'kaila˘" the Silver Dragon said.

"horoa ' sai ini summan selin amal sylveria˘"

"dryka ' tera immkaila jork unis tera iimglodarg'kaila ink astu kitetai' aril'kaila era iim respon'kaila˘"

"If we cannot talk to them, then how are we to have them answer our questions?" Sveraden asked.

"We must learn their tongue, or they ours," Adaashar said.

"All we can do is wait," I added. "It looks to me as if they are discussing *us*. And is it only me, or does it seem that they are as astonished by us as we are them?"

The others agreed, for though we could not understand their many words, when they did look at us, they did so with a strange fascination in their giant eyes.

"maura jorka iimvormuko kian etselin garen'kaila˘ vaira os'sai kalum os erimem'nawar˘" the Black Dragon asked of the others.

"etkoume'sai amal'nawar ' okan etkova˘" the Copper Dragon explained. *"sai epskort eiminii kiniialda emirk ' uinkort'sai non iimmorothay'nawar gol aril'nawar˘"*

"tera iimolen kaila armi˘" the Black replied.

"keyner'sai init˘" the Gold said. *"osrasan selin bodin'sai init vaira iim'sai sertak bodin omaliases˘ aisau˘ armikort'sai eps alet kitetai' masograth ' loashen iim jorka uin peal˘ jorka esfa iimjorka ' kovot jorka uin thormar oskenanas' gagupog'kaila ' lulwar'kaila etkort tera priilan'kaila uinausmo'sai˘ tera numen heses'kaila bralk sai osivero ' tera*

beldren'kaila oskaras˘ nonliases'sai os ' aril'kaila et kort˘"

Then the Dragons moved away from us and separated into two groups. Those that were of metallic colors—the Gold, Silver, and Copper—stood upon one side of us, while those of natural colors stood on the other. The Blue, Green, Black, and Crimson Dragons, standing only upon their back legs, moved their great clawed hands to their heads, covering what must have been their ears, and then closed their eyes. And the others were silent.

"osvormuko'sai init glodarg non nelf˘ init unis˘" the Gold Dragon said, and he slowly moved his clawed hand high overhead.

And then what seemed to be an unnatural sleep overcame us.

I awoke with the first light of the golden sun. Just as it had retreated into the west the night before, consumed by some distant wonder, so did it emerge in the east. I had not seen this time of day previously, as I had still been sleeping this early the day before. Now, at this hour, the blue sun appeared higher over the gold and seemed overpowering, for the morning was a deeper purple than the latter day would be. The green moon hung in the west, showing faintly with its lonely light.

The Dragons were gone; the only sign of them was the imprints their massive bodies had left upon the landscape. Whatever mystical sleep they had put upon us had concealed their flight away. I wondered when we would see them again.

Alunen and Norandar were already awake, and they sat together leaning against a large boulder that was nearby. When they saw that I had risen, they stood and came closer.

"What has happened, Alak'kiin?" Norandar asked.

"Where are the Dragons?" Alunen wondered.

"I have not seen them since last night. They were doing something, but I know not what. Then, I think, they put a spell upon us to make us sleep." The others stirred and slowly began rising. "Maybe they didn't want us to see something."

"What are we to do now?" Alim'dar asked.

"That did not go as I would have hoped," Sarak'den said. "We got nothing from them, no answers. We can't even speak their language!"

"Maybe we can learn it with time," Adaashar said.

"If we can even find them again," Sveraden said. "Look how long it took for us to find them before."

"And what do we do now? Where do we even look?" Norandar wondered.

"We can still go to the mountain," Sarak'den said. "We are halfway there already." Some of the others nodded, showing their silent assent.

"I cannot speak for all of you," I said. "But I feel like there is more to this.   The Dragons… Their strange behavior in putting us to sleep. Something more has happened."

"I do not understand what you mean, Alak'kiin," Norandar said.

"I am not entirely sure what I mean either," I admitted. "Just that even though we could not grasp their words, I got the impression that they were perhaps… bewildered by our presence here in the world."

"I felt that too," Alim'dar said.

"If that is true," Sveraden said. "Then what answers can they give us anyway?"

"We will have to wait until we find them again," Alunen said, then changed the course of our conversation. "I was thinking, all day yesterday, about our lives. For on the first day of our awakening, when the day was coming to its end, Sarak'den, Sveraden and I all thought that it was the end of our lives, when the complete darkness came, at the hour of attrition, and we drifted into slumber. But we awoke again in the morning, and we had memories of the previous day. And I cannot help but have the feeling that we are here for a purpose, or at least a reason. We did not awaken by mere accident, surely. If we did not perish on that day or yesterday, then surely we will not tonight either, and maybe never."

"What is it you are trying to say?" Sarak'den asked.

"I am saying that we likely have all the time we might need to get the answers we long for, even if the Dragons cannot help us. So why should we worry about it?"

"Yes," Sveraden said. "I felt certain urgency about finding answers too, but that was before, when we did not know how long we might have left here in this world. But now it seems that our time has not been determined."

Adaashar added, "Just as the moon and the gold sun leave us when the day ends, they both return. The creatures of this world sleep and then wake. All things seem to move in cycles, with purpose and order. So indeed, why should we be concerned? What has been will be again."

The others agreed, as did I. So we decided then that we would not hurry to find the answers to the many questions that would tell us what was the purpose in this life. And we spent that morning just enjoying the world around us; we didn't stray far from where we had slept, for there was much to see right there, much to consider about the plains and the creatures that inhabited the region.

From there, the great mountain was just to the west and north, towering over the plains, its mysteries waiting to be uncovered. To the east was the valley of our awakening, where there was much still to be explored, for we had but seen parts of the western side. Northward, to the very extent of our vision, there seemed to be plains, though further still there was a thick haze set upon the land. And to the south were endless plains as well; beyond that, more mountains... What wonders and what creatures might exist in the far away places that we could not even see?

Once again, when the golden sun had reached its apex in the sky, long after the moon had been taken by the west, the indiscernible shadow from the north fell upon us, upon our spirits, and the dark and jagged lines across the horizon appeared. What was it about this hour that cast such dejection upon our souls? Still we could not fathom... However, it was not so despairing this day, because having experienced it before, we knew it would pass. And when the time came, the distant features indeed vanished, and the world returned to normal.

Then, just after this time, we had a lone visitor arrive.

Adaashar and Sveraden had been gone for a time but had now returned with handfuls of berries that they had found. Giving some of them to each of us, we ate, sitting upon the soft grass of the plains, paying little mind to the sky, or anything other than one another's company.

Then we heard the great swishing of a Dragon's approach, its wings cutting through the air. We quickly stood to see that the great Gold Dragon had returned, but nowhere around were the others. He landed firmly upon the plains, not far from where he had been the night before, and he looked to us.

"*nelf,* he said. "I am Ashysin, your *patral,* your *enaril."* His words were strange, seeming a mix of our tongue and his.

Astonished that some of his words were like ours, we then introduced ourselves to Ashysin the Gold, and as each of us did so, the great Dragon nodded his head.

"I do not yet... *aldrun...* your words, *woko.* But I will. *Kronaggas* is... *araril* we. Now you must do what is *keyner."* His words were slow and strained, and it was clear that he was having great difficulty in saying what he intended, at least in our tongue.

"What do you want us to do?"

"I do not want. Kronaggas *toraw* you go the Valley of *Naiad.* For something *neskra* has there *aril'nawar.* You must find it."

"What is 'neskra'," I asked, confused by his words, unsure what he really wanted us to do.

"*neskra... nefa...* no... evil. *Neskra ai."*

"We do not understand 'evil'," Alim'dar said.

"We will do whatever you want, great Dragon," Alunen said. "But what does this mean?"

"*Kronaggas keyner* to *inukku* others. *irtta* you. Go, find them. They are *arool* and *toraw* you. Go, *inukku* the *nefa.* I must return to *vorma.* Others wait."

I nodded to Ashysin, for I was fairly certain that I knew what he wanted. The others looked to me then, understanding that I must have grasped the meaning of the Dragon's words better than they. I was not so sure. But before I had time to protest Ashysin had taken flight once again, his massive wings creating huge gusts of wind that nearly toppled us, and in a moment he was gone, flying back toward the giant mountain of the plains.

"I presume you know what he wants us to do?" Alim'dar asked.

"Maybe," I said. "The valley in which we awoke... I think he called it *Naiad.* Something is there, something that was not before. Something evil that he wants us to find."

"What is *evil*?" Sarak'den wondered. "The word sounds somehow familiar, but I do not understand it."

"Nor do I," I admitted.

"It does not sound good or pleasant," Norandar said. "The word inspires something... uncomfortable... within me."

"What should we do?" Sveraden asked.

"We should do what Ashysin asked us to do," Alim'dar said. "Or what we think he asked us to do. For even if we are wrong, it will be but a chance to further explore the Valley of Naiad, and if we are right, we must trust what the Dragon told us. For have we not, since we first cast our eyes on these great creatures, put our faith in them, trusting that it was they who could offer us answers to our many questions?"

"We have," Alunen said. "I agree that we should return to the valley and see what it is that Ashysin wants us to find."

That day we erected a pillar of stacked stone to mark the location, and we later called it *Kal'Taisin,* because it was where we first met the Dragons face to face.

So we all agreed that we would return to the valley and search for whatever evil the Dragon had told us about in his strained and confusing words. We left immediately and headed north, having decided that we would take a different route back into the valley. Rather than returning across the land bridge and through the Razorgrass Field we would take the slopes on the northern edge of the west side of the valley.

A MEETING WITH THE DARK

As we crossed the plains, we followed within view of the great river that flowed out of the Valley of Naiad, which was the place of our awakening. Here we were on the west side, and at the place where the river bent back to the east the ground began to slope upward, for the hilly lands of the valley were higher still than these vast plains. As it always had, the blue sun was hanging in its place in the east. The gold sun had moved onward to the west, and the moon had yet to make its appearance once again. If all were to be the same as on the previous days it would not be long until it emerged from the distant veil that seemed to obscure the heavenly bodies.

The slopes of the western valley were an arduous task to overcome, for they were steep, rocky and wet with water that was coming up from the ground itself, not in springs or streams, but covering the entire face of the slopes, so far as we could tell. Even Saxon found it difficult to pass through as his paws continually became embedded in the mud that was formed. He protested with snorts and moans but continued on with us nevertheless.

By the time we had overcome the slopes the green moon had indeed begun to show itself—a tiny spot in the distance at first, but as the moments passed it fully egressed from the vault that kept it concealed for more than a third of the day. As well, it was at this hour that the light upon the landscape was spread evenly, for the two suns seemed equally distant from one another, and from us. This hour of the day came to be called *Evenlight.*

There, at the top of the slopes we were slowed even further, for the land was covered in vines that were overlaid with thorns. Our protective clothing, made from the barathea of the Dragonscales, protected us from harm, but as we traversed this region we would often become entangled in the bristly growth. For this reason we called this area *The Knotted Lands.*

By the time we had escaped these hindering hills and crossed over another river by way of a land bridge, the gold sun was fast approaching its time of fading. Here, we were in the hills that were just west of the wooded land where I had first met Alim'dar and my other brothers. As the sky began its envelopment of the gold sun we mounted a hill and could then see the forested expanse. And by the time we reached the tree line, the sun was nearly extinguished. This was the time of the last light of the day. Thus, this hour became known as *Lastlight.*

"How are we to find this evil, this *Neskra ai* that Ashysin told us to find?" Sarak'den asked as we rested by the trees, eating of the same kind of fruit that Alim'dar had given me two days before.

"I do not know," I said. "I assume that all we can do is search and explore. Then we will find that answer."

"Perhaps it will make itself known to us," Alim'dar suggested.

"We should wait for Firstlight," Adaashar said.

"Indeed, for what can we find in the darkness of night?" Sveraden asked. "When only the blue sun casts its dim glow and the moon barely gives any light of its own."

"Then we will make camp here," Norandar said. "In the morning we will eat to keep our strength, and then we will explore and search until we find what we were sent here for."

As we made camp, Saxon, knowing the area at which we were, began howling, and a short while later, the other Dains appeared from the south, trotting over the hills to us. These were the same as those who had first found me, when I first met Saxon. They stayed with us that night, curling up close to us, and we were glad that they did, for the night was cooler than those previous, and their warm bodies gave us comfort.

Some of the others had fallen asleep; Alim'dar, Alunen and Norandar were still awake with me, and the four of us were discussing what we might encounter when we found whatever it was that Ashysin had sent us after. We came to no conclusions, of course, for it was just the excited speculations of our tiring minds in the last moments of the day.

Then, we heard something. Each of the Dains perked up, their eyes darting to the forest to the east. We too looked, and it was not difficult to see that peering through the darkness, between the tightly packed trunks of the trees, were several pairs of eyes, glowing seemingly of their own power, for there was no sunlight to be reflected. The Dains did not seem alarmed, but only curious, and they stared, waiting.

"What are they?" Alunen whispered.

"Animals, perhaps," Alim'dar said. "Some creatures we have not seen before. Something that lives only in the woods."

"I entered the woods two days ago," Norandar said. "Just after I emerged from my cave that is not far to the north of here. There were animals in there—Birds and Squirrels and horned Pigs. But nothing with eyes like those."

"You could not have seen everything that lived in there," Alim'dar said.

"Perhaps not. Who knows what mysteries that dark wood conceals?"

"There are six of them," Alunen said, still whispering, still staring into the trees. "That I can see. Twelve eyes… what could they be? For look… they do not look away, their eyes darting about as do most of the animals we have seen. No… they stare straight at us."

"Their eyes are like ours," Alim'dar noted.

Curiosity was overtaking me, and I stood up; the others followed. Adaashar, Sveraden and Sarak'den still slept; the Dains that were near to them seemed more intent on staying with the others than on investigating.

I took a few steps closer to the trees, studying the eyes, watching for their reaction. The eyes blinked as they stared, but they did not otherwise move.

"Hello," I said in more than a whisper.

"What are you doing?" Alunen said.

"I want to see what they are," I explained, now more quietly. "Maybe they are what we came here for."

"I sense no... *evil*," Norandar said.

"Neither do I," Alim'dar agreed. "And when the Dragon said the word *evil*, I felt disquieted, for something in that word held a kind of power that made me uncomfortable. But I do not sense it here. Whatever these creatures are, they are not evil."

"Then let us go to them," I said.

"No," Alunen said. "See if they will come to us."

I nodded and took several more steps toward the trees. "Hello," I said again. "I am Alak'kiin. We were just wondering what kind of creature you might be... for we have not seen eyes such as yours since we awakened in this world. Will you come out so that we might see you?"

Only one of the eye pairs seemed to react, and they shifted in the darkness. Then, moment by moment they grew just a bit larger, and from out of the trees one of them moved. Still, it was too dark to see anything but a silhouette, the outline of something that may well have looked like us...

It said nothing, and stopped. I did not know if it was for fear of us, or something else entirely. Then, the remaining five pairs of eyes vanished. This figure then slowly retreated back into the woods, watching me all the while, saying nothing, barely making a sound, then its eyes vanished.

"Are they gone?" Alunen said.

"Yes."

"If they leave we may never find them again," Alim'dar said. "For they will flee from us all through the night. If they are what we have come for, let us catch up to them now so that we might uncover this mystery!"

He started forward into the trees, and none protested. Alunen was the next to follow. "Alak'kiin," Norandar said. "Let us go around the woods, me to the north and you to the south, so that we might cut them off."

"What about the others?"

"Go wake them and tell them. If they wish to join us, then let them. If not, tell them we will meet them back here later. Now go!"

I went to the others and shook them awake. Sveraden said, "What is it, Alak'kiin?"

"We may have found them... the ones we came here to find! But they run from us. Alim'dar, Alunen and Norandar have already given chase." Each of the others rose from their brief sleep, and the Dains followed. "They were in the woods, and then they fled!"

And so Sarak'den, Sveraden and Adaashar spread out, all three of them entering into the woods, followed by the Dains. Only Saxon and I remained, and we made haste to the south, hoping to find these strangers so that we might learn more.

The darkness of night grew deeper. I was awake later than I had ever been. Once I turned around the bend of the forest to the east, the landscape was better lit by the faint glow of the blue sun, which remained far ahead, still lingering high in the night sky. I was able to move faster now, not so concerned about stumbling over rocks or brush in the darkness. I moved quickly, always keeping my eyes on the woods, hoping that one of these creatures would emerge.

In the distance I heard a voice shouting but could not make out what had been said or who had said it, only that it came from deep in the woods. I stopped for a moment to listen but did not hear it again. Saxon was panting, and so I decided to rest for a few moments so that we would be ready to run again if we saw one of these strange new beings. When he saw that we were resting, he sat down and waited, recovering his own breath.

I sat too, breathing deeply, but not heavily; I had not been over-exerting myself. Staring as far as my vision could see I looked to the east. Soon I should be coming away from the forest and into the hills south of the cave of my awakening, where I had first been greeted by the Dains. Beyond that were more hills, rising higher and higher, and I could barely make out the dim outline of the mountains to the north.

The night held a certain charm; it was quieter, calmer, and if possible even more peaceful than during the day. There were sounds unique to it— night Birds squawked in the distance, Bats flittered overhead, and even the sound of the rushing waters of the rivers was more distinct.

Although I wondered what my brothers and sisters might be doing, if they had found the strangers, I realized that I was actually in no hurry to resume my own search. Despite my earlier urgency in finding them, I realized once again that my time in this world was indefinite, and that there was really no reason to be concerned. It was, I deemed in those moments as I considered it, more a matter of anticipation for things that were new, here in this wonderful life that caused the urgency that I sometimes felt.

For we had felt great determination to find the Dragons, so that our questions might be answered, and we had been disappointed when we could not even speak with them. But that had resolved itself, for we *had* found them, and upon our last meeting with Ashysin we had seen that very quickly he was somehow learning our language. Surely, in my estimation, we were beings that would be here for a long time. Indeed, there were many questions left unanswered, and many more would certainly present themselves as time carried on. And what exhilaration it would bring to discover new things… what a wonderful world!

I was filled with unwanting peace in those nighttime moments, and I wondered if my siblings might be having the same epiphany, or if they were simply intent upon finding the strangers as quickly as possible.

And it was this peace, I soon discovered, that opened my mind to a new perception of the world. For in it existed all of the wonderful creatures and places that we had seen—and all of those that we had yet to see—and there were many things to learn. There were the suns and the moon in their successions through the heavens to learn about, the vast lands that only existed at the extent of our vision and our imaginations, and the gloriousness of the Dragons, whom we knew so little about; all of these things were the natural world.

Yet there was so much more, surely, for had the valley itself awakened us? Or had the suns and moon given rise to our lives? Perhaps it was the Dragons. But how could such things have been? For all things in nature moved with a pattern, it seemed, in a cycle, and it clearly was not common that people such as we were awakened, otherwise the world would be filled with them.

So I was left thinking that surely it was something else that had willed us into existence, some special circumstance. If it was special, then it was outside of the natural realm and this opened an understanding of the fullness of what we were and of what we were capable to a world unseen— to a spiritual aspect of our existence. And if beings such as us could be created, what force would it be that was capable? What could create not only us, but the moon and suns and mountains and rivers and the entirety of the world itself?

As I considered these things, one word came into my mind, and it was *magic.* Magic…

What could this force be, this unnamed power or influence that was not seen with the eyes or perceived with any of the other senses? It was surely nonphysical, for I could not interact with it… or could I? For at that moment I realized that if this magic did exist then it could only be a force of intention, a power that pervaded all things, for all things were created by it. Magic.

As I sat there south of the woods considering these things, I decided to focus my own intent upon that which I was here to do in these moments of my life—to find the strangers who were in the land, whom Ashysin had sent us after.

And what is my intent, the heart of the matter? I asked myself, and words—whether my own thoughts or some other force—came into my mind, saying, *"To see the others and where they were at would bring greater success than wandering around in the dark of night."*

I closed my eyes and concentrated, focusing my thoughts, my imagination, upon where each of my brothers and sisters might be, whether or not they had found any of the strangers, and what my next action should be. I relaxed my mind and breathed easily, taking in the coolness of the night air, and finding myself at great peace, at one with nature, and absolute calmness came over me.

Then, when at last I opened my eyes, I saw the world that I had seen surrounding me before, but now I could see new things as well, things that had been there previously—I knew—but that had been unnoticed. There was a faint glow that permeated all things, all life, an aura of a kind. All things had their own presence, their own power within them, and this was part of the spiritual realm, now perceivable by me, through my meditation.

And then I saw it, first peering at me through the woods—one set of the strangers' eyes—and when I took notice of it, it moved away quickly, along the edge of the forest to the east. It was within the woods, yet I could see its aura moving swiftly, unobscured by the trees. Had it not been for this new ability, I would not have seen it at all. My intent, my will, had awakened within me this magic, and I knew then that I could use it to achieve the things I desired.

Exhilarated by this, I quickly rose and started running after the glowing shade as quickly as I could so as not to lose sight of it. Saxon followed, as excited as I was, but surely not knowing why.

Invigorated, I was able to not only keep an eye on my objective—catching up with the stranger—but also to take notice as more and more of the auras of the world came into view. This magic was growing in intensity and the awakening of this new sense was quickening all things within me. Every creature glowed with this aura, every blade of grass, every stone, and though the darkness of night encompassed me, I could see as if it did not. Even distant entities were perceivable; far away, to the north, I could see others, perhaps my brothers and sisters or the strangers, also running over the hills, some in pursuit of the others.

In this heightened state I found myself able to run without tiring so quickly, and I guessed that my siblings may also have uncovered this power within, for the distant figures continued onward through the night just as did I, following the others, surely as euphoric as I. And it occurred to me that the strangers must have realized this ability as well, for so long as we gave chase, they continued their flight through the dark.

The night was fully set in as we continued the pursuit; though I had not realized it before, there had been a lingering and faint residual light in the west. But now, even that had faded and there was the light only cast by the blue sun, and by the glowing auras... I realized then that the color of the magical impression surrounding all things was the same shade as the light cast from the night's sun. I stopped running then, just for a moment. Saxon kept on until he realized that I was no longer moving, and then he too stopped and turned back to me.

I looked at my hands, holding them out in front of me, and I could see that the blue aura also was upon my own flesh. I raised one of them up to the heavens, and held it in front of the night sun, and could see that indeed the colors were indistinguishable. I concluded then that the magic of seeing auras might be given by this heavenly body. But it mattered little at that moment, for I could see that the distance between my objective and me was again widening. Again I ran, and though he grunted slightly in protest, Saxon followed.

The height of the hills through which we ran was lessening the further east we went. Small streams flowed between many of them, but they were easy to surmount with leaps and vaults across the terrain. As the chase pressed on, clouds moved in from the west, obscuring the night sun, but the auras never lessened. Gusts of wind sprang up and for the first time since I had awakened a heavy and warm rain began to fall upon the world. Soon thoroughly soaked—I in my barathea clothing, Saxon sodden and whining—we continued on.

Several spans after the rain began I saw as the stranger whom I pursued stopped and kneeled down, for weariness was surely overtaking them as well. I thought that this might be my opportunity to overtake them, and so I ran harder; I ignored the fatigue in my muscles and body, as I was intent on reaching my goal. Still, to the north of me, others ran eastward, still chasing or being chased.

Then, when I felt certain I would either have to stop for exhaustion or I would fall of natural enervation, the stranger turned toward me, now not far ahead. I slowed myself, still walking, but unable to continue at my quickened pace. The person was not moving anymore, but only standing still, and I hoped they would stay that way so that I might recover my breath before arriving. Saxon sighed, seemingly thankful that the night run was over.

As I drew closer, somewhat sure but mostly hoping that the stranger would flee no more, I looked around. In the far distance, to the north, I saw the auras of several of my kind, though I knew not if they were my brothers or sisters or the strangers, for all of them had ceased the chase. And as I panted to recover, the blue glow that had allowed me this magical sight slowly faded until I could see nothing save for that which my natural vision granted me. But now I was close enough that I could see the stranger without the magic, and I could see that it was a woman by the curves of her body.

Under the light of the night sun I could see that the hills ended there, where she was, dropping off into places unseen. I would have hastened my pace if not for the aching in my chest, but it was such a short distance that I felt mostly sure I could make it.

As I approached I could see that her hair was a dark shade, and she was a full hand shorter than my sisters. Her skin seemed to be a different shade than my own, yet I was unsure if it was a trick of the light, for her body seemed covered with a deep sapphire tint. I held my hand out, not to the woman, but to compare the shades of skin under the light of the sun. They were different, no doubt... She was different, but indescribably beautiful. And she was humming a soft melody, a wordless song that was enchanting.

For long moments I listened to her refrain. Then, when my breath was recovered enough, I asked, "Why did you run?"

She was silent for a moment then softly said, "Why did you follow?"

"We... I just wanted to know who you were, you and the others like you. My brothers and sisters have given chase to the others who were with you."

"But why?" Now she turned, facing me, and I could fully see her face. "Why do you care who we are?"

"We were told to come find you."

"Told?" she said, raising her eyebrows. "By whom?"

"By the Dragon, Ashysin."

"What is a Dragon?"

"You will have to see for yourself."

"Why would this Dragon want you to find us?"

"Well, I'm not entirely certain," I admitted. "He told us that something evil had awakened here...."

"And where is here?"

Considering her reactions and questions, I thought for a moment, then said, "Tell me, do you know who you are or where you are, or why you are here?"

She shook her head, saying, "No. My name is Nirvisa'nen. I know only this. I know that we awoke here, between these two great ranges of mountains, over a full day and part of a night ago. There were six of us, awakened together, near the trees where you first saw us. None of us knows why."

"That is a mystery that my brothers and sisters and I are trying to unravel ourselves," I explained. "For we too awoke in this valley nearly three days and nights ago. We have no memories of a time before our awakening."

Nirvisa'nen looked deep into my eyes, curious, intensely searching for something—whether truth or answers to her questions, I was not sure. Then she asked, "What is *your* name?"

"I apologize," I said, realizing I had not yet introduced myself. "I am Alak'kiin."

"Have you been here before, to this place, Alak'kiin?" I shook my head. Calmly then, she took my hand in hers and gently pulled me to face the east. Here, the hills were gone, dropped off to a large body of water that I had not even noticed before. This lake glistened and gleamed under the blue light of the night sun. I could hear water in the distance flowing or falling, and I imagined that this place was beautiful in the light of day. But it was dark, and the full view could not be seen at this late hour. "I call it *Iidin*," Nirvisa'nen said. "But I do not know why it should be called this. I only know that it is enchanting and stunning."

I looked again out over the water and then returned my gaze to hers, for moment by moment I was feeling more drawn to her beauty. "I would much like to see it in the light of day," I said, but I was not certain that I meant the lake anymore, for I felt stirrings in my body when I looked into her dark eyes, which was something I had not felt before.

Nirvisa'nen smiled faintly and said, "You do not have to wait until Firstlight." She released my hand then and turned to face the water. She moved slowly down the hillside until she was on the shoreline of the lake, and then into the water, only ankle deep. "Watch and listen, Alak'kiin."

And then she began to hum again, and I was entranced, for I had never known that such a thing was even possible—for someone to use their voice to create an aria that flowed so perfectly in tune with nature.

As her music pierced the night the waters shimmered even brighter. All sounds of nature faded away, drowned out by her soft and gentle song.

The light that was before reflected of the night sun seemed to take on a life of its own, stirring within the waters, swirling and spiraling about, and then leaping out—tiny points of light that danced about the surface, rising into the air and skipping about in perfect harmony with her magical tune.

Her sweet humming carried over the surface of the waters and the entire lake was lit with countless dancing lights that were subservient only to her song. And the beauty of the entire scene before me—the glowing waters, the jittering lights, and Nirvisa'nen herself—overcame me, and I sank to the ground, still watching, enticed...

As she finished her song and her voice trailed off into the night, the lights dropped back into the water, fading back into their previous place. The waters were still, as was my heart.

Nirvisa'nen looked over her shoulder at me, smiled, and then quite unexpectedly dove into the water and disappeared under the surface. I leaped up and hurried into the shallows. Saxon followed. The water was uncomfortably cold.

"Nirvisa'nen!" I cried out.

She swam to the surface, her head poking out of the lake and she said, "Join me, Alak'kiin."

But as I considered doing so, I was drawn away from the side, abruptly and forcibly. A hand had grasped my shoulder and pulled me away, distracting me from the woman. I looked about, and standing there was a man as tall as I, but he was not one of my brothers...

"You are not one amongst us," said the man; he was azure-skinned like Nirvisa'nen. "Leave her."

I backed away from him, from the shoreline onto which Nirvisa'nen was now emerging.

"I mean no harm," I said.

"I do not doubt you, stranger," the man said. "But you are not like us, and you should keep your distance."

"Why should he?" Nirvisa'nen said.

The man had no response to her and instead said to me, "Who are you?"

"My name is Alak'kiin, and I mean no harm. You say we are not the same, but we—my brothers and sisters and I—are much the same, for we are newcomers in this land as well, and like you, we do not yet know why."

"I am Norgrash'nar," he said. "And I apologize for the harshness of my tone. But we have... my own brothers and sisters... been in this world for some time now and we do not even know what we are, or why we are."

Then, though I had not heard their approach, I saw as others appeared, coming out of the darkness. There were four others of cobalt skin, and they walked together. And not far behind came my own siblings, all of them. The Dains who had been with them were nowhere to be seen and I supposed that they had grown bored with the run and returned to their own endeavors. Only Saxon remained amongst us.

"We have already met the others of your kind," Norgrash'nar said. Nirvisa'nen had come fully out of the water and was standing amongst her sisters.

"You keep saying that we are not the same *kind*," Alim'dar said, walking to stand near me. "But from what you have told us, we *are* the same—we have all awakened into this world and do not know why. Whatever magic has awakened us all is surely the same."

"But you look different," said one of the women, whose name I had not yet learned. "Our skin is like the blue night sun, and yours is more like the sun that rules the day."

And it occurred to me then what Ashysin had meant, when he was telling us to go into the valley and find what had awakened... something *evil* he had said; but in not fully knowing the tongue which we spoke, the words were likely misunderstood. He had said at first the words *Neskra ai*... and this surely was a word that meant *dark*, and not *evil*, for there was nothing disquieting about these people.

"You are... Neskra ai," I said.

"What do you mean?" Norgrash'nar asked.

"That is what the Dragon called you, what he sent us here to find. It must mean something like *dark*... dark-skinned people, perhaps."

"Why did this Dragon send you to find us?" Norgrash'nar asked.

"What is a Dragon?" one of the other men asked.

"Can you tell us why we are here?" one of the women asked.

"We do not know much more than you," Alim'dar replied.

"We are new to this world as well," said Alunen.

"Let us sit and talk," Norandar suggested. "Though I know you want answers, understand that we all do as well. That is why we have come here to find you. There are great mysteries about our existence, and it seems that now we have all found one another. Now we can discover this world together."

And all of the others, both my brothers and sisters, myself, and the *Neskra ai* agreed that we would sit together and see what we could learn. But it was not long thereafter when exhaustion overcame us all, and we slept through the remainder of the night.

The Oath of Dragons

When Firstlight came we all awoke. In the light of the day the true beauty of the *Neskra ai* became apparent, for the deep tone of their skin was so unlike the golden hue that my brothers and sisters and I adorned. They were unclothed, as we had been, for it had not occurred to them that they might want to cover themselves, but seeing that we were not naked, they soon found themselves covering the parts of their bodies that were different between man and woman. With thick leaves that grew by the lakeside that Nirvisa'nen had called Iidin, they made rudimentary coverings for themselves.

Iidin itself was a beautiful region, for the vast lake extended to the north and to the east as far as the mountains went. Along the north edge a waterfall poured out of the extreme heights of the mountains, visible even from this distance. It was here, in Iidin, that the northern mountain range of the valley curved southward and eastward.

Despite the urgency of the *Neskra ai* the night before—their many questions—the morning found them much more patient, for as we all awoke to this new day we were finding new companionship. For to me, there were no longer just my six siblings and me in this world, but now six others—thirteen of us in all to enjoy the delights of the world.

Nirvisa'nen and her two sisters, who were named Kalenen and Kuranen, left with Alunen, Sarak'den and Sveraden for a short time and when they returned they had gathered and brought us large fruits and leaves to eat for a morning meal. While they were gone we spoke with the other men, learning that Norgrash'nar's brothers were named Haldus'nar and Garonar.

After eating, when our conversations were starting to turn toward matters deeper and of greater significance, Haldus'nar stood abruptly and pointed silently to the west. We all followed his gesture.

"What is that?" Kuranen said.

"I have seen nothing like it before," Garonar said.

A great white creature was in the westward sky, soaring toward us. And though I had not seen this particular one before, I knew well what it was, for it was unmistakable. "That is a Dragon," I explained, my heart leaping, as it always did when one of these great beasts was within sight.

"How big is that thing?" Kalenen asked, astonished as it drew closer still.

Now, gusts of wind were rushing over us, stirred by the Dragon... then the others came into view. Gold and Silver, Copper and Blue, Green, Black and Crimson, and White, the Dragons all approached, shining in the sunlight and within our hearts. Excitement filled me, not just for the sight of the Dragons but also for the *Nescra ai*, because this was the first time any of them had seen these great creatures.

The Dragons came to land upon the tops of hills to the west. The great white was near the center, with the Crimson Dragon next to him. The Silver and Copper Dragons were directly next to Ashysin the Gold, who was himself next to the White Dragon. And next to the Crimson Dragon were the Black, Green and Blue Dragons. These were the same as those we had seen upon the plains. Only in regard to the great White Dragon was this a new meeting for my siblings and me.

They all looked down at us, from an even greater height upon the hills, but it was the White Dragon that spoke first, saying, "Greetings, *nelf*, children. I am Kronaggas, and I welcome you to this world."

I was astonished that the Dragon spoke with such clarity in a tongue that we understood fully.

"Kronaggas," Alim'dar said, but then nothing followed. He too was overwhelmed, as I'm sure were all of the others, for this great beast spoke with more eloquence and exuded more power and grace than did all of the others.

"You speak our tongue?" Alunen said.

"Yes," he said. The tone of his voice was gentle, despite the deepness that came naturally to him. "For yours is a language more ancient than either I or any Dragon. The others will learn it as well soon enough, so that you might speak freely with them."

"What do you mean it is more ancient?" I asked. "For we are new creatures, are we not, awakened just days ago into this world of Dragons."

Kronaggas turned his giant head slightly, hesitating it seemed, then said, "You are... and this is the doing of my *draiko*... my children. For if you have not yet discovered this, Sylveria is a world of great beauty and magic. It is with this magic that the others have awakened you."

"What do you mean *awakened*?" Alim'dar asked. "Does this not imply that we were asleep? For as we fall into slumber at night, when the golden sun vanishes, we then awaken in the morning."

"It is not the same," Kronaggas said. "But in your tongue there is no word to better explain. For this awakening is one of magic... you are... new creatures, not born into this world, but brought into it...." He glanced to his side, toward Ashysin, then added, "By those who inhabit it."

"So what are we?" Norgrash'nar asked eagerly.

After considering this for a moment, Kronaggas, the great White Dragon, said, "You are the *Naiad,* which in the tongue of Dragons means *companions*. Those of you who first awoke, those of you with golden skin, are the *Sylvai,* which means *beautiful creatures*. Those of you with skin like Vespa, the sun of the night, are the *Nescrai*. "You are the children of Dragons, and we welcome all of you to this great and glorious land that is *Sylveria.*"

Each of the other Dragons rumbled and roared, seemingly with delight, and it was clear to me at that moment that they held a great affection for all of us, for in their reactions and observance of our interaction with Kronaggas, they had appeared to hold back their fervor. Their enthusiasm for us was equal—at least—to that which we held for the other small creatures of the world; it was a passion for the beauty and mystery of something new and exciting in the world.

And as I looked amongst the Dragons, amongst my brothers and sisters, and amongst the Nescrai, who were our cousins, I saw expressions of elation and love. The world had grown even more fascinating, and it was with great eagerness that I awaited all of the wondrous things that were certain to follow.

The Dragons stayed with us that day, talking, learning our language, bathing in the waters of Iidin, and I found it most interesting that although these great creatures seemed so powerful, so mightily divine and so transcendent, they had the same playful spirits as the other creatures of the world—the same as Saxon and my siblings and my cousins, and all other living things. It was a world of nothing but tranquility, and all of its inhabitants were filled with the joy of life.

That day, when the golden sun, which the Dragons called *Aros* had reached its high point, we all rested upon the hills near the lake of Iidin, both Dragon and Naiad. For long moments we had all been silent, but at last, Alunen said, "What is to come?"

"What do you mean, Alunen?" The Copper Dragon, who was named Sharuseth, asked.

"The future," she said. "Days will come and go as they have before, right?" The Dragon nodded, intensely interested in the woman and her questions. "What will come when many more have passed? How long will we be here, in this wonderful world, with you?"

"Time is eternal," Sharuseth said. "Our lives continue on as they always have. For more than three thousand cycles of the world we have dwelled here. And now that you have come, the world is even more stimulating." Alunen nodded, not fully understanding but content with the answer for now.

"Time..." Alim'dar said thoughtfully. "How can it be eternal? For just as we have awakened, so too did we have a beginning. And just as the day begins when Aros pierces the eastern Veil and ends when it fades into the oblivion of the west, will there not be an end to all things?"

But none of the Dragons spoke; each of them—save for Kronaggas— seemed bewildered by the deep rendering of Alim'dar's thoughts. He, the great White Dragon, appeared not so disconcerted, but rather as though he would only keep silent on the matter.

"I am sorry, Alim'dar," said the Silver Dragon, who was named Merilinder. "But I do not think we understand what it is you ask. For the day begins and ends, but it always returns again."

"And what if it did not return?" Alunen asked. "What if the world remained in darkness?"

"Things do not work like that, Alunen," Ashysin said. "It *always* returns. And I do not understand what it is that troubles you so... for life will always be what it is... beautiful and wonderful."

"But cannot things change?" Alim'dar wondered. "Just as there is night and day, just as there is up and down, is there not something that is... *not* wonderful. And is there not that which is unpleasant, for I felt pain two days ago, when I grasped the Razorgrass that is to the south and west of here. Yes, I healed, but it was unpleasant for a short time."

Kronaggas interjected now, thoughtfully saying, "I understand your concerns, though I do not know why it consumes your thoughts, for never in three thousand cycles have the *draiko* pondered such things. These are things that are best left unknown... unexplained, for they are those things that do not matter. Only peacefulness and love matter here in the world."

"Your words are a mystery to me," Norgrash'nar said. "For the others speak truly... what if things are not always so pleasant, so perfect."

"What would ease your minds, children?"

Each of us, Sylvai and Nescrai looked to the others, all of us sharing in the perplexity of questions unanswered, but still not really knowing what it was we were asking of the Dragons. None responded, for none had an answer to the question.

Finally, I had a thought and I said, "Great Dragons, as I have walked and ran amongst the fields and hills of this beautiful world I have had fleeting thoughts of the small creatures of the lands, those which are far smaller than am I. And I have taken care not to disrupt them too much—moving clear of them if I get too close, for I have wondered what would happen if I were to step upon them. Would they be harmed by my great weight upon them, just as the grass is sometimes broken beneath our steps?"

The Dragons listened intently, particularly Kronaggas the White, and I continued. "So it has entered my mind that we, the Naiad, are tiny to you, as the Insects are to us. Would it be possible that either you or something else might cause us... harm?"

Each of the Dragons seemed taken aback, for it had not occurred to them that such a thing might be possible. My siblings and cousins were nodding, and I surmised that my words had abridged their own thoughts and concerns.

"Now I understand," Kronaggas said. "And there is but one thing that we might do to ease your worries...." Everyone present, Dragon and Naiad, looked to him. "There is a natural force that is set upon the order of this creation. It is called the *Law*, and by it oaths might be sworn. This is not a matter to be taken lightly, for the Law is severe in its actions and stern in its demanding that all who swear by it must uphold their word. As you might fear harm by Dragons, one should even moreso fear harm by the breaking of an oath taken to the Law.

"And it is this that we will do to alleviate your concerns. Draiko, let us here and now make a vow to the Law that never will we harm, in any way, any one of the Naiad. And if we do, let the full force of the Law fall upon us."

The Dragons, each of them, agreed, and in a strange and ordered manner, they repeated the words of Kronaggas, each swearing that they would never bring harm upon us. And our minds were put at ease, for somehow this action taken by the Dragons brought us a sense of comfort, and we were certain that peace and love would always be upon us.

These were the first days of the meetings between the Naiad and the Dragons. Twenty-one of us there were—thirteen of my kind and eight of the Dragons in all of Sylveria.

The Sylvai were:

♂ *Alak'kiin—with silver hair, gold skin, and brown eyes*
♂ *Alim'dar—with brown hair, gold skin, and blue eyes*
♂ *Norandar—with blonde hair, gold skin, and green eyes*
♂ *Adaashar—with black hair, gold skin, and black eyes*
♀ *Alunen—with gold hair, gold skin, and hazel eyes*
♀ *Sarak'den—with brown hair, gold skin, and blue eyes*
♀ *Sveraden—with black hair, gold skin, and black eyes*

The Nescrai were:

♂ *Norgrash'nar—with black hair, azure skin, and black eyes*
♂ *Haldus'nar—with black hair, azure skin, and green eyes*
♂ *Garonar—with black hair, azure skin, and brown eyes*
♀ *Nirvisa'nen—with brown hair, azure skin, and green eyes*
♀ *Kuranen—with brown hair, azure skin, and blue eyes*
♀ *Kalenen—with brown hair, azure skin, and black eyes*

The Dragons were:

☿ *Kronaggas the White, with eyes equally pure*
☿ *Ashysin the Gold, who had eyes of green*
☿ *Sharuseth the Copper, with eyes of blue*
☿ *Merilinder the Silver, with black eyes*
☿ *Drovanius the Black, who had golden eyes, fierce and determined*
☿ *Verasian the Green, who had silver eyes*
☿ *Merobassi the Blue, who had eyes of brown*
☿ *Aranthia the Crimson, who had eyes of red, the same as his scales.*

THE BOOK OF

SEASONS, TIMES & TIDES

THE ESTABLISHMENT OF NAIAD

In the days that followed the Oath of the Dragons we continued to explore the Valley of Naiad. The Dragons would come and go as they pleased, and though we never knew when they might show up again, we always knew that these great creatures were nearby, somewhere in the world.

All of us, both Sylvai and Nescrai, stayed together in those days, getting to know one another, learning about our world, talking and enjoying the beauty of the land together. We learned much in those times, and speculated even more about the future and what great things we might be able to accomplish in the world.

On the ninth day after our awakening, we together decided to make a journey to the east, having already explored much of the Valley of Naiad.

The lake of Iidin extended farther to the east than I had first realized, and there was one long hill that passed between the lake and the great river that cut through the valley. For this we began calling this the River of Iidin. The land tapered as it moved eastward until it was but a narrow plateau with the lake to the north and the river to the south. Then, the land came to an end, for there the lake showed itself to be the source of the river.

Just past the mouth of the river was the point where the northern and southern ranges of mountains came together. There was no path by land across the river there, and so we were forced to swim the distance. Ever eager to accompany us, Saxon remained at my side. It seemed I had made a lifelong companion who enjoyed my company even more than that of his own kind.

When we came to the southern shore of the river, we were upon rocky ground, for here there was little soil and even less vegetation. To the south were the vast fields upon which Alunen and Sveraden had first seen the grazing Bison. Even from here we could see the great herds moving across the landscape, enjoying life in their own way.

To the east, at the point where the two mountain ranges met, there was a steady and rocky slope that we knew would be surmountable, passing right between two high mountains. The way certainly led to another region of this vast world, and since we had seen most of the whole of Naiad, we prepared to take the mountain pass to the other side.

But it was as we were moving up the first segment of the incline that Merobassi the Blue came to visit, landing upon the rocky ground.

"Where are you going?" he asked inquisitively.

"We were going to see what is on the other side," Kalenen said. "Can you tell us what is over there?"

"Of course I can! The land there is different, and strange creatures inhabit it. Rain falls there most days, at least during this season."

"We want to see it," Garonar said.

"We want to see all of it!" Kuranen added. "All of the lands of this beautiful world."

"In time you will," Merobassi said. "But there is so much to see! Go, climb to the top of Yor'Kavon and see the western lands for yourselves; they are vast and are the domain of Verasian."

We continued our march up the incline; Merobassi accompanied us, walking alongside, his strides so much longer than ours that he had but to take a step only every so often. But his giant neck slithered around so that his face was always near us, looking at us, watching, waiting to engage us in as much conversation as we desired.

"Yor'Kavon?" Alim'dar asked. "What does that mean, in your tongue?"

Merobassi thought for a moment; our language was still new to him, and so he had to translate. "Tight... or Narrow Pass," he said. "That is the best rendering."

"It doesn't look so narrow," Norgrash'nar said.

The Dragon laughed—a deep and powerful chortle. "Indeed, for one such as you it is not. But try having these enormous wings and flying between the mountains!"

Norgrash'nar laughed as well.

The rocky slope became steeper and more strenuous to climb. Our breath was taken away much more quickly than walking upon the hilly lands of the valley. Judging by this terrain, I only imagined how different the other side of the pass might be. We did not quickly wear out, but our progress was slow.

"Merobassi?" I said after a time.

"Yes, Alak'kiin?" his mighty head weaved through the air and came to face me.

"It would be much easier if you would carry us."

"I wish that I could," the Dragon said. "But Kronaggas has instructed us not to take you anywhere, for fear that you might fall off and our oath be broken!"

"It is the suspense that drives us onward, Alak'kiin," Nirvisa'nen said. "If we were just shown everything upon the wings of Dragons, how quickly might the world grow boring?"

"Dear girl," Merobassi said. "This world could never grow boring; from the Zenartha of the western plains to the great Druugal of the Southern Reaches there is always something delightful to observe."

"And how long have you flown the skies of Sylveria?" Norgrash'nar asked, moving to stand between me and Nirvisa'nen, where he could more easily engage the Dragon.

"It has been more than three thousand cycles of the world since we were awakened. Since then we have soared the firmament and established our own domains over the lands of the world."

"Your domains?" Norgrash'nar said. "What is your domain?"

"My domain is the far northern reaches, the great land that would, in your tongue, be called *Skyreach*. In Draiko it is called *Maris'Borthrin*. It was there, in my lands, where we Dragons were first awakened, and indeed it is sometimes called *Dragonswake*."

"The north land?" Alunen interjected, drawing the Dragon's attention, who nodded. "Then perhaps you can tell me of a great mystery that has bewildered me since the first day of my awakening." Merobassi nodded. "When the Hour of Highlight comes, and we are in the southern valley, far to the north, over the heights of the mountains, a dark contour strokes the sky, and for a time, we are filled with an ominous sense, and we are drained of our pleasant thoughts. Can you tell me what this is?"

"I cannot," Merobassi said. "Not because I do not want to, but because even I do not know. The dark landscape you see is indeed the Skyreach Mountains of my land, but the shadow cast upon Sylveria is not of my domain; there is nothing there to cause such despairing thoughts. Yet it does, even in Dragons."

We were nearly to the top of the pass of Yor'Kavon, and at the top where it leveled off were the peaks of two tall mountains. It would be there that we could see that which had been hidden from our view thus far, whatever was to the east.

"And does this shadow fall upon all of Sylveria, wherever we might be? Even in the lands to the east?" I wondered, still moving toward the peak.

"No," Merobassi said. "Not from the ground. Only from the sky. For when one is upon the ground, much further to the south, Skyreach is not seen at all, for it is hidden beyond the perspective of the eye. Only if the mountains of my domain can be seen at all is it influential."

As we mounted the highest peak of the pass, the eastern lands came within view, and what I saw was far different than what I had expected.

For even though Merobassi had said that it was a rainy land filled with strange creatures, it was a region not entirely unlike the Valley of Naiad. In some ways it seemed like a reflection of Naiad, for there was a new range of mountains along the northern edge, and another along its southern. But the resemblance ended there.

From here, the pass of Yor'Kavon sloped downward to the east, just as it had risen from the west. But it did not level off below us onto a plain or hills or any other landscape that I was familiar with, but rather into a vast and desolate marshland.

"What is this that we see?" Garonar asked.

Merobassi, still on the western incline, extended his long neck in between the peaks to look over into the east, and said, "This is the region we call *Forthran*, for it is sometimes a sea and sometimes is not."

"I don't understand this, Merobassi," Garonar said.

"You must come to realize," the Dragon said. "That there is much you do not yet know about our world." The Dragon's eyes lit up then with a thought, and he looked at the northward mountain top of the pass, still rising far higher than we. "Go to the right of this mountain, for there is a pathway there that leads around to the north side. The Paken of this region often take this path, for there is succulent grass that grows along it. Go there and observe, then come back here."

"Will you not go with us?" Garonar asked.

"No. It is far too narrow of a trail for me, and though I could fly, I fear my wings might blow you off the mountain!"

Garonar led the way, and soon we were upon a stone path that was narrow even to us. When it was too slight for us to walk more than two side by side, Saxon turned and went back the way we had come, uncomfortable, it seemed, with the heights, for to the side the path dropped off down the steep side of the mountain. It led around the eastern face of the mountain top, then opened up onto a wider natural terrace upon which we all could stand. And there before us was the most incredible view that we had seen...

To the north was a great sea that met with the entire coastline, which was the northern mountain ranges of both this new expanse as well as the Valley of Naiad. As far as the eye could see to the east and west this vast body of water extended. But beyond the ocean, to the north were the lands that Merobassi had spoken of, which were his domain, the land of Dragonswake.

From such a distance as this our view of Dragonswake was hazy and few features could be distinguished. There seemed to be small ranges of mountains on the western side of this new land, and flatter, maybe hilly ground upon the eastern. But beyond that, little could be seen.

"How big *is* this world?" Sarak'den asked in wonder.

"Unimaginably so," Haldus'nar said, standing beside her. "For as far as my vision will go I can see land, far larger than Naiad, and this that we can see must only be a small part of it all."

"Look!" Alunen said suddenly, almost alarmed, as she pointed northward. "The hour has come."

And indeed, Aros was directly behind us, and to the north the faint outline of the distant mountains of Skyreach began to show itself, casting its gloomy shade upon our souls once again. To distract ourselves from this ominous affair, we turned away, each of us unwilling to look upon it.

To occupy ourselves, we looked around—in any direction but to the north. Just to the east, at the base of the mountain upon which we stood, the waters of the sea formed a cove that was just north of the marshlands; and from this view we could see that there was but one narrow stretch of land that separated the ocean from the lowlands. It seemed that it was only this stone barrier that held back the great waters of the sea.

After taking in the darker beauty of this scene we returned to the top of the pass where both Merobassi and Saxon waited.

"Did you see the great waters of the world?"

"Yes," Garonar said. "But why did you want us to go there? It is the Hour of Highlight, and that brooding darkness fell upon us again— whatever it is that emanates from your domain, from Dragonswake."

"I just want you to understand some things about our world," Merobassi said. "For nature is a far stronger force than you can imagine."

"We were already aware of the shadows coming from the north," Alunen said.

"It is not that of which I speak," the Dragon said. "And I have not finished showing you. For now we must wait here."

"Wait?" Alim'dar asked. "For what? I would much like to go down to the east, into this new land, and investigate."

"If you can but trust me for a while," Merobassi said. "You will see that this is not a good idea." His voice was stern and convincing, and though we could not yet know why, we agreed that we would wait and see what the Blue Dragon wanted to show us.

The Hour of Highlight passed entirely, as did another long stretch of the day. Aros moved from directly overhead and further to the west. Vespa, the night sun that showed even during the day lingered in the east, and still the moon, which the Dragons called *Imrakul*, was out of site, somewhere upon the northern stretch of its circuit through the heavens.

And when even more time had passed, Merobassi said to us, "Look! The Paken come!" He pointed with his giant claw to the east, down the slope of Yor'Kavon.

As we stood from our rest, Sveraden asked "What exactly is a Paken?"

"But another creature of the world," the Dragon replied.

We looked down the slope, and indeed there seemed to be an endless line of these Paken coming toward us in numbers so great that I would not even have tried to count them. They moved at a steady pace, neither running nor strolling, but they came with intent.

"Why are they coming up here?" Sveraden asked, sounding somewhat worried.

"They are harmless. As to why, you will see soon enough."

And the Paken drew closer. They were relatively small animals, at least compared to many others we had seen in the west. Standing with their head just above waist high they walked upon four legs with hooves like the Bison. Some of them had small horns protruding from their skulls, while others had giant spiraled projections.

As the first of this legion mounted the pass, many of them came up to us, sniffing at us, snorting, nearly pushing us over. Most of my companions laughed, for these were indeed harmless creatures, but Sveraden did not find it humorous and took to clinging to Adaashar as if she needed his protection.

Soon, we were so completely surrounded by the Paken that we could not have moved if we wanted to. Still they came, up over the pass and to the west, toward Naiad.

"Where are they all going?" Kalenen wondered.

"They will go into Naiad, to the plains along the southern mountains."

"Do they go there to feed upon the grasses?" Kuranen wondered, fascinated by the creatures.

"No," the Dragon explained. "For they have already eaten for this day. They love the taste of the quick blooming flowers of the marshlands below in Forthran."

"Then why are they going into Naiad?" Garonar asked.

"It is not what is in Naiad that they desire," the Dragon said. "It is what they wish to avoid." The herd of Paken was thinning now, and the end of them was in sight. All of them had moved through the pass. "And that is what I wish to show you. The time is drawing near."

"The time for *what?*" Alim'dar said impatiently. "We have waited here for a great stretch of the day."

"Be patient, Alim'dar," Merobassi said firmly. "It is of the utmost importance that you understand."

And so we waited longer. When at last the time came for the Dragon's revelation, he rose up, craning his neck to the northeast and said, "It comes! The Hour of Feltide!" And it was just as Imrakul, the green moon, pierced through the veil and showed itself once again that we saw it... From the north, from out over the stone barrier, a great wave of water rushed onto the marshland, sweeping southward, covering everything in its path. Moment by moment it proceeded to the south, flooding all in its wake.

Here on the pass we were safe from this mighty force, as were the Paken, now safely on the eastern side. For long moments the water rushed in until at last it struck against the range of mountains to the south.

Staring wide-eyed at this great and powerful natural wonder, all of us were now thankful that Merobassi had been with us this day, for if he had not, we might have gone down into the lowlands and been swept away.

"Now you see...." The Dragon said. "The world is a great and beautiful place, but we must understand it. There are places even a Dragon dare not go... You see, when the Hour of Feltide comes, the tides all across Sylveria rise quickly and ferociously. It is only the earthen mound to the north of these lowlands that holds back the sea during the day. But even this is overcome by the rising of the oceans. The Paken know this, and for it they migrate, knowing instinctually that they must. Throughout the day and night the tides will fall and a sea will be left there in Forthran. And in the early hours, beginning at Firstlight, this sea will drain deep down into the underworld below. As the day warms, the rocky ground will dry out again, and the Paken can return to graze upon the new growth and the seaweed that comes in with the ocean and is left behind. This is but another cycle of nature."

We did not go down into Forthran that day, but instead returned to Iidin, for we had gained a new respect for the world in which we lived. Though we did not, in those days, fear death—for death was then not a part of our existence—we did hold a kind of apprehension for things unknown, for things that might be dangerous or bring us harm. Merobassi's warning had been heeded by us all.

That day—the day we learned from Merobassi—was the 9th day of the season that the Dragons called *Springtide*. For they had in their three-thousand-year existence come to understand that the world moved all things in cycles and seasons. Though there were many other seasons that the Dragon told us about that day, we could not fully comprehend them, for we had not yet experienced them. But time would bring us understanding.

Together, we the Sylvai and the Nescrai, decided that we would remain in the Valley of Naiad, for it was our true home, the place of our awakening. And so we returned to the hills near to the cave where I had awakened, the place we now called *Nightrun*, for it was this region where we had all ran through the night, where our two kinds of people had met for the first time.

THE TIMES OF SYLVERIA

Understanding now that the world of Sylveria was a world to be respected, for the forces of nature were powerful, we made our homes in Naiad, which seemed a calm and innocuous region. The days passed slowly, and our time was filled with leisure and pleasure, for now that we had settled in the Valley of Naiad we had lost the inclination that we had suffered before to have all of the answers of our existence. There was much that we still did not know, but much of it was simply about the world, and with time we knew we would learn it all. Still, there was much that we did now understand: We were the children of Dragons, awakened by their magic into the world. Two separate awakenings there were, one of the Sylvai and one of the Nescrai—cousin races that were different only for the time of our creation.

As we discovered our world—both on our own and with the guidance of the Dragons—foremost of importance to me was in understanding the days and the hours. I took an interest in this, moreso than the others, and I made it my profession to understand the heavenly bodies inasmuch as it was possible.

It was in the early days of my study of these matters that I realized that not only did Aros and Imrakul make a journey over the world, but so too did Vespa, the blue sun, though ever so slowly... for since the first day of our awakening, it had seemed stationary in the eastern sky, but as the first season passed into the next, so too had Vespa moved in relation to the land. I surmised from what I had learned—and it was confirmed for me by the Dragon Ashysin—that it took a full year for Vespa to make its journey over the face of Sylveria. Yet the blue sun itself was an anomaly, for while it too progressed into the Veil in its latter seasons, its light was not obscured, still shining even through the mysterious shroud that dwelled somewhere far to the north, both day and night.

Now, in regard to the Veil itself—that distant and enigmatic wonder where the suns and moon vanished—I could learn nothing; neither the Chromatic Dragons nor their Metallic brothers could tell me anything. For three thousand years they had been in the world and had never uncovered its mysteries. They had never flown into it, beyond the lands of Merobassi, for it seemed too far a distance across the seas, and when they asked Kronaggas about it, the great White Dragon would tell them nothing, forbidding talk of it, saying only that it was a dismal region that none had a need to visit. So, for the time, I could know only that which I could observe with my own eyes, and I occupied my time during the first seasons of my life by studying the cosmos above.

Below is a list of the Seasons and Times of Sylveria according to my observations, as perceived from the Valley of Naiad. Knowledge of these matters will provide a better understanding of many of the events that followed.

The Seasons of Sylveria

There are twelves seasons that cycle through a single Sylverian year. Each of these lasts twelve days, and is marked by significant changes in the patterns of nature. The Seasons are:

Springrise	Autumnturn
Springtide	Autumntide
Springend	Autumnfall
Summerstorm	Winterfel
Summertide	Wintertide
Summerfade	Wintermelt

Times of Day

There are twenty Times of Day that cycle through each day of Sylveria, each of them referred to as an Hour. Each of the Hours is marked by a distinct position of the gold sun, Aros, and the green moon, Imrakul, in the celestial realm, or by other events that occur naturally each day. These Hours of the Day are:

The Hour of Distinction
The Hour of Gathering
The Hour of Firstlight
The Hour of Elation
The Hour of Awakening
The Hour of Midlight
The Hour of Eventide
The Hour of Passions
The Hour of Meeting
The Hour of Highlight
The Hour of Devotion
The Hour of Darkening
The Hour of Feltide
The Hour of Evenlight
The Hour of Concession
The Hour of Mourning
The Hour of Lastlight
The Hour of Attrition
The Hour of Pondering
The Hour of Midnight

Other Measurements of Time

In order to understand the passage of time upon Sylveria, the following measurements of time should also be understood.

A _Year_ is the passage of twelve seasons. Throughout a single year, the blue Night Sun, Vespa, makes one entire circuit above the face of the world, while both Aros and Imrakul make many.

A _Season_ is comprised of twelve days, which is twelve cycles of Aros and Imrakul over the entire face of the world.

A _Day_ is understood as the length of time that it takes for the gold sun Aros to make a full circle over the entire world. It encompasses both daytime and nighttime, one of each per Day. Imrakul, the green moon. also makes an entire orbit above the face of the world, and is always opposite to Aros in the heavens, no matter the Time of Day.

An _Hour_ is defined as one part in twenty of a Day, and each of them is marked by either a celestial event or a natural occurrence. The Hours of the Day are named either for these occasions or for things that occurred during the first days, seasons and years of our time in Sylveria.

A _Course_ is one fourth of an Hour. To fully grasp the length of a Course, and thus Hours and Days, this unit of the measurement of time is further broken down below.

A _Span_ is one part in sixty-four of a Course. A Span is the length of time it takes to walk the distance of a Dragon's wingspan from one end to the other.

A _Pulse_ is one part in sixteen of a Span. The term is a reference to the length of time it takes for a Dragon's heart to beat when it is at rest, which is much slower than our own.

A <u>Moment</u> is one part in four of a Pulse. It is a unit that is commonly considered to be the length of time it takes for a single thought to be enacted. It is the shortest measurable period of time.

These are the measurements of the Seasons and Times of Sylveria that I discovered during my first years in the Valley of Naiad. There are further details that have not been described in this section, such as celestial eclipses, equinoxes and solstices, but their explanations will be best given in the context of the story, and in the remainder of my writings.

THE BOOK OF

PASSIONS

THE FIRST PROFESSIONS

Those first days passed away, Hour after Hour, and we were content now in our own small piece of the world, the Valley of Naiad. The Dragons often came, for their affinity with us was at least as great as ours for them. While there were a great number of creatures, both large and small upon Sylveria, there were none others with whom they could commune, no others with a higher intelligence that brought them above instinct. Though the Dragons loved all of the creatures of the world, they loved none more than us, for we were their companions.

Then the seasons passed, the Spring Seasons into the Summer, then the Summer into the Autumn, and finally into the Winter Seasons. When Winter ended, Spring rose again. This cycle of nature was eternal, the Dragons said, and had gone on for as long as they had existed.

And as years cycled through, we, the Naiad, began to learn how to use the resources of the world to make life better, and to keep ourselves occupied. We constructed homes for ourselves, shelters from the heavy rains of Summerstorm and the fierce cold of the Winter Seasons. We learned to harness fire so that we could keep ourselves warm. And most of all we learned of magic.

Now, magic in those days was not a mystical power that was only learned by a select few, but it was a natural force that permeated all of creation. One had only to understand it to learn how to use it, though some were more gifted than others. Even some of the animals of the world were able to harness the smallest portions of magic. None were so great with it as were the Dragons, of course, but even they were conservative in its use, saying that it was a force of the natural order of the world and should not be abused. And so we practiced it with moderation, using it only to accomplish goals that were not possible through other natural methods.

We made our homes in the hills of Nightrun where we would be sheltered from the Shadows of Dragonswake—which was what we came to call that ominous event that happened every day at the Hour of Highlight. We desired to be close to one another in our dwellings, but to each have our own space, and so we selected thirteen adjacent hills upon which to raise our homes. And from our abodes we each pursued our own endeavors.

My dwelling was larger than the others' for the sole reason that there were two occupants—myself and Saxon, who still preferred to remain with me rather than return to his own kind. From here I began studying the movements of the suns and moon through the heavens, and I learned much in the first years. While I occupied my time with the learning of celestial matters, the others found their own interests.

Alunen was the most gifted in the magical arts and communed with Sharuseth the Copper frequently on such matters. She became strong in manipulating inanimate things around her to do her will. When one of the Naiad needed to cross the rivers of the valley to seek resources for our projects, Alunen could create a land bridge to span the distance. Nature became compliant with the magical workings of my sister.

Norandar, who had constructed his home on a hill near to Alunen's, for there was a developing affection between them, became fascinated with the forest to the west, in which we had first seen the Nescrai. He studied the trees and discovered that the bark, the sap, and the pith of the trees possessed interesting and very usable properties. He never harmed the trees, but only gathered what he could from the fallen branches and shed bark. He used these to make the planks of wood that were turned into our dwellings. His method was to lay out the broken bark and then soak them in the sap. After a time of baking in the sun it hardened into nearly unbreakable boards that could withstand the harsh elements of nature. He called the forest that was in Naiad *Sternwood* for the trees themselves were strong, and the material forged from it nearly as indestructible.

Sarak'den spent much of her time in the working of stone and metal ores. So too did Haldus'nar take an interest in these things, and in Sarak'den. They carved images into the stone faces of the mountains, creating the first symbols that represented the language which we spoke. Later, they began carving sculptures and working the stone into structures and tools that could be used by themselves and others.

Sveraden became fascinated with the weaving of cloth. She made frequent journeys to the Razorgrass fields to gather Dragon scales and to use the barathea from the inner side. (As it turned out, the Dragons did *not* want their scales back.) She learned to harness fibers from plants and from the shed hair of animals and to create beautiful pieces of material that could then be used for clothing, blankets and various other items that made life simpler. She made brushes for the grooming of our hair and became a crafter of jewelry.

Adaashar preferred to be outdoors, and spent little time inside his own home. During the warmer seasons he would sleep on the roof of his dwelling or upon the hard ground in the Hills of Nightrun. He spent much of his time gathering food, discerning which fruits, vegetables and herbs of the valley were the best. Often, while the rest of us would be occupied with our own undertakings, he would be gathering and preparing meals for all of us. Although their interests were not complimentary, Adaashar and Sveraden seemed to be developing a deep closeness to one another.

Garonar was greatly fascinated with the larger animals of the Valley of Naiad—particularly the Bison and the Paken. He befriended them and with his own kind of magic he even seemed to be able to communicate with them. He often would arrive at Nightrun in the evenings with a small herd of the creatures at his side; he did this so that Sveraden could brush the shedding hair from them and use it for her creations. Though Sveraden was thankful for the ease of gathering the hair offered by Garonar, in truth he did it for his own reasons—because the animals themselves were more comfortable and content when their hair was not unkempt. He did these things not to gain Sveraden's favor, for his heart and his interest were in Kuranen.

Kuranen spent her days learning about the Birds of the valley; she was fascinated by them and often longed to be able to fly amongst them. The Falcon was the most interesting to her, and with time she learned, like Garonar, to commune with them. This was accomplished not with magic, but by understanding the needs and desires of the animals. Naturally, Kuranen was also drawn to Garonar, for their love of the attendance of animals.

Kalenen was a lover of the earth, and she spent her time in observance of the growth of vegetation throughout the Valley of Naiad. It was she who first discovered that it was the seeds of the plants that allowed them to spread over the landscape, and she was able to cultivate the land and produce plentiful crops for all of us. She was also fascinated with the soil itself, and by digging deep into the earth she discovered clay and used it to form bricks and pottery. She also learned the art of making inks and dyes and parchments upon which we could write. Kalenen held a fondness for Norgrash'nar, but he did not share in this affection.

Alim'dar became a forger of tools; in close cooperation with Sarak'den and Haldus'nar and their understanding of stone and metal, he was able to use fire to forge stronger tools—iron hammers, knives, chisels and axes, all of which made the professions of the others easier. He was also greatly interested in woodwork, and in the early years he crafted rafts that could not only cross the rivers of Naiad, but also move up and downstream with the use of oars. He often carved detailed wooden statues depicting the Dragons, the animals of the world, and even depictions of the other Naiad. But he favored making images of nothing more than of Nirvisa'nen.

Nirvisa'nen was the founder of song and dance and she loved nothing more than performing. After a time she learned to construct musical instruments of various types, which only added to the beauty of her performances. In the early years of our time in Naiad, she did not show a particular interest in any of the men, either Nescrai or Sylvai. Nevertheless her melodies inspired love and peace amongst all of us. Even the Dragons would come to listen to her songs, and were greatly fascinated by them, for they were unable to sing.

Norgrash'nar was, like Alunen, a lover of the magical arts. Though he was not as strong in the use of this natural force, he nevertheless spent much of his time seeing what he could accomplish. With time, he could reproduce nearly any simple object such as a tool or carved wooden statue simply with his magical prowess. For this, he eventually began creating small items that were mechanical in nature, trinkets to impress the rest of us, and even more complex devices that could aid the rest of us in our own undertakings. He mastered the art of glass-making and was able to construct the first spyglass that allowed us to see over greater distances. He became the first engineer in the world of Sylveria, and his development of mechanics was an art that was used all throughout the ages of the world thereafter.

THE FIRST DRAGONFLIGHT

Twenty years passed as we developed our own passions and gained knowledge about the world around us. Each of us was content in our workings and we found nothing but love for the world, for each other, and for the Dragons. Every day of our lives seemed to bring something new— something we had not seen or heard or known before, and these years were a time of rich discovery.

Our fondness for the Dragons grew, and slowly they began showing us more and more of the world around us, outside of the Valley of Naiad. Although they were hesitant at first to take us into flight upon their backs for fear of us falling, when Norandar, Garonar and Norgrash'nar were together able to fashion great saddles that would mount upon the Dragons' backs which we could sit upon, safely strapped in, Kronaggas at last gave approval for us to be taken by air upon great journeys that showed us all the lands of Sylveria.

Although we could all easily fit upon the back of a single Dragon, the saddles had been made to hold but two people. They were affixed to the great beasts by way of hooks, clamps and ropes that held fast to the scales along their backs and sides. The ropes then attached to the saddles, each seating having its own cords that would hold the riders in place. So effective were these that a Dragon could fly upended and in any direction, and we would stay perfectly in place.

When we took our first flight it was the first day of Summertide in the twentieth year since we had awakened, and we were divided between the Dragons: Alunen and Norandar rode upon Sharuseth the Copper, Sarak'den and Haldus'nar upon Verasian the Green, Sveraden and Adaashar upon Merilinder the Silver, Garonar and Kuranen upon Merobassi the Blue, Kalenen and Norgrash'nar upon Drovanius the Black, Nirvisa'nen and Alim'dar upon Aranthia the Crimson, and I rode alone upon the back of Ashysin the Gold.

Though we had thought to stay together as we soared over the lands, the Dragons each had their own ideas, and when we left Naiad, flying at first low over the landscape, each of them went in their own direction, wishing to first show their riders the lands of their own domain. Each of us would, in the coming seasons, be given the opportunity to see all of the lands of Sylveria upon the backs of the different Dragons.

Ashysin took flight from the hills just outside of the village of our settlement, and he moved westward toward the plains where Kronaggas' mountain towered, and where we had first met the Dragons. We had, in the past years, rarely ventured onto these plains, staying mostly in the Valley of Naiad because everything we needed could be found there.

I was amazed by the swiftness at which we flew; the wind rushed past me with great ferocity and the landscape below blurred by even faster. I had seen the Dragons fly with great speed before, but only from the perspective of the ground. Now that I was aboard the Dragon itself, it was astonishingly swift... and frightening!

"Are you all right, Alak'kiin?" Ashysin asked as he turned his head around to face me, still flying.

"I... I think so!" I yelled back, wondering how we could even hear one another with the wind whipping past with such intensity. I held tightly to the handles on the saddle and struggled to keep my eyes open. "I... I think we are going too fast!"

The great Gold Dragon laughed. "This isn't even my fastest speed!"

After perhaps only half of a course we left Naiad and were high above the Plains of Kronaggas, for the western slopes of the valley dropped down and we were left relatively high above this region. From there Ashysin flew me westward until we neared the great Mountain of Kronaggas, and then higher he went until we were level with its great pointed peak. There, upon the pinnacle of his mountain home was perched the White Dragon, waiting to greet us, for he had known we would be flying by; as we passed he let out a great shriek of reception, and we flew onward.

"Where would you like to go, Alak'kiin?" Ashysin asked.

"Closer to the ground!"

Laughing again, the Dragon took us to a lower height where the blurring of the landscape seemed even greater as we soared. After circling

Kronaggas Mountain several times he headed in a southward direction, across the southern plains of the White Dragon's domain. I could not see the details of the lands immediately surrounding us—rivers and rises blurred past—but as I found my bearings and grew more comfortable upon the wings of a Dragon I recognized that the best way to view the world from this height was from a distance. For the higher we were in the air, the farther I could see, and those places most distant were the clearest for my vision to behold.

To the southeast I could see the River Iidin flowing out of the valley and draining into an even larger river that flowed from the west to the east, and beyond; to the south was a fantastic land covered in verdant hills that must surely be near the size of the mountains of Naiad. This was the extent of my vision, even from this great height. The world beyond continued, but it was held in the haze of lands not yet visible.

"How big *is* this world?" I yelled to Ashysin.

"Bigger than you can imagine!" he answered joyfully.

"Where are we going now?"

"I will show you my realm, my domain... the great Mountains of Ashysin!"

And as we continued, Ashysin slowly rose higher and higher. Over my shoulder I could still see the edges of Naiad, but even that was quickly diminishing. On the southern side of the mountain range of Naiad I could see that there were darkly shaded green plains that exceeded my eastward sight. Bordering the north side plains was another river—a smaller one that branched off from the Iidin river at the western tip of the mountains and which ran along as far as I could see.

To the west of us was more of the same—dark and beautiful green lands that seemed endless. Then, finally, after we had been airborne for two courses, I could see that ahead must be the domain of the Gold Dragon, for mountains even taller than I could have imagined rose up from the hills and extended onward in all directions save for north.

Soon we were above these mountains and it seemed not so far a distance to the ground, for the great mountainous terrain was high above the level of the plains and hills—so high in fact that the tops of the mountains were covered in snow.

"It is Summertide, Ashysin," I said. "Why does snow fall here, in these high places?"

"Because the air is thin and during the night it gets very cold, Alak'kiin. Enough snow falls so as to stay unmelted all throughout the day."

"Where are we going?" I wondered.

"I am taking you to my favorite place in all of Sylveria... Vindras Vale!"

We flew a while longer; Aros had moved westward and so I thought it must be the Hour of Darkening, but it was difficult to tell, as I no longer had the Valley of Naiad as the reference point of my location. Until now, all of my studies of the positions of the suns had been relative to but one small region in the whole of these unfathomably large lands.

Then, we came to a break in the mountains, and below a great hilly land came into view… this must, I assumed, be Vindras Vale, for I could see why it was preferred by Ashysin. It was more beautiful than perhaps the Valley of Naiad. Great rivers and streams cut the land, grasses of the greenest hue blanketed the entire area, tall trees of kinds I had never seen grew in woodlands, and incredible creatures of a kind unknown grazed and galloped through a region that I estimated to be perhaps twice the size of the Valley of Naiad, and all of it was secluded high in the mountains, and never would have been seen from the ground.

Then, in the center of the Vale, Ashysin landed. "Take a few breaths before you dismount," he said.

I was so eager to get down and touch the ground again that I did not heed his warning, and I unstrapped myself and slid quickly down his wing and came to stand upon the grassy fields. But when I tried to walk, I tumbled to the ground.

Ashysin laughed, saying, "I tried to warn you, Alak'kiin. Your body will take time to adapt to *not* moving so swiftly."

Finally I was able to stand as my balance returned and I looked about in amazement, for none of the creatures of this realm were small, and a great clowder of beasts that stood taller than I while upon four legs was coming toward me, sniffing at the ground curiously, for they had no more seen the likes of me than I had of them.

"What are these?" I asked.

"These are the Mountain Leopards of Vindras Vale. They are of a kind known to us as *Cats*."

There were four of the Leopards coming toward me, their thick coats of hair were yellow and they were each covered in a multitude of black spots in various patterns. They were gentle as they approached, taking in my scent, nudging me with giant heads that were even larger than Saxon's. I wondered then if the Dain had ever even seen the likes of these creatures, and how he would react to their presence if he could have come along.

I reached out to one of the Leopards, and laid my hand upon the side of its giant face; it made the strangest of sounds that were like a humming vibration and it pressed its head further against my hand, twisting its neck as it rubbed against me.

"What is it doing?" I asked Ashysin.

"These are amongst the most curious of creatures in Sylveria," the Dragon said. "And playful." And as he said this, the Leopard fell to the ground and started rolling over, still purring. The others followed, save one, which leaped on top of the other in an effort to establish some spirited dominance.

"Wait here for a moment," Ashysin said, and he turned away, walking now upon his great legs over to a nearby wooded area. The Leopards continued their frivolity, each of them now engaging the others. When the Dragon returned, he held in his great claw a clump of some long strands of a kind of grass I had not seen before, and he dropped it directly on top of the Cats.

They leaped up and began sniffing at the grass, and in a matter of moments their eyes grew larger and filled with an intensity that startled me. Each of them leaped and ran as fast as their legs could take them, but only for a short time, and then they were back on the ground, wrestling and growling and tearing up the landscape with playful and passionate growls.

Ashysin laughed deeply, saying, "I will never get tired of seeing that!"

"What did you do?" I wondered, smiling myself, for the joy of watching these creatures was great. "What was that?"

"That is the Nephata plant. For some reason it attracts and exhilarates all cats of the world." The Leopards soon darted away, chasing one another, but I could still see them in the distance, thumping and rolling upon the earth.

I looked around, wondering what other interesting creatures might be in the Vale. And to the west I saw something… a new animal that was unfamiliar… or at least its head; for hidden behind my view by the tall grass I could see only long necks and small heads poking up. They were gray in color, and their heads bobbed up and down, as they tromped through the fields.

"Now what are those?" I wondered.

"Go see for yourself, Alak'kiin."

I started walking toward them, wondering all the while what this creature's appearance would be. As they came into better view I could see that these were large animals, taller than any other I had seen in Sylveria thus far, but only for their excessively long necks that towered over my own head, perhaps four times my own height. They walked upon four giant legs. When I came close they looked at me curiously, and then, seeming to smile, one of them lowered its great head down and stroked its tongue across my face.

Laughing again, Ashysin said, "This is the Gray Giraffe of Vindras Vale."

I wiped my face upon my tunic sleeve and said, "Sveraden would not care for the Giraffe."

We spent the entirety of the Hours of Feltide and Evenlight in Vindras Vale exploring as the Dragon showed me the other wonderful creatures of the vast region. Herds of Elk tromped through the gentle, hilly grasslands, grazing upon the plants and flowers. Wide-eyed Owls soared the skies along with various other kinds of Birds. Foxes darted across the landscape and in the wooded areas; large funny creatures that walked more like the Naiad than like other animals swung from branch to branch in the high trees. Ashysin called them *Monkeys*.

When the Hour of Concession arrived, the Gold Dragon said, "I would like to show you one other place, Alak'kiin, before I take you back to Naiad."

"Where is it?"

"To the east, over another great range of mountains." He lowered his wing to the ground so that I could climb back onto his back and into the saddle fashioned by my brother and cousins. And again we took to the air, now to the east.

In this latter Hour of this Summer day Aros was far to the west, Imrakul was just opposite in the eastern sky, and Vespa was lingering out above the eastern lands that I had not yet seen. We flew over the mountains, a different segment than before, and after a course I saw a great flat-topped mountain that was a plateau amongst the otherwise jagged mountain tops. We flew over it and past one final mountain and then we were in a long and narrow valley that ran north to south. Ashysin swayed to the left and lowered our altitude to pass into it. A great river seeming as liquid silver and as shimmering as my own hair cut the valley in two, and all along the sides of the mountains the stone was speckled with gold that was as beautiful to look at as the Dragon himself.

"This is the Golden Valley, and we call the river *Enar'uduk*," the Dragon said. "And this is another of my favorite places."

Countless streams drained along the valley into the river which flowed from north to south until it reached its end at a giant crevice just below where we had entered into the Golden Valley.

"Where does it go?" I asked Ashysin.

"The river? It falls into a great cavern deep beneath the surface of the world, a cave that I am far too large to go into. I have never seen where it flows from there."

To the north we soared through the valley for the rest of the day until at the Hour of Lastlight we came to its northern end, where the river was fed by a waterfall coming out of the very top of a mountain and was higher even than the waterfall that fed into the Lake of Iidin in Naiad. Ashysin circled this mountain to the west and we were suddenly upon the eastern end of the Valley of Naiad, at Yor'Kavon, back home after making a circuit around the domain of Ashysin the Gold, which was only one small part of the whole of Sylveria.

THE GEOGRAPHY OF SYLVERIA

In the subsequent seasons the Dragons took each of us upon flights to their own domains, showing us all of the wonderful places of the lands of Sylveria. The world was far larger than I could have imagined and its wonders were unimaginably stunning.

As I was shown all of these things, I developed a new interest in mapping the lands of Sylveria upon parchment made by Kalenen, for though I had now seen the reaches of the world, it had only been in large segments viewed from high above, as well as small and select regions within. I knew that in the future I wanted to visit every corner of Sylveria by way of land. Cartography became my first profession.

And so I spent another year establishing, as best I could, the geography of the world, drawing maps and distinguishing the names of places as given by the Dragons, as well as those that we, the Naiad, had named ourselves.

The whole of Sylveria consisted of five landmasses. First and foremost was the Mainland, within which Naiad had been laid. Upon the Mainland were the Domains of _Kronaggas_ the White, _Ashysin_ the Gold, _Sharuseth_ the Copper, _Merilinder_ the Silver, and _Verasian_ the Green. To the north were the lands of _Merobassi_, and directly to the east were the lands of _Aranthia_ the Crimson, which comprised two of the land segments, which were called Aranthia and Aranthia Minor. To the northeast of there were the vast lands of _Drovanius_ the Black. Throughout the Mainland there were also two regions unclaimed by any of the Dragons. These were called _Whitestone_ and _Goab'lin_.

Before describing the lands of Sylveria in further detail, it is necessary that I here record the units of measurement that we established in the early years, so that the scope and size of the world can be understood. Please note that each of the units below is considered an imprecise measurement, as variations in the objects of comparison make each of them only estimates. However, as we, the Naiad, developed our crafts and instruments in our early years, tools were designed to assign more precise dimensions.

Measurements of Distance

A _Length_ is described by the average length of a Naiad's index finger.

A _Reach_ is defined as the distance between the center point of a Naiad's chest and the tip of their index finger. It is about twelve Lengths.

A _Height_ is equal to the tallness of a Naiad man, and is about one and a half times a Reach.

A _Breadth_ is a measurement of the width of a Dragon's breast at the point where its wings meet with its body. It is roughly equal to seven Heights.

A _Span_ is the distance between the tips of a Dragon's wings when they are fully extended out to the sides. It is equal to about six Breadths.

A _March_ is the average distance that the Naiad can move over flat terrain in one Hour[1]. It is about equal to three-hundred and forty Spans.

A _Flight_ is the average distance that a Dragon can fly in one Hour. It is about eight Marches.

An _Extent_ is the average distance that a Dragon can fly in a full day. However, this accounts for rest that must be taken throughout, as a Dragon cannot fly continuously for a full day without. It is equal to about five Flights.

[1]   Note that an Hour, as described here, is not the equivalent of a sixty-minute hour as was adopted as the Clavigar Standard(CS) in later ages. Rather, an Hour is equal to 4 standard CS hours.

    The entire domain of _Kronaggas_ the White was the plains just west of the Valley of _Naiad_. Although he was the oldest of the Dragons he had selected for himself only this moderate region. There was little variation in the landscape of the Plains of _Kronaggas_, other than the massive mountain that was the Dragon's home. This mountain tore up through the plains and resembled a giant talon, curved and dominating of all the bordering regions that could see it, for it was the tallest mountain, save perhaps for those in the northern land of _Skyreach_.

There were two entrances into this mountain, one high toward the heights of the mountain, before its curve began reaching eastward, and the other was near the base, at the end of a rocky red-soiled path that led from the plains up to it.

The sides of the mountain appeared scored, as if perhaps a Dragon even larger than Kronaggas had tried to climb it; but this was just the effect of the creation of this structure, for the great White Dragon had in fact raised it from beneath the surface of the earth in the early years after his own awakening. Using his great magic Kronaggas had drawn molten lava up from the underworld in a great fountain that cooled into what we saw to that day. He had then carved out the interior of the mountain to suit his desire.

The Valley of _Naiad_, unclaimed by any other Dragon, was often considered to be a part of Kronaggas' Domain, though it was largely used as a gathering place for all Dragons, exceptionally after the awakening of the Naiad.

Westward and southward from the Plains of _Kronaggas_ was the domain of _Sharuseth_ the Copper. This realm was largely covered in shallow hills and sparse woodlands and extended westward all the way to the distant mountains that were along the western edge of Sylveria. His domain did not include the lands north of there, which were called _Kort'Lograk_ by the Dragons, but which we called by our common equivalent, which is _Whitestone_. It was in these lands of the Copper Dragon that the great Trees of _Mara_ would one day rise, seeded by the sorrows of one of the Naiad.

South of Whitestone, within the western part of _Sharuseth_'s domain was a great inland lake, which the Dragons called _Abai_. And south of _Abai_ was the _Goab'lin_ Plateau, which was not considered to be a part of his lands. And east from _Goab'lin_ was the rest of the Copper Dragon's domain, extending all the way southward and eastward to the mountains that were south of the Valley of Naiad.

The Mountains of _Ashysin_, which were the Gold Dragon's Domain, covered the greatest range of distance of any of the lands of the Dragons. His included all of the ranges that were south of _Naiad_ and which extended all the way to the southern coast of Sylveria, and included the _Golden Valley_ and _Vindras Vale_. Likewise, all of the Vales of the Mountains were considered his. So too did he claim all of the mountains that extended north to south that divided the east from the west.

The far southwestern lands, beyond the Mountains of _Ashysin_, were called the _Southern Reaches_, and were the domain of Merilinder the Silver. This was a relatively small domain, but the Dragon was content with the land he had claimed.

Although the region was small, it had the most varied range of landscapes of any of the other places in Sylveria. The western side was covered in deserts of great sand dunes, which supported many different kinds of animals. The next eastward stretch was covered in grasslands; one river flowing out of the Mountains of _Ashysin_ fed three lakes in this small region, which then drained into the _Southern Ocean_. Eastward from there were the plains of _Merilinder_, which were populated by incredibly powerful creatures known as the Plains Viper—a snake that when fully extended was nearly as long as two Breadths. The Dragons referred to these creatures as the Druugal. The eastern part of the Southern Reaches was rocky terrain upon which little vegetation grew, but which exhibited a great variance of wildlife.

The region of _Whitestone_, north of _Sharuseth_'s Domain, was not, as stated before, claimed by any Dragon. All of it except for the central part of the region was covered in mountains that were comprised not of the dark stone of the rest of Sylveria, but of a nearly pure white rock that existed only here in this part of the world. Though the mountains were amongst the largest in the world, they were easily passable, as many valleys rifted the great stone heights. The central region was covered in rolling hills that were divided by rivers and many streams.

Coming out of the region of Whitestone, all along the western coastline of Sylveria, though not considered part of any region, were two narrow ranges of mountains, side by side. This stretch was called _Etakos_, and high between these two lines of mountains was a valley with a river uninterrupted that ran all the way from Whitestone—where it was fed by the mountains and springs—to the sea, where it drained into the _Western Ocean_, just north of the most distant reaches of the Mountains of Ashysin. In later years this waterway would be used as a transport system for the people of _Whitestone_ to quickly move along the western side of Sylveria.

The _Goab'lin_ Plateau was a large, elevated region that extended from the southern coast of the Lake of _Abai_ down to the western sea, near where _Etakos_ drained. The entire region was raised to a higher elevation by steep earthen slopes that extended all along the northern and eastern edges. By ground there were but two paths that led onto the plateau; one was along the eastern side of the region, while the other was along the north.

The *Goab'lin* Plateau was thus named for a strange cycle of nature that was evident here, but nowhere else in Sylveria, for the name in the tongue of Dragons meant *Fertile Decay*. It was a lush land, where great fruit-bearing plants grew in such abundance that even the great *Ilveros Boars* and other unique species could not keep the growth at bay, so fast did the vines and brush of the region produce. Nature here was only balanced by the presence of large Insects—Beetles of various kinds that swept the landscape, destroying large sections of the vegetation all at once, not consuming them entirely, but only there to impede the growth from spilling over into the rest of Sylveria. Giant Worms lived in the soil, helping to consume that which was left behind by the Beetles. Though it was a unique region it was also dangerous, for those animals there considered everything upon the plateau to be destructible or consumable. *Goab'lin* held its own beauty and it was later discovered that magic was rich in the soil of the plateau.

The remainder of the Mainland of Sylveria, which was all of the lands to the east of the Mountains of Ashysin, was the domain of Verasian the Green. This was the largest single domain of any of the Dragons, and was covered with a great variety of landscapes. It extended from the lowland region of *Forthran*, where *Merobassi* had shown us the destructive effects of the tides, eastward onto higher lands that were not affected, then southward across a vast and wild grassland.

Along the eastern coast, the region was surrounded by earthen slopes that were very reminiscent of those around *Goab'lin*, except that these dropped off into the *Eastern Sea*. This region was called *Onilmar*. Further south still were more grasslands, and a region that was called *Etharg'Heron* and was a sparsely forested area. It extended from the Mountains of *Ashysin* to a southern point in the grasslands near the *Southern Ocean*. This land was set off from the rest of the region by rivers that flowed both from lakes and from the mountains to the west. There was also one lone mountain that rose above the rest of the landscape in this area.

South of *Etharg'Heron* were the further lands of *Verasian*, which were a mixture of both grasslands and fertile plains.

The northern most region of *Verasian*'s domain was the region called *Forthran*, which was home to the lowlands, the higher lands and the realm of Felheim.

The northern land mass was the domain of *Merobassi*, and was a vast region. We had seen only a small segment of the land when the Dragon had taken us to the top of the mountain pass of *Yor'Kavon* and shown us his domain from a distance.

The entire northern stretch of the island was covered in the massive *Skyreach Mountains*, and these were indeed mountains that reached higher than anywhere else in the world. Even the Dragons themselves could not properly explore this region, for there were great gusts of wind that poured over the mountains from the north and would ground the winged beasts.

South of *Skyreach* there was a large mountain lake that was distinguished from the northern mountains; it was a range that was raised like a great bowl, meant only to hold these waters within. It was said by the Dragons to be the best place in all of Sylveria for a Dragon to bathe, and was thus named *Groam'Tharomar*, which meant *Washing Waters.*

Following Groam'Tharomar in a southward way were the Plains of Merobassi; to the east within this region was a plateau that was called, *Goren Tong*, which meant *Granite Etching*; for upon its top were great carvings etched by the great claws of the Dragons long ago. These were the first characters written in their own language, in the time just after their own awakening. The plateau was now overgrown, but from the air, the markings could still be distinguished.

West of the plains was the specific region known as *Dragonswake*, for it was here that the Dragons were first created and took their first breaths in the world. This was a hilly and mountainous region, with two ranges, one extending along the northern peninsula and one along the southern. These mountains were known as *Koal*.

Most interesting was a mountain that the Dragons called *Luen'Aril*, for there was a large hole in the stone that passed all the way through from west to east, more than large enough for a Dragon to fly through. It was upon the slopes coming out of this hollow to the west that the Dragons specifically awoke, and for which the region was named. It was through this hole that the Dragons emerged for the first time, into the rest of the world of Sylveria.

The two island regions to the east of the Mainland of Sylveria were the domain of *Aranthia* the Crimson. The major island was simply known as Aranthia, while the smaller came to be called *Aranthia Minor*. The small island was nearly all one range of mountains, not so tall as many of those in Sylveria, but its base was nearly the length of the entire island. There were but four smaller mountains on the island as well—two on the northwestern edge, and two on the east. Rivers poured through the valleys between the mountains, and though it was a rocky region, it was tropical and one of the most beautiful places in all of Sylveria. Strange magic was present in those lands.

The Major Island consisted of two primary stretches that came together at the northern end. The smaller and western most stretch was called *The Horn of Aranthia*, and it was covered with high hills and plains. There was one mountain in this region and it was there that was closest to the lands of *Verasian*, separated only by a small segment of the ocean.

As the land went northward, it became hillier and finally gave way to great highlands that rose high above the plains all along the eastern stretch of Aranthia. Though these highlands were not mountains, they stood nearly as tall as they ran all along the entire north and east coast of the island. At their top were great stretches of plains and grasslands. From there, the highlands fell off into the ocean, steep and perilous cliffs that could not be scaled.

Also, along this eastern stretch, the highlands declined quickly southward onto hilly plains that were much like the western stretch.

The final island that was a part of Sylveria was the far northeastern region that was the domain of *Drovanius* the Black. The entirety of this domain was vast plains, forests, swamps, and mountains. Along the eastern edge of the island were the labyrinthine mountain ranges of *Hinliss*. In the southern segment of the Island of Drovanius, encircled on three sides, was the great swamp known to the Dragons as *Tarik Bokompun*, which meant *Wetland of Alligators*, for great land-dwelling reptiles lived there amongst the other lesser species.

There were three other small mountain ranges upon the island—one to the far northwest end of the vast plains, one in the north-central region, and the third in the northeast, just set apart from the Mountains of *Arge'Kort*. Here, at this third location, were three mountains massed together, two in the front and the third in the back. It was in a cave at the peak of the backside mountain where Drovanius made his home. It was unreachable by ground, and the only way one could visit was to be carried by a Dragon.

All of the rest of the lands of *Drovanius* the Black were plains that were in those days very fertile. Only one major river flowed out of the mountains of *Arge'Kort*, but there were countless streams that flowed across the vast landscape.

And so these were the lands of Sylveria, created long ago by Kronaggas, raised up out of the sea and made into the world of Dragons. There are many more locations other than those listed here that are of great interest, and great beauty; these will be best described in the context of the story that follows.

The Hour of Passions

By the Season of Springtide, twenty-one years after we had awakened, my brothers, sisters, cousins and I had settled well into our lives in the Valley of Naiad and we were continuing to learn much about our world. We had become proficient in our crafts and content with the workings of our hands. We each had interests that the others did not, and this made us unique in all that we did. Our abilities and artistries often complemented one another, and we freely gave to the others anything they needed that we could produce or gather.

But as time pressed on, there was an awakening inside each of us, a longing for something more than what we had... Each of us loved one another, for we were a family of the same awakening, but rising up out of our small civilization were natural desires that drew some of us to others with a bond that surpassed our relationships with the rest.

Garonar and Kuranen had developed a special bond with one another, and spent much of their time together. Likewise, so too did Adaashar and Sveraden, and Haldus'nar and Sarak'den. But foremost in this matter were the affections that arose between Norandar and Alunen, for not only did they spend all of their days together, but so too were they warmly close to one another—holding hands, leaving Nightrun for long periods of time, choosing to spend much of their time alone and away from the rest of us.

Norgrash'nar and Alim'dar had both developed an interest in Nirvisa'nen, as had I—for to me she was the loveliest of all of the women, both Sylvai and Nescrai. Her songs and music and voice were enchanting and they inspired something deep inside of me that I could not understand. But Nirvisa'nen had not revealed to us for whom her affections might be greater, since three of us had expressed our fondness for her. Likely, she knew that whichever of us she chose, there would be two others who were disappointed. Only one other woman remained, and it was Kalenen.

Now, Kalenen was beautiful, and her heart was kind and sharing, but she was most interested in Norgrash'nar, who did not share in her affections. And the one thing that was clear to all of us who remained uncoupled was that one of us men would be left without a partner, once Nirvisa'nen chose for herself. She likely knew this too, and it was for this that she would not reveal who her true interests were with.

It was on the seventh day of Springtide in that year, during the Hour of Passions, that something arose within each of us. It was not something comprehensible, and why it happened at that time I did not know, but I did know that rising even moreso than ever before was an intense longing for Nirvisa'nen that welled up from deep inside of me. And this did not affect only me, for each of the others—particularly Alunen and Norandar—were incited with passion for one another as well.

This inflammation of passion was something that intensified as the Hour passed. It was a longing for something more with the person with whom we shared our greatest affections, a desire to be even closer, to be intimate. But this was something that we did not understand in those days.

As the Hour passed so too did the intensity of the longing, but upon each subsequent day, at the same time, it returned. At last, after a full season of this, we decided to take the matter to our Dragon fathers. But none of them could tell us what was happening, for they did not have such things as intimate desires and longing for physical contact. The seven told us then that only Kronaggas might have an answer as to what was happening to us.

And so we set out on the last day of Springend for Kronaggas Mountain.

Down the Westward Slopes we went onto the Plains of Kronaggas. It was a full day journey, for as we had developed in our habits of life, we allowed only half of the Hours of the day to be used in travel or work, for the days were long and our bodies needed both rest and relaxation—time to be spent in communing with one another.

This was to be our first journey into the Mountain of Kronaggas, for we had not in our twenty-one years needed to seek his counsel. Although the White Dragon did come to Naiad on occasion, he held not the same kind of affection for us as did the others. He had not been a part of the spells of awakening that had brought us into existence. Still, this did not diminish his love for us, for we were creatures of this world, and he held a profound love. When he did come to visit us in Naiad it was often for several days at a time, and he would talk to us at great length and always showed interest in the things we were accomplishing.

When we reached the outer edge of the Mountain of Kronaggas we followed the red soiled path that led from the plains and higher up to the cave opening that was the entrance into the mountain.

As we moved up this path we looked upward, and from this perspective we were amazed at how truly tall this mountain was. Without using tools or instruments of measurement, we could only estimate that it was at least a full March from base to peak. Its scored sides were unclimbable, though Garonar and Norgrash'nar discussed as we made the journey how they might build a device that would allow them to climb the face of the sheer mountain.

When we reached the entrance we were again amazed at the size of the cave opening, for it was large enough for any Dragon to easily fly through. Without hesitation we entered.

The cave was cool inside and it was reminiscent of the cave from which I had emerged twenty-one years earlier, though much larger. The light from the outside extended only so far in; it was the Hour of Devotion, and much of Aros' light filtered inside. But even this luminescence diminished and the way began to grow dark.

"Kronaggas!" Norandar yelled into the blackness. "Can you hear us?" But there was no response.

"We can't keep going in the darkness," Sarak'den said.

"We can if we make light," Alunen said, and she closed her eyes, summoning from within her the will to make magic, and a glowing sphere of mystical light appeared in front of her. Thereafter it was subservient to her and followed before us, lighting the way.

All along the giant cavern were rough stone walls, damp and cold, and as we delved deeper we began noticing that there were great masses of mineral deposits gathered on the walls. So too were there deposits of gold and silver and diamond and all other kinds of beautiful rocks embedded in the stone. There were many passages off this main corridor that would have been far too narrow for the Dragon to pass through, but which we could easily traverse. We stayed to the main passage, as our intent was to find the Dragon.

The ground seemed to be sloping downward, deeper into the earth, and then after at least a Course of walking we came to a massive cavern that was larger than what we could see fully by the magical light, and was surely where the Dragon lived and spent much of his time, perhaps where he slept. For there were mounds of gemstones and golden ore and fragments of shining stone that were used as decoration. And above this cavern was a great opening in the mountain that went upward as far as Alunen's light would allow us to see. This, I supposed, was the vertical passage through which Kronaggas would reach the upper exit at the height of the mountain.

"Where is he?" Alunen wondered.

"The other Dragons said he should be here on this day," Norgrash'nar said. "Kronaggas!"

"He is not here, I think," Norandar said. "Should we wait?"

Then a great puff of warm air rushed over us followed by a bellowing grunt, and ahead, opposite the way we had come, two great eyes came into view out of the darkness, the reflected light of Alunen's magic.

"I am here," said the deep and strong voice of the White Dragon, and his head snaked outward into the light, where he could see who his visitors were. "All of you have come here, to visit me in my mountain?"

"Yes," Alim'dar said. "The others said that you would be here and that we should seek your wisdom."

"There is some matter that Ashysin could not resolve?" Kronaggas asked.

"Yes," I said. "Even he said that you would be the only one who could give us an understanding of our troubles."

"Your troubles? What troubles might you have, here in Sylveria?"

"Nothing is wrong..." Alunen said.

"Then you are here just for a visit?" Kronaggas said. His tone seemed inspired. "It is not often that I have visitors in my mountain. Sometimes the creatures of the world wander in here by mistake, but most are frightened away when I try to talk with them."

"The animals can talk to you?" Garonar wondered.

"In a way much like you speak with the Bison and other creatures of the Valley of Naiad. Mostly it is I who do the talking."

"What about the other Dragons?" I asked. "Do they come in here often?"

"Perhaps once every year or so," he said. "But that is often enough. I enjoy my solitude."

"What do you do in here all day?" Sveraden asked.

"Oh, I sleep, and rearrange my hoard... and ponder many things."

"What things, might I ask, does a Dragon have to ponder?" Norgrash'nar wondered intensely.

"There are many things that are of a deeper and spiritual nature that you have not yet experienced, Naiad. Perhaps with time you will."

"What kind of things?" Norgrash'nar asked, his curiosity peaked.

"Matters you cannot comprehend... things you do not need to know just yet."

"But we want to know everything there is to know!" Kalenen said.

"Only with time can you learn all things. Only with time... And even then there may not be enough of..."

"We have come to seek your counsel, Kronaggas," Alunen said suddenly, trying to turn the conversation back to our purpose.

"On what matter?" Kronaggas asked, his interest now alight.

Norandar explained, "For the past season, perhaps, we have been aflame with passions for one another. Before this time, in years past, there have not been such feelings."

"What do you mean by *feelings*?"

"We have loved each other, all of us," Alunen said. "For all of our lives since our awakening, we have developed affections for one another. We are a family. Yet for this past season we have, most of us, felt a greater pull toward another individual. I feel an intense longing to be... intimate with Norandar, for through all of our time I have grown closer to him than to any other."

The White Dragon's head bobbed up and down in understanding. Still he listened.

"And all of us have felt this same pull," Kuranen said. "Toward another of our kind. I have become infatuated with Garonar, and he with me."

The others as well expressed their passions to Kronaggas. Only Norgrash'nar, Alim'dar, Nirvisa'nen, and I refrained.

"Can you tell us what is happening?" Sarak'den asked. "For I do not know if I can for long resist the longings I have for Haldus'nar. Yet we do not want to engage these passions, for we do not know what they are, or what it would mean."

Kronaggas considered this for a long moment before finally saying, "I can tell you what is happening; for have you not observed the animals of the world and how many of them are paired together, male and female? They are awakened creatures of Sylveria, as are you, and it is a natural thing that you would be drawn to one another. Though you were awakened greater than the animals, for you are *arein,* and of a higher order, you remain children of Sylveria. And you are more...."

"What do you mean?" I asked curiously, for it seemed a peculiar thing to say, that we were *more....*"

"You are physical creatures of the world... but you also possess *nas'alak*—the spirits of those who do not belong... I say more than I need say...." He paused long then, and all of us were considering his words, but none of us would speak. Finally he said, "As it is, you are drawn to one another, and to one another you should be bound. Male and female, together like the animals of the world. And this will bind your spirits, your souls, to this world. This is good..." another pause... "Yes, this is what Numen wills...."

"Numen?" I asked, unfamiliar with the word.

"Numen... the first of everything, the creator of all that there is. Numen wills that you would be bound to one another. And to make this so, there must be a ceremony."

"What do you mean?" Norandar asked, now confused by the Dragon's apparent ramblings.

"A ceremony," the Dragon repeated. "A ritual... I will show you. Who amongst you wishes to be first? Who would bind themselves to another here, this day?"

Although we were not entirely sure what Kronaggas was talking about, each of us trusted the Dragon, but none so much as Alunen, and she said, "I would be bound to Norandar, as you say. Though I do not understand what this entails. Nevertheless, if you say it should be so, great Kronaggas, then it should be so."

"Then prepare yourselves," the Dragon said. "Come to the back of the cavern, and down a path I will show you—just you Alunen, and you, Norandar. There is a fountain of the purest water. You must bathe in it and be cleansed. The rest of you must remain here... to observe, to witness… we will return."

Alunen left the glowing sphere of light there with us, so that we would not be plunged into darkness. And she made for herself and for Norandar another light which followed them as they were led by Kronaggas into the darkness.

When they returned, they held hands, and the smiles alight on their faces showed the love they held for one another. Kronaggas followed, though still we could see only his long neck and massive head.

"Stand before me," the Dragon said in a slow and steady tone. "Keep hold of one another."

"What is going to happen?" Sveraden asked.

"Be silent," Kronaggas said firmly. "You are here as silent observers to what is coming." He turned back to Alunen and Norandar. "Do you love this man, Alunen, more than any other?"

"Yes," she said.

"And will you accept that his soul and yours will be one every day of your lives? A bond unbreakable, a love unmatched?"

"Yes."

"And Norandar, do you love this woman more than any other, and will you take her soul into your own?"

"I will," Norandar said.

"Will you both bind your souls to this world, to Sylveria, and in this will you accept the cleansing of your spirits as you are reunited?"

Though they did not really know what it meant—none of us did—they both said, "We will."

"Then let it be so," Kronaggas said, and he closed his giant eyes. He murmured under his breath words that we could not understand, and then he audibly said, "Repeat the words that come out of my mouth, both of you together…." They nodded.

"omanas' loashen egreen'nawar lirawister'paiat'sai numen˘"

Norandar and Alunen repeated the words slowly, still unfamiliar with the tongue of Dragons, for it had shown itself to be more difficult to learn their tongue than it had for them to learn ours.

Kronaggas continued, *"iim'sai loashen utusk'kaila˘"* And the two repeated his words once again.

"iimbrangius'kaila loashen galgrun esfa etamaranthi milant˘"

And when Alunen and Norandar had finished saying this, a silence fell on the cavern, a quiet moment that was suddenly interrupted by a burst of golden light that blinded us, though only for a moment. Then Kronaggas said, "It is done. Alunen, you are now wife of Norandar, and Norandar, you are her husband. You will love one another for all time, and in this your souls will remain bound to Sylveria. You have done something great this day, and when the remainder of you are ready to do the same, return here, to my mountain, and you too will be wed. Let it be henceforth that there will be eleven witnesses to the marriage of two Naiad."

Still not fully understanding what had happened, we all returned to Naiad then. Norandar and Alunen seemed happier than before, and they soon abandoned his dwelling place and both then resided in hers. They were married now, and in this the inflammations of their passions were satisfied.

The Book of

Bondings

Alunen's Troubles

Although Alunen and Norandar were satisfied, now that they were married, the remainder of us were still affected by the longings stirred at the Hour of Passions, and each of us knew that we would only find reprieve when we too were wed. But there was a problem with this, in my mind and in the minds of some of the others, for there was an odd number of us—seven men and only six women. This was not a consideration for any of the Naiad other than Norgrash'nar, Alim'dar and myself, for it was one of us who would be left without a mate once Nirvisa'nen revealed for whom she held affections, and when one of the others had chosen Kalenen.

In the days following the marriage of Alunen and Norandar, both Alim'dar and Norgrash'nar made frequent pleas for Nirvisa'nen's attention. I, on the other hand, chose not to behave as were they, for in their longings they were made fools by their incessant engagement. Yet I knew all the while that this was but an excuse—for in truth I simply did not know how to attain her affections, for it seemed obvious that when she chose, it would be one of them. So too did I consider that even if she were to choose me, this would leave both of the others unhappy, and I did not want this at all.

I considered turning my attention instead to Kalenen, who was an attractive and appealing woman, but I felt not the same longing for her as I did for Nirvisa'nen. And she only seemed to have affections for Norgrash'nar; and regardless, the problem remained that there was an odd number of us. It seemed to me like an insurmountable obstacle that everyone might be satisfied... Someone was going to be hurt, and I considered that most likely it would be me. At least, I often told myself, if this happened, I still had Saxon as a companion, though assuredly he could not effectuate all that I desired.

The courtships of both Norgrash'nar and Alim'dar went on throughout the remainder of the Spring Seasons and into the Summer Seasons, and still Nirvisa'nen did not make a choice. Seeing how contented Alunen and Norandar had been made by their marriage, Haldus'nar and Sarak'den, Garonar and Kuranen, and Adaashar and Sveraden all made plans to together go to Kronaggas early the next Springrise to be wed as well.

Their only reason for deciding to wait this long was because each of these three men wished to build new homes that were large enough for two occupants.

Now, while all of these other things were happening in the Valley of Naiad, Alunen was experiencing something troublesome that she did not wish to bother the others with. She confided in me in this matter, rather than in her husband, for though she loved him greatly, she was concerned that her problem might drive him away. For it was that since she had become wed to Norandar, there had been a change in her body that she did not understand. Her abdomen had swelled, and her body seemed to her to be disfigured.

Her husband eventually noticed—as did we all—but was unable to give her comfort. As that season of the year passed away, she became more and more upset over it, fearing that Norandar might begin to desire one of the other women more than her, for to her own eyes she was no longer so beautiful. Norandar tried to reassure her that his love was only for her, but this did nothing to assuage her concerns.

Then, on the fourth day of Autumnturn of that same year, Alunen disappeared.

Norandar came out of their home that morning looking for Alunen but he could not find her. It was very unusual that she would leave Nightrun without him, for they had spent nearly every moment together. Soon, we all became concerned and began spreading throughout the village to find her. But she was nowhere in Nightrun, and so we looked elsewhere—to the east into Iidin, to the west into Sternwood, and then even further, all throughout the valley, but she was nowhere to be found. Norandar was distraught, and we all promised that we would not rest until we had found Alunen.

We prepared packs for traveling longer distances, with all of the necessities for being away from home for a longer period of time. Food would not be a concern, for the world was filled with edible fruits and plants. Extra clothing, tools and utilities might be needed. A pack was also prepared for Alunen, for we did not know what she might have taken with her, if anything at all.

"Surely she would not have gone through Yor'Kavon, into Forthran," Sarak'den said. It was two days since Alunen had disappeared and we had not yet found her.

"No," Norandar agreed. "She must have gone to the west, onto the plains."

"But why would she leave?" Sveraden wondered.

"Have you not seen the way that she has grown fat?" Norandar said. "I have told her that she is beautiful regardless, but she was uncomfortable in her own skin. Surely this is why she has left, for the shame of her appearance."

"I don't understand," Sveraden said. "She is loved here, by all of us, by you."

"It doesn't matter why she left," Alim'dar said. "It only matters that we find her... Alak'kiin, do you have any ideas?"

I considered this and was about to shake my head, when I noticed that Saxon was near Norandar and Alunen's home, sniffing the ground. He too seemed concerned. I turned my attention to him and said, "Saxon!" He came running to me. I said to the others, "This Dain can smell far better than we... Saxon, can you smell her, Alunen?" And he wagged his tail, his mouth open, seeming happy and not so distressed as the rest of us. "Can you take us to her?"

"This creature doesn't understand what you're saying," Norgrash'nar spat. He had, of late, been peevish in his words toward both Alim'dar and me. He knew that it was we who also longed for Nirvisa'nen.

I ignored his derision and said, "Go, Saxon, take us to Alunen!" And the Dain went again to their house, sniffed at the ground, and then headed westward, out of Nightrun, looking quickly over his shoulder to make sure we were coming. The rest of us followed, thinking now that we might have a chance at finding her.

Saxon led us through the Valley of Naiad, down the Westward Slopes, and onto the Plains of Kronaggas.

"Maybe we should go find Kronaggas," Sveraden suggested.

"We don't know if he's there, in his mountain," Adaashar said. "We don't know where any of the Dragons are right now."

"But they could help us find her."

"We will lose too much time looking for the Dragons," Alim'dar said. "If it rains, the Dain might lose the scent."

Throughout the day Saxon took us onto the northern side of the Plains of Kronaggas. We rested that night when we could travel no more, when weariness overcame us, despite our urgency in finding Alunen.

But that night the rain came, and in fact Saxon did lose the scent of Alunen, for in the morning when I told him to continue on, he looked around, befuddled, and knew not where to go.

"Foolish creature," Norgrash'nar said. "He has led us nowhere."

"It's not his fault!" Sarak'den said harshly. Norgrash'nar snorted and turned away.

"He was taking us westward," I said. "Let us continue there and maybe we will find some sign as to where she has gone."

We continued on, but as the day progressed we became discouraged, for we had found not even a single footprint that might reveal where Alunen was going. That evening as we camped, when we were perhaps halfway across the plains, Norgrash'nar and Alim'dar became incensed with one another, for their competitive aggressions put them at odds with one another, all over the affections of Nirvisa'nen.

Now, Nirvisa'nen had grown close to Alunen, as had all of us. But she held a particular fondness for her because Alunen had been a lover of song and dance, and had even been learning to sing herself, under the instruction of Nirvisa'nen. And Nirvisa'nen became angry with Alim'dar and Norgrash'nar when they argued, and said to them, "Can you not put aside your petty disagreements until we find Alunen? I know why you fight, and that it is for me, for you both wish to wed me. I will be the one who decides this, not the victor of your senseless vying!"

And so the two men were silenced by her stern reprimand. Although I felt guilty about it, I wondered then if I might thereafter have a greater chance with Nirvisa'nen, for she had scolded the others. But I knew I should not even be thinking about such things when my dear sister was missing and nowhere to be found.

We continued onward the next morning, still westward, and again by the Hour of Mourning we had found no sign of Alunen. But as we made camp we were visited by Sharuseth the Copper, for we were on the very edge of his Domain.

"Naiad!" the Dragon said enthusiastically, landing on the ground not far from us. "What has brought you here, to my domain? For is this not further than you usually venture out of Naiad?"

"It is," Norandar explained. "But Alunen disappeared three days ago, and we cannot find her anywhere. Have you seen her?"

"I have not," the Dragon said. "Yet I have not looked either. Where would she have gone? And why?"

"We don't know," Norandar said. "Something odd has happened to her of late, and she has become disheartened."

"Why do you think she might have come this way?" the Dragon wondered.

"Saxon, this Dain that follows Alak'kiin everywhere, led us this way, then lost her scent," Alim'dar explained.

"Ah, yes, the nose of the Dain is great, so long as there is a scent to be found."

"We don't know what to do," Norandar said.

"Can you help us find her?"

"I will, of course," Sharuseth said. "But understand that if she does not wish to be found, it may not be easy. Alunen is intelligent and if she sees me coming from a distance she might hide. For I am much larger than she and she will see me coming long before I can see her. I will find my brothers in the morning, and we will search until we find her."

"Whatever you can do...." Norandar said. With each passing hour he was becoming more distraught.

Sharuseth stayed with us that night, promising that he would go in search of Alunen at Firstlight.

When Firstlight came, Sharuseth was already gone. Norandar had already risen and was pacing about the camp while the rest of us were just awakening.

"Alak'kiin," he said, coming to me when he saw that I was stirring. "Get out your scope." Still blurry-eyed, I reached into my pack and pulled out the small telescope that had been made for me by Norgrash'nar. Into the side of it was engraved the words, *For Alak'kiin, my Cousin, my Brother: Norgrash'nar*. As I handed the telescope to Norandar and felt the engraving, I frowned, for just since the time that Norgrash'nar had given it to me, there had been feelings of discord arising between us.

Norandar took the scope and looked to the west, scanning the terrain. "What do you see?" I asked. The others were rising from their sleep as well, and they began to gather around.

"A fire, I think... a small one."

"Might Alunen have lit a campfire?" Sarak'den wondered.

"Maybe," Norandar said. "But it is far away, nearly as far away as this scope can see. Sharuseth has already gone to investigate." He handed the scope back to me and I looked through it. After a moment I was able to find the faint trace of the fire, but could make out nothing else, for it was only the single point of light that was faintly visible. "Let us make haste. We may have gained ground on her."

"We don't even know if it's her," Kalenen said.

"What else should we do?"

"We could divide," Adaashar suggested. "Split up. Some of us go toward the fire, the rest of us spread out over the land, from northwest to southwest."

"That is good," Norandar said. "Surely then we will find her." But let us wait until Sharuseth returns before we do so. Let us see what he discovers."

Sharuseth returned before the end of Firstlight. "There is no sign of her. The fire was caused by a Lightning Bug, I think. Alunen was not there."

Frustrated, Norandar said, "We are going to split up to cover the lands. We will meet back here at this spot within four days' time." Everyone agreed. Norandar looked around and gathered some scattered stones that were strewn about, and he started stacking them. "Let this serve as a marker for where we divided, and to where we should return." The rest of us gathered stones as well, and piled them together.

Then Sharuseth took his hands to action and spoke words of Dragon

Magic and the stones were fused together. "Let this place be called *Tiden Kort,* for here we will gather."

"Will you keep searching?" Norandar asked.

"Of course. And I will find the other Dragons so that we may scour the lands until we find her."

Then we decided who would go in which direction; Norandar and Alim'dar would be going toward the fire, which was due west. Adaashar and Sveraden would go due south, Sarak'den and Haldus'nar due north, Garonar and Kuranen to the southwest. Norgrash'nar was expecting to go with Nirvisa'nen, but the woman refused, saying, "You should go with Kalenen. I will go with Alak'kiin." And so with great reluctance and indignity Norgrash'nar left with Kalenen, going in a southwest direction, though separate from the others. Nirvisa'nen and I left as well, going to the southeast; Saxon—as always—was by my side.

"Where do you think she might have gone, Alak'kiin?" Nirvisa'nen asked when we were a fair distance divided from the others.

"I really don't know. I know only that she was upset. But I never thought she would just leave."

"What if something terrible has happened to her?"

"What could have happened?"

"I don't know," Nirvisa'nen said. "What if she is lost and hungry, or has fallen into one of the deep places of the earth?"

I considered this. Although there was little concern of Alunen going hungry, for there were ample supplies of vegetation everywhere in Sylveria, there was a real worry that perhaps she had fallen into a crevice in the ground, for the world was littered with holes and hidden places. Sylveria was a very large world and I wondered how we would ever find her. "Surely with the Dragons' help we will find her soon."

"I hope we do."

We continued on in our assigned direction until the others were completely out of sight. It was the Hour of Concession on the eighth day of Autumnturn. It was then that Nirvisa'nen said to me, "Alak'kiin, there is a matter that I wish to confide in you."

"Of course," I said, knowing that it was going to be in regard to Alim'dar and Norgrash'nar. Though my heart was already hanging low for the troublesome disappearance of Alunen, it sank even further, for I knew that in her seeking of my counsel she was confiding in me as a friend, as a brother, and nothing more.

"My greatest concern right now is finding Alunen, but I'm certain you have noticed that both Norgrash'nar and Alim'dar have shown affections for me." I nodded. "Both of them are men of charm—Norgrash'nar a man of eccentric passions, and Alim'dar a man of fierce character. And I love both of them. But... only one of them can have my affections."

"Have you chosen between them, then?"

"My heart has decided for me, Alak'kiin. Norgrash'nar says the sweetest things to me in his fondness. He is poetic and charismatic, and I will always love the attention he gives me. But it is Alim'dar who I will be bound to, ultimately. This I know, in my heart."

"We cannot help who we love," I said, and though I was disappointed, for my affections had fallen on this woman who was now telling me whom she had chosen, I was pleased that at last it would come out, that it would be resolved, regardless of the consequence.

"No, we cannot."

"Are you concerned about how Norgrash'nar will take such disappointment?"

"A bit," Nirvisa'nen said, and her eyes turned away from me. "But... that is not my greatest concern. I know that Kalenen will convince him to love her. He is not the one... I worry about. It is you, Alak'kiin. For how unfair it seems that we were awakened such, with one more man than woman. And why it is you that should be left alone is something I don't understand, for you are the kindest of us all, and the wisest."

I frowned, embarrassed that she knew of my affections though I had tried to conceal them from her over the past seasons. But it didn't matter, I knew, for Nirvisa'nen had made her decision, and I had always known it would not be in my favor. I nodded, then, not knowing why, and I said, "It is all right, Nirvisa'nen. It does seem unfair, but perhaps it is for the best."

"How so?"

"I don't know. You are not wrong that I have felt stirrings when I look at you. Ever since the night we first met, on the shores of Iidin, I have been entranced by you. But you were never so drawn to me as to the others and—"

"Alak'kiin, do not misunderstand. It is only Alim'dar whom I am drawn to. Only him that I love like this. I find in Norgrash'nar a friend, in a different way than you, even. But in you I find someone who is filled with wisdom, someone I can talk to about this, about anything at all. And I just want you to know how sorry I am for this—that it couldn't be you...."

"It is all right, Nirvisa'nen. That is what I'm trying to say. I would not have you come to be with me, or with anyone who was not what you truly desire. It is for the best because it is what is right for you. And yes, there remains none for me, but I am blessed in that I have Saxon here to fill in at least some of the emptiness, for with no others has any animal bonded so greatly."

She looked from Saxon to me and nodded sadly. "Perhaps he knew," she said.

We continued on, searching for any sign of our dear friend and sister, Alunen. But the days passed and we found nothing. On the last day of Autumnturn we returned to Tiden Kort, where we had made a meeting place, hoping that one of the other pairs had found Alunen.

Nirvisa'nen and I were the first to arrive, and soon after were joined by the others. Norandar and Alim'dar were the last, and no one had found any trace of Alunen.

Sharuseth, Merobassi, Ashysin, Merilinder, Drovanius, Verasian and Aranthia also arrived that day, at the Hour of Devotion, and none of them had found her.

We vowed then, that day, that we would not return to the Valley of Naiad until we found Alunen, so distraught were we all. But had we known then where Alunen was, we would not have been so concerned.

Alunen's Bondings

When Alunen awoke on the fourth day of Autumnturn, she was uncomfortable in her skin. Her abdomen was swelled moreso than ever before and she wondered if this ailment would ever pass. She edged her way out of the bed while Norandar remained asleep. She placed her hands on her belly and said silently to herself, *"What is happening to me?"*

After resting for several moments—for the act of simply rising had strained her—she stood up and looked down at her husband, speaking inaudible words. *"I love you, Norandar, but I cannot stay... I cannot bear the thought of you casting me aside for my ugly appearance."*

Alunen slowly and quietly dressed, then gathered into a bag the berries and fruits and leaves that had been attained the day before. Taking this over her shoulder she quietly left the house.

Outside, it was a cool morning. Summer had passed away and the night gave a comfortable air, which in her current state Alunen found most appealing. It was the Hour of Distinction, long before Norandar or the others would rise. She had not been sleeping well of late.

She looked around the Hills of Nightrun, then across the valley. Though Aros had yet to emerge, a strange and unique thing was happening in the heavens... As she observed, Vespa and Imrakul were side by side in the sky, west of Naiad. But moment by moment the two bodies were merging, and Imrakul was eclipsing Vespa. Although this was not a rare event, as it happened to some degree every night during this season, it was unique in that it was a full eclipse, and as she watched, the green moon completely blocked out the blue sun.

"This is a sign," she whispered to herself. And when Imrakul

departed, leaving Vespa in its wake, so too did Alunen leave Naiad, following after the westward moon. She looked back at Nightrun, sadly wishing that she did not have to leave, but in her heart she was certain that it was for the best. Whatever was happening to her was becoming a burden on Norandar.

By Firstlight she had traveled beyond Sternwood. She knew the others would be rising and would start looking for her. But she did not want to be found. In her wisdom she knew what they would do—they would search Nightrun first, then the northern valley, then the southern, and if they found no trace of her they would look elsewhere. But just maybe eventually they would stop looking.

She considered that the Dain would be able to track her scent, for she had seen him do so before, but she also knew that the rain would wash it away, and so she only had to stay ahead of them until the first storm came.

Onto the Plains of Kronaggas she went, gaining ground all the while, for as the other Naiad were searching the valley, she would be getting farther ahead. Alunen did not know where she would go, what she would do, or what would become of her, but in her state of mind she cared only that she was not found, for she felt great shame in the appearance of her body given by this afflicting ailment.

Westward she continued, day after day, and when the rain came she was thankful, for her tracks would be hidden. In order that she would remain unfound, Alunen then thought to use magic so that she would walk without leaving footprints, and she turned sharply to the south, once she was past the Plains of Kronaggas and well within the domain of Sharuseth... and she realized then that eventually the other Naiad would seek the Dragons to help them, and still she did not want to be found, even by them.

And so she used her skills that did not involve magic to further hide, taking from the plants of the land and covering her clothing in thick layers of leaves that would make her blend in with the landscape. When she did first see Sharuseth in the skies overhead, she dropped to the ground and further hid amongst the foliage. Doing this she was certain she would remain unseen, even from the eyes of Dragons.

On the ninth day of Autumnturn Alunen began to feel lonely and she missed her husband and the other Naiad, for she was not intended to be alone. She considered turning back, but when she looked upon her own ever-growing abdomen, such thoughts were diminished. But that day she began crying fiercely for she was in such misery, both physical and emotional. The first tears of the Naiad fell upon the fields of Sylveria that day, and though she did not yet realize it, this was causing something wondrous to happen...

For it was that such sadness had never been known or felt in all of

Sylveria and the magical world was perplexed. Always had the world been a place of joy and contentment, but now it had been touched by melancholy. And the natural order of the world compensated for this, and transformed the tears of Alunen into something more, and they became the seeds of the largest organism that would ever be formed upon the world of Sylveria—the trees of Baobab. Everywhere that her tears fell thereafter, new life began.

Alunen turned westward again that day, crying all the while, and she committed herself to continue on, never wanting to be found so long as she was afflicted.

All through the remainder of the season and well into Autumntide did Alunen wander through the wilderness; then finally she came to the eastern shores of the lake called Abai. She found plentiful food along the way but was nevertheless growing weary, not only for the lengthy travel, but also for her infirmity. She was unsure now if she was still being pursued by the others, for she had not seen any sign of them in days. On occasion she would still see a Dragon soaring the skies, usually Sharuseth, but she did not know if they were searching for her. Still, she retained her disguise and remained invisible, so far as she knew.

At Abai, Alunen turned northward and edged around the lake, coming at last, a day later, to the northernmost point of this inland sea. There, she crossed the great river that flowed out of the northern lands of Whitestone, which was the Isyn River. This she accomplished with the use of her magic, for she had become proficient in manipulating the earth itself and she created a land bridge across. She had done this before on this journey, passing over numerous rivers throughout the fields of Sharuseth, and now she did like before, then dispersed the magic walkway after crossing so that there was no sign of her passage.

Now, this far north, along the ranges of the Etakos Mountains that spread all the way to the south, there were two mountains that rose separately, standing as a gateway into a valley between them. On the tenth day of Autumntide, Alunen went through this gateway, and she knew that she would be unable to go any further. Whatever lay beyond in the shadow of these mountains would be her home, her resting place, and she could only hope that she would be concealed behind these mountains.

But as Alunen came into this small region she stopped suddenly as she saw something far stranger than she had imagined possible. For there was an illusion of her perspective, or so it seemed. Her eyes squinted and her mouth draped open in perplexity. She could, through her perceptions, see the Etakos Mountains extending along the west, to the north and south. But there along the wall of the mountains were several great creatures moving about that should have been far too small to see, if in fact they were considerably smaller than a Dragon. For to be so large in comparison to the mountains they would have to be larger than any other creature she had seen throughout Sylveria, save for the Dragons. And before now she had seen nothing so massive, not even upon her flights on the wings of Dragons in years past. Still, though she had seen this region from the air before, it had been from at a distance far greater than she now was.

She went onward toward them, wanting to see them closer... The creatures were gray or brown in color, covered in exceptionally long fur, and they blended well with the stony terrain. They moved very slowly as they went about their tasks, which seemed to be the gathering of vegetation that grew out of the sides of the mountains. And for this slow movement, Alunen called the creatures *Sloths*.

Alunen was fascinated with them, for she had seen nothing of this kind before, and she was amazed even, for no haired creature that she had seen anywhere in Sylveria came even close to this size. It was a creature that even a Dragon would not be able to lift, so great was its mass.

They had giant claws that seemed as if they would be even longer than a Dragon's, if they were compared side by side. Their front paws were like hands but with four fingers that were able to grasp. And it was with these that they easily scaled the mountainsides and pulled from between the stones great clumps of vegetation that must not have grown anywhere else, for they went to great lengths to retrieve it.

There were seven of the Sloths there in her sight, but more could easily be blended into the distant stony landscape, much the same as she had concealed herself from the Dragons.

Then Alunen was astounded again as one of the great creatures let out a bellow that rang through the valley. And suddenly the Sloths were coming out of the mountains, not so slow and sluggish now, but with a strange rapidity that caused thunderous sounds. Rocks fell before them—a small avalanche—but the creatures were unaffected as they came to stand on the valley floor, perhaps half a March away.

Although it surprised her to think it possible, the Sloths must have seen her, for several of them began moving with a sudden purpose, for they were running now, not at all slow as they had seemed before, in her direction. It did not occur to Alunen that the creatures might try to harm her, but still she backed away, up against the side of large boulders, so that she would not be trampled if they came close.

For long they ran, continuing toward her, and she became alarmed as they drew nearer, for their charging thundered through the valley as their weight fell upon the earth, and with each passing moment they grew larger to her perspective and even the ground shook.

And at last they came to a halt, just to the west of her. Now, after such a run, the Sloths breathed deeply, and it must have been strenuous for them, for each of them lay down upon the ground and closed their eyes as if to sleep. But one of them remained alert enough to keep its eyes upon Alunen.

Seeing its gaze upon her, she thought to reassure it that she was not there to hurt it, but then realized how ridiculous it was, for surely nothing could harm a creature so large as this. Even lying down, with its head upon the ground in front of it, the creature towered over her, rising three Heights tall perhaps.

The Sloth that watched her did so with great interest alight in its eyes. There was no malicious intent apparent in its gaze; of this she was certain. They had, most likely, seen something new entering into their domain, and charged at it with great curiosity. But now that they had arrived, most of them were too tired to even stay awake, for it must have expended a great amount of energy to move such an incredible weight.

Alunen slowly inched her way toward the Sloth. Her pack was empty and slung over her back; her hands were in front of her, resting upon her abdomen, which felt great pressure from within. The Sloth continued staring at her but moved not at all, even when the woman came to stand right in front of its giant snout. She could easily have reached her entire arm into the giant creature's nostril, so large were they, but she instead reached out one of her hands and laid it gently upon the side of its nose.

"I am only here to retreat from my own troubles," she said softly. "I hope I have not disturbed you."

The Sloth rolled its head ever so slightly and it seemed to Alunen that perhaps it understood. Then, with curiosity in its eyes, it took a deep breath in through its nostrils, and she felt certain that it was smelling her, much like Saxon often did. After its long inhalation, it began to let it out and Alunen moved off to the side so as to avoid a blast of warm air. Still she kept her hand upon the creature. The Sloth turned its eyes downward and she could tell it was looking into her own, and then shifted them downward further, toward her abdomen. And something in its gaze told Alunen that it related to whatever was afflicting her.

The hour was getting late and soon Lastlight would fall upon the lands, and so Alunen deemed it wise to stay there, with the Sloths, at least for this night. It did not seem to her that they were going to awaken any time soon, and so she lay down upon the ground just a short distance away, preparing herself for the cool night.

But the Sloth was not content in letting her be so far away, and it reached its giant paw toward her, and curled its hand around her, gently, shielding her from the coming cold. And Alunen knew that she had somehow made a friend of this wonderful creature.

At the Hour of Firstlight, when Alunen woke, she was covered with giant leaves that must have come from some distant plants, for there was no vegetation so large here in this valley. She wondered how the Sloths might have accomplished covering her without disturbing her sleep, but she was thankful. All but one of the Sloths had moved on; the one with whom she had bonded remained, and when it saw that she was awake it rose from the ground and ever so slowly turned to the north.

"Where are you going?" Alunen said, entirely unsure if the creature could even understand her at all.

The Sloth turned its head to look at her, and when it was certain it had her attention, it rolled its head in what seemed a gesture for her to follow. She did not know if this was the true intent of the beast, but nevertheless she went along.

Great masses of hair covered the Sloth, for theirs was not a hair of a short variety, and clumps of it dragged along the ground as it moved. Although it seemed a slow pace, each giant lurch forward by the Sloth covered more ground than she could have herself in the same time. Growing tired in her ailing condition, Alunen took hold of a clump of the Sloth's dangling hair, and took a step onto a mass that was dragging, and thus she was pulled along, without expending any of her own energy. The Sloth did not object.

And so it was not long before they reached the greener fields that were north of the two disparate mountains that stood as a gateway into the lands of the Sloths. These were greener lands, lush and cradled by the place where the mountains met, a secluded retreat where she thought the other Naiad might never find her. This, she thought, might be the perfect place to remain forever hidden.

When they came into the fields, there were present several other Sloths, but one of them in particular caught Alunen's eye, for it was lying upon the ground amongst thick foliage, and it was toward this beast that they went. When the Sloth that carried her stopped, Alunen stepped off. The lying Sloth looked at her curiously, but with weakness in its eyes. It breathed heavily, as if it too suffered some ailment, and when, after just several moments, it stretched out, it seemed that its belly was also swollen, for it was fatter than the others.

And Alunen wondered if there had indeed been some force guiding her westward and to eventually find this place, for here was a creature that may well be suffering the same as was she. For in its eyes she saw the same despondency that she felt.

As coincidental as it was, that night the Sloth gave birth to its offspring, something that Alunen had not ever seen in the natural world in the Valley of Naiad, for coming out of the Sloth was a small version of itself, and she was amazed. She was certain then that this was her affliction too... that since her marriage to Norandar, and since they had known one another in the most intimate way, she too was with child.

Autumntide passed and Autumnfall came, and still Alunen stayed with the Sloths. The infant Sloth was incredible to behold, for though it was newborn, it was still larger than most animals she had seen before. But she found herself wondering why it was that neither she nor the other Naiad had ever seen such a wondrous thing in nature—for they had been around the animals of the Valley for more than twenty years.

She supposed it was because it was only the Dain, Saxon, whom they were around constantly. When Garonar brought a herd of Bison or Paken around they were no longer in their native environment. Perhaps in the fields to the south there were places where their females went to give birth to their young, just as the Sloths had come to this most secluded part of their region.

They had seen smaller versions of all of the animals in the Valley of Naiad, and these must have been their young; now that Alunen had seen firsthand the nature of birth and reproducing she felt foolish in not having considered it before. She had always thought before that there were simply variations in the sizes of the same kind. So was it true that at their most infantile ages, the mothers must surely keep their young away from the others.

Although the infant Sloth was itself far larger than was she, Alunen helped to care for it by bringing it branches and leaves upon which to lie while the father—the Sloth who had brought her here—was out gathering food for his small family.

By the time Winterfel came the newborn was able to move about on its own and had grown considerably. She spent the first few days of this season preparing her own shelter, for she did not have the same thickened fur as the Sloths to shield her from the cold. Although she was not the clothier that Sveraden was, she was able to create for herself a warmer covering from the excess hair of the Sloths.

The Sloths cared for Alunen as well, for they recognized that she was with child. When she would work too hard, the mother would nudge her either with a claw or a giant snout until she stopped. The father would bring food for all of them, for their diet was not far different than hers.

It was on the third day of Winterfel when Alunen went into labor, and though it was not a painful experience, it was neither comfortable. She relied on her instincts to get through the struggle, as well as on what she had seen when the mother Sloth had given birth.

At the Hour of Feltide, Alunen gave birth to the firstborn child of the Naiad. It was a male child, and she called him *Mara'non*. She immediately bonded, cared for the child and loved him more than she loved anything else. And although she had also fallen in love with the Sloths, she longed now to return home to Naiad, to her husband, and to her own family.

THE TRAIL OF TEARS

All through the Autumn Seasons did we search for Alunen. At that time we left little of Sharuseth's domain unexplored. By Winterfel we had made no progress and were beginning to grow weary, for even the Dragons had been unable to find her. On one occasion even Kronaggas had given to using his magic to try to locate her, but to no avail. He concluded that either she was out of the reach of his magic—an unlikely possibility—or that she had found some way to shield herself from it. Alunen was strong in magic, and so this was the more likely case.

We never returned to Naiad during this time, for we had vowed that we would not until we had found our sister; rather, we spent all of our time in scattered parties scoping the landscape, looking in every hollow, every shrubland and everywhere else we could think to look. By Wintertide some amongst us were losing hope, and by Wintermelt there was some talk amongst them of returning to Naiad regardless. But Norandar would not give up, for he loved his wife, and so despite the complaints and discouragement, we kept on.

During these seasons there was much else transpiring amongst us. Those who had already determined their mate were ready to forego their previous plans and to go on and be united in marriage as had Norandar and Alunen. Nirvisa'nen had yet to tell either Alim'dar or Norgrash'nar whom she would wed, for she considered it a minor matter in comparison to finding Alunen. Although I knew her heart in this matter, I kept my silence and said nothing. I had been excluded from the possibilities, and so it was not my concern.

Still, I had my own moments of discouragement, for all the while that we traveled, Kalenen continued in her engagement of Norgrash'nar, so that if Nirvisa'nen were to choose Alim'dar, she would be the next for his consideration. This meant, of course, that I would be the man left without a mate, and I struggled with this often, especially when I was in close proximity to Nirvisa'nen, for there was always a reminder of her beauty and grace right there in front of me, and I could not escape it.

For this, I also spent much time in consideration about what it meant... Why had seven of the Sylvai awakened but only six of the Nescrai? Was it not the same magic that had awakened us all, though at different times? These were questions that I would bring before Kronaggas at some time in the future, perhaps. I was disheartened, for it seemed that all of my brothers and sisters and cousins would have someone else to be bonded to, yet I would be left alone. And though having the companionship of Saxon was some kind of recompense, it seemed that it was not enough.

When Springrise came, so too did a new year begin, and it would not be long before the first day of our awakening would be marked, and we would begin our twenty-second year. We still had not found Alunen and most of us had committed to living our lives in the wilds rather than in the comforts of our own homes. But finally, as Springtide began, we were at last given hope of finding our sister.

We were camped along the northern seashore of the region. That morning, just as we were rising from slumber during Firstlight, Sharuseth arrived, excited in his demeanor, talking fast in his gruff voice, saying, "I have found something!"

"What is it?" Norandar said. "Have you seen Alunen?"

"No, but it is something wondrous!"

"What is it?" I asked.

"New growth in my domain... trees!"

"It is Springtide, Sharuseth. Why is this so surprising?" Norgrash'nar asked, frustrated.

"Because," the Dragon said. "It is new... it is *masograth*... new! It is life that was not there before, last Autumnfall when the earth reclaimed the leaves!"

"Is this so unusual?" Kalenen asked.

"It is, because there are many of them, and they are in a great line that spreads all throughout my domain. It is a kind of tree that I have not seen before!"

"Sharuseth," Alim'dar said. "Tell us how this helps."

"Because I asked Kronaggas about it, wondering if he had awakened something new in my lands, and he had not. He went and looked at them and he said that they were magical trees, formed by some magic he did not even understand."

"Again, how does this help us?" Norgrash'nar asked.

"Kronaggas said that only one of great magic might produce such things as new life... who is the strongest amongst the Naiad with magic?"

"Alunen!" Norandar said excitedly, then more somberly added, "You think she left Naiad to plant a forest?"

"I do not know, but it can only be she, surely. Follow the trees and you will perhaps find Alunen!"

It was not at all an unsound plan, for if indeed Alunen was responsible for this new growth then perhaps these trees would serve as a trail for us to follow. It was as good of an idea as any, for we were quickly running out of places to look.

"Can you follow the tree line in the air?" Norandar asked.

"No, I cannot. They are saplings only. It was only by chance that I found them at all. I cannot even see them from the air."

"You say there is a great line that goes throughout this region?" Adaashar asked. Sharuseth nodded. "Can you take us to them, to some of them?"

"I can. I know that the trail starts far to the east, but there is a place not far where it passes by."

And so the Dragon led us to the southwest, away from the seaside and farther into his domain. There, during the Hour of Passions, he showed us the way, and indeed there were small trees that grew all in a line, extending as far as we could see them. They were no taller than we were, and few leaves were budded. Some of them grew close together, others further apart.

Norandar came to stand beside one of them and gently touched it, closing his eyes and whispering, "Alunen, I will find you...."

We followed the saplings to the west, but after a while they turned back to the south, and then west again, snaking through the fields in an unpredictable manner. As we moved slowly onward, often backtracking— going wherever the trees led us—Sharuseth flew off, again in search of Alunen. He too was excited by the possibility of finding her, for in truth, she was one of his favorites.

For days we followed the young trees all about the fields of Sharuseth, around the hills and over the rivers wherever we could. And at last, on the final day of Springrise, we came to a place in the far northwestern corner of Sharuseth's realm that we had not searched before. Etakos came into view, as did two other mountains that seemed separate, and it was to these very mountains that the trail of trees seemed to lead. It was there, inside that valley, that we at last found Alunen.

Like Alunen before us, we were astounded when we saw the Sloths of the valley, for never had we imagined that creatures so large existed, save for the Dragons, of course. As we beheld them, I considered that if we had first encountered them, rather than the Dragons upon our awakening, perhaps we would have been equally enamored with them.

It was the first day of Springtide when we entered the Valley of the Sloths, exactly twenty-two years after the awakening of the Sylvai. When they saw us, they came to us with not so much enthusiasm as they had Alunen four seasons earlier, for now that they had seen our kind, they expected such visitations. Instead, they came to us in not an unfriendly or aggressive manner, but in a guarded state—not for their own sake, but for that of their resident, Alunen. In this they blocked our way into the northern valley with their giant masses and simply would not let us pass.

Then Sharuseth landed upon the northern mountain, which came to be called *Glotiro Mariarne*, and he cried out to the Sloths in a shriek that caused them to divide—not for fear of the Dragon, but for an understanding of trust that they were given by his shrill cry.

We hesitantly went between the Sloths, moving northward, knowing that we must be near to our long sought-after objective. And indeed, when we came to the end of the valley, Alunen rose from a bed of vegetation and ran to us, embracing first Norandar and then the rest of us. There were three Sloths at this end of the valley and they watched us with interest.

Alunen took us to the place where she had rested, and showed us the most amazing thing we had ever seen—the firstborn child of the Naiad, the boy child named Mara'non. And she explained to us what she had learned—first of all why she had left, where she had gone, and how she had come to be here. Each of us held the child for a time, trying to understand the implications, and then passed the baby back to its mother.

"How did you ever find me?" Alunen wondered.

"We searched everywhere," Norandar said. "We left Naiad as soon as you vanished, and we have not returned since. Each of us has been searching for you this entire time, for over half of the year. I thought we would never find you. Then at last we followed a long line of saplings, new trees that were growing in the fields, for the Dragons had told us to follow it. And here we found you. I have missed you so...."

Alunen embraced Norandar again, and he held in his arms both his wife and their child. Alunen said, "I am so sorry I left as I did. I was ashamed and could not bear the thought of losing you... I was getting so fat... If only I had known that I would give birth and would be slim again."

"It is all right. It doesn't matter now... will you return with us to Naiad?"

She looked over at the Sloths and a dismal frown fell upon her mouth, but she nodded. "I want nothing more, and I will return. But I will miss these creatures. They have taken care of me. Rest here, tonight, with us. We will leave in the morning."

When the morning came we all prepared to leave. But Alunen first took Mara'non over to the mother and father Sloth, so as to say farewell. And she said to them, "My friends, I am so thankful for what you have done, and I will never forget my time here. But I must return to my own home, to be with my own kind...." The three Sloths each let out a slow moan of sadness, but it was apparent that they understood. "I make a pledge to you now that this child and our descendants will always be lovers of the Sloths."

NORGRASH'NAR'S TROUBLE

We left the Valley of the Sloths and began the long trek back to Naiad. It was the first day of Springend when we arrived back home at last. Alunen and Norandar took their child into their home and made for it every comfort that they could. The rest of us took great care as well to provide everything that might be needed for this firstborn child of our people. Even Saxon took to spending time outside of their home at night, for his instincts were on alert and he was by nature a guardian.

Once we had rested from our long absence, plans were made for most of the Naiad to go to Kronaggas Mountain to be wed, as Norandar and Alunen had done, for to see Mara'non made all of us want children of our own.

It was during this time that Norgrash'nar began to plead with Nirvisa'nen to wed him, foregoing now the pleasantries of courtship. For long hours she listened to him as he told her of his love for her, and how they were meant to be together. To him it was destiny that they bear children. I could see that she was flattered by his affections, even encouraged it, in those days... For this, I pulled her aside one evening, during the Hour of Concession, for there was something I needed to say to her.

"It is cruel what you are doing, Nirvisa'nen," I said.

"What do you mean, Alak'kiin?"

"You know that your heart has chosen Alim'dar, yet you inspire hope in Norgrash'nar. Or has something changed?"

"It has not...." She looked away from me now, knowing that I was right and feeling shame. "I do love Alim'dar, and it is him I will wed. But I do not have the heart to tell Norgrash'nar."

"You must find it in yourself. You cannot keep doing this to him. He knows, I'm sure, by his instincts, that you have not chosen him. But he fights it because of his love for you. Every part of his soul longs for you, and you give his mind hope that maybe his instincts are wrong. It is delirium, Nirvisa'nen, that will be inspired by this."

She was grimacing now, knowing what it was she had to do, but feeling great guilt. "He will not take my decision so well as did you, Alak'kiin."

"I did not take it well," I admitted. "I have struggled with it for a long time. But I have accepted it because I have no choice. I care for you, Nirvisa'nen, and because of this, I want you to be happy... I want you to be where you belong, and I can see that my brother Alim'dar is what it will take."

"But Norgrash'nar is not like you... he will not take it so well."

"No… I think you are right. And this is why you must tell him now, without further delay. He will be displeased, even angry, I think. But how much worse will it be if you delay any longer?"

She was sulking now. "Will you tell him for me?" she asked.

"You know I cannot. It must come from you."

"How do I tell him, Alak'kiin?"

"Just tell him. It is the only way. I think it will hurt you to hurt him, but when it is all over, you will feel better."

"But what of him? What if he cannot accept it, as you have? He does not have the same patience and humility as you."

"I don't have an answer for you, Nirvisa'nen. He will be hurt, and angry, I think. But he still has an advantage over me, remember? He has another to fall back on, for Kalenen still longs for him. They will have children. I will not."

Frowning still, her heart low, Nirvisa'nen said, "All right, Alak'kiin. I will tell him tonight, for he is going to appeal to me again… but I will not let him. I promise."

Later, when I was in my home considering many things, a heavy knock came upon my door. When I opened it, Norgrash'nar was there, scowling, but from the look in his eyes I knew that Nirvisa'nen had not yet told him, for the fire in his eyes was not of disappointment, but of his passion. He pushed his way inside and paced about.

"What did you talk to her about, Alak'kiin?" he asked.

"I think you should talk to her about that," I said.

"I am asking you!" When I said nothing, he said, "You were making your appeals to her heart, to try to sway her to marry you…."

"No, Norgrash'nar. I am not. I have given up on that. I know that she is not meant to be with me."

He snorted, "If that is true, then you give up too easily!"

"It is not a matter of giving up. It is a matter of wanting what is best for Nirvisa'nen—"

"What is best for her? You think *you* are best?"

"No, that is not what I said. Norgrash'nar, though you are my cousin, I consider you a brother. For many years since our awakening we have been friends… all of us have been friends. Only since the awakening of our passions has all of this become so confused… I do not know what to tell you, except that we must both accept her decision. Only she can determine who is best for her."

Norgrash'nar now sat; his heart was low, and I could see the turmoil upon his features, for his infatuation with Nirvisa'nen had grown so great that it was nearing obsession. He could no longer see reason. "It must be me…" he said in a deep whisper. "I cannot be… I cannot live without her."

"Cousin," I said, sitting beside him and putting a hand on his shoulder. "I have had the same thoughts. If it were me she chose, then my heart would be saddened, for your sake. But it will not be me, I can assure you."

"Then you know..." he said. "You know... That is what you talked about with her!"

"Again, you need to speak with her about this. I will not break the confidence she has in me."

He stood quickly, heading for the door, muttering, "Then I will! I will talk to her now. I will make her tell me." And then he was gone, slamming the door behind him.

At that moment, I envied neither of them—Norgrash'nar or Nirvisa'nen. I could only be relieved that my heart had been broken long ago, whereas Norgrash'nar's troubles remained ahead of him.

As she had promised, Nirvisa'nen told Norgrash'nar that night that she had chosen Alim'dar. This was apparent to all of us in Nightrun, for his indignation echoed throughout the hills. So harsh were his words against both Nirvisa'nen and Alim'dar that in the morning, when we realized that he had left Nightrun, none amongst us felt compelled to go in search of him, as we had done for Alunen.

Norgrash'nar did not return that day, or any day for the remainder of the season, and beyond. As these days passed, everyone decided to go on with their plans to wed those whom they loved, including Alim'dar and Nirvisa'nen. And so on the first day of Summerstorm, when we saw that the skies were clear and that we still had time before the seasonal storm would arrive, we went to Kronaggas Mountain once again.

But Kalenen remained behind, for she was upset in that she would not be marrying the man she loved, for Norgrash'nar was gone, and we did not know when he might return.

When we went to Kronaggas, he said to us, "You wish to wed, but I told you before, such a bond must be made in the presence of eleven witnesses. Yet there are but nine here present for each of the bondings. Where are Norgrash'nar and Kalenen?"

"They were not so well disposed to be a part of this," I explained to Kronaggas. "For she loves him, but he loves another."

"Another?" the Dragon wondered. "Who?"

"He loves Nirvisa'nen," Alim'dar said. "As do I."

Kronaggas looked at Nirvisa'nen and said, "And you love Alim'dar?"

"Yes. It is to him I should be married, for I know in my heart that he and I will be lovers of one another for all time."

"Hrmmm." The Dragon growled thoughtfully, then closed his eyes.

"Cannot this child serve as one witness?" Norandar asked, raising up the infant for the Dragon to see.

His eyes remaining closed, he said softly, "A child cannot bear witness to such sacred affairs...." Then, after a long pause he said, "This is what the Numen wills... only seven will be the number of witnesses required, henceforth, for there will be a division amongst the Naiad. Seven and the two to be wed... nine will be the number kept whole, and four will depart."

Though we didn't understand what his words meant, we took it as practice, and in the coming years, when the Naiadic children would grow and themselves be wed, there would always be seven witnesses.

The next day, Kronaggas performed the same ceremony as before, and bonded together in marriage Adaashar to Sveraden, Garonar to Kuranen, Haldus'nar to Sarak'den, and Alim'dar to Nirvisa'nen.

And in Nightrun all were happy save for Kalenen and me; somewhere else Norgrash'nar was surely incensed in his dejection.

Then, a season later, at the Hour of Passions, while all of the other Naiad were busy with their tasks and professions, Kalenen came to my home and knocked on the door. When I opened it she stepped in without invitation. She wore an outer robe tied about her waist, her arms crossed about her abdomen. There was upon her face an expression that I could not discern.

She said, "Alak'kiin, Norgrash'nar is gone, maybe forever. The others are trying to make children of their own. Yet you and I are alone."

Not approving of where I thought this might lead, I said, "We can go out into the world and find Norgrash'nar. I understand your sorrow. We can convince him to come back. I know that you love him."

"I thought I did. But love cannot be one-sided, Alak'kiin. There is a longing within my thighs; I need to feel what the others have. I cannot wait for Norgrash'nar. You are free, though, Alak'kiin."

Now, I had, in previous days, taken note of Kalenen's demeanor, and seen that she had taken to looking upon me. While there remained within me a longing much like what she described, I would not give in to such yearning. For it was that truly, while I loved Kalenen as much as all of the others, I felt no special connection to her. Still, deeper feelings remained for Nirvisa'nen, but these were feelings that I suppressed, for I would not succumb to jealousy or such lechery. And neither would I acquiesce to temptation with Kalenen.

"I cannot give you what you want. As I said, we will find Norgrash'nar, and though it may not come so easily as it did for the others, I am certain he will come to love you, to appreciate you for your beauty. You are no less than the other women. As beautiful as them, surely as desirable."

"Then why will you not have me?" she said sullenly, and her arms dropped to her sides. The tie upon her robes loosened.

"Because it is not meant to be. As Nirvisa'nen had to choose between others, so too have I decided that I will choose none."

"Because you cannot have her?"

"Because I no longer want her. I will not entertain such things. Alim'dar and Nirvisa'nen are bonded by the power of Kronaggas and the Numen. My desires died with their marriage, and I am well pleased that they have found such happiness with one another."

"Could you not find such with me?"

Frowning, I said, "I cannot. It is just not meant to be."

"Why not!" she barked, and stomped her foot against the wooden planks of the floor. As she did, her robe fell open and revealed that she wore no other clothing beneath. She made no attempt to cover herself.

Now, when we had all first awakened, there had been no shame amongst us, for we were all unclothed. We were as children, innocent and unabashed. But as time had progressed and our passions had arisen, so too had it been recognized that the flesh of the body was the flame that could ignite our longing.

Kalenen stepped toward me; I stepped back. I would not be tempted, for what her eyes then proposed was something of which I would not indulge, for I had witnessed five marriages of the Naiad to one another, and I had seen the sanctity of the rituals performed. Anything outside of the bond established by Kronaggas and the Numen would be irreverent, and I would not partake.

Yet it seemed that she cared little for this in that moment, so strong was her desire, and I was reminded of what Kronaggas had said before, when he had proclaimed that only seven witnesses would be required. For he had said that there would be a division amongst the Naiad. Nine would be the number kept whole, and four would depart. And again, I wondered at this, thinking that perhaps the present behavior of Kalenen was tied to this prophetic statement of the Dragon.

She advanced again; this time I stepped toward her and reached for her shoulders. But my hands touched not her skin, but instead the collar of her robe, and I pulled it back into place to cover her bareness. Then I gently turned her away toward the door and nudged her outward.

When she looked back over her shoulder at me, her eyes revealed both sadness and anger at what she perceived as rejection. But she said nothing and departed.

When Winterfel came that year, each of the newly wed couples of the Naiad announced that they were with child, as were Alunen and Norandar once again. All were filled with joy, for they were beginning new lives in which they would be blessed with children. Only Kalenen was left out of this, and though I knew it saddened her to see the others so happy, she then seemed not too displeased in her life. I surmised that after I had turned her away she had considered my words and had regained hope that Norgrash'nar might return. In this, she thought that surely she could eventually tame his affections.

And much to our relief, the cold season finally drew Norgrash'nar back to Nightrun, and though he seemed distant much of the time, the rage that he had suffered before was quelled, and his rationality returned. He resumed his previous works, growing ever stronger in his magical abilities and more proficient in his technological creations. He spoke little to the others—not at all to Alim'dar or Nirvisa'nen—but to both me and Kalenen he made frequent visits. At first I was concerned that he would contend for her, causing a rift between us as he vied for the affections of the last unmarried woman. I assured him that neither she nor I had any interest, and his previous lunacy in regard to Nirvisa'nen seemed vanquished, and we were, as I had hoped, friends once again.

Kalenen and Norgrash'nar began spending more time together, and her previous indiscretion was never discussed.

In Springrise of the next year Norgrash'nar proposed to Kalenen and they too were soon married. Quite strangely though, when it came time for the ceremony, they insisted that there should only be seven witnesses, as Kronaggas had decreed, and they selected Alunen and Norandar, Sveraden and Adaashar, Kuranen and Garonar, and me as these witnesses, leaving out Alim'dar and Nirvisa'nen, and Haldus'nar and Sarak'den.

Kronaggas insisted that it was but seven witnesses that were required, but that all could certainly serve as attestors. Nevertheless, they invited not the Naiad who had chosen to intermarry between Nescrai and Sylvai. Divisions were forming, and I was greatly troubled for it.

On the first day of Springend, Norgrash'nar and Kalenen announced that she was with child.

So it was that all of the Naiad, save for me, were married and beginning families. Strangely, though I still found myself longing for what the others had, I also found contentment in my own workings in life, and I concerned myself little with such matters.

Saxon and I would take long hikes together, exploring the deeper places within the crags of the mountains, the depths of the river valleys and the extents of the Valley of Naiad. In him I found the most fulfilling companion and friend, and I could not imagine anything greater.

The Book of

DESCENDANCY

THE FIRSTBORN CHILDREN OF THE NAIAD

These are the first children of the Naiad, the Firstborn Sons and Daughters of the people of Sylveria:

The Sylvai, Norandar and Alunen, became the parents of the following children (they were gold-skinned like their parents):

 ♂Mara'non—born 3 Winterfel, 21
 ♀Dadriinen—born 4 Summerstorm 23
 ♂Malanar—born 7 Springtide, 25
 ♀Manis—born 8 Autumnturn, 28
 ♀Imara'nen—born 12 Wintermelt, 30

The Sylvai, Adaashar and Sveraden, became the parents of the following sons and daughters (they were gold-skinned like their parents):

 ♀Ingridven—born 2 Summerstorm, 23
 ♀Avis'sin—born 4 Summertide, 24
 ♂Barvan'nar—born 8 Autumnturn, 25
 ♂Riiska'nar—born 11 Winterfel, 27
 ♀Aisaven—born 4 Springtide, 29

The Sylvai, Alim'dar, and the Nescrai, Nirvisa'nen, became the parents of the following children (they were a brown-skinned people, mixed of both of their parents):

♂Lakail'sor—born 5 Summerstorm, 23
♂Maivusar—born 3 Wintertide, 24
♂Kalan'nar—born 7 Springtide, 26
♀Versailen—born 7 Summerfade, 27
♂Umonar—born 10 Winterfel, 29
♀Sora'nen—born 4 Autumntide, 30
♀Estor'nen—born 4 Autumntide, 30

The Nescrai, Haldus'nar, and the Sylvai, Sarak'den, became the parents of the following children (they were a brown-skinned people, mixed of both of their parents):

♂Kyrik'nar—born 6 Summerstorm, 23
♀Olais'sin—born 6 Summerstorm, 23
♀Tiiga'sin—born 1 Wintertide, 25
♂Duhekiin—born 2 Autumnfall, 26
♂Varis'sar—born 6 Winterfel, 29

The Nescrai, Garonar and Kuranen, became the parents of the following sons and daughters (they were azure-skinned like their parents):

♀Rohiimen—born 9 Summerstorm, 23
♂Gamloar—born 12 Summerstorm, 25
♀Daiad'sin—born 11 Wintertide, 26
♀Siianen—born 8 Autumntide, 28
♀Aneka'nen—born 5 Autumnfall, 29

The Nescrai, Norgrash'nar and Kalenen, became the parents of the following children (they were azure-skinned like their parents):

♂Rhinusor—born 3 Summertide, 23
♂Relanar—born 3 Summertide, 23
♀Rekasen—born 3 Summertide, 23
♀Kalniisin—born 7 Autumnturn, 25
♀Dugazsin—born 9 Wintermelt, 26
♂Lavanar—born 3 Winterfel, 27
♀Miiganen—born 8 Autumntide, 28
♂Miithinar—born 10 Springend, 30

With time these children grew into adults, and many of them learned the crafts of their parents, while others pursued things of their own interests. Our civilization developed and when these sons and daughters married one another their children began to move out of the region of Nightrun and into the surrounding areas of the Valley of Naiad.

Now, in the first generations, the sons and daughters of the First Awakened Sylvai and Nescrai married amongst their own families. Each of the children retained the physical traits of their parents—the golden skin of the Sylvai and the azure tones of the Nescrai. In later times, there were unions between various people groups.

But amongst the children of Alim'dar and Nirvisa'nen, and Haldus'nar and Sarak'den, the offspring were born with brown skin, for they were mixed of Sylvain and Nescraian blood, and they inherited the diverse traits of both parents. Likewise, these children tended to marry within their own families, and the characteristics of them were preserved.

Life in the Valley of Naiad remained pleasant and as the second generation began to have children of their own, who also grew into adults, it became vibrant and ever more interesting as they learned and evolved their parents' crafts. By the third generation, we had grown to a hundred and fifty-nine people in number, and by the fourth there were nearly nine hundred. It was in this latter generation that some of the Naiad began feeling crowded in the valley, and they began to separate into people groups, which were named for their fathers who were of the fourth generation.

For this, each of the Dragons invited the families to move out of the Valley of Naiad and into their own domains, where they promised to watch over them. And so in the fifth generation, in the year 100, many of the Naiad went their separate ways to begin filling the lands of Sylveria.

The Noranites—who were the descendants of Norandar and Alunen—settled in the forested region of Sharuseth, where their Awakened mother had once sought refuge. By this time, the trees that were seeded by Alunen's tears had grown and the lands were largely forested. These were the great Baobabs that would persist in Sylveria throughout the ages. The Noranites became strong in magic and in the power of interpreting dreams. So too did many of them become stoneworkers, guided by their cousins, the Haldusians. Also they had an affinity for crafting and carving wood; it was these people who built the great city of *Floran'Adar*, deep within the woods near to the lake called Abai. In time, these lands became known as the Trees of Mara, named for the Firstborn Son of their people.

The Adaasharians—who were the descendants of Adaashar and Sveraden—settled in the southern lands of Merilinder, which was a vast prairie. These people became nomads, wandering the beautiful plains and building only a single city, which was called *Oman'Tar*. It was raised upon the southernmost tip of Sylveria, overlooking the Southern Sea.

The Garonites—who were the descendants of Garonar and Kuranen—settled in the mountains of the region of Ashysin. Although they were a Nescraian people who moved into the lands of the Metallic Gold Dragon, they lived in peace with Ashysin, and for a time they visited with him frequently. The mountains were difficult for them to work, but the Garonites thrived in the region by befriending the mountain goats and other wild animals of the vales, which helped them in cultivating the large mountain meadows. It was in this region, upon a great flat-topped mountain in that region that they built the great old city of *Hest'Vortal*, which overlooked the Golden Valley, far to the south of Naiad.

The Norgrasharians—who were the descendants of Norgrash'nar and Kalenen—settled in the Grasslands of Verasian, and they built great cities to live in. The grandest of these cities was *Mar'Narush*, which was so tall that it could be seen from anywhere upon the grasslands. These people loved the cities and they later hired others to farm the lands so that they could remain within their comforts.

The Haldusians—who were the mixed descendants of Haldus'nar and Sarak'den—settled upon the highlands of Aranthia. These brown-skinned people became, under the noble and watchful eye of Aranthia the Crimson, the most honorable of all the Naiad in Sylveria. Upon the Aranthian Highlands they built the great city of *Eswear'Nysin*, and it was there that the orders of the Knights of Haldus would one day be formed. This land would forever be known as Aranthia.

And finally, the Darians—who were the mixed descendants of Alim'dar and Nirvisa'nen—settled in the region that was north of Sharuseth's domain, in the region called Whitestone, which was land unclaimed by any Dragon. They too were brown-skinned, and they built the great city of *Nirvisa'Iinid*, which was commissioned by Alim'dar himself and named in honor of the wife he loved more than anything else.

The Dragon Temples

Throughout these years all of the First Awakened Naiad survived, for in those times there was no death. Eventually our homes in the Hills of Nightrun were abandoned as my brothers, sisters and cousins moved into the lands of their descendants, where they remained somewhat isolated, seeing one another far less frequently than when we had lived on the thirteen small hills in Naiad.

I had no descendants, no people of my own, and I spent much of my time traveling between the various lands of the offspring of my siblings and cousins, observing them, teaching them, and learning from them.

For ten more generations the Naiad multiplied and the lands of Sylveria flourished. What had begun with only twelve (excluding myself, for I had never married or had children) had grown innumerable.

The lands were at peace and thrived while the Dragons watched over the people, and it was in these fruitful times that the Dragon Temples were constructed, for the Naiad had grown so numerous that the Dragons could no longer keep intimate contact with each of them. These temples were made to serve as places for the people to seek the Dragons' counsel and companionship. Eight of these temples were made with the assistance of the Dragons themselves, one to honor each of them. These were the names of the temples and their locations:

The Temple of Kronaggas was carved out of the deep caverns beneath his mountain home. There was the great opening into the mountain and the road covered in crimson soil that led up to its entrance; this pathway was called the Sanguine Artery. The people would often make pilgrimages along this path and into the mountain to pay homage to the oldest of all Dragons.

The Temple of Diras'Vorma was built into a mountain at the southern end of the Golden Valley to honor Ashysin. The Gold Dragon would often wait upon the stone façade of the temple, looking out over the river that had been named *Steel*, eagerly watching for the arrival of both Sylvaian and Nescraian visitors.

The Temple of *Norad'Taun* was grown deep in the western woods, northwest of the city of Floran'Adar, to honor Sharuseth the Copper. When the Naiad came to visit him, he would create magical spectacles to enchant the people and he would teach them magic to take back to their homelands.

The Temple of *Nysin'Sumuni* was built within the city of Oman'Tar to honor the Silver Dragon. To fascinate his guests, Merilinder would dive beneath the waters of the Southern Sea, and as he resurfaced, the falling water would come off his scales and reflect the light of the suns, creating brilliant shows of dazzling colors. Although Merilinder loved both the Sylvai and the Nescrai, few of the latter came to see him, for his lands were far to the south and too hot for their liking.

Although no people had yet settled in the domain of Drovanius, the *Temple of Bela'Goreb* was built near the Hinliss Mountains of the east to honor the Black Dragon. After a time, only the Nescrai would come to visit him, for his lands were too cold for the Sylvai; or rather, this was their pretext. In truth, after a time when other matters unfolded that will be discussed further, the Sylvai were often made to feel inferior by Drovanius.

The Temple of *Luen'Aril* was built in the icy mountains of Merobassi, to honor the Blue Dragon. Though few—either Sylvai or Nescrai—came to visit his cold temple, Merobassi had a loyal following that chose to migrate into his lands and live in the caves and the mountains and upon the plains near Dragonswake. Rather than put on displays or entertain his modest guests, Merobassi would instead indulge himself by asking them ceaseless questions about themselves and their lives, for he too had chosen to remain isolated in his own domain, leaving only when he was called upon by the other Dragons.

The Temple of *Atim'Unduri* was built upon the Aranthian Highlands to honor the great and noble Crimson Dragon. Aranthia spent his time with all of his visitors whether Sylvai, Nescrai, or the mix-blooded, teaching them about how to respect and love all of the natural world, and each other. It was these teachings that would be carried on in later times to become the Code of the Knights of Haldus.

The Temple of Aleath'Weryn was built upon the Plains of Verasian to honor the Green Dragon. Verasian would often entertain the people by proposing great riddles for them to solve. In those days he did this for the Naiad of all shades, but in later times he favored the Nescrai.

Roads were built all across Sylveria, paved in local stones; they extended the breadth of the land masses, giving easier passage from each of the Dragon Temples and the first cities. These were later called "The Old Roads."

From the time of the construction of the Dragon Temples, which were completed in the year 310, the Naiad visited their fathers yearly so as to keep the presence and love of the Dragons in their hearts. They would bring gifts of their prosperity—the fruits of the lands and the objects of their crafts. And as it was, the lands of Sylveria were full of life and peace.

A TALE FROM NAIAD

Now, before all of these things had happened—before the Dragon Temples had been raised, before the cities of the people had been built, before even any descendent of the First Awakened Sons and Daughters had wed, there was the time when Norgrash'nar had vied for the affections of the beautiful Nirvisa'nen. He had professed his love for her, but when she told him that it was Alim'dar she loved and would marry, he became enraged, and he left the village of Nightrun and was gone for four seasons. None of us knew where he had gone, and never questioned him about it, for we knew that the entire ordeal with Nirvisa'nen had crushed his spirit. It was only in later times when I learned of where he had gone and what had occurred.

Norgrash'nar was greatly distressed when Nirvisa'nen firmly told him that he must stop his pleadings for her affections, because she had decided to marry Alim'dar. Now, all the while that he had been courting her, he had held on to a hope that maybe she would choose him—for to him, she was the most lovely, the most beautiful of all of the Naiad. And so too did he believe that she belonged to him, for the other two men who had shown interest in her were both Sylvai. He became convinced in his heart that only he had the right to be with her, because they shared the same blood, were of the same awakening.

When she crushed his heart, Norgrash'nar could do nothing but flee Nightrun, for he could no longer stand to face any of his own kind. He felt ashamed that he had not been able to win the heart of the woman he loved, and he decided that if she would not wed him then neither would she have to suffer his presence. And so that night he fled, no longer caring what happened to him, for his heart and his spirit were in dismay.

He went eastward, wondering if the others would try to follow him, as they had all followed Alunen to the west. In part, Norgrash'nar wanted to be followed, for perhaps if Nirvisa'nen did come for him, she would tell him that she had made a mistake, and did wish to marry him instead. But from a distance he watched them the next day, and those that followed, and there seemed not to be a single inclination by any of them to find him. Instead, they advanced in their previous plans to wed one another. Amongst the others, Alim'dar and Nirvisa'nen married as well, and now he was certain that there was no hope.

So he left Naiad entirely, traveling through Yor'Kavon Pass, and then down the other side onto the lowlands of Forthran. Norgrash'nar knew that the fierce tides would rise at the Hour of Feltide, but he cared not if he was broken against the mountains of the south by the crashing of the waves. As he moved along through the lowlands, indeed, the Hour of Feltide did come, but he was not destroyed by the rushing of the sea, for in his sorrowful rage, the depths of the magic he had practiced protected him, forming a field around him that kept the waters at bay. That day, Norgrash'nar passed safely through Forthran and onto the higher grounds of the eastern lands, the domain of Verasian the Green.

He went then through the northern lands and turned to the south when he found the Eastern Sea, which was the Sea of Repose. He did not know where he was going, only that he wished to get as far away from the Valley of Naiad as possible. It was along this route that Verasian found him one day, and the Dragon landed before him, saying, "What are you doing here, Norgrash'nar?"

"I don't know. I only know that I must get away."

"What is wrong? Why are you here alone?"

"I cannot stay with my people anymore," Norgrash'nar said. "They have rejected me… I am not wanted."

"Oh, now, why would they do that?" the Dragon wondered.

"I do not wish to talk about it, for if I do, you will tell the others of the thoughts of my mind and where I am."

"I will not do so, if you ask me not to."

"Still, I would keep my troubles to myself, if it is all the same to you."

"Of course," Verasian said. "But do you mind if I stay with you for a while? I was going to the Valley of Naiad for some company when I saw you here. If you would be pleased, I will talk with you instead."

"I am in your lands, Verasian, your domain. I would not contend to tell you what you cannot do here—or anywhere."

"I don't want to be a bother…"

"You will only be a bother if you keep on bothering…"

"Very well, I will walk with you a while."

Norgrash'nar and Verasian continued southward all that day. He spoke not a word to the Dragon until that night when he said, "Nirvisa'nen has married Alim'dar."

Verasian took this offering of information as an invitation to inquire further. "And this distresses you?"

"Yes! Have you not known that it was I whom she should love?"

"How so?"

"Because she is like me, Nescrai. He is not!"

"And why does that matter? Why does that make you more fit to be her husband?"

Norgrash'nar did not have an answer, but he fumed at the notion, and said, "I am like her, and she is like me!"

"You are all of the same kind, Norgrash'nar. Yes, you are of different awakenings, but you are only different in that you were awakened at night, while the Sylvai during the day. The light of Aros and Vespa determined this. Nothing more."

"Are you not understanding that I don't care about that?" Norgrash'nar asked. "It matters not anymore, for she has married Alim'dar, and I will be alone…."

"So what will you do?" Verasian asked.

"I will stay here, if I may, in your lands, as far south as I can go. As far away from Naiad as possible."

"There are places further away than my domain," the Dragon offered. "Have you not flown over the distant realm of Drovanius?"

"I have, but I had not considered this, for in my misery I thought only to keep going and never stop."

"I will watch over you if you stay in these lands," Verasian promised. "But if you wish to go to Drovanius, to his vast lands, I will take you there."

Norgrash'nar took the offer of the Dragon to heart, and the following morning he rode on the back of Verasian across the seas and lands of Aranthia the Crimson and then deep into the domain of the Black Dragon. Across the vast and dark prairies of this domain they flew until they reached the high mountain cave that was the roost of Drovanius.

"Brother!" Verasian called deep into the cave.

He was answered by the deep voice of Drovanius, "Verasian, what brings you here, to my domain? For I was lost in slumber… it is not time for our assemblage yet, is it?"

"No, it is not. But I have brought you a visitor. Norgrash'nar wishes to speak with you."

"Ah, Naiad! I have been longing to visit the Valley. Come in, come in!"

Norgrash'nar walked down the steep slope that went into Drovanius' cave, his way guided by a magical light that the Black Dragon immediately produced. Verasian did not join them, but instead waited outside upon the rostrum of the mountain.

Once inside, Norgrash'nar came to face the Dragon, who said, "What can I do for you, favored son?"

"I wish to stay in your lands, and make a home here for myself."

"Just you? What of the other Naiad?"

"Just me. I do not wish to be with them anymore."

"You may stay here as long as you desire," Drovanius said. "But please tell me what has happened that makes you wish to be away from your own kind."

Norgrash'nar was silent for long moments, considering his words, then said, "For all of my life I have loved Nirvisa'nen, and I have given her my affections and told her the trueness of my heart. And for a time she hung upon my every word. Her eyes told me what her mouth would not, that she longed for me as well. I always thought that she and I would become wed. But then Alim'dar came to her and stole her affections from me, and I find now that my heart is filled with bitterness. I loathe him, for he has taken what should not be his, for he is not worthy of her."

Drovanius had sympathy for Norgrash'nar and he tried to console him, saying, "Although I am not like you, in that I have no longings for another, I see the anguish within your soul, and for this I am most remorseful. You are a child of my awakening. Yet what of the woman Kalenen? Could you not give your love to her?"

"She has not captured my heart as Nirvisa'nen has," Norgrash'nar said. "As you said yourself, you do not have the same longings that we have, and it is not so simple as choice."

"Everything is about choice," Drovanius said. "Everything is done with our own will. For does even the Bison not choose its own mate? The Paken does not look twice when he is rejected by the doe, but finds another that is willing."

"I am not a beast of the fields, Drovanius!"

"No," the Dragon agreed. "You were awakened greater than the animals of the world, and with this there is a greater responsibility."

"Responsibility? To do what?"

"To tend to the needs of the world, and those creatures who surround you."

"This is foolishness!" Norgrash'nar spat, but settled his tone when the Dragon glared at him. "What of my needs? Is it not Nirvisa'nen's responsibility to tend to my needs, above those of the Sylvai?"

"What needs, nelf?"

"The need to be loved, to be bonded together. I am Nescrai, like she, and she has given her love to Alim'dar who is Sylvai. You cannot know what this pain is like, this aching in my heart and my soul."

"Indeed, I cannot. I can only offer you my sympathy. But what am I to do for your sorrow? For Nirvisa'nen is free to do as she will, and to love who she will love."

"But do you not understand the unfairness of this, Drovanius?" Norgrash'nar's words were growing fiercer, the bitterness in his heart mounting. "Alim'dar is not like us, and I do not understand how the trueness of love could transcend such differences. Have you not noticed that our skin is akin to the deepness of the night, while theirs is like the day? We are as different as darkness and light! And it is not right that we should blend together, for if the day and the night were to mix, what would we have but a fusion of half-darkness and half-light, like at the Hour of Lastlight, in the Winter seasons, when the suns cast little light upon the world and everything is gray?"

"What does this mean?" the Dragon asked, confused perhaps by the madness-etched tone of Norgrash'nar's words. "Are you saying that there should not be a mixing of the blood of the Nescrai with the blood of the Sylvai?"

"Yes! And it is not Alim'dar and Nirvisa'nen alone who will bring this about, but Haldus'nar and Sarak'den have already wed. As it is, one-third of our people will be mixed with theirs! And what then, Drovanius, will happen when future generations arise and our children and their children mix even further? I tell you, there will be no distinction between our people and our own uniqueness will dwindle away."

Drovanius listened to his son's words and though he could not understand Norgrash'nar's agony, here a seed was planted deep within the Dragon's mind by the bitter rantings of the man; for it was true that Drovanius loved his children as they were, always having held a greater fondness for his own than for the Sylvai. And if the Nescrai were to be blended with the Sylvai, their descendants would all be changed. And this was something that the Dragon did not care for—for how much more sorrow might arise in the conflicts of the heart? He could see the wisdom in his child's words.

Still, there was nothing Drovanius could do to ease the pain of Norgrash'nar, for like all creatures of the world, Nirvisa'nen was a free spirit—free to love who she chose. He explained this to Norgrash'nar, that there was nothing to be done to change what had been. For this, Norgrash'nar grew even more bitter, and he vowed to himself that he would defy this until his last breath.

Norgrash'nar left Drovanius' company then, and upon the wings of

Verasian he returned to the Green Dragon's domain, and there dwelled in contemplation for several seasons. He spoke with Verasian sometimes, but most of his time was spent in silent consideration of all things. Then, as the seasons turned cold, he at last decided to return to Naiad.

Once there, he made amends as well as he could, and he consented to marry Kalenen, the only remaining woman of his kind, the Nescrai. They, like the others, had children and grandchildren who multiplied in number. And when many generations had passed and they grew too numerous to remain in Naiad, Norgrash'nar took his descendants to the east, to settle the lands of Verasian the Green. And by the year 300, the Norgrasharians had grown greatly in number, out-populating perhaps any of the other peoples of Sylveria.

But never did the father of these people forget his true longing, the love he had lost in Nirvisa'nen, and though he showed it not outwardly, he grew all the more bitter within.

The Book of

Dissidence

Journey to Nirvisa'Iinid

In the year 310, I—Alak'kiin—had been set upon a task by Alim'dar to retrieve something that Haldus'nar had made for him. It was a trinket, an amulet that encased a pink stone of unknown origin, the likes of which I had never seen before, and was meant as a gift for his wife, Nirvisa'nen.

This was how I spent much of my time in these days, traveling between the lands of my brothers, sisters and cousins, recording the events of their peoples' progress... and sometimes making deliveries. With no family or people of my own, I became a historian, a bearer of news from one region to another, and a favored guest nearly everywhere I went.

On the third day of Summerstorm I was upon the Plains of Valor, which was southeast of the lands of Alim'dar, just south of the Bay of Diin'gar. During the Hour of Eventide. storm clouds began gathering in the west; at the Hour of Meeting the rains began and the warm winds surged across these plains. I took shelter in a burrow near the Umonar River. I wondered what kind of creature might have dug this hole, for I could tell that it extended out from the bank of the river into the hillside. There was little threat of it flooding, even if the river overflowed, as the tunnel elevated away from it.

I had to crawl through most of the passage, as it was not quite high enough for me to stand upright. It grew darker as I progressed, and darker outside as the storm intensified. Reaching into a pocket, I pulled out a fist-sized stone that had been given to me by my sister, Alunen. Willing it to activate, the stone began beaming with a light bright enough to guide my way. Although I did possess the magical prowess to simply summon a small sphere of light myself, I nearly always used this artifact, as it was a reminder of my sister, whom I saw far too infrequently during these years. Always, it seemed, I was busy exploring or visiting so many places throughout Sylveria that I found it difficult to stay in one place for more than a day or two.

Deep inside the burrow I encountered the occupant and maker of this subterranean home—it was a creature known as a Maran Fossa. Strangely orchestrated, the animal seemed an amalgamation of a Cat, a Mongoose and a Beaver. These creatures typically were around a Height long, were quadrupedal and stood about half a Reach tall. They had long bodies, feline legs and the tail and facial features of a Beaver. When I encroached on its den, the Fossa hissed at me, but this was hardly a sign of displeasure, for these creatures only ever made two sounds and one of them was this. The other was a deep and intense purr, which the creature initiated once it had gotten over the initial surprise of my entrance. This was a sign of its contentment, a welcoming gesture, and I found that its presence was as comforting to me as mine must have been to it.

The storm was intense; lightning flashed and briefly lit the long tunnel; thunder shook the air and torrents rained from the heavens. This went on for perhaps a full Course before it finally settled into a rhythmic, heavy rainfall. Leaning against the side of the dark den, the Fossa pressed up against me, and I soon fell asleep as boredom overcame me while I waited for the storm to pass.

When I awoke, the rain had calmed, and I rubbed the animal's ears as a show of gratitude and began crawling back through the now soaked and muddy burrow. When I emerged, the worst of the storm had passed and the sky was clearing. It was the Hour of Concession and most of the day was lost to the Summer storm.

To the north and west I could see the towering mountains of Whitestone. These were mountains drawn of the purest rock and were unique in all of Sylveria. If anywhere a stone structure was found that was white in its natural tint, it came from this region. Whitestone was the domain not of any Dragon, but only of my brother Alim'dar, his beautiful wife, Nirvisa'nen, and their mixed children. All of the offspring of these two were of a beautiful brown skin tone, a mixture of the golden and azure shades of their parents.

As I surveyed the scene of the Plains of Valor I found that the ground was saturated with mud and sand that had washed over the banks of the river. When I arrived at Alim'dar's city I would certainly be ready for a good bath in one of the region's hot springs.

When I started walking northward, struggling to pass through the mud-caked ground, I heard the hissing of the Fossa, and when I turned, it was emerging from its den, squinting its small eyes and gazing at me. With it were two small pups which must have been hidden behind the mother in the burrow, for I had not before noticed them.

"You want to come along?" I asked her. I had long held a fondness and an affinity for the animals of Sylveria, and they seemed drawn to me as well.

Slinging the pups onto her back, where they clung tightly to her, the mother leaped toward me and followed along as I moved northward. "I suppose I should give you a name then," I said. "How about... *Ferris?*"

The Fossa hissed and sneezed which I took as an objection. "Then how about... *Molley?*" She hissed and purred. "Then Molley it is." As I continued on, Molley followed, ever curious about what I was doing, as was her nature.

I was, of course, reminded of my oldest and first friend in Sylveria, the Dain I called Saxon. Thoughts of him could never do anything but brighten my spirit, and though it had not been long since seeing him, I missed his companionship and his happy playfulness. He had remained behind in the Valley of Naiad, taking time when I was away to visit his own kind, who had multiplied just as we Naiad had, and they dwelled north of the Valley, in a place behind the mountains called Kaliim. Oh yes, I longed for his company, always wishing him to be by my side. But he rarely ventured outside of the small region of Naiad. So, for now, Molley and her cubs would keep me company.

As we followed along a northward trail that followed the river, we came to Hargid Cliff; from there we could go west across a land bridge that crossed the Umonar River or rise up a slope to the top of the bluff which would lead into the eastern realm of Whitestone. We took the land bridge, as this would lead us onto the central plains of the region and toward my destination, which was the city of Nirvisa'Iinid.

Nirvisa'Iinid was laid out quite unlike any other city in Sylveria. This was one of the old cities, the first places that the people dwelled in large groups after leaving the Valley of Naiad. The Darians had made this region their home, and Alim'dar had named this central city in honor of his wife.

The city was still three Marches away and we would not arrive at Nirvisa'Iinid until well after night fell, so I committed to taking it slow and planned to camp outside of the city until Firstlight.

The southern region of Alim'dar's domain was farmland, resting upon the rolling Hills of Estor. There were two other districts in the central area of Whitestone, which were the habitable lands encased on three sides by the mountains. To the west was the district of Sora, and to the north was Versailen; each of the three regions was named after one of the daughters of Alim'dar and Nirvisa'nen. The borders of these regions were established by the river that flowed out of Lake Umon, which split into the Umonar and the Isyn Rivers. The City of Nirvisa'Iinid was set upon the confluence of these rivers, dividing the city itself into three sectors that were named after their first three eldest sons, Lakail'sor, Maivusar, and Kalan'nar.

Called the White City, for it was carved and constructed from stone drawn from the nearby mountains, Nirvisa'Iinid was not even visible until one was within a quarter of a March because it blended in with the backdrop that was the Whitestone Mountains. This realm was one of the most beautiful and enchanting places in Sylveria, as great care had been taken to cultivate the land and preserve the natural essence of Whitestone. Even the roads that cut through the region were made of moss-covered stone that blended into the landscape.

With Molly and her pups at my side, I approached the main roadway that would lead into Nirvisa'Iinid at the Hour of Lastlight, and there made camp for the night, under the cover of the eastward Hills of Estor.

Here in Whitestone we were nearly equal distance from where Aros receded in the far west and Imrakul hung in the east; Vespa too lingered there in the east, just beside the green moon. The heavens were beautiful in all of their glory as the light of these three bodies cast their respective glows upon the world.

Resting upon my bedroll, Molley and her pups lay up against me. Although it was the early Summer Season, the nights were often cool so far to the north. As the three animals drifted into slumber, they purred loudly, creating a soothing hum that brought me quickly to sleep as well.

When we awoke at Firstlight on the fourth day of the season, there was a bit of a disturbance alongside the road. We had camped just a short distance off the lane, to the east. Just to the south we were greeted with an unusual sight, for there, spread across the road and extending far to either side, was one of the giant Maran Sloths that lived typically to the south, journeying, it seemed, alone toward the city. The two Fossa pups each leaped onto my shoulders to curiously watch as the great beast approached. Molley too was at my side, excited in her interest as well. As the Sloth passed us by, it looked at me and lifted its massive head as if in greeting, and then continued on its way. Though it appeared to be moving slowly, even from a close distance, it would in fact have been difficult for me to keep its pace, as its giant legs carried it in long strides, and soon it was out of sight as it fell over the hills upon its route to Nirvisa'Iinid.

"I wonder where he's going?" I said to Molley. She sniffed at my arm and purred.

It was the Hour of Elation when Nirvisa'Iinid first came into view; a heavy fog still lingered in the air, obscuring the city walls. As it was, we were but a Course's walk from the south gate, and as the lines of the city sharpened, coming into focus, it seemed as if we had been transported from afar and into the clear view of the outer walls, so quickly did the city separate from the mountains in our perspective.

The city's outer walls stood nearly a Breadth tall, the tops reaching even higher than a Sloth's back. Though I could not see all of it as we approached, I knew the walls extended all the way around the city, passing even over the rivers. Now, in those days, there was no great enemy to keep out of a city, but still the walls served two purposes. One was to keep the appearance of stone, so that the city would blend into the mountain landscape beyond: this was an intentional design. The second reason was to keep out the White Bears that lived in Whitestone.

Although as harmless as all of the other animals of Sylveria, the White Bears were creatures driven by their appetite for honey, and as honey was one of the largest yields of Nirvisa'Iinid—which was famous for its Bee farms—it seemed most crucial to keep the animals out. It was not uncommon in the early years of the construction of the city for a Bee farmer to lose an entire season's harvest to a sleuth of voracious Bears.

But the White Bears were not looked down upon, for frequently the farmers would carry a portion of their harvests in barrels and drop them over the city walls, so that the Bears would be satiated. The people of Alim'dar were quite fervent in caring for the native creatures of Whitestone. The Bears, thankful for the treat, would often bring bundles of scarcely found berries from the mountain regions and drop them at the city gates in exchange for the kindness of the Darian honey farmers.

The Darians were regarded by the other people of Sylveria as lovers of the creatures of the world, and so when I approached the closed gate of the city with Molley and her pups, the watchmen gave no second thought to opening it for us. These watchmen were both well known to me, as I had come this way many times before. One of them was named Varusar, the other Petrusan, both of them the great-grandsons of Alim'dar, through the line of Maivusar.

"Welcome back to Nirvisa'Iinid, Alak'kiin," Petrusan said as I entered the gate with the Fossa.

"It is good to be back," I said. "Give my regards to your mother and father." He nodded and I continued on into the city.

As far as land area, Nirvisa'Iinid was the largest of all of the cities of Sylveria, but this was not for a greater population. Rather it was because both Alim'dar and Nirvisa'nen fancied very large things. From east to west and north to south, the city spanned a full March, and would take the entirety of three Hours to encircle.

Inside the gate was the great Plaza of Nirvisa'Iinid, which was a marketplace so large that it was difficult to see from one end to the other on a foggy day, as it was this morning. But there within the Plaza I saw the same Giant Sloth that had passed us by on the road into the city. Farther away, there was another. It was not uncommon for the Sloths to be here in the city, as Nirvisa'nen considered herself a friend to these creatures. They were here not to perform any task or for any reason other than that the Darians allowed them to come and go as they pleased. Ever since we, the Naiad, had first encountered these creatures in our pursuit of

Alunen, Nirvisa'nen had been as fascinated with them as had my sister. This had been a common thread between the two cousins.

I, along with my animal companions, had crossed perhaps half of the Plaza when I heard hoof beats upon the white stone pavement beneath. Two riders appeared through the fog and approached upon the horses that were native to this land, and which had been present in such numbers that they were exported to all of the other realms of Sylveria.

"Alak'kiin!" the soft voice of Nirvisa'nen said. "You have returned!" She dismounted from the horse, as did the second rider, who was my brother, Alim'dar.

"Your way from Aranthia has found you well, Brother?" Alim'dar said, clasping my shoulder.

"It has, as always."

"We heard you had arrived," Nirvisa'nen said.

"And I see that you have brought some friends," my brother said, gesturing to the Fossa.

"They decided to come along when I hid in their burrow to weather the storm," I explained.

Nirvisa'nen bent down toward the pups, and each of them leaped into her arms. "They are adorable!" she squealed.

"You always were a fool for the creatures, Alak'kiin," Alim'dar said, smiling at the pleasure his wife was deriving from the small animals.

"You're one to talk, Brother," I said, looking over at the Giant Sloth. Alim'dar nodded; he knew that he too was an easy mark for a friendly beast.

"Will you come with us to the Keep?" Nirvisa'nen asked, still petting the Fossa pups as they nipped at her face and neck.

"Of course," I said. "I still have a taste for your honey wine, if you have any to spare."

"Always," Alim'dar said.

"Ride with me," Nirvisa'nen said, releasing the pups to be with their mother again, and I mounted the horse just behind her. As we galloped to the north, toward the Keep of Nirvisa'Iinid, her and I upon one horse, Alim'dar upon the other, she turned and whispered to me, "I need to speak to you in private, later, before you leave the city again." I nodded, wondering why there seemed a kind of secrecy about her manner.

We rode the horses into the Keep, wherein there were stables amidst the other buildings and structures. The Keep of the city was little more than another set of walls that had been raised around the interior of the city. Within the center of the Keep was the castle that stood as the highest part of the city with four outer towers upon each corner and one in the middle. The heart of the castle was where Alim'dar and his closest family resided.

At the stables, we dismounted again. Nirvisa'nen thanked the horses and the three of us walked toward the castle. The Fossa, who had run their fastest to keep up, there decided to stay, as these creatures found themselves in need of frequent naps, and the hay in the stalls was irresistible.

"Nirvisa," Alim'dar said. Often he would leave off the latter part of her name; this was, to him, a show of his affections. "I believe you have matters to attend?"

"I do," she said, smiling softly at her husband. "I will see you at mealtime, Alak'kiin." And as we entered the front door of the castle, she went off on a different path than Alim'dar and I.

"You have something for me?" my brother asked.

"I do," I said, as I reached into a pocket and pulled out the carved medallion that was decorated with gold encasing a strange pink stone. I handed it to him and he held it by its cord and studied the details with great admiration.

"It is perfect," he said finally. "I am always amazed at the craftsmanship of Haldus'nar."

"Indeed. He was happy to do it for you."

Still he held the amulet, dangling it by its chain, staring deep into it, as if it was a treasure that he himself longed for. "There is power in the craftsmanship of our cousin," he said. "This is a very special item."

"Is it enchanted?" I asked, knowing full well that I could discern if magic was embued within it, should I choose.

"No. But there is power in it. Have you ever seen a stone like this before, Alak'kiin?"

"No, I never have. I thought it unique when I first saw it. What is it?"

Still staring into the stone, Alim'dar explained, "Some time ago, Haldus'nar and I were exploring the Shallow Lands. We came across this stone, pushed up from the depths of the earth, I suppose by the tides. He was fascinated by it, for he had never seen anything like it. He took it home and studied it. He said that it had the power to bring souls together. And he said that he would make it into a gift for Nirvisa'nen. She will be pleased."

"When will you learn, Brother, she loves *you* and not the trinkets and jewelry you give her, and the cities you build?"

"Let us be honest, Alak'kiin. She loves both."

I accompanied Alim'dar into the dining chamber of the castle, which was near the center, and there we sat and discussed my travel from Aranthia to Whitestone. After that, the midday meal was brought to us and Nirvisa'nen joined us once more.

"My business is complete," she said. "I am yours for the rest of the day."

"You are mine till the end of time," Alim'dar smiled, a display she returned.

"You know, Alak'kiin," Alim'dar said. "Aside from you and Norandar and Alunen, few of our kin visit us here in Nirvisa'Iinid."

"Well, it is a long journey from the Southern Reaches," I said. "Adaashar and Sveraden always send their regards. As do the others. Haldus'nar and Sarak'den are kept busy, but they plan on coming soon, I think. I do not know why Norgrash'nar and Kalenen do not come...."

As I said this I noted that Nirvisa'nen withheld words that nearly escaped her lips. Her eyes looked to Alim'dar—who did not notice—then quickly back to me. There was something she had to say... But I didn't know what, only that it must have to do with Norgrash'nar or Kalenen.

"It is just as well," Alim'dar said. "He is always too keen on his own brilliance and technologies. He has little regard for a city like Nirvisa'Iinid."

After this we ate and talked about many things regarding the advancement of the civilizations of the Naiad and how they had spread across Sylveria during the last three hundred years. When this conversation had run its course, Alim'dar had brought into the chamber a favorite pastime of the Darians, which was a game developed originally by the Garonites. The game was called Maassen, and the field of this activity was upon a large table covered in felt with surrounding edges that kept large marble balls from falling off the sides. The object of the game was to strike one ball with another and to land it within an area of the table marked with numbers that granted points.

Unlike the Garonites, Alim'dar and I played this game only for entertainment, and we felt little of the true competitive spirit as our cousins. As we rolled the balls across the surface, drinking the famous honey wine of Alim'dar, Nirvisa'nen sat patiently watching. Still, behind her eyes, I sensed that she was distracted... After losing several rounds of the game, Alim'dar left to go and retrieve more wine, and Nirvisa'nen stepped in to play.

"We don't have time right now," she said quickly, softly. "But after Alim drinks more, he will go to bed. Then we will talk." I nodded just as my brother returned. I didn't like that Nirvisa'nen seemed to be keeping something secret from her husband, but I also considered that it was maybe just a small matter... perhaps she knew of the medallion that he was about to give her, and in secret she wanted to devise a plan to acquire something for him.

"Has she bested you yet?" Alim'dar asked.

"Of course I have," she smiled affectionately at him. "You know that no one can beat me at this silly game."

Alim'dar nodded. "And I can't seem to beat anyone!" he said jovially.

"That is because you drink too much wine!" Nirvisa'nen said. "It dulls your senses, and your aim."

She was not wrong; long I had noted this, and long had I refrained from telling him. If he were to realize it, he might stop drinking while playing, and that would give him an advantage.

We played late into the day, until Lastlight, by which time Alim'dar had consumed as much of the honey wine as he could, and he retired at last to their bed-chamber, which was behind the dining hall.

Nirvisa'nen looked about the chamber to make sure no one else was present, and when she found us alone, she pulled me by the arm and we sat upon a lounge in the corner of the chamber. "Alak'kiin, will you come to my garden at the Hour of Gathering? I need to talk to you, alone."

"I will, but why?"

"I do not want anyone else to know, to hear what I have to say."

"We are alone now. Tell me now."

"I am tired now; I need sleep."

"Then why so early?"

"I always tend to my garden at that hour," Nirvisa'nen said. "I like to prune it and feed it under the light of Imrakul. It is a quiet place, where we will not be disturbed."

Reluctantly I agreed to meet her there; reluctant not because I didn't want to hear what she had to say but rather because the whole matter seemed too reticent.

There remained five hours still to rest before Gathering, but I slept only part of it, awakening late during the Hour of Distinction and venturing out into the halls. The keep was silent; most of the Darians still remained asleep. It was peaceful there as I walked along the halls toward Nirvisa'nen's garden.

Then as I drew nearer to the stone-encased botanic I heard soft and beautiful singing. Though I felt guilty, for I was arriving early, I could not help but stop just inside the egress to listen.

It was Nirvisa'nen, her voice unmistakable as she sang a melody I had never before heard. Her voice was enchanting, beautiful, as much so as the first time I had heard this woman hum, long ago in the waters of Iidin, near the Hills of Nightrun. Now though, she used words, which at first I did not even listen to, for the simple tone of her voice was soothing. Then finally I began listening to the words, for it was a song I was unfamiliar with. She sang:

Into the dream I have finally awakened,
The greatest of things I have finally seen;

Hozuiim, Hozuiim, just what could this mean…
Please tell me, please tell me in your blessed dreams.

Hozuiim, Hozuiim, Hozuiim, Hozuiim,
Please let me know by this what you mean.

Listening to the words I found it most peculiar, for the word *Hozuiim,* was not a word that I had heard before. Clearly though, neither did Nirvisa'nen, for the sake of the words of her song displayed the mystery.

She repeated the song over and over as she pruned the branches of her plants, and in those moments, as I peaked around the corner into her garden, I could see how truly happy she was. For she had found the love of her life in Alim'dar, and I would never begrudge this. I could, I knew, appreciate the beauty of Nirvisa'nen without ever possessing her as my own. Not all love had to be of an amorous nature.

I stepped into the garden loudly enough to announce my presence.

"Alak'kiin…" she whispered softly. "I am glad you came."

"What is it, Nirvisa'nen?" I asked. "I have seen all day that you were eager to speak with me."

"I have been… There is something you must know." She was silent then, for a moment, gathering her thoughts. "But I don't know how to tell you… I don't want Alim'dar to know about this…."

"What could there possibly be that you want to keep from your husband?"

"It is about Norgrash'nar," she said. "He came here, to Nirvisa'Iinid, just half a season ago."

"He did?" She nodded. "Last I spoke with him he mentioned specifically having no intention of coming."

"He was here, and apparently no one else knows about his arrival, not even the watchmen."

"Then how did he get in?"

"I don't know. But he came to me in my other garden outside the Keep, the one with the honeysuckle. It was late in the evening and I was tending the plants. No one else was there. But he came up from behind and startled me."

"What did he say?"

"Well, first he told me how good it was to see me… that I was more beautiful than ever. He was very seductive…" She looked away, somewhat embarrassed, then continued. "He took my hands and told me that he still longed for me after all these years. I pulled my hands away and told him that he needs to get over this, that I am Alim'dar's wife, and that I love only him. All he said was '*I know you love him, but you know that I love you*'. Then he tried to convince me that he was nothing without me."

"Does he really hold on to all of this, after so very many years?" I wondered. "He has been wed to Kalenen since all of us—all of you—were married. What is he doing?"

"I don't know," Nirvisa'nen said. "I thought he had gotten over this long ago, before we even had children amongst us."

"As did I. What did he say next?"

"Then he tried to convince me that Alim did not truly love me, that it was impossible for him to, because I was different than him... that I was better than him, because I am Nescrai, and he is not. I don't know what madness has overtaken him, Alak'kiin. He said that someday Alim'dar would betray me."

"Betray you? What did he even mean?"

"I cannot discern it," Nirvisa'nen said, shaking her head and shrugging her shoulders bewilderedly. "He spent the whole of the Hour going on about it, how Alim would turn on me, how he was deceitful and how I should leave this city and go with him to Mar'Narush."

"You listened to him for an Hour?" I asked.

She looked away ashamedly. "You know I have a weakness for this, Alak'kiin," she sighed. "You know I have never been able to be too harsh with him. Norgrash'nar has such affection and such passions...."

"You cannot entertain his delusions, Nirvisa'nen," I said firmly. She was right, though; always was she one to listen to all of the renderings of Norgrash'nar's heart. It was I who had had to convince her long ago to finally make her decision to marry Alim'dar known.

"You're right, I know," she said. "But it all worries me. I don't want Alim'dar to know about this. He would not take it well."

"I agree. For now, say nothing to him. I will be with Norgrash'nar come the first of Summertide. I will address this with him... try to convince him to stop."

"Thank you, Alak'kiin," she said, and she hugged me tightly.

I turned to leave, but then stopped, asking her, "That song you were singing when I entered into the garden... what is it?"

Nirvisa'nen blushed slightly, and said, "You heard me singing... It is just a melody. I sing a lot, Alak'kiin, and sometimes silly words just come to me."

"Hozuiim," I repeated the word. "What does that mean?"

"Well, that is the question of the song, isn't it?" she smiled. "I don't

---

know. I dreamed of an old man with a strange blade in his hand. There was a word carved upon it. It said, 'Hozuiim', but I never understood what it was."

"Strange enough. But dreams do strange things in our minds."

"Yes. But it is a beautiful word, I think. I have probably been smelling the honeysuckle too much."

Though I would never act upon my own feelings for Nirvisa'nen as was Norgrash'nar, I was enticed by the smell of her honeysuckle perfume and the sweetness of her words... she truly was the most beautiful of all the Naiad, and I understood in a certain capacity my cousin's fascination with her.

Alim'dar did not rise until after the Hour of Awakening the next day. He asked if I would stay another night with them, but I declined, saying, "I need to be at Yor'Kavon on the first of Summertide. I would like to stop along the way in Floran'Adar to see our brother and sister." He understood, first that I had other engagements, and second that it was not uncommon for me to stay but only one day in any one place. I was a vagabond by nature and circumstance. And so I said my farewells to them.

On my way out of the Keep, I looked to the stables, but Molley and her pups had already departed. At the city gates, the watchmen told me that they had left the city—probably to return to their homes—the night before. Though I had enjoyed their company, and would even miss it, I was pleased to know that I had bonded with yet another of the wonderful creatures of Sylveria. And I wondered if I would ever see them again, for the world was large and all animals were not always as predictable as Saxon and the Dains.

JOURNEY TO FLORAN'ADAR

My next stop would be the city of Floran'Adar, the greatest of the cities in all of the lands of Sharuseth. Out of the city of Nirvisa'Iinid I was able to take a small charter boat down the river of Isyn, which would take me to a small port town that was upon the north point of Lake Abai. From there it would be no more than a day's journey to my destination—the city of my brother and sister, Norandar and Alunen.

They were not expecting me, as I often arrived unannounced; my travels usually kept even me guessing as to where I might go next. It had been several years since I had seen either of these siblings, and it was long overdue.

Isyn flowed out of Whitestone with rapidity until it came onto the lower forested lands of Mara, where it then widened. As I passed through the forest aboard the boat I was amazed—as I always was—at how much the trees of the region had grown, even since I last visited. These were the descendants of the trees that were first seeded by the tears of Alunen, when she had fled Naiad, and had since grown to be the largest woodland in all of Sylveria.

Passing through the northernmost realm of this region I was interested to see that to the west of the river several of the giant Sloths had ventured from their valley that was further still to the west. In times past, these fantastic creatures had kept to themselves. Yet now, since the mother of all of the people of this land was Alunen herself, they and their own descendants seemed content to come into the forests to gather the fruits from the great Baobab trees. So too did they, as I had seen in Nirvisa'Iinid, venture much further to the north.

The Hour of Mourning brought me to the end of my travel by water and I thanked the oarsmen and stepped off into the village of Geth. The people of this town were always friendly, even to strangers, and several of the villagers offered to take me in for the night, but I chose instead to stay just outside the town, camped under the night sky, which was nearly always my preference.

In the morning I took a path that I had traveled before—not one that would lead me directly to Floran'Adar, but instead to the Temple of Norad'Taun, for I much longed to see both how the temple had grown and the one whom it had been made for—Sharuseth the Copper. It was a level road, one that was often used by those making pilgrimages to the same destination as I. It was a path too narrow to be traveled by horse and carriage and was intended only for those traveling on foot. The quiet atmosphere of the woods gave those passing through it a great sense of serenity that prepared them for their visit with Sharuseth. Birds swept through the air between trees, flighty and happy; squirrels leaped from branch to branch, sometimes playfully dropping seeds and nuts down upon passerbys. Gentle winds breezed through the high leaves, whispering and soothing.

It was the Hour of Midlight when Norad'Taun came into view; it was a magnificent sight, for unlike all of the other temples of the Dragons, it was not constructed, but had instead been grown. The entire temple was a great dome, a hundred Spans across, and had been started in the earlier years of the settlement of the region. Small saplings had been planted in a great circle, and as they flourished, so too were their trunks twisted, shaped and directed into the dome form they now took.

There were three entrances into the temple—one to the east, one to the north, and one large opening at the very top through which only a Dragon could pass. I ventured through the northern entrance and into a hallway that would take me around the outer edge of the temple, then into the central chamber where Sharuseth now dwelled.

The inside walls were not as one might expect, but rather seemed solid and impervious, for the leaves and branches had been so tightly woven throughout time that no light could penetrate anywhere. These walls were lined with wood carvings of every creature of Sylveria, depictions of the time of Dragons, the times of the Naiad, and the times of the Maran people. The hallway was lit by magical orbs spaced about and were said to have been sustained since the first day they were summoned by Alunen, over a hundred years earlier.

As I moved through the corridor I was passed by several other visitors who were leaving the temple, having already paid their respects to the Dragon. They gave a silent greeting and I nodded in acknowledgment. This was not the usual season for pilgrimages to this temple, but Sharuseth always welcomed visitors.

I followed the passage as it curved eastward, and then finally northward, turning into the way that would lead to the heart of the temple. Light filled the sanctum, a glowing coppery shade that was warm and welcoming. When I entered, Sharuseth was awake, standing in the center, looking about him at the walls, where piled on the floor was mound after mound of baubles, shining gems, flakes of gold and silver and platinum, and many other proceeds.

"You grow wealthy, Sharuseth," I said loudly.

The Dragon turned his head quickly. His eyes lit up when they fell upon me, and he said, "My, Alak'kiin! It is good to see you, my son!"

"And you as well. I see you have acquired even more of these treasures."

Sharuseth rolled his eyes and his head, saying, "I tell you, Alak'kiin, one Dragon decides it is most comfortable to sleep on a bed of these shining stones, and the whole of Sylveria thinks we desire a hoard!" Since the building of the Temples, when the people would visit the Dragons, they would treat them as if they were gods who desired tribute be paid. Thus, each of them had acquired goods far beyond their needs or their wants—ornaments of the labors of the Naiad, the objects of their crafts.

"They mean well," I said.

"Of course they do!" His eyes lit up again. "And between you and me, Alak'kiin, I really do not mind. But don't tell Merilinder I said so!"

"I promise I will say nothing. How are things with you, Sharuseth? It has been some time since I saw you last."

"Has it?" the Dragon asked, genuinely unsure. "It doesn't seem so long… and things are as they always are, Alak'kiin. Nothing ever changes for a Dragon. The last thing new that I can recall was when these irksome creatures were awakened in the Valley of Naiad." He grinned a toothy grin.

"Do we bother you so much?" I asked, knowing that the Dragon's words were entirely in jest.

"Nah... not at all. You know that you and your kind are always welcome here. The world has become much more interesting since you came."

"Indeed it has," I said. "The descendants of my brothers and sisters and the Nescrai have come so far. It is a pleasant world we have inherited. Do you ever regret the spell that you and Ashysin and Merilinder once cast to awaken us?"

"Never! What else would we be doing if not entertaining the whims of the Naiad?"

"So things are well here, in your domain?"

"As well as it is, I suppose. What is it that brings you here today, Alak'kiin? Some matter to discuss? Some new rendering of your mind?"

"Nothing at all. I am on my way to see Norandar and Alunen, for it has been longer since I last saw them than you. Do you know if they are in the city?"

"They are in Floran'Adar, so far as I know. They don't leave often. Their children and their children's children keep them busy, always nagging them to help them with some matter or another."

"See, and that is why I sometimes think I was the fortunate one, Sharuseth, to not have married."

"Indeed," the Dragon said. "For you are as free as are we Dragons, to go where you will go and do what you will do, without obligation. Speaking of which... whatever became of that Dain of yours?"

"Saxon. He stays in Naiad most of the time, still amongst the hills of Nightrun, with his own kind. I make sure to go there at least twice each year. It keeps me grounded to be there alone, with nature, with him, for since it was abandoned and the people discovered more interesting lands, it has been left untouched. And Saxon is always elated to see me. And I miss him. Always."

"I can go and get him for you if you would like."

I laughed, "That is not necessary. He would not appreciate being carried by a Dragon through the air. He is not a lover of heights."

"I see the Dains sometimes, when I fly over Naiad. They move about happily in their packs and their numbers have grown greatly as well. They are marvelous creatures, wholly good and pure. They have even migrated to the north of the mountains, to the isolated realm of Kaliim."

I began walking around the circle of the sanctum, looking at the treasures brought here by the Naiad as gifts of tribute. "The people truly have come far, Sharuseth, in all of the things they can do." I lifted from the floor a device called a sextant, which was invented long ago to help track one's position upon the face of the world only by using the suns and the moon. "Even I never thought to build something such as this."

"Yours are the labors of the mind, Alak'kiin. None amongst your kind has ever been so wise, or had such understanding. You say you were fortunate to not have found a mate; I say you are gifted with solitude."

"Thank you, Sharuseth." I laid the sextant back down.

"You may keep that if you wish. I have nine others just like it!"

"That is all right," I said, smiling. "What this device can do with its calculations I can do with my own eyes."

"How long can you stay, Alak'kiin?"

"Not long. In fact I would like to get to Floran'Adar by the Hour of Darkening."

"Well…" Sharuseth said, seeming a bit slighted. "Take whatever supplies you might need from my stores. The food in the adjacent chamber will spoil before I can eat it all."

I conversed with the Dragon for another course, and then set out again, leaving now through the eastern entrance of the temple and going southeast, for there along the road I would find the city of my brother and sister.

The city of Floran'Adar was a testament to the creativity and ingenuity of the people of Alunen and Norandar, for as one approached from any of the roads that made their way into the city, there would be no sign whatsoever that the city even existed. The name of the city, when translated from the tongue of Dragons, was *Carving Mound*.

As it was, when the descendants of my brother and sister came to this region there was a great mound of stone that was covered in many years of undergrowth. They cleared the vegetation, leaving only the raw stone that was half a March in diameter from east to west as well as north to south. Many of the Noranites were stone workers—a craft learned from Haldus'nar and his children—and they went to work in delving deep into the stone of the earth, to a depth of a full Breadth and a half. Yet they made not just a massive hole in the ground, but with careful planning and expertise, large pillars were left in a concise and concentric pattern, radiating out from the very center. These pillars were then carved into the buildings that would serve as homes and places of work, each of them six levels high and mountable by stone stairs.

And so from the ground level outside the first signs of the city were the very tops of the structures of Floran'Adar. From all around the outer circle of the city stairs had been carved, descending into the city depths.

So large a city was Floran'Adar that of the pattern designed by the stone workers there were nine circles that came outward from the central park of the city. Each of these were called districts, and each was named after a different color, for each of the buildings were painted accordingly.

There were likewise ten streets that moved in a circle between each of the districts; as well there were sixteen straight streets that came out from the center, dividing each of the districts into sectors. Thus, each District had sixteen sectors, and each sector had nine structures, each considered part of a different district. And so there were one hundred and forty-four structures within the city of Floran'Adar and each of them was six levels high.

The city was kept from flooding during heavy rains by way of two methods: first, an intricate series of pumps powered by magic drew water out from drainage grates that were all along the streets, and secondly by a magical canopy that could be raised as a dome over the entire city. This barrier had been designed with the intent to keep only water out, and thus, even visitors could enter during storms, passing easily through the magical ceiling.

I entered the city that day—the sixth of Summerstorm— from the west and descended the stairs where first I came into the White District. The streets were sparsely populated, though it was a typical day, for so large was this city that it had yet to reach its full occupancy. It had been designed so that coming generations would always have a place to go, and it was thought that every Noranite in all of Mara could probably have their own home in the city, though this was likely an exaggeration; so too had the population grown since the city had been constructed.

Alunen and Norandar made their residence here in Floran'Adar, near the central park of the city. I traversed the streets, district by district and sector by sector until I reached the center. There, the park was thirty Spans across and growing from within its epicenter was one of the largest Baobab trees ever grown. Though it was not the first of these trees, it was the most well-tended in all of Mara, receiving the full care and love of all of the people who lived there. The top of the tree rose higher now than it had last I visited, and it would certainly continue to grow and would eventually be a marker for distant travelers to see.

I found Alunen by the tree, there in the park, covered in a sequined dress, her hair braided with shining ornaments clipped into it. *So far we have come*, I thought to myself, *since the days when we first donned the clothing made from the innards of Dragonscales.* I came up behind her and said, "Do you have time to tend to the needs of a weary traveler?"

She spun around with such excitement and the brightest smile beaming from her face, saying, "Alak'kiin!"

"Yes, dear Sister, it is I."

"Where have you been all these seasons?" She embraced me tightly.

"You know the way I travel, Alunen, never knowing where I will be from one season to the next."

"Last I heard you were in the Southern Reaches, with Merilinder."

"I was, but that was a year ago, I think. I have been to many places since."

"Someday we will have to find a way to keep track of you."

"I don't know about that," I said. "I kind of prefer it like this; springing up unannounced makes for better surprises."

"I wish you had come sooner," Alunen said, the smile slowly dwindling from her features as she released her embrace. "We will be leaving at Lastlight."

"Traveling at night? For what reason?"

"It is better that we talk together with Norandar about it. But I will say it is a matter of urgency."

"Urgency? What could be of such importance that you would leave the city at the end of the day rather than at Firstlight?"

"We just want to get started early... walk with me, Alak'kiin." She bowed her arm—a gesture for me to take it—and we started walking through the park.

"Where is Norandar now?" I wondered.

"He is meeting with a council of settlers from the south. He will be done soon, and he will find us then... So tell me, Brother, where have you been of late?"

"Well, two days ago I was with Alim'dar in Nirvisa'Iinid, delivering a medallion from Haldus'nar."

"A gift for his wife, I assume."

"Indeed. He does love her dearly, showering her with gifts."

"So you were in Aranthia?"

"Yes. I spent three seasons there."

"How is—"

"Sarak'den is well," I interrupted, knowing full well that Alunen was about to ask about our sister.

"She is happy still?"

"Why wouldn't she be?"

"Just making sure. You know I have always had a special bond with her. She was the first of our siblings that I met."

"Ah, that seems so long ago, does it not?"

"That's because it was! More than three hundred years have passed... we were so young, so inexperienced in the simplest of things."

"And yet even after so long this world offers us wonders and new adventures."

"Well to you it does," Alunen said. "Tell me, Alak'kiin, do you think you will ever settle down? There are many women now. You need not be alone."

I shook my head. "You know my heart, Alunen. There once was love

163

in my heart for another. But it did not work out so well. And I am glad for it. Alim'dar is well deserving of his wife, and I would not have it that I had taken her heart."

"But there are so many others…."

"And I suppose you would have me marry one of your own descendants, so that I might settle down here, in Floran'Adar?"

"Of course!" she laughed. She knew well that I was not interested any longer in marriage, but every time I saw her she reveled with me in this regard. "I know you are content as you are Alak'kiin. But in all seriousness, do you not get lonely at times?"

"Maybe sometimes," I admitted. In truth it was more often… I truly was content in my solitude, but I had not ruled out someday settling down and marrying. But never had I found anyone who could capture my heart as Nirvisa'nen had long ago. "But when I do, I just go and see family. You are spread all across this world."

"Yes—"

"Alak'kiin?" a familiar voice cried out from a distance.

I turned to see my brother Norandar coming toward us, a broad smile upon his face. His pace quickened and he came to me, placing his strong hands on my shoulders and then embracing me. "How good it is to see you!"

"You too, my brother." I then proceeded to catch him up by answering nearly every question Alunen had already asked.

"Come," Norandar said. "Let us go to our dwelling and talk."

We walked to the north side of the city, to the innermost district where the entire ground floor was but one residence. Inside, we sat around a table and Alunen offered to make tea. As she brewed it, Norandar talked.

"It is true that we are leaving at Lastlight."

"What is of such urgency?"

"There is dissidence in the south, in the Hilly Lands that border the mountains."

"Dissidence? In what regard?"

"A territorial dispute. Some of the Garonites are claiming that the Hilly Lands are theirs to settle and to farm, that these are the lands of Ashysin and not Sharuseth."

"And your people disagree?'

"Yes," Norandar said, shaking his head. "Unfortunately."

"What will you do there?" I asked.

"Negotiate, I suppose. But it will be difficult."

"How so?"

"Because I don't know whose land it is. I don't know if Sharuseth or Ashysin has truly claimed this region."

"Have you asked either of them?"

"Of course we have," Alunen said, delivering the tea in clay mugs. "Sharuseth says to ask Ashysin, because he doesn't know."

"And Ashysin says to ask Sharuseth. Neither of them cares."

I nodded, saying, "I would expect as much. The only reason the Dragons divided the world into domains was to have relative points of their preferred regions. They never cared about borders."

"I have told my own people to give ground to the Garonites, because we have far more land than do they... the mountain vales are nearly all they have to farm. But they say that our land is becoming overgrown everywhere by the Baobab Trees, that it is being wasted."

"I suppose that is my fault," Alunen interjected. "But it doesn't matter. We retain plenty of land good for farming in the north and west. We have even begun taming the outskirts of Goab'lin."

"But this doesn't help the settlers who have made their homes in the south and who are now trying to move into the hills." Norandar seemed frustrated.

"And what of the Garonites?" I asked. "What is their claim to the land?"

"Only their need for it," Norandar said. "And they do have a greater need. But our people are afraid that if we give to them, they will keep taking, and that it is not our fault that they chose to settle in the mountains."

"Scuffles have even started to erupt there, in the hills," Alunen said. "The likes of which we have not seen before. One side will build upon a hill and the other will burn it down. We cannot have this going any further. The Garonites are our cousins, our family. We must convince them all to settle this matter peacefully."

"Why can they not just divide the land?" I asked.

"Because they are stubborn!" Norandar said, his frustration peaked.

"Would you like me to go with you?" I asked. "To be a mediator, someone who has no reason to be on either side?"

"You are welcome to join us," Alunen said. "But it is not necessary. Truthfully, if anything, we are more on the side of the Garonites. It is a matter of convincing our own people."

"Your presence is always welcome," Norandar said. "But if you have somewhere else to be, some other engagement...."

"I am supposed to be in Mar'Narush on the First of Summertide," I said. "Norgrash'nar has an unveiling that he has invited me to attend."

"What kind of unveiling?"

"I don't know yet. Some new technology, I suppose. But he was very insistent on me being there. I am to meet him at Yor'Kavon just one day prior, if I am going to attend."

"One day?" Alunen said. "It will take longer than one day to get to

165

Mar'Narush."

"That is what I thought as well. But he insisted that I come there, on that day."

"Well, if you're going to make it, you will have to leave here soon," Norandar said. "Do not worry about our matters here. It is nothing that Alunen and I cannot resolve."

"Are you sure?"

"Of course," Alunen said.

"Keep me informed, if you will, about it."

"We will."

My thoughts drifted. This news was troubling, nearly as much so as what I had heard from Nirvisa'nen in regard to Nogrash'nar's secret visit. I had thought to discuss this with Alunen and Norandar, but thought better of it. They had their own troubles, it seemed. So too was it a matter that I would learn the most about by talking to Norgrash'nar himself. Considering their own troubles, I thought it best not to address the issue with my siblings.

"Is there something on your mind, Alak'kiin?" Alunen wondered.

"Yes, but it can wait. Perhaps I will return when I know more."

"Now you've got me curious," Norandar said. "But if you think it best to remain silent, then do so. And Alak'kiin, I hate to put you off, but we really must start preparing for our own departure."

"What can I do to help?"

"Nothing," Alunen said. "Just enjoy your tea."

That evening, at Lastlight, I saw Alunen and Norandar off, and I remained in their home until morning. At Firstlight, I departed as well. It was a long journey back through Naiad and to my meeting place with Norgrash'nar at Yor'Kavon.

JOURNEY TO MAR'NARUSH

On the last day of Summerstorm, 310, I entered the Valley of Naiad. It had not been long since I was there last, just prior to going to Nirvisa'Iinid to make my delivery to Alim'dar, but I made it a habit of coming as often as possible. So too was it that this valley led to Yor'Kavon—the northern pass into the east. Now, there were other ways through the mountains, passes that led from the Golden Valley into the grasslands, but it was there that I was to meet with Norgrash'nar.

The Valley of Naiad had long ago been abandoned, when the growing populace had decided that there were more resourceful places in Sylveria.

It had taken time of course, but now, after so many years, the land had reclaimed all of the structures we had built there. Even in the Hills of Nightrun, where just thirteen of us had lived for many years, there was barely a reminder of a time when the hills were alive with laughter, joy and love. The Valley existed now more as a refuge for wildlife and for the Dragons.

Naiad was not now a dreary place; it was as beautiful and serene as ever, seeming just as it had at the time of our first awakening. Although the Shadows of Dragonswake unfailingly continued to fall upon the region during the Hour of Highlight every day, the land held a special place in my heart, and always would.

But there was another reason that I frequented the Valley of Naiad, and he stood before me, waiting, even as I mounted the Westward Slopes, as if he had known I was coming. Perhaps, I thought, he always kept a watchful eye.

"Saxon!" I cried out, always ecstatic to see the Dain who had been my first encounter after awakening three hundred and ten years ago. He was, like all of the creatures of the world in those days, the same as always, unchanged by time—except that he had grown. Once he had stood at the same height as me; now he was a head taller.

When he hurtled forward he stopped just short of plunging into me, so excited was he as well. His giant tongue stroked my face and he whined in his happy way as he bounded about.

"I have missed you too, my dear friend. Where are the others?" He just stared at me and cocked his head. Once he settled his fervent emotions, I drew close to him, facing east and stared out toward Sternwood. "Let's go home," I said, and together we continued on toward Nightrun.

I expected to see the other Dains along the way, but they were absent from the journey, and I wondered why they should be off wandering elsewhere in Naiad when Saxon was here alone. But the ways of the Dain were sometimes mysterious, and always comical.

The Thirteen Hills of Nightrun stood as they always had. Our homes had since decayed away, and there seemed not a trace of them anywhere. But there was nothing for me there, and I had long since reminisced over the times long gone, and so we moved eastward, toward Iidin.

There, around the Lake, was a greater trace of a civilization than anywhere else in Naiad, for surrounding the large body of water along the northern edge the mountains had been carved into and a walkway which still remained, an alternative route that Haldus'nar had created simply for having a private and tranquil place to walk with Sarak'den. The path followed the line of the mountains, under the Falls of Iidin, and then onto the plains; beyond that it led to Yor'Kavon, which was my destination.

I made early camp at the Hour of Evenlight; I had made good time coming across Mara, and I wanted time to spend with Saxon before meeting with Norgrash'nar the next day.

Late that Hour the other Dains showed themselves, coming from somewhere in the west. Saxon seemed as excited to see them as he had me, and though I had partially hoped for a quiet half-day with my old companion, I took great pleasure in watching them splashing and swimming in the waters of Iidin. We were not at all far from where I had first met Nirvisa'nen, where she had brought the magic of the lake alive with her sweet song.

Night came and the Dains remained with me throughout. In the morning, all of them except Saxon departed. Together we broke camp and went around Iidin—the slowest route—so as to have the most time with one another. He would not go with me beyond Yor'Kavon; he rarely ventured beyond the Valley of Naiad and the Plains of Kronaggas.

When we were halfway up the pass, Saxon began barking, looking ahead—an alert to someone or something's presence.

"I never could sneak up on you when that beast was at your side!" the familiar voice of my cousin rang out, just as he stepped from behind a cleft in the side of the mountain.

"Norgrash'nar!"

"It is good to see you, Alak'kiin." We embraced, for like Alunen and Norandar, it had been too long since I had seen him. Saxon sniffed at him, but when Norgrash'nar reached out to him, the Dain pulled away. My cousin scowled ever so slightly, but then turned his attention back to me. "How long has it been since you have been here to Yor'Kavon?"

We continued our ascent of the mountain pass. "Twenty years, perhaps," I said. "I have been through Naiad many times since, but have usually been taken eastward across the Golden Valley on the back of a Dragon, or walked through the lower passes."

"So you have neither seen Forthran since then?"

"No. There is not a lot to see... it is a wasteland in most regards," I said.

"Not anymore," he said slyly.

"How so?"

"You will have to wait and see."

We continued up the pass and though the Hour was now approaching Feltide, the Paken were not, as in years past, mounting the eastern side and making their daily migration into Naiad. This was most unusual.

"What is going on?" I asked, now curious.

"You will see," Norgrash'nar said, now smiling.

When we came up over the peak I looked eastward; the region of Forthran that was before a kind of desert region was now lush and green.

There was no fear in the hearts of the Paken, though the flooding hour approached, and they grazed in the green fields, far below.

"How is this possible?" I wondered aloud.

Pride in his demeanor, he said, "The ingenuity of men. All it took was a simple wall, Alak'kiin." And he gestured to our left, toward the gorge between the mountains through which the sea once flowed when the tides rose. And indeed, a great wall rose up from the earthen embankment, spanning the whole of the ravine.

"That is amazing," I said, truly impressed. "Truly a testament to technology. How did you build such a wall?"

"I cannot take credit for it," he said, but pride was still in his tone. "It was my son—Miithinar—who engineered it; he and his children."

We began our descent, still talking, me still wondering at the size and scope of the efforts that must have been involved in such an undertaking.

"It was built in sections using steel reinforced concrete, layer by layer, until it was tall enough to withstand the tide. It rises ten Heights over the stone beneath and is over twenty Spans wide."

"How thick is it?"

"Miithinar calculated that it would have to be a quarter Span thick to withstand the force of the tides, and so he built it twice that, to be sure."

Although we were a quarter of a March away from the wall itself, I thought I could see movement upon the top of it. "Are there people there, on the wall?" I wondered.

"Yes, the descendants of Malanar live here, in Forthran, tending the wall, making sure it remains strong."

"Malanar?" I asked. "He and his wife live in Mara, I thought."

"They do," Norgrash'nar said. "But their grandson Mikaalnar and his progenies came to Mar'Narush perhaps ten years ago, looking for work. They wanted not to live in the woods, they said. And so Miithinar put them to tending the wall."

As we came to the floor of the lowlands, east of the pass, I took my first step into the fields of Forthran, for in the past, upon every other visit to the region there had been not a single reason to come this far. From there I looked around—the wall of Miithinar seemed even taller from this lower elevation, and more impressive, though I was still filled with an uneasy sense, for it was written into my mind that these were dangerous places. Still, the Hour of Feltide came, and I could hear the crashing of waves to the north, against the wall, and the lowlands remained unflooded.

"How will we get to Mar'Narush?" I asked, suddenly realizing that I saw no method of transport. "How did *you* get here?" I added.

"You will see, Alak'kiin." He turned us toward the north, toward the great wall that held back the seas.

It was then that Saxon decided to depart from my company once again.

Saying our farewells in our own way, I promised him that I would return as soon as possible.

As we approached the Wall of Miithinar I was astounded at how tall it actually was, for while it was ten Heights, it also sat upon an earthen mound that itself was another three. At the base of the wall was a village which was called *Sharanid*. There were perhaps fifty houses and other structures in the town, and as we entered into it I could see that the residents here were indeed of the bloodline of Malanar, for nearly every one of them had the golden hair of Malanar, who was Alunen's son. Although at least some of the people likely knew who I was, and most assuredly knew Norgrash'nar, they were strangely silent as we passed them by.

Along this southern face of the wall were steel scaffolds rising from the ground to the uppermost heights, which were permanent fixtures and used for inspection, maintenance and repairs on the concrete structure. Concrete was a relatively recent invention by the Norgrasharians, and was made by mixing gypsum and lime, or so I had been told. It was a solid construction material and was made even stronger when reinforced with steel beams that ran throughout. Here, at the very base of the wall of Miithinar, I had little doubt that this structure could withstand the tides for a very long time.

"Ready for a vigorous climb, Alak'kiin?"

"A climb?" I looked up at the towering wall. "Up there?"

"Our way to Mar'Narush is there, at the crown of the wall." He laughed then. "Do not worry, there is an elevator."

"An elevator?"

"Yes, let me show you."

We went to the eastern end of the wall where there was a box-like construction with a steel base and a wire screen about it. Steel beams extended upward, gripping the four corners of the cage and amongst them were chains and ropes rising toward the top. Norgrash'nar opened a door upon the face of the enclosure and stepped inside, gesturing me in as well.

Inside there was a brass horn and my cousin blew into it, sending a bellowing signal throughout the village and up the wall, and with a sudden jerk we were being pulled upward along the guiding rails. Higher and higher we rose, until the lift had brought us to the very top.

"I am glad that Saxon decided to return to Naiad," I said. "He would not have liked this at all."

"Come, Alak'kiin," Norgrash'nar said, sliding the gate open and stepping out to the north onto the top of the Wall of Miithinar. I followed.

We walked to the northern side of the wall, which was as Norgrash'nar had said—half a Span wide. "How did you ever acquire the materials to make so much concrete?" I wondered.

"The Southern Grasslands are rife with mineral deposits and the remaining ingredients are made by the process of the chemists of Mar'Narush. Again, the ingenuity of our people is astounding."

"Indeed," I agreed. We had made it to the northern edge of the wall, where we looked out over the Northern Straight of Merobassi, which was also called the Dragonmere Channel. Below, the rising waters of Feltide pummeled the wall.

"How will we get to Mar'Narush?" I asked again, wondering, though not doubting, how we could possibly get from here to there.

"Come, I will show you." He gave a gentle nudge on my shoulder, turning me to the east, and we began to walk. Ahead, the wall met the mountain, and there was a tunnel that had been drilled out of the stone, and emanating from within was a faint blue light. "Magic is strong in Verasian's domain, Alak'kiin."

I wondered when we entered the tunnel if we might be teleported from one place to another, from here to Mar'Narush, though I did not think that such magic was possible. What followed, however, was even more astounding than if it were.

The blue light came from two parallel rows of magic-infused steel tracks that lined the ground of the tunnel. Hovering just over these rails was a large and sleek-shaped compartment with glass windows all along and a single door that opened to the inside.

"Welcome to the Guidetrain of Mar'Narush, Alak'kiin."

"What is this?" I asked in wonder.

"The likes of which have never been seen before. This is our way to the city, to Mar'Narush."

"And this is what you are unveiling there?"

"No, no! There is much more than this to see." He did not elaborate, but instead led me onto the Guidetrain. The inside was lined with cushioned seats. "Sit where you will," he said. "But I would recommend a southward view."

Norgrash'nar then uttered a word of magic under his breath, and I suddenly felt like we were beginning to move. Though I could see only the dimness of the tunnel through the window, I could feel and hear a gentle hum as the machine picked up speed.

"Hold on to the rails, Alak'kiin."

I held the bars that were mounted to the seat ahead of me and was glad I did, for as the Guidetrain continued, it accelerated at such a rate that I felt my innards pulling back into the seat. "Is this safe?" I asked, a bit uneasy.

"Of course it is!"

And in a Pulse I saw a flash of light and a glimpse of scenery through the window, then darkness again. A short time later, light and green and mountains beyond... then darkness. In this I surmised that we were passing through tunnels of the northern mountains, heading eastward as the transport sped up exponentially. And after perhaps a quarter of a Course, we were clear of the tunnels, moving along the Ledges of Aisorath high in the mountains, uncovered now by stone.

I could see out over the higher lands that were east of Forthran, all the way to the mountains to the south, and it was a wondrous view; my eyes were wide with excitement as we were carried ever gradually down the side of the mountains. Then a great sight came into view—a Dragon! Verasian was flying beside us, the tip of his wing not more than a Breadth away, and he arced his head and looked into the window, directly at me. And he let forth a shriek of delight, for he too was fascinated with the ingenuity of the men and women of his domain.

Soon the Guidetrain was moving too fast, and even the Dragon's swift speed could not keep up, and Verasian veered off to the south, left behind by the advent of technology.

Thereafter, we descended gradually until we were on the northernmost plains of the region. To the left were the seaside cliffs that here held back the tides; to the right, the forest of Felheim darkened the landscape. When we curved to the south, the Guidetrain seemed steadier and I let loose my tight grasp upon the bars.

"What do you think, Alak'kiin?"

Nearly speechless, I said, "Norgrash'nar... how have you achieved so much?"

"Again, I cannot take credit. The engineers of Mar'Narush have imaginations as grand as their talents."

"This will take us all the way to the city?"

He nodded. "We will be there by the Hour of Concession."

"This is simply... amazing...." I said. "In three hundred years we have gone from using simple stone tools to... this!"

As we passed upon the Guidetrain from the northern region of Verasian's domain to the central plains, I took the opportunity to discuss something that had been on my mind ever since leaving Nirvisa'Iinid.

"Have you ever played the game of Maassen?"

"I have little time for games, Alak'kiin. Though I'm sure my brother would much like it. Garonar is a fancier of such things."

"Yes. I have played with him. I cannot win against him. I recently played with Alim'dar at Nirvisa'Iinid." Briefly, he looked strangely to me, for his eyes flared at the mere mention of the city's name. I added, "Have you been there in recent times?"

"I have not visited Alim'dar in many years," he said, looking out the window rather than at me. I discerned by this and a sudden quiet tone that he wished to avoid this conversation.

"Strange, I had heard that you were seen going there, within the last Season."

He glared abruptly at me, saying, "And who told you that?"

"Just a traveler I met on the Plains of Valor." I was not being truthful with my cousin, but he had already lied about going to the city. "Could he have been mistaken?"

"Obviously he was," Norgrash'nar said harshly. "I told you, I haven't been there in many years."

I was not sure how best to approach this. I had promised Nirvisa'nen that I would address his inappropriate visit to her with Norgrash'nar, but now he was entirely denying that he had even gone to the city. I sat in silence for long moments, still trying to find the best tactic, but soon, Norgrash'nar was talking again, his voice now sounding different, more cheerful.

"I would like to see that city again, and Alim'dar and my sister. Nirvisa'Iinid is more...primitive than is to my taste, but I can't deny its beauty." Though he had said the name of the city, I wondered if he was truly speaking of Nirvisa'nen. "How do they fare these days?'

"They are well," I said. "Alim'dar still loves his wine. Nirvisa'nen is as striking as ever."

"Still not over her, Alak'kiin?" I was taken aback by this question. Whereas I had long ago relinquished my hope and interest in Nirvisa'nen, I knew for certain that he had not. And now he was bringing his refusal to let go down upon me... But, I recognized that this was but his tactic in trying to convince me that what I thought was not the truth.

"It is true that I loved her long ago," I admitted. "But she is happy where she is, with Alim'dar." I now hoped to provoke the truth out of him.

"Is she?" he asked.

"So far as I can tell, yes."

"Not likely, Alak'kiin. We both know that she chose wrongly."

"What are you talking about?"

"You know that she was supposed to marry *you*." Now he was conniving...

"Me? I was never in the running, Norgrash'nar, not really. It was always between you and Alim'dar."

"I am happily in love with Kalenen, Alak'kiin. And I don't know what your intent is, but I will not be ensnared by your words."

"Then I will get directly to the point, Norgrash'nar. You *were* in Nirvisa'Iinid recently. Nirvisa'nen told me of your visit to her in the garden." He said nothing and I continued my reproach. "You cannot keep doing this, Cousin. How long has it been since she married Alim'dar? Since you married Kalenen? You must let this go."

"Clearly the woman lies, Alak'kiin. I have not been to Nirvisa'Iinid in many years. Surely she now regrets her decision to marry Alim'dar and she is drawing you into her fantasies."

I let it go then. Most assuredly, Norgrash'nar was not going to admit to his inappropriate visit with Nirvisa'nen. But at least now he knew that someone other than she was aware of his obsession.

Thereafter, for the rest of my time with Norgrash'nar, he seemed to have moved on from the charged exchange, making no more mention of it, and he further spoke to me as if the conversation had never taken place.

It wasn't long before Mar'Narush came into view—at least the highest spires of it—for it was a city unmatched in magnificence. It was only a matter of functionality and spectacle that the city needed be so tall, for the high spires collected the light and energy of the suns and transferred it to the streets below. And it was not for being close in proximity to the city that I could see it not long after turning south out of the northern region of Verasian, passing by Mount Hearin and Faigor Landing, and then onto the Central Plateau, but rather for its great height.

The east central region that was north and east of Mar'Narush was sometimes called *Diras'Onilmaria* which meant *high flatland*, but was most often simply called *Onilmar* in recent times. The land here was almost entirely soil and it was a well-known fact that this region was slowly eroding into the sea. Because of this, Onilmar was covered in fertile soil and was one of the best lands for farming in all of Sylveria.

Many farmsteads lined the way along the magically enhanced tracks of the Guidetrain, and it was at one such grange that we made our first stop.

"The train must recharge," Norgrash'nar said, standing as soon as the transport came to a halt. "Care to join me?"

"Of course," I said, following him off onto a wooden platform. "I cannot believe you have come so far in so short a time with your technologies." We were perhaps a quarter of the way across Onilmar. I looked around and could see that the blue lights that lit the tracks had grown faint. "Where does it get its power?"

"From the collectors of Mar'Narush. The energy travels all the way from there to Miithinar's wall. It is only consumed by the motion of the train. I wish to build these tracks all across my domain, so that no place is without quick transport, but we need more collectors."

"So you only have to bring it to a stop and it will recharge?"

"Yes. Now, I apologize, Alak'kiin, but I have a short matter to attend to here in Naivar. Would you mind waiting here?"

"Not at all."

"Very good. I will return shortly. The track will be recharged within a Course."

Norgrash'nar left and disappeared behind one of the many buildings of the small ranch. I wondered what his business might be, but did not give it much thought. Upon the platform was a bench, and I took a seat.

It was growing late in the morning, the Hour of Evenlight was approaching, but judging by the distance we had come we would be in Mar'Narush in plenty of time before the end of the day. I contented myself to consider the tracks of the Guidetrain, which were recharging simply by the train's immobility. Indeed, as the moments passed I could see that the faint glow was deepening. And I thought to myself once more about how truly impressive the achievements of Norgrash'nar and his people were.

Then a strange sensation flooded over me. I squinted my eyes and listened, but heard nothing. I looked over my shoulder and saw nothing unusual. There was nothing odd in the heavens—it was not an hour of eclipse. This was a sense that I had not felt before... and I did not understand it.

I stood up and turned around to face the structures of this homestead. There were a dozen of them—one main house, two others, and the rest were barns and stables. Everything looked ordinary—several Nescraian men and women moved about, tending the horses and other chores. A bit further away people tended the fields, both Nescrai and Sylvai. It was unusual, I thought, that there were Sylvai here, in the heart of Verasian, but something more was out of place...

I focused my intent, which was the method of my own magic, and I bent my will to give me insight... to listen, not with my ears, but with the magical energy that flowed around me, and through me. And I could then hear—or sense—a voice calling out. I attended to this thought, this voice in my mind, but it was incomprehensible...

Then Norgrash'nar returned, having come out of one of the barns, and he must have seen that I was disturbed, for he said, "What is it, Alak'kiin?"

"I don't know... something feels wrong, out of place."

"Like voices in your head wish to speak?"

"Yes. What is it?"

"It is a strange after-effect of the train. The fast motion does something to us. But it lessens the more you travel it."

"What would it be about motion that would cause such a sensation?"

"The best I can imagine, it is the waves of our thoughts catching up with us."

I was skeptical. Still, while it did not entirely explain the uneasiness I felt, this technology was something that I had never before experienced and it was possible that Norgrash'nar's explanation was the reality.

"Give it a few more moments and it will pass," he said. I nodded and he explained, "We are expecting crop yields better than ever this year, here and all across Onilmar.

After a short time passed, the sensation did fade away, and though I was not convinced that my thoughts had been left behind by the speed of the train and had just now caught up, I did feel better.

"Are you ready to continue to our destination?" Norgrash'nar asked. I nodded and we boarded the transport, took our seats, and were on our way once again.

"I have been with Norandar and Alunen," I said once we were fully in motion. "They are having disputes with the Garonites... or rather their people are."

"Disputes? Over what?"

"Land, they said. The Hilly Lands of Southern Mara. The Garonites want to farm the land, and so do the Noranites."

"I have heard nothing of this," Norgrash'nar said. "And I keep in frequent contact with Garonar and Kuranen. I received word from them just yesterday. She has mastered the art of Falconry and sends and receives words upon the wings of Birds."

"Maybe it has been resolved. Alunen and Norandar were going there, to the Hilly Lands, when I left Floran'Adar. I noticed at Naivar that there were Sylvai living and working... is this common in this region?"

"Yes. Many of the Noranites and the Adaasharians have come here to work."

"Have there been any disputes between them and your own people?"

"None that I have been made aware of. We all live in accord."

As we continued on, coming ever nearer to Mar'Narush, the plains were more densely settled with farmsteads and fields. Most of these passed by in a blur, and I could see little of them. But it wasn't long before I started getting the same uneasy sense as before. I considered telling Norgrash'nar about it, to see if he could explain it away, but instead I thought that I needed to find understanding within myself. So again I focused my intent and again I could sense that something was crying out to me... But I could not grasp the voices in my mind.

Then I considered my will, which was the source of magic as I understood it. I wished that I could see what was happening on these farms, for it seemed only when I was near to them that the sensation came, first at Naivar, now here... But everything was going by too quickly. My desire was to see more of the farms, more of what might be going on, for I had a darkening sense that something was not right.

And whether it was time that slowed down or my perceptions that sped up, I suddenly was able to see that which was transpiring, mostly in glimpses... and several images that flared before me seemed the source of disturbance... a Sylvaian man was tied to a post, struggling... another was being struck down... a woman being dragged across a field...

"Stop this train, Norgrash'nar!" I demanded, leaping from my seat.

"What is it?" He made no effort to stop our forward motion.

"Just stop it."

"We will be late for the unveiling," he said coolly.

"Stop it or I will."

"With what?" Norgrash'nar barked with harsh derision, then quickly changed his demeanor. He raised his hand, uttered another magical word, and the train came to a quick stop, just on the edge of one of the farmsteads, one that was farther beyond than where I had seen the unsettling visions. "Why are we stopping, Alak'kiin?"

"I want to see the people." I went to the transport door and it opened. Stepping out, Norgrash'nar followed. Here was a more bustling farm than had been Naivar. So too were their Sylvaian men and women and children working the fields, doing the tasks of operation, and all would have seemed normal if not for the near-complete absence of many Nescrai amongst them. There were Nescrai there, at this farm, but of them not one was doing labor.

Instead, the Nescrai seemed to be lording over the others, directing them, telling them in harsh words to work faster. The Sylvai had no inclination to defy them, and they hurried even more swiftly about their assigned tasks.

I turned quickly to Norgrash'nar. "What is going on here?"

"The labors of farming are intense, Alak'kiin. Do not forget that most of the fruits and vegetables that feed Sylveria are grown here in Verasian."

"And what of the beatings... the abuse... I saw these things, Norgrash'nar."

"When? While the train was moving? You could not possibly have seen anything...."

"Do not think you are the only one with mastery over magic, Norgrash'nar."

"Alak'kiin, please, come with me." He took me by the arm—not forcibly—and walked me into the fields, up to where several of the Sylvaian men were tending crops. "Stop working for a moment," he said, and the three men stood, their eyes not meeting with Norgrash'nar's but with mine. "Tell me, gentlemen, who are you?"

One of them said, "I am Avosar, and these are my two sons. I am of the seventh generation descended from Adaashar."

"And why have you come here to my lands, to Verasian?"

"We needed work. We were not content wandering the southern lands, scrounging the wilds for food."

"And are you paid for your labors here, on the farms?"

"Yes, *varethaiad*," the man said, his eyes still not meeting with Norgrash'nar's. I thought it strange what the man had said... *varethaiad*... this was a word used by Dragons; it meant *with respect* and I had never heard anyone use the word, only the Dragons and only in regard to the proper way to treat nature. It was their way of saying that they held esteem for the natural order of the world. Though language did have a way of evolving over time, this seemed an out-of-place usage of the term.

"And are you or your sons treated poorly here?"

"No, *varethaiad.*"

"You see, Alak'kiin... there is nothing untoward happening here."

To Avosar I said, "Is all well with you?" He nodded unconvincingly. "Tell me, are you paid a *fair* wage?"

His eyes darted to Norgrash'nar and then back to me, and he said again, "Yes, *varethaiad.*"

His voice seemed a subtle hint, his eyes told me something more, and I knew that something was not right here. But with Norgrash'nar here present, Avosar would likely not tell me everything, or anything at all.

"How far are we from Mar'Narush?" I asked.

The man replied, "Perhaps a Flight."

I committed then to going on to the city, not to see Norgrash'nar's unveiling, but to instead further investigate. I intended to return to this farm, for something was not at all right.

"Let's go," I said to Norgrash'nar. "Let us make haste to Mar'Narush."

He boarded the train with me. Once we were seated, as it began to move once more, he said, "They *are* paid a fair wage, Alak'kiin. I don't know what you think is going on here, but remember, these people came to me for work. They have agreed to all terms of labor."

We will see, I thought, but said nothing. The rest of the journey was made in silence.

Snaking across the grasslands, the Guidetrain rails crossed rivers and streams, went around hills and through valleys, and passed directly by the Temple of Verasian, which was called Aleath'Weryn, which meant *Tall Structure* in the tongue of Dragons. Indeed, it was the highest of all the Dragon Temples, and it swept up from the plains of Onilmar like a great billow of earth dragged by the wind. For it was designed with a metal frame at its core, shaped like a great wave, and it was covered first with a steel screen and then with earthen reinforcements, and it appeared as if a great wind had swept the land itself into a great crest of earth and vegetation, as if it were about to cascade down upon the ground below. Yet it was stationary, standing nearly six Breadths tall, and it was a sight to behold. For had I not been witness to its construction I would have thought it a unique aberration of nature's ability to create wonderous formations in itself, so fluidly did it blend into the landscape.

Small trees and other vegetation grew upon its summit and so wide was the structure of this temple that even a small village had once been established upon its top by those who felt most at peace when near to a Dragon.

The inside of the temple structure was no less spectacular, for it was designed with one main chamber which was a dwelling place for Verasian himself. The walls were wooden carved structures depicting the glory of the Dragons as seen through the eyes of the Naiad who had constructed this place. As with all of the Dragon Temples, Aleath'Weryn was not a place of worship to the Dragons, but rather a place to commune with them, for in the days that the temples were built, the people still held their fathers in great esteem, before the people had become more centered upon their own affairs and ambitions.

Quickly passing by the temple, the Guidetrain continued southward toward our destination. Norgrash'nar remained silent, staring out a window, consumed with his own thoughts. There was a strange detachment in his silence, and I knew well what it meant—that my confrontation of his actions had caught him unexpectedly. Though I did not desire conflict with him, for I still considered him a cousin, a friend, a brother even, something was certainly amiss with him and his people. There were secrets within his mind, things that he was not willing to share with me at this time. It would not be until our ride was complete that Norgrash'nar would speak to me once more.

Mar'Narush was a city of great commerce—in fact this was exactly what the name meant in the tongue of the Dragons. It had not always been called this; when it was first founded by Norgrash'nar and his family a hundred years earlier, it was called Azeria, which meant *loose land*. For it was built at the base of the Central Plateau that was the eastern edge of this region, overlooking the Eastern Sea, and beside the bay that was also called Azeria. The plateau was soil land, thick and compressed, but not held in by stone as was the Goab'lin Plateau far on the other side of Sylveria. Slowly time was eroding the land into the sea, and so at its base, here where the bay met with the slopes, the ground was soft and loose. But as the city developed, Norgrash'nar had changed the name to one more fitting.

Riverways from the north central plains led here and were also routes to other parts of the entire region of Verasian, from the northern lands near Felheim, to the central mountains of the west, and all the way southward into the southern lands.

Mar'Narush had become a center point of trade between much of the Mainland of Sylveria and Aranthia. So too were there trade routes established with the people of Adaashar and Sveraden in the Southern

Reaches. This city was the go-between of major commerce, and the center of the most advanced civilization in all of the lands of Sylveria.

The Guidetrain stopped on the outer edge of the city. We debarked and Norgrash'nar said shortly, "The unveiling will be at the Hour of Concession. Go to the southern square." His tone was now more somber. "I hope you will not miss it."

It had been a long day, from the meeting with Norgrash'nar at Yor'Kavon, to the scaling of the Wall of Miithinar, to the long but quick transport ride all the way to Mar'Narush. If there was something untoward going on in the region, there was little I could do about it this day. It would have to wait until Firstlight. Whatever would be unveiled by my cousin was something I wanted to see, no longer for the excitement of some new technology that would be shown, but to discover what else Norgrash'nar might be up to, for something most certainly did not seem right.

The Hour of Concession came and much of the city's populace had gathered at the southern city square, which was a sector that was typically used for trading. Mar'Narush was laid out such that there were three major areas of commerce—open city squares on the north, west and south sides. Few of the homes and shops there were permanent structures that stood more than one or two stories high, unlike the towering domiciles of Floran'Adar. The eastern point of the city was the Bay of Azeria, where cargo boats and ships brought their wares into or out of the city. In most regards, Mar'Narush was fairly ordinary.

But it was the city spires that made Mar'Narush spectacular. Arranged upon eight points spread equally around the border of the city, the spires each towered more than four Spans tall. These were hollow structures, designed to do only two things—to glorify the city and to gather the light of the suns. The two most northern spires collected from Vespa, drawing its usable light and transforming it into magical energy that kept the streets lit at night. The remaining six spires were used to gather from Aros, though I was uncertain what power they derived was used for.

The spires themselves were each diamond-shaped, but seemingly stretched from ground to sky with each of the edges arced—either a design to make it more efficient or more stunning; for by design the outer surface of each was made up of thousands of small cells, each capable of taking in the light rays that fell upon them. For this, light also reflected off the small gaps between these cells, casting their light out across the grasslands as a beacon to welcome visitors.

The southern square was crowded when I arrived. In the center of it was a huge wooden crate, concealing something within—no doubt it was that which Norgrash'nar was about to unveil. In front of it was a makeshift stage and podium. The people in the crowd were almost entirely Nescrai, which I did not find particularly strange, as this city was the center of Nescraian civilization. However, I did notice that toward the southeastern corner of the square there was a small gathering of perhaps fifty or sixty Sylvaian women and men. They were segregated, it seemed, kept apart from the regular citizens of Mar'Narush. Again, this was not suspicious in itself, for it was natural that visiting or even migrant Sylvai might remain close within a group of their own family or friends.

Soon, my cousin arrived and was upon the stage at the podium, preparing to make a speech once the murmuring of the crowd died down.

And when at last it did, Norgrash'nar spoke in a voice that sounded out over the crowd through means other than with his natural voice, for it was too audible across the whole of the square to have been anything but magically enhanced.

"People of Mar'Narush, and all of those visiting from foreign lands, I have brought you all here this evening to demonstrate once more that the inventiveness of the people of this city is unmatched anywhere in Sylveria. For our greatest achievements have been the convocation of the suns in the spires of this city and the demonstration that this power can be drawn to the ends of the world.

"Just this day I brought an old friend here upon the Guidetrain from the north. I do hope you are in the crowd, Alak'kiin!" People in the crowd looked around, for the mention of my name surely sparked their interest. To the Norgrasharians—a people entrenched in their love of technology and audacious in their fascination with acclaim—it would be a great thing to have another of the First Awakened among them; for in these times, when the people were too numerous to intimately know one another, it was a highly uncommon event that one of renown might be present.

I lowered my head, hoping not to be recognized.

Norgrash'nar continued, "Now, so that others amongst us might not think the new technology that I will soon unveil is for any reason other than for the betterment of all people of Sylveria, let it be known that schematics for these devices, and for all of our machinery, will be sent to all corners of the world—freely given!"

The crowd seemed only moderately enthused. The people of Mar'Narush had always taken pride in their unique place amongst the cities of Sylveria as the most advanced. But there was some stirring to the southern end of the square from where I had seen the Sylvai... but now, they were dispersed, and I wondered where they might be, or what was going on, for I felt a sudden, inexplicable uneasiness. Slowly, still wanting to see Norgrash'nar's newest invention, I started edging my way to the south.

"And so I present to you now the technology that will take us into the future, and into the heavens!" As he said this, the sides of the giant crate were broken apart and fell to the ground, revealing that which was inside. It was a strange device, shaped similar to the spires of the city, but more rounded. The tops and the bottoms were narrow, each widening as they came together in the middle, as if two cones had been affixed to one another at their larger ends. They were covered in shaped sheets of metal and held the same appearance as the spires, and I supposed it was at least in part the same technology.

Norgrash'nar finished, "The Turbine Engine! A wonder of our age that converts the light of the suns into energy, just as we have done in the past. But its wonder does not stop here—"

I did not get to hear the remainder of his speech; someone grasped my arm and whispered into my ear, "Alak'kiin, please, come with me." I tried to see who it was; the voice sounded familiar. But his face was enshrouded in a hooded cloak. He was pulling me, urging me backward, and I allowed it, for I felt at my very core that something was amiss in Mar'Narush, and that this strange encounter might have something to do with it.

"Where are we going?" I asked.

I could see that the man guiding me was Nescraian, for his hand upon my arm was an azure tone. I did not sense any animosity in his manner or in the pitch of his voice as he said, "We need you to see something. You will *want* to see it."

I nodded my assent. To the south we went through the area of the square where had been the Sylvai onlookers; there was no sign of them anymore. After passing through the densest part of the crowd we came onto a street that was lined with businesses that were permanent stores for selling and trading. It was behind this row of structures that we went, between several of the buildings, then across several more streets until we were in a residential area. Only then did the man let loose of my arm and remove his hood.

A familiar face was presented before me. It was the grandson of Norgrash'nar himself, a man named Aivus'nar, who had been with us in Iidin, before the expansion of the people.

"Aivus'nar! What is going on?"

"I will explain it to you soon. Put this on." From inside his cloak he produced another and thrust it at me. "We don't want you to be seen. Let Grandfather think you are still in the crowd."

I wrapped the cloak around my shoulders and raised the hood. "Where are we going?"

"To the old docks, along the southern shore of the bay."

I knew this area well, for long ago, when the Norgrasharians were first settling this area, it was here at the old docks where they launched their first seafaring vessel. Then, it had been such an exciting and innovative time, when something so new as a boat was the talk of the people of the region. Now, such new technologies had risen that one day the ship itself may be obsolete.

We turned down a street, and then another, moving eastward. We were already on the south side of the city and so it was not too long before we were at the edge of Mar'Narush.

"What do you think of the newest invention of the engineers of Mar'Narush?" Aivus'nar asked, a note of derision in his tone.

"I didn't really get to hear what he plans to do with them."

"You'll see soon enough. It truly is for the betterment of the people— his people anyway."

"What are you talking about?"

"Just wait," he said shortly, still leading me eastward.

In less than a Course we were at our destination. The Bay of Azeria was to our north east. Great ships larger than any building of Mar'Narush, save for the spires, had made port. Some of them were cargo ships, others extravagant vessels for touring the South Sea. Many small boats were harbored there as well, but none here, at the old docks, for they were long ago abandoned. But there remained an old boathouse still standing, and it was into this that Aivus'nar led me.

Inside, we removed our hoods and found ourselves amongst perhaps twenty men and women who were split evenly between Nescrai and Sylvai. I recognized some of the faces, but most were strangers. Yet all of them seemed to know who I was as soon as I revealed my face.

"Alak'kiin!" they cried out. "It is true that you are here," one woman said. "We need your help!" a man said pleadingly.

"Everyone be quiet!" Aivus'nar demanded, and they quieted. To me he said, "Be seated, Alak'kiin. Can we offer you a meal?"

"I have not eaten since... yes, please. Whatever you have on hand is fine. But you must tell me... what is going on?"

"This is what's going on!" one man said, one I knew to be Aivus'nar's own nephew. He dropped a pile of bound papers onto the table in front of me.

I inspected the cover... on it was etched what appeared to be a mountain citadel, a city carved out of a mountaintop, perhaps. Underneath it was the word *Kor'Magailin*... another word in the tongue of Dragons.

"What does this title mean, Alak'kiin?" one of the women asked. "You are proficient in Draiko, are you not."

"Yes... somewhat," I said. "But it is difficult to translate this word... *Kor*... that is a description of something like the way in which the suns move over the surface of the world in an orderly and timed manner. *Magailin*... is something like an impenetrable place, a place that cannot be reached. What is this book?" I asked.

"It came from Norgrash'nar's study," Aivus'nar said. "I took it myself."

"Are these the schematics he is planning on sending out to all peoples, as he said?"

"No. You can bet he doesn't want anyone seeing *this* volume. It does have schematics, not just for his turbine engine but for something much larger. Something more complex and mechanical."

"Ah," I said. "Perhaps then *Kor* is best translated as *mechanical*. Mechanical Fortress."

"That is a fair description of what is shown within," Aivus'nar said.

I opened the book then, to see what might be there. But all I saw were drawings of intricate components of a greater machine. I had never had much of an inclination to these things. That had been my cousin's domain. Ever since Norgrash'nar had first moved beads along a string so as to do simple mathematics I had been disinterested. There were few words in this volume, only schematics used by the engineers to create things such as city spires and turbine engines.

"I don't understand," I admitted. "What is it you think is going on? What is this?"

"It is most certainly something untoward!" A Sylvaian man said.

"It is just a representation of something he wants to build. He has been making these since the Naiad were but thirteen living in the Valley."

"We need your help to understand this," Aivus'nar said. "We need to know what my grandfather plans to do."

"What are you talking about?" I was growing mildly frustrated because I did not understand what these men and women wanted of me. I had expected to learn of something more disreputable than a book of Norgrash'nar's drawings, something in regard to the potential mistreatment of the Sylvai in the city.

"Alak'kiin," an Adaasharian man said. "I am Dinrisar. Two years ago my brother and his family and I came here to Mar'Narush. We wanted to labor here and start a new life. Some of us are not content in the Southern Reaches. We thought that maybe his sons—my nephews—could become engineers, or learn some other trade. But we have been made to work on farms ever since. My brother's name is Avosar, and I believe you met him just several hours ago."

"Avosar, yes, I did meet him, upon the farmstead outside of Mar'Narush. How did you get word so quickly of this?"

"Avosar and I are twins of the same birth. Our mother is gifted in magic, and we inherited it in part. You see, we have a connection that is magical in nature, for it requires that we both will it, but we can communicate through the power of our minds."

"It is hard to believe, I know," Aivus'nar said. "I scarcely believed it at first either, but Dinrisar has seen things through his brother's eyes that he could not have divined on his own."

"I don't find it hard to believe," I said. "I have seen others possess this magical ability. They called it *telepathy.*"

"Anyway, I saw your coming, Alak'kiin. I saw your face through his eyes, but I wouldn't have recognized you. But your name… I heard Norgrash'nar speak it. You have seen what is happening on the farmsteads, haven't you?"

"I have seen things that I do not understand," I said.

"And here in the city, how many Adaasharians have you seen? How many Noranites, or Darians or Haldusians?"

"Very few."

"Yes!" Dinrisar said, exasperated. "Because most of them are made to work the fields."

"Are you saying that their labor is *forced* upon them?" I asked.

Dinrisar frowned and said, "Not so much forced, but… encouraged. When we first came here we were greeted by Aivus'nar, and we were thrilled with the prospects because Norgrash'nar's own grandson was to tend to us."

"Yes," the Nescrai Aivus'nar confirmed. "I took them in, as I did many and offered them rest after their long journey. I learned of what their current skills were and what they might aspire to achieve and learn in Mar'Narush."

"Mostly we wanted the boys to have the opportunity to be a part of this technological revolution. Avosar and I would have been content in doing more menial tasks."

Aivus'nar continued, "I took them in, and set them up with those who would help them achieve their goals. And they were well on their way. Then the *Culling* happened."

"The Culling?" I asked.

"About a year ago they came, many of the near relations of Norgrash'nar. They took most of the Sylvai out of the city and constrained them to the farms. They were offered work there, and indeed they are paid a fair wage. But when and for what will they spend their wage?"

"Are they not allowed to visit the city?" I wondered.

"Once every season," Dinrisar explained. "They are given two days off, days of their own choosing. They can do as they please. Avosar and my nephews are lucky in that they are close to the city. But what of those who are on the distant farmsteads? Where are they to go?"

Aivus'nar added, "They are more or less stuck where they are."

"Are they kept from leaving?" I asked.

"No. But where would they go? Back to the cities? They would be fine there for a time, until they ran out of their wages. Then they would be taken back to the farms."

"Why not return to their own people if they are unhappy?"

"Some have," Aivus'nar said. "But most of them remain because they hope things will change. Not everyone in Mar'Narush approves of what is happening. I am one of them."

I sat at the table in consideration. One of the Sylvai men brought me a plate of fruits and prepared grains. I poked at it with a fork and ate a few bites, but suddenly I had little appetite.

"We love this city and its innovations," Aivus'nar continued. "But how much greater would it be if it had the minds of both the Sylvai and the Nescrai working for its advancement?"

"I think this city has advanced too swiftly," I said. "But this is hardly my greater concern. I have seen the way some of the Sylvai are treated, and I do not approve. Yet if they are free to go, then what wrong has Norgrash'nar committed? Is it not their own ambitions that are keeping them there? I certainly do not like that some are being mistreated, but if they allow it, then what can be done for them?"

Aivus'nar stood up and paced around, saying, "I think I have perhaps... not explained myself very well. Everything you say is true. The problem is not that the Sylvai are being kept against their will, forced into labor, or even mistreated. The problem is that the Norgrasharians are intentionally segregating our people. Do you not see that most of them look down on the Sylvai?"

"I am starting to," I said thoughtfully.

"And this is why we are concerned about this book... The turbine engines just unveiled are drawn in its pages, as are many other things that have not yet come to invention."

"But what does this mean?"

"We don't entirely know, yet," Aivus'nar admitted. "But I do not get the impression that Norgrash'nar intends to use any of his technologies for the betterment of anyone other than his own people, and perhaps the Garonites."

"Yet he plans to send his schematics all around the world, to all of the people..." Dinrisar said. "To all corners of the world."

"This doesn't make sense, then," Aivus'nar said. "What other technology has he shared with the world? Where else have these advancements been seen, other than Mar'Narush? Nowhere... but perhaps in Hest'Vortal."

"So," I said. "Norgrash'nar is lying?"

"Yes, that is our point," Dinrisar said. "That is our concern. This book of drawings shows us what he wants to do. But why would he be untruthful? If he wants to hoard his inventions, he is free to do so. If he wants to only allow the Sylvai to work in the fields of Verasian, he is free to do so. And we are free to leave if we want. But there is something more going on...."

"You may be right," I said. "For what reason would there be to lie to the people?" My mind was not set at ease. Between apparent lies and definite mistreatment of the Sylvai, something was indeed amiss in Mar'Narush. "I will investigate all of this," I promised.

"We are already doing that here," Aivus'nar said. "Not that we wouldn't benefit from your assistance. But we just received word from Oman'Tar. The Adaasharians have been looking into this as well. Sveraden does not trust Norgrash'nar any longer. We thought you might like to go with some of us there, to see your sister and brother."

"I would very much like to see them," I said. "But I am still unclear on what your concerns are here, in Mar'Narush."

"I am sorry, Alak'kiin. Our thoughts have been scattered. Our words are too vague. Let me show you something." Aivus'nar then took the bound book of schematics and flipped through the pages until he settled on a certain arrangement of images that showed the interior of one of the intended cities. "There, look," he said, pointing at an image. "This is inside the city, at the very top of the *fortress*. Those are living quarters, wouldn't you say?"

I studied the diagram, and from the little ability that I did possess in reading these kinds of blueprints, I concurred.

"Alright, now look here...." And he flipped the page. "This is a more detailed image of those quarters. Inside the walls, there are mechanics... locking mechanisms to seal the doors."

"So? It is not uncommon in Mar'Narush for the people to secure their homes and belongings, is it?"

"Not at all. It is rare but there have been some instances of thievery here. But that is not the point, Alak'kiin. These drawings show that the doors not only lock from the inside, but also the outside... in a way that does not allow them to be opened from within."

"What are you saying then? These pictures detail chambers that can be used to detain the inhabitants?"

"Precisely!" Aivus'nar said. "Now do you see our problem?"

"Yes..." I said, now contemplating exactly what this meant. "Why would they need prison cells, if not to imprison someone?"

"And who do the Norgrasharians despise most of all?"

"Any who are not Nescrai," I said. "They have always thought too highly of themselves, starting with your grandfather."

"Yes."

"We have to do something about this."

"What can we do?" one of the women asked. "These are just plans.

There are none of these cities even being constructed. This is long in the future, I think…"

"But it does show Norgrash'nar's growing animosity toward the Sylvai and the Haldusians and the Darians."

"It does," Aivus'nar said. For this we are making efforts here in Mar'Narush to sway the people, to convince them that we are no better than any other people in Sylveria."

"Your efforts seem not to be going so well," I said. "As you said there is segregation in the city and on the farms. But there is nothing we can do if the Sylvai will not stop working for the Nescrai here…."

I could only acknowledge that there was little that could be done to change the progression of this civilization. If there was a growing enmity between the Nescrai and Sylvai in this domain, the only thing that could stop it would be internal workings. The people here, both Sylvai and Nescrai who shared not their kin's acrimony were already doing what they could. My presence here would do little to help. And so I thought it best to consult with my brother and sister in Oman'Tar. "I would like to go to the Southern Reaches," I said.

"Then we depart in the morning," Dinrisar said. "I am returning home. The rest of our family has sent word that there are other problems there as well, something coming out of the mountains."

"I will continue observing things here, Alak'kiin, and doing what I can to quell this malice," Aivus'nar promised. "And I will send word if I learn anything new."

I rested that night in the boathouse and was prepared to leave by morning. My rest was troubled by the events of this day. I always knew that Norgrash'nar was ambitious, even self-important, but until this past day I had never known him to be malicious or so deceitful. This seemed a characteristic that had been inherited by many of his descendants.

JOURNEY TO OMAN'TAR

We left Mar'Narush on the second day of Summertide, 310, by way of boat. There were no restrictions in those days on the coming or going of any sea vessel, and so we left the Harbor and headed eastward. Now, not far ahead a line of ships had begun to accumulate, and just beyond were the Tidegates. These were huge, solid steel gates that opened and closed to block the harbor, though not intended to seal the way into the city. Instead it was to keep the rising tides from flooding all of Mar'Narush.

Every day during the Hour of Darkening the gates were closed. No ship could either come or go after that hour, until the next day at Eventide, when the waters had receded. Now, when Feltide came, the waters struck the Tidegates, much like at the Wall of Miithinar, and the waters were pushed aside to the north and south. To the north the waters struck the southern slopes of Onilmar, while to the south there was no natural barrier to hold the water away. And so the tides pushed inland and to the south.

This had, ever since the construction of Mar'Narush and the Tidegates, caused the land to be flooded with twice the water than would naturally occur, and it backed up more than three Marches all around the coast. This region was known thereafter as the Drowned Lands, and little vegetation would grow there, for the ground was tainted by the ocean salts.

It was still the Hour of Midlight when we reached the ship line and took our place. Once Eventide came, a horn would sound and the Tidegates would open. On the other side would be a fleet of ships ready to enter the city, but those leaving always had priority.

Dinrisar was with me on the small sailing vessel, as well as the crew and captain, who was an Adaasharian man named Horas.

The crew was made up of just two other men, both of them Haldusians. This was a boat made not for transporting goods, but for luxury and speed. These men were friendly, and like all of their people their skin was a light brown shade, which was a perfect mix of their First Awakened ancestors, Haldus'nar and Sarak'den.

"Any news from Aranthia?" I asked the men.

Both men shrugged, and one said, "There is not much trade between the Haldusians and Mar'Narush these days."

"Why not?" I asked. In years past there had been much exchange of goods between the two regions. Though a sea separated them it was actually easier to transport goods and materials to or from the island region than to cross over the Mountains of Ashysin to trade with the Noranites or the Garonites, and not as far by sea as to the Southern Reaches.

"Our father and mother know that something is awry in Mar'Narush," the second man said. All Haldusians referred to Haldus'nar and Sarak'den as their *father* and *mother;* it was a cultural show of respect, for they held their ancestors in high esteem.

"The Aranthians have become greatly self-sufficient," Dinrisar added. "I spent some time there years ago, learning of their farming techniques. Both the highland and the lowlands are fertile ground. They once shipped gypsum and calcite to Mar'Narush in exchange for the Felheim, but even that has been stopped. Norgrash'nar will not confirm it, but it has been rumored that Haldus'nar has refused trade with his brother."

"There are tensions between Norgrash'nar and Haldus'nar?" This was indeed strange and unusual. Haldus'nar had always been closer with Norgrash'nar than with their other brother, Garonar. They had chosen the lands of their people's settlements partly because of their proximity.

"Yes," one of the Haldusians said, then explained. "And it is for the same reasons as all the troubles in Mar'Narush... because Norgrash'nar looks down on the children of our parents because we are not *pure.*"

"Pure what?"

"Pure Nescrai. We are mixed, tainted if you will."

The great horn of the Tidewatch sounded, marking the beginning of Eventide, reverberating out over the Bay of Azeria. Almost immediately the Tidegates began to open, and the many ships began to move.

Once we were through the Tidegates, Horas veered the boat to the southeast, following the coast of the Drowned Lands. This shoreline would take us all the way to the Southern Reaches, to Oman'Tar, which was the only established city in all of Adaashar and Sveraden's realm.

It would be an all-day journey by sea even with the speed granted by the heavy southern winds upon the sails. If the winds were strong we would be there by the Hour of Concession. We talked little during the journey, mostly because the wind rush was deafening and we were forced to wear dampeners. And so there was little to do but sit in consideration of recent events.

Through the Hour of Passions we sailed around the southeastern edge of Verasian's Domain, where we turned due west. From there the way would be slower as the eastward currents of the Southern Sea became strong. The winds were exceptionally in our favor and we made good time; by the Hour of Highlight we had reached the southernmost point in all of Verasian—*Taken Point Lighthouse.*

This was but one of numerous lighthouses that lit the way to the west all along the southern coast of eastern Sylveria. These served as markers for trade vessels and were spaced about every three Marches, and their lights that showed both day and night were powered by technology similar to the spires of Mar'Narush.

When the Hour of Devotion came, we passed beyond the Southern Grasslands and could see only the mountains to the north. There, high up in the massifs, I knew was the hidden Vale of Noramas. This was a forested region where grew the only Cambium Trees in all of Sylveria. This isolated area was otherwise home only to a few native species of small animals and Insects, and was considered one of the most secluded places in all of Sylveria, as the only way to reach it was with the help of a Dragon. The surrounding mountains were too steep, and no passes reached into it.

But in the time when Oman'Tar was being constructed there were many visits to Noramas by Merilinder the Silver, for the trees were harvested for their bark and the Dragon would strip them with his giant claws and drop it down into the sea below, where it was gathered by the

Adaasharians. It was a unique property of the Cambium Trees that the bark was both strong and lightweight enough to float in the seawater. The removal of the bark did no lasting damage to the trees, and within a matter of several years they had regrown their bark and were ready to be stripped again.

It was also the bark's lightweight attribute that made it desirable, for it was a major component in the construction of Oman'Tar. The plainsmen of Adaashar and Sveraden had built only one city throughout all of Merilinder's domain, preferring instead to live in nomadic camps, never staying in one place too long. It was largely the need for trade with other people that created the necessity of having a central point at which to conduct such exchanges. So too was it a place for the people to come to visit the Silver Dragon, for his temple, which was Nysin'Sumuni, was built in the center of the city.

Oman'Tar was a name derived from Draiko, which meant *Ocean Rest*, and it was a fitting name as the entire city sat upon the sea. Nysin'Sumuni had first been constructed ten Spans out from the Eventide coastline. Merilinder was such a fancier of the water that he desired his temple to be made out to sea, and when Adaashar and Sveraden decided to build their great city, it was around the temple that seemed most fitting.

Now the Temple of Merilinder was mounted to a small outcropping of loose stone that had there risen from the sea. It was made of carved stone drawn from the Mountains of Ashysin; its shape was like a pyramid, with its base twenty Spans square. Its northern face was covered in stairs of a size appropriate for the Adaasharians that went from bottom to top, where an entryway opened into the temple. The east and west faces of the temple were smooth stone, and the southern side was entirely open to the Southern Sea.

The city itself surrounded Nysin'Sumuni on all sides, and itself was afloat upon the sea. Constructed of a strong composite of gypsum, lime and the Cambium bark from Noramas, its low density kept it resting solidly upon the water. Great chains had been forged by the Darians and were attached to both the temple island and to great boulders upon the mainland. When Feltide came the city simply rose with the ocean level and was otherwise unaffected.

Oman'Tar was of a pentagonal shape with each side named for one of the children of Adaashar and Sveraden. There was but one roadway that went around the city, and there were very few structures. Instead, even the streets of Oman'Tar were set up so that residents could move around freely, living in tents or other temporary shelters. There was very little personal property amongst the Adaasharians, and so wherever one found a place to set up their havens they could freely do so. Moveable walkways passed from the city to both the temple and the mainland and could be raised and lowered as needed.

The southern stretch of the city was lined with moorings at which incoming and outgoing trade vessels could dock. Ships could come at any time, day or night, as the city was unaffected by the tides.

It was at one of these berths that we arrived just after the Hour of Concession had begun. We thanked Horas and the crewmen and set foot upon the floating city of Oman'Tar. To the north, the open side of the temple was facing us, and we could see that Merilinder was not present.

Dinrisar and I were almost immediately greeted by a man and woman, who were Kavonar and Elysanen, Dinrisar's mother and father. They took us a short way to the east and then brought us into their tent.

"It is good to meet you, Alak'kiin," Kavonar said kindly after Dinrisar introduced us; I had never met either of them.

"You as well," I said. "Who are your *naukal*?" This was a customary way of asking the Adaasharian people about their heritage, as they took pride in those from whom they had been descended.

"I am the firstborn of the ninth generation of Riiska'nar," Kavonar said. "Elysanen is of the same generation, daughter of Vanuson."

"Vanuson... son of Raithor?"

"The same."

"I know your grandparents well, then," I said to Elysanen.

"Father," Dinrisar said. "There are things uncouth happening in Mar'Narush. Alak'kiin has come here to speak with his brother and sister."

"What is happening in Mar'Narush?" Kavonar asked.

"We do not yet know," I said. "That is why I have come, to seek the assistance of Adaashar and Sveraden. Have you heard of where they might be?"

"They are with Merilinder, or so I believe," Elysanen said. "They came to the temple two days ago and left with the Dragon, flying to the north."

"The plains are vast," I said. "It may be best if I just wait here for their return."

"But who knows when that will be?" Kavonar said. "If it is a matter of finding them, then we can help. They have probably gone to Sairvon Pass. There are stirrings in that place."

"Stirrings?"

"That is the rumor," Elysanen said. "Word does not always travel fast in the Southern Reaches. We do not know what is transpiring. But it is something abnormal."

"It is a long journey by land to Sairvon Pass," I said. "Can you arrange transport, by chance?"

"Go to the north of the city, on the shoreline," Kavonar said. "You will find a man named Aisar near the north point."

"Aisar, the keeper of the Druugal?" Both Kavonar and Elysanen nodded. "I thought he had gone to Aranthia, to tame the Felheim."

"That was many years ago, and he has returned. Seek him out, Alak'kiin, and he will get you to Sairvon Pass as swiftly by land as is possible."

I thanked them for their help and said my farewell to Dinrisar; I could not be sure that I would be coming back this way.

Like all creatures of Sylveria the Druugal were affable with the people, living amongst them while both benefited from one another's presence. Compared to others of its kind, the Druugal, however, was much larger, reaching nearly two Breadths in length. Other than a Dragon, there simply were no lengthier creatures.

Called a *Plains Viper* by visitors from other regions, these giant serpents were native to the Southern Reaches, and were in fact a part of what had compelled Adaashar to first bring his people to the domain of Merilinder. The Dragon too had been fond of the Druugal, finding a certain unique kinship with them.

The average Druugal was as long as fifteen men were tall, and as big around as the trunk of a juvenile Baobab Tree. They were strong and their demeanors were well suited to the needs of the Adaasharians. As they were, one could be mounted in saddles upon its ventral region, just behind the hood of its head. They were unobjectionable even when reins were used to guide them.

While all creatures of Sylveria lived in harmony with one another, the Druugal was the only animal that consumed not the grass or vegetation of the world, but instead the discarded shells and remnants left behind after the hatching of the eggs of other species; as it was with the Raphus Birds of the plains, so ordered was the natural arrangement of the world, that these Birds layed infertile eggs just to serve as food for the Druugal.

In order to gain the cooperation of the Druugal, one had only to provide it with such food. The supply of Raphus eggs was not in short supply, as the Birds were abundant upon the plains of the Southern Reaches.

It was not difficult to find Aisar at the northern end of Oman'Tar, for there with him was one of the Druugal, coiled upon a large rock, basking in the sun.

"Alak'kiin!" he said enthusiastically as I approached.

"My old friend," I said. I had known Aisar for a long time. He had been of the last generation born in the Valley of Naiad, and was the son of Aisaven, the firstborn daughter of Adaashar and Sveraden.

"It has been many years since I have seen you, Alak'kiin."

"At least a hundred, I think. How have our paths not crossed more often?"

"You are always going to and fro," Aisar said. "And my talents have kept me occupied all over Sylveria."

"Last I heard you were in Aranthia."

"I was. Haldus'nar had imported some of the Felheim. They were an unruly harras if I've ever seen one."

"How did that end for you?"

"Very well. I've yet to find a beast that I could not handle."

"And now you have returned to the Druugal…"

"Yes, they are my first love… but… I see urgency in your eyes, Alak'kiin. It is not just a social visit that brings you to me, is it?"

"I wish it were," I said. "I am searching for Adaashar and Sveraden. I have heard that they are with Merilinder in the north, at Sairvon Pass."

"Well, where they are now I cannot say, but two days prior Merilinder flew overhead, heading that way, and I thought it likely that your siblings were with him."

"Can you get me there?"

Aisar looked over at the Druugal, then back at me. "That depends. How long has it been since you traversed the plains the right way?"

"Well over a hundred years," I said. "The first and last time was at your suggestion."

"Ah yes," he said, smiling. "That did not end well for you, as I recall."

"I handled it fine. My stomach did not." In fact, the winding motion of riding upon the Druugal had made me queasy, and I did not long to feel it again. But the urgency I felt in finding my brother and sister outweighed my need for a stable belly.

Laughing, Aisar said, "Do you want me to go with you?"

"That is not necessary. Two mounted on it will slow it down, will it not?" He nodded. "Then if you don't mind, I will go alone."

"Of course. It is late now," Aisar said. "Vaysa will not travel at night. Why don't you rest in my tent tonight, and you can leave at Firstlight."

We stayed awake late into the night, talking. I told him of my travels of the past years and of the problems arising in Mar'Narush. This news of Norgrash'nar's segregation caused Aisar concern too, for he had family that had moved to the east. He too had heard rumors of stirrings here in the Southern Reaches, but knew nothing more defined.

On the third day of Summertide at Firstlight, I mounted Aisar's Druugal, who was named Vaysa, and left Oman'Tar for Sairvon Pass, far to the north. By foot, it would be a three-day journey, accounting for plentiful rest. Upon the Druugal, it would be much shorter, as their quick and sidewinding paths could take them across the plains in half the time. Accounting for Vaysa's needs, I estimated I could reach the pass by Highlight the next day.

As we swayed along the plains, the queasiness in my stomach was ever present, but looking skyward seemed to ease it. This was for the best anyway, for I needed to keep my eyes out for Merilinder. Along the route, we passed many encampments, which were tents lined up in various arrangements by the Adaasharians. Kind gestures passed between us as we navigated the land.

That night found us two-thirds of the way to Sairvon Pass, at a place called the Mainar Outpost. Here people would occasionally set up shops for travelers, trading for provisions and other needs. At this particular time there were no merchants and so we had the campsite to ourselves.

In the morning I hesitantly mounted Vaysa once more, ready for this journey to be over. We crossed over the Sairvon River soon thereafter; the Druugal easily passed over the surface of the water and we came to the other side, which was flatter grasslands and more easily traveled by the mount.

It was the Hour of Passions when the first sign of the stirrings in Merilinder's domain showed itself...

There, upon the plains that were narrowing as two ranges of the Mountains of Ashysin came together at Sairvon Pass, were more animals gathered together than I had ever seen, all creatures of the mountains... Mountain Goats and Gorillas, Black Bears, Baboons and Beavers, Tamarins and Tigers, Wolves, Weasels and Wombats, and every other variety of creature that found its home in the mountains; all had now come down onto the plains in such numbers that it was uncertain if the whole of the Southern Reaches could support them.

Amongst them all, near Loch Sairvon, Merilinder lingered, and, I assumed, Adaashar and Sveraden would be there as well. I directed Vaysa to continue on and she parted the way between the gaggles and gulps, the clowders and cackles, the herds, hosts and hordes—countless legions of the creatures that were now crowded onto the plains. Finally reaching the Dragon, I dismounted from the Druugal, and amongst the confusion found my brother and sister.

"Sveraden!" I said loudly, to be heard above the cacophony. "Adaashar!"

Both turned to look at me, as did Merilinder, and their stressed features brightened. They rushed to me, Sveraden warmly embracing me as Adaashar clasped my shoulder.

"Oh, Alak'kiin, it is most pleasant to see you here," Merilinder said, himself appearing in a state of uncertainty.

"What is going on?"

"We're not sure!" Sveraden said. "We heard rumors that there were animals here, coming out of the Pass, from the mountains. We came here to see ourselves..." she looked around, nervous, and continued, "We never thought it would be such a mass migration."

"Migration?" I wondered. "Why would they be migrating?"

"What else would it be?" Adaashar asked.

"Something is not right about this," Merilinder said. "For two days we have been trying to bring order to these beasts, but they won't listen! They just run to and fro!"

"These animals have never come down from the mountains have they, Adaashar?" I asked.

"Not in numbers such as these. Occasionally some will come, exploring, seeking food. But never such multitudes."

"Merilinder," I said. "There's no reason for them to migrate... what if they are fleeing from something? Have you flown over the mountains?"

"Not even as far as Vindras Vale. Most of these little pests have come through there!" The Dragon was clearly upset, for Merilinder had always been a lover of the creatures of the world, and now his frustration was surely not for any nuisance they posed, but rather his concern for what was causing this mass evacuation of the mountains. The animals were crowded in, clearly themselves agitated, but unwilling to return the way they had come, through Sairvon Pass. "It's a scourge upon my lands!"

"Don't worry, Merilinder," Sveraden said, placing her hand upon the very tip of the Dragon's tail, which was curled in a great circle around us now, keeping us apart from the packs. "We will figure this out and take care of them all."

"I hope so...."

"Merilinder," I said. "Where is Ashysin?"

"I suppose in Diras'Vorma, his temple in the Valley of Gold."

"Perhaps you should go to him, get him to help uncover this mystery. You can cover a lot more ground than we."

Merilinder looked to the east, toward the Golden Valley, then his eyes scanned the creatures that swarmed the plains. He said, distressed, "I cannot leave them...."

"They will be fine," Adaashar assured. "We will take care of them."

"How? There are only three of you."

"We will manage," Sveraden said.

Merilinder looked back over the masses, and if it were possible for a Dragon to do so, he frowned. Hesitantly he said, "I will leave at Lastlight. Let me help you to bring some order."

So we agreed that all we could do would be to spread the animals out through the plains; the more sparsely their populations in a given area, the more food there would be available.

Now, the animals were already mostly arranged by kind—they sorted themselves out as they came from the mountains, each of them finding themselves more at ease with their own. In this our task was made easier, as all we had to do was urge some of a particular kind to keep moving southward, and generally the others would follow. Merilinder was best at this, as he possessed a certain affinity with the other creatures of the world. Additionally, he was able to compel Vaysa, as well as the other Druugal that were in the area, to aid in this as well. Adaashar and Sveraden were no strangers to the handling of animals, and they too were able to accomplish much. But still the animals kept coming out of the mountains…

When the Hour of Mourning came, the animals had spread out far moreso than when I had first arrived. There was still work to be done, but it would have to wait until Firstlight. Hesitantly still, Merilinder departed at Lastlight, disappearing to the east as he went to find Ashysin the Gold. We camped near the western mountain range where we would be safest from the possibility of stampede.

"Let us see what morning brings," Adaashar said as we lay down to rest. "But if these throngs are under control still, I would much like to investigate Sairvon Pass. Something must be driving them southward."

"I agree," Sveraden said. "I have never seen any creatures behave this way. Something is amiss…."

"Speaking of which," I said. "I have come to the Southern Reaches from Mar'Narush. Things there are unsettling as well."

"We have heard rumors," Sveraden said. "Whisperings that Norgrash'nar is not treating our people well."

"That I can confirm is true…." I said. "At least some of the Norgrasharians are not. I have seen this with my own eyes. But not all of them are guilty. Some of the Nescrai helped me to get out of Mar'Narush. But Norgrash'nar is up to something… I just can't yet discern it."

"I do not trust him, Alak'kiin," Adaashar said. "Too many ill words have been spoken of him. Some of it must be true."

"He seems to be segregating the people, creating a wealthier, more distinguished class, which are his own people. The Sylvai and the Haldusians are lower citizens to them. But there is more…."

"What do you mean, Alak'kiin?"

"Norgrash'nar unveils new technologies at a numinous rate. On the first of Summerstorm I was at Yor'Kavon. He has built a great wall there to hold back the tides. Forthran is a dry land now. From there he took me upon a transport that moved along the ground at such a speed that we were in Mar'Narush well before Lastlight. Then, he unveiled something new, what he called a turbine engine. And he was promising his people that he would take this technology to the ends of the world."

"What does it do?" Sveraden asked.

"I don't know. I was pulled away before I saw it all. There are those in Mar'Narush who are amongst your own people, and some of the Nescrai... they have found schematics, plans for the use of the engines, I think. But I cannot say more; I don't know what he is doing, but his advancements are happening too swiftly. He will overtake all of Sylveria with it."

Both Adaashar and Sveraden seemed concerned, for as they were, they were lovers of the land, and they liked their quietude. Norgrash'nar, they feared, would bring his ways of busyness to all of Sylveria if allowed. And this was assuming that he had nothing more sinister planned.

"There is more news, too," I said. "From Mara. There are disturbances in the Hilly Lands, conflicts between the Noranites and the Garonites."

"Conflicts over land, I presume?" Adaashar said.

"Yes. You have heard."

"No, but it is unsurprising. Some of them—the Garonites came down onto the plains a year ago, claiming quite ardently that they were going to settle there. We did not object. The land does not belong to us. We welcomed them. But when the Summer Seasons came, it grew too warm for their liking, and they returned to the mountains."

"It was strange, Alak'kiin," Sveraden said. "The way they acted, the tones in their voices. Their attitudes have changed over the years, toward us, and probably toward the Noranites as well."

"I think we may well find that the Garonites are responsible for all of this as well," Adaashar added, gesturing to the multitude of creatures. "Let us sleep now and begin our journey tomorrow."

I awoke in the early morning, even before Firstlight, to the sound of bickering; Adaashar and Sveraden were already awake, packing their gear, which was considerably more than I had brought. Adaashar was wide awake, hurrying her along. Sveraden seemed groggier, her black hair a mess, and she was not so pleasant as usual; as I recalled, she never was fond of mornings.

"Ah, Alak'kiin, you're awake!" Adaashar said cheerfully.

"Good morning," I said.

"Watch out, Sveraden is not so exultant at Firstlight."

She glared at him, but said nothing, turning her attention instead to completing her task.

"Did you sleep well?" I asked; it was directed at both of my companions, but Sveraden took offense.

"It's hard to sleep with a plot of Lemurs picking at my hair all night!"

"Oh, *Erhayl,* they only do it because they are as enamored with you as am I." Again, she glared, but then her eyes brightened and she fought a losing battle with a smile that played on her lips.

I looked around, and indeed there was a large assemblage of the small creatures not far away, some of them staring at us, chittering playfully, others picking at each other. Not far from them was a pride of Lions and their many cubs, and just a little further were the Gray Giraffes of Vindras Vale. I was reminded then of my first visit to the vale, long before the Garonites had inhabited the mountain regions.

All across the prairies the animals had spread, moving southward, and it seemed this morning like not so a daunting task to get them apportioned. The various clusters of creatures now extended as far as we could see toward the lower plains. No longer were they coming out of the mountains in such numbers.

"They will spread across the savannah," Adaashar said.

"But will there be enough food for them all?" Sveraden asked.

"Doubtful. We need to figure out why they left, and hopefully get them to return."

We broke camp, just as the faint glow of Aros's light broke the eastern sky, and headed for the Sairvon Pass, now assured that there was little more we could do for the animals.

It was through Sairvon Pass that the Adaasharians had first gone when they made their exodus from the Valley of Naiad into the domain of Merilinder. At the entrance into the pass was a lake that was fed by many mountain streams and was itself a source for the Sairvon River. Called Loch Sairvon, it was a watering place for many of the creatures of both the northern prairie and the southern mountains. So it was not unusual that a variety of animals would be seen near it, but never before in the numbers that had come this way of late.

Past the lake, to the north, a small valley came to an end after only a short distance, but there was a well-worn trail that had been passed over for many years by both animal and Naiad, leading into the western end of Vindras Vale. This was a major trade route between the Garonites and the Adaasharians. The way through the mountains was not an incredibly strenuous trek, but it was a winding path that would take some time to traverse. The snaking route was nearly five marches long, almost entirely uphill.

Vaysa, the Druugal, had remained near us, as well as several others of her kind. Typically, when one of the Plains Vipers was called to assist, they did not leave until they were released. Adaashar, Sveraden and I mounted the Druugal, but they would go no further than Loch Sairvon. Something to the north made even them uneasy. And so we released them from service and they slithered southward across the prairie.

"This is going to be a long trek," Adaashar said. "I hope you have kept in shape, Alak'kiin."

"I have walked these lands more than most," I said.

"How many years have you been traveling, Brother?" Sveraden asked, walking between Adaashar and me as we started the incline up the pass.

"Over two hundred years," I said. "Since everyone started leaving Naiad. Once my brothers and sisters were gone there was little reason for me to stay in Naiad."

"There is always Saxon."

"Indeed. I still go there, to Naiad, as often as I can. I was there just before meeting with Norgrash'nar at Yor'Kavon."

"And he is well?"

"Yes. Naiad has been reclaimed by nature. It is little different than it was when we were first awakened. It is a timeless place, and to Saxon it is always the same."

"Do you ever miss those first years?" Adaashar asked.

"Nearly always," I said. "The world is full now; most of the lands explored. Remember when anything that was beyond our range of sight was a mystery? When the world was so big that we couldn't even imagine it?" They were both nodding, reminiscing. "I miss the mystery."

"There are still mysteries in the world, Alak'kiin," Sveraden said. "Still places in the mountains unexplored, and Drovanius and Merobassi… their lands are not settled, are they?"

"No. They are too cold for most of the Sylvai. The Nescrai are content where they are, I think. I may well explore those regions one day. But I always seem to find something else to do with my time. Perhaps I've seen most of the world, but I suppose I have been occupied for two hundred years, and still the world is not boring."

"I suppose it's hard to get bored when there is always something new happening…." Adaashar said just as a flock of Ostriches came wobbling around a bend in the trail ahead, coming at us, heading out of the mountains. "Alak'kiin, what do you think might be causing this migration?"

"I really don't know, Adaashar. But I admit that I have an uneasy feeling about what we will see ahead, in the Vale."

"The Garonites are nearly as fascinated with technology as are the Norgrasharians," Sveraden said.

"But why would they drive the animals out of Vindras Vale?" Adaashar asked. "Garonar and Kuranen were always caretakers of the animals, if not their people."

"They were porters, yes," I said. "But it was always for their own benefit. And the Garonites may be even less concerned. They have tolerated the presence of the creatures in the Vales only for the sake of

Ashysin."

"But it's not just the animals of Vindras Vale," Sveraden said. "This many animals could not have come from there alone. And who knows how many have fled to the north, into Mara?"

There was nothing that could be resolved by talking about it, only by observing, and we still had a full day of travel before we would reach the Vale, where we might find answers.

Solemnly I considered all that had happened in just the past season, since I had visited Nirvisa'Iinid. Before, upon my many journeys, the lands of Sylveria had always seemed serene and peaceful, functioning as they always had, the ecosystems and orders of nature always flowing and following a determined course. But now, there were troubles throughout, seeming to quicken along; it was as though the influences of the Naiad had reached a tipping point, where they no longer lived in perfect harmony with the world, but instead were influencing its course with progress. In but a season, the natural structure had been altered. So, as we continued on through the pass, I addressed these matters with my siblings.

"There is change in the air. I have noticed it just in recent times." Sveraden and Adaashar both looked at me, curious. "Who knows what we will find in Vindras Vale; certainly something is upsetting the natural order. There are the strange things happening in Mar'Narush, and all of Verasian's domain. Arguments over land rights in Southern Mara… and at the center of it all seems to be Norgrash'nar."

"You think he has caused this, the animals to flee the mountains? And the Garonites to fight with the Marans?" Sveraden asked.

"Perhaps. But I can't be sure. I was in Nirvisa'Iinid in early Summerstorm. Nirvisa'nen pulled me aside to tell me something; something she wanted to be kept from Alim'dar."

My companions raised their eyebrows in wonder; Adaashar asked, "What could that possibly be?"

"I wondered the same at first. After she told me, I understood. Norgrash'nar came to her one day in her garden. He pleaded with her to leave Alim'dar for him. He has not moved on past her, it seems. He still is infatuated with her, even after all these years."

"Even after marrying Kalenen…." Sveraden said. "I have never understood his obsession. For love is only true if it is two-way, and clearly Nirvisa'nen has always loved Alim'dar."

"I confronted him about it as we traveled to Mar'Narush. He denied even visiting her. He lied."

"Yes…" Adaashar said somberly. "There has always been something different about him, about Norgrash'nar. And something certainly is amiss in these times. As you said he may well be at the center of it all."

"We should not assume too much," Sveraden said. "There may be other explanations. But indeed, we should be cautious in regard to him. Perhaps we will find answers in Vindras Vale."

Slowly, Sairvon Pass rose higher into the Mountains of Ashysin, winding northward one moment, then east the next, and back south before turning back again. Still some animals were migrating, though it was mostly small Rodents and Raccoons, Hedgehogs and Hares, and many Insects. Overhead, Birds of all varieties were flying south—a practice usually only occurring during the Autumn Seasons.

It was late in the Hour of Awakening when we began to hear a strange and unnatural sound—a distant humming—coming from the east, toward Vindras Vale. Whatever this clamor was, it was likely to be the source of the disturbance in the region. As we drew even nearer there were sounds of scraping and grinding, gritting and groaning, as of metal upon stone. And when Evenlight came and we entered into Vindras Vale, we were met with the most distressing sight that I had seen in all three hundred and ten years of my life...

Vindras Vale, a place once so beautiful so as to have been Ashysin the Gold's favorite place in all of Sylveria, had changed. Once, it had been covered in thick, lush fields of green grasses and colorful flowers, small woodlands, and filled with many beautiful creatures—Giraffes and Monkeys and the Mountain Leopards, Giant Butterflies and Birds of a hundred varieties. It had been silent and serene, isolated as it was from the rest of the world. But now it was quickly becoming a wasteland.

The Garonites had settled in the Vale in their early years and had tended and farmed the land, much to the approval of the Dragon. He loved all things that lived in harmony with one another. I had not heard any word that this had changed, and I was with Ashysin just two years earlier. He had said nothing about any of this...

The grounds of the Vale, so far as I could see, had been upturned, reduced to soil with clumps of grass slowly withering. The trees of the forests were gone—no doubt to be used in the construction of buildings and structures for the betterment of their civilization. Giant machines rolled across the once green fields, tearing the landscape, and near the mountains, even more enormous apparatuses carved into the stone mountains themselves using giant circular steel blades that cut through the rock with ease, destroying the natural formations of the Vale. These terrible machines rivaled the size of the Sloths of Mara.

Adaashar and Sveraden looked on in revulsion, their eyes wide, their jaws clenched furiously—the same look that must have been apparent on my own face, and I could not believe what I saw, for never had such destruction been seen in Sylveria. Silently we stormed into the Vale, disgusted at the demolition that was transpiring before us. None of us could speak, but woe to the first of the Garonites who might come before us—for the rage that was increasing within us was never before imagined in all of Sylveria—at least for that moment...

For then we saw, coming out of the east, two Dragons—Gold and Silver, soaring swiftly and furiously above the wasteland that was now Vindras Vale. Together they let out a shriek so loud that I would not have been surprised to later learn that it had been heard even in the far reaches of Drovanius. It silenced the machines, for their operators ceased their tasks and looked skyward for the source of the uproar.

Now, this was all in the westernmost end of the Vale, but by the rage that filled the Dragons' eyes I felt certain that this was not alone isolated to this side. Ashysin and Merilinder landed in the now dry bed that once had been Devor Lake, and Ashysin cried out, "What have you done to my Vale?" And their giant heads snaked in all directions, looking for anyone to blame for this atrocity. They stomped through the Vale, Ashysin, coming to the north and west, toward us, and toward one of the great grinding machines. And he repeated in a fierce growl, *"What have you done to my Vale?"* The fury in his tone was frightening, even to us, for we had never heard a Dragon speak with such indignant rage.

But the Garonites seemed not so intimidated—or perhaps they could not hear the Dragon's words for the deafening that must be present in their ears by the loudness of their engines. And even with Ashysin so close, one of the grinders started up again, as if to resume its destruction... And Ashysin would not contend with this. In a concerted leap he was airborne, but only for a moment until he came to land with his massive claws upon the top of the contrivance. He flapped his wings, creating gusts of wind and he shook it fiercely until the several Nescrai who were inside leaped out onto the ruined ground. Then, considering it unoccupied, Ashysin lifted it into the air, rose higher and higher, and came out over the mountains to the north of Vindras Vale, where he flung the machine with such great ferocity that it went crashing into the stone below.

The Garonites then scattered—any who witnessed this who were not before intimidated now were terrified and they fled their own vehicles. Together, Ashysin and Merilinder tore through the machinery of the Garonites that day, and I felt not even slightly inclined to stop them.

When the Hour of Devotion came, the Dragons came to us, having seen us earlier. They were tired from their destructive efforts, but remained furious.

"What have they done, Alak'kiin?"

I shook my head, my own anger still infused. "I don't know. I swear I did not know what they were doing here, that they had such destructive power."

"They must answer for this," Merilinder said. "Garonar and Kuranen must answer...."

"They have disrupted the natural order of this land," Ashysin said.

"I agree," I said, as did Adaashar and Sveraden.

"They have done a great wrong," my sister said.

"We will go to Hest'Vortal and confront them," Adaashar promised.

"We will all go..." Ashysin said solemnly, looking around the once beautiful Vale that was now a sundered, desolate waste, devoid of life, devoid of the creatures he loved so dearly. I was certain then that if a Dragon were capable of crying that Ashysin would have flooded the whole of the Vale at that moment.

"We must remember our vows," Merilinder said, almost with spite. "We vowed that we would never harm them."

"I will not harm them," Ashysin said, now sounding not so incited with rage, but with sadness. "But they must fix this...."

"Look!" Sveraden said suddenly, and she was pointing to the north. There, coming over the mountain tops was another Dragon—one with gleaming white scales. "Kronaggas!"

The great White Dragon came into the Vale and landed amongst the others. Upon his back were two riders, who slid down his wings onto the ground near us. It was Norandar and Alunen, who were themselves horrified by what they saw all around them.

"The Garonites have done this?" Norandar asked.

"Yes," Adaashar said, embracing his brother, and then Alunen. Sveraden did the same, for it had been long since they had seen one another.

"The land cries out...." Kronaggas said; his voice too was filled with ire.

"We are going to Hest'Vortal," Ashysin said. "To deal with Garonar and Kuranen. They have brought this upon the land!"

"You do not know that, yet," Kronaggas said. "The mountains are a vast region... perhaps... no, it is unlikely that they do not know of this, for the Garonites tell their father and mother of all that happens...."

"All of the animals of the Vale and the Mountains have flooded onto the prairies below, into Merilinder's domain," Sveraden said. "We don't even know if food will be plentiful enough for them."

Kronaggas, calmly resolute, affirmed, "No creature will go hungry. We will bring them food from every corner of Sylveria if we must. Ashysin, Merilinder, this is our task."

"No!" the Gold Dragon shrieked. "We must go to Hest'Vortal and confront them...."

"Let the Sylvai do that," the White Dragon said. "They are of a better temperament right now." Kronaggas turned to the five of us and said,

"Will you do this? Will you go to Hest'Vortal and do all you can to stop this profanity?"

"Of course," we all said in unison.

"Very well. We will tend to the creatures of the world. Then, if you need us, we will tend to Garonar and Kuranen."

We had not the saddles necessary for travel by Dragon and so the five of us set out to the east while Ashysin and Merilinder reluctantly followed Kronaggas out into the world to gather food for the legions of displaced animals.

Journey to Hest'Vortal

It was the fourth day of Summertide, 310, when the Dragons left us in the western Vale. It had been a long day of travel through Sairvon Pass and so after covering just a short distance we made camp. We talked throughout the last hours of the day.

"So, Alak'kiin," Norandar said, "You have been all the way to Mar'Narush, across the Southern Sea to Oman'Tar, then all the way here since we last saw you?"

I nodded. Alunen said, "How is that even possible?"

"You know how I travel—but I cannot take all of the acclaim..." I told them about Norgrash'nar's Guidetrain and about all the other things that had occurred since I had seen them not so long ago. They too were concerned over the events in the east. There were, most definitely, strange stirrings all across the lands of Sylveria. "What happened in the Hilly Lands?" I asked.

"We left that night," Norandar explained. "When you remained in Floran'Adar. Once we were nearly there, the way to the troubles was lit by firelight. A Garonite settlement was ablaze. By the time we got to it, it was too late to do anything. The family seemed distraught, though the settlement was not much more than a makeshift shack. Others were around, too, other Nescrai infuriated at this atrocity."

"In the morning," Alunen continued the story. "We found the people who were responsible—some of the Sylvaian settlers—and we scolded them for behaving in such a way. They freely admitted that they had started the fires. When we asked them why, we were *very* taken aback by their answer."

"They had not burned the settlements of the Garonites... They had burned *their own*—for just a day earlier the Nescrai had forced them out, claiming the work of their own labor. This is happening all across the Hilly Lands... Our people go and build settlements, prepare the land, and then the Garonites come and take it away, having to do little work for themselves."

"At first, from what we gleaned, the Nescrai came, claiming to be settlers from the mountains, asking for work. But the kindness of our people was soon turned into duplicity. They would take over and make the Sylvai do their bidding, or they were thrown out."

"And thus the fires. Some of our people are a bit vengeful, I suppose, but I can hardly fault them. This thievery has not been seen before in our lands."

I asked, "Did you confront the Garonites, any of them?"

"Yes, we did," Norandar said.

"But what *could* we do?" Alunen said, looking suspiciously toward Norandar, who returned the expression.

"What *did* you do?" I asked.

"Well, we observed all the next day, throughout the hills. We saw it happen with our own eyes—the Garonites taking what was not theirs. So... we helped our people to burn it all."

Sveraden and Adaashar laughed; she said, "I'm sorry, but I feel as though they deserve it."

"I don't understand what has overcome the Garonites," Adaashar said.

"It didn't matter anyway—what we did," Norandar explained. "Because the next day, the animals started coming, flooding onto the hills, trampling everything that our people had built."

"We too were inundated in the south. That is what brought us here."

"We had no idea what to do," Alunen admitted. "So we went to Kronaggas. And he brought us here to Vindras Vale."

"Garonar and Kuranen have much to answer for," I said. The behavior of their people as of late was unprecedented, for never had any of the people of Sylveria shown such disrespect for one another, and for the natural world.

At Firstlight we continued on our journey, eastward across the remainder of Vindras Vale, which was a wasteland from one end to the other. We encountered numerous Garonites, who, recognizing at least some of us, veered away rather than engage us. We too thought it best to avoid them.

By the Hour of Devotion we had come to the northeastern end of the Vale, where the Tybor River bent northward and passed through the narrow mountain gorge into far eastern Mara, which was south of Naiad. From there we would travel east into the mountains over Gnok'Gerthorn Pass. This was not a pass at all alike to Sairvon, with an easy incline leading steadily up. Instead it was a trail that traversed the ridgeline of several mountains before coming to Hest'Vortal. This was the only simple route by land into the old city, for it was built upon a great plateau that was just west of Diras'Vorma—Ashysin's Temple.

The high pass was six marches long, but took much longer to traverse than if it had been upon flat ground, for there were many rises and falls, and the landscape was rocky and difficult to trod. We would be able to cover the distance by Lastlight, but we did not want to cross over into the city until the next day, for spanning the last mountain peak before the plateau was a rope bridge that swayed wildly in heavy winds and bounced just from simply walking upon it. This span was called *Boris'Thirith*, which translated literally as *Air Way*. None other than the Garonites had ever been comfortable crossing the ten Span long bridge as it rose equally high above a deep gorge far below.

Along Gnok'Gerthorn Pass, at places where the path was more than just a Height wide, there were sites set up for travelers at which to camp. We took advantage of one of these that was perhaps a Course's walk away from Boris'Thirith.

When the darkness of night came, no one dared to travel the narrow path—save for the Garonites, for they seemed to have developed an instinct for moving around and through the high places of the mountains without fear, even without much light. And so, as we lay down to sleep in silence, several of them passed us by, likely unaware of our presence as their torchlight extended only so far. But we could hear their words…

And they were not kind words, either to the Dragons who had destroyed some of their mechanical equipment or toward the Sylvai in general. There was animosity in everything they said, and it was unnerving, for why there should be such acrimony was beyond my understanding. Until these recent events the Garonites had always gotten along with and traded with the Adaasharians and the Noranites.

When the Garonite travelers had passed beyond earshot, Sveraden said, "It would seem that they have adopted the same attitudes toward our people as have the Norgrasharians. Perhaps our cousins have colluded."

"I don't understand why they would have grown to despise us," Alunen said.

Although I didn't speak of it that night, I was pretty sure that I did understand, for dawning within my mind was a deep suspicion that Norgrash'nar's continuance of spite was leading a great portion of the Nescrai to despise their cousins. It seemed that perhaps the Garonites were following in his footsteps, thinking themselves more important, even better, than the Sylvai.

We approached the bridge of Boris'Thirith halfway through Firstlight on the sixth day of Summertide. The city was barely in view as we took our first steps out over the chasm that fell before us. It was a wide enough path that four men or women could stand side by side, and so it was no issue to have others coming from the opposite direction. It was an unsteady and frightening trek across, but within the Hour we had come back onto solid ground.

"I hope we don't have to do that again," Sveraden said. She had never made the walk across Boris'Thirith.

"Except by Dragon, there are only two ways in or out of Hest'Vortal," I said. "This bridge, and the Trenches of Avaron."

We entered the city a short time later. Hest'Vortal was, as I have stated before, a city built entirely upon the plateau. Translated literally, it meant *insightful plateau*, but this name seemed deceptive in that the intent behind the designation of the city was to mean *the height of insight,* or *of higher understanding.*

The city had only short walls, not intended to keep anything out—for what could come against a city such as this—but to serve as a boundary to keep its drunken people from falling off during the late-night escapades that they had become fond of in recent years. The wall ran the entire circumference of the city; otherwise, Hest'Vortal was fairly plain in appearance. Much of the city had been carved out of great stone boulders that Ashysin had brought to them in the early years of its construction.

Most notable was that at the very center of the city was an enormous coliseum that covered nearly a fourth of the entire plateau. This was used for public meetings, bartering, exhibitions and competitions, as the Garonites had always had a fondness for trying to best one another at physical and menial tasks. The Coliseum had enough seating to hold every Garonite man, woman and child, as well as room for visitors, so large was its design. Additionally, there were eight towers that were spread evenly around the outer circle of the stadium, each with a horizontal perch intended for a Dragon's comfort. This structure was designed to be a spectacle for all of the intelligent creatures of Sylveria—Naiad and Dragon.

At the north end of the Coliseum was an entire residence for Garonar and his wife Kuranen. This was their palace, and its ornamentations and fine craftsmanship were beyond what most in Sylveria could either afford or desire.

Through the Coliseum gates we walked; there were no special events this early in the morning. Around us were hundreds of rows of stone seating, all arranged in circles. The walkway declined downward into the center, giving all seats a better view of whatever might be going on. From the center of the base the carved pillars which served as the outer boundaries of the Coliseum were a full span high. The floor of the arena was covered in tightly packed dirt, and as we went over it there seemed to be dark markings upon the surface that I could not identify. Later I would realize that the Garonites had also become fond of bloodsports, which were games in which opposing factions would physically assault one another in contests of strength, continuing in brutality until one or the other could fight no more.

As we approached Garonar's palace steps we were greeted by his wife, Kuranen.

"Ah, Cousins!" she said delightfully. "I had no idea you were coming for a visit."

"This is no social call," Adaashar said firmly. "Where is Garonar?"

"He is inside, bathing. Come on in and I will have a meal prepared for you."

We accepted the invitation; though we were filled with intense umbrage, Garonar and Kuranen still deserved a measure of respect. After all, we were not entirely sure how responsible they were for the happenings in the west. Though they were the leaders of their people—generally taking an active role in all of the activities and planning of the Garonites' endeavors, it was not unreasonable to think that things might be happening without their knowledge. Unlikely, but not unreasonable...

Kuranen led us into a fancy dining hall within the palace and made a gesture to a woman who was standing nearby—a Sylvaian woman. "Prepare our guests a meal of crudites and lecso." The woman nodded submissively and disappeared into what I supposed was a kitchen. I eyed this exchange with misgivings, as did my companions. Something about it had seemed... inapt.

"Did you come by way of the Trenches or Boris'Thirith?" Kuranen asked. It seemed either an unmindful question, or one of slight insult, for had we come through the Trenches of Avaron, we would be covered in far more than the dust that permeated our clothing.

"Boris'Thirith," Alunen said shortly.

"Why don't you all sit? Delva will bring your food shortly. I will go and let Garonar know that you have all arrived."

We sat at a large ornate table made of marble, in chairs made of finely polished wood with intricate designs.

"Is it just me or does Kuranen seem oblivious?" Adaashar asked.

"She's been this way ever since Hest'Vortal was constructed and they started living in luxury," Norandar said. "Garonar is not much different."

"Our tempers are hot right now," Alunen said. "Let us give them the benefit of the doubt. We never had issue with their lifestyle before."

"Look at what their people have done, Sister," Sveraden said. "They must answer for Vindras Vale."

"I agree," I said. "But let us hear them out... try to keep our anger under control." The others hesitantly agreed.

Moments later, the Sylvaian woman named Delva brought our meals to us upon a cart, giving each of us a porcelain plate filled only with moderate portions. None of us were of the mindset to take an extravagant meal anyway. Delva's eyes met mine; she was Noranite, though neither Norandar nor Alunen seemed to recognize her. But there was something in her eyes that made me feel uneasy—not for her sake, but because it seemed that she was trying to use them to tell me something that she could not say with words. I was reminded of the look in the eyes of the farmhands in Verasian, days earlier... there, the men and women were paid a fair wage for their work, but they had felt trapped in their professions. I wondered if something similar was happening here.

I was about to speak to Delva about it when Kuranen returned and the servant rushed off back to the kitchen. "My husband will be with us shortly," she said. "How are the crudites and lecso?"

"Insipid," Adaashar said shortly.

Kuranen sat down at the lavish table with us and traced one of the intricate line carvings on its surface with her finger, and she said, "Garonar is very eager to talk with you."

"Why is that?" Alunen wondered.

"Because he knows what happened in Vindras Vale. He wants to offer you an explanation."

"He will answer for—" Sveraden said, but I cut her off.

"We will hear him out," I said.

"I understand your concerns," Kuranen said, as if to cajole us into thinking she was on our side. "You must understand that our people have the least favorable land in all of Sylveria."

"And is that the fault of any one of us?" Norandar said harshly.

"Or the animals that these mountains are also home to?" Sveraden added.

"It was your husband who brought you and your people here, was it not?" Alunen said. Kuranen did not answer.

"And it was all for the enticement of the gold and ore and gemstones that all of the Garonites followed," Adaashar finished.

"Why are you all so angry?" Kuranen asked, seeming genuinely surprised; her mind was enthralled by nescience, oblivious entirely as to why any of this would upset us so. Or she was faking it...

"You should be well pleased that it is we who have come," I said. "Rather than Ashysin."

A door swung open upon the wall opposite the kitchen, and Garonar—dressed in his immoderate robes—came through, smiling broadly as he said, "Cousins! How good it is that you are here."

"Save your mendacity and embellishments for your own people, Garonar," Adaashar said harshly.

"Excuse me... have I offended you in some way?"

So far this exchange was not going well. Our tempers had not been cooled by the long trek to Hest'Vortal, our outrage sustained, and we were in no mood for Garonar's verbal antics. But if we were to get anywhere with him we would have to approach this differently. I said, "Let's calm ourselves. Garonar, please, sit with us. There is much to be discussed."

"Well, of course," he said, seeming perplexed by the hostility.

"It is good to see you again, Garonar," I said, now with discretion, knowing that if we piled upon him all of our anger he would only resist. Though they did so with hesitancy, the others followed my lead, nodding. Garonar and Kuranen were, after all, amongst the first of our kind, the First Awakened, and had lived peacefully with us in the Valley of Naiad. They deserved a certain respect, an opportunity to explain the atrocities of their people.

"Uh, well, yes, you too, Alak'kiin," Garonar said. "And all of you. I must say I am surprised by the abhorrence in your tones though. What have I done to offend you all so greatly?"

The others visibly resisted lashing out. We knew his words were only to misdirect our wrath. Calmly I said, "I think you know well why we are here. And as I said, you should feel fortunate that it is we who have come to address this. Ashysin was not pleased."

Now knowing that his cajoling was not going to work, Garonar changed his tone and demeanor. "Yes, Alak'kiin, I have heard of the Dragon's rage. He destroyed our mining operations in the west. It took many men's ingenuity to build the excavators."

"Will you defend your own people in this?" Adaashar asked. "Did you direct them to upturn the whole of Vindras?"

"Of course I did," Garonar said. "There is nothing done under the suns by my people that I am not a part of."

"Why?" I asked. "What are you trying to accomplish there?"

"Our people have grown numerous, Alak'kiin. The vales are the only places we have to farm. The excavators accomplish much for them, expanding the grounds of the land fit for farming, while crushing the ores from the stones of the mountains."

"What of the animals you have displaced by this?" Adaashar said, still holding back. "They have been driven from their homes given to them by the Dragons by your odious contraptions. What of their kind? Where will they find food?"

"They have bred too rapidly," Kuranen said. "Overtaking more land allotted to them than they deserve."

"Nonsense!" Alunen spat, unrestrained. "For since the beginning of this world, long before any of us were awakened, the creatures of Sylveria never multiplied more than what the land could support. It was a world of harmony and balance. It is you and your people who have bred beyond your means!"

"And what am I to say to our people?" Garonar said, now raising his own voice. "Should I tell them that they cannot have children? Shall I allot them only one child per family? And if so, then why should the Garonites be made to suffer this fate while the rest of Sylveria enjoys their large families?"

"You have to be reasonable," I said. "There is always a better way. We cannot unbalance the world for our own gain. The Dragons will surely not suffer us this."

"We have tried moving northward, out of the mountains, into the Hilly Lands, but your people, Norandar and Alunen, have stopped us at every turn, destroying our settlements, coercing our—"

"Stop there, Garonar," Norandar said firmly and fiercely. "We have seen how the Garonites settle the lands. We have seen it with our own eyes. They come and take what is not theirs. We offer to share the lands, but they always want more."

"The Noranites have burned the shacks and cabins of my people!"

"Shacks and cabins built by *our* people," Alunen said, standing, now furious, now even ready to unleash… "Taken from them by yours.…"

"This is not the story I have heard," Kuranen said. "Gamloar was here two days ago, straight away from the Hilly Lands. He said the Noranites would not consent to let the people settle there."

"I cannot vouch for every one of my descendants," Norandar said. "But for all that we have seen, it is not them who are so confrontational."

"So you do not claim the Hilly Lands as part of your land?" Garonar asked.

"I don't claim any of Sylveria as my land! The world is not a place to be divided up and demolished for its resources. It belongs to all of us. So far as I am concerned, your people may settle in the hills, so long as they do not take from the labors of the Noranites."

"Shall we divide the lands there, then?" Kuranen said. "Place a border between that which is part of our domain and yours?"

"Did you not hear Norandar's words?" Adaashar said scathingly. "The land is not a possession. We do not have domains. We do not have anything but what the Dragons have given to us. And what you have been apportioned you are destroying!"

"You cannot keep doing this, Garonar," Sveraden said. "The mountains belonged to the creatures of this realm long before you."

Garonar buried his face in his hands, now seeming careworn, now that his deceptive tactics were not working. "It is not so simple," he muttered. "My people demand more, and I must provide. They are my children, my offspring. It was I who led them into this harsh realm. How are we to survive if we cannot provide ample food for ourselves?"

"Trade with your brothers, the Norgrasharians," I said. "Their farmland is plentiful."

"We do. But they require as trade the gems and ores and compounds derived from the mountains. If we cannot mine the mountains, we have nothing of value to them."

"Take the Hilly Lands then," Norandar resigned. "Our people will be disconcerted, but take the hills as land for farming. We will stay out."

"We cannot compromise like that," Alunen said. "We don't rule over our people as king and queen. They do as they please."

"You are willing to give ground?" Garonar asked, his brow raised, and he seemed astonished that Norandar would compromise.

"Of course. We are willing to help in any way we can. Why didn't you come to us, or someone else, even the Dragons, before you decided to start rending the world?"

"Your people and mine divided long ago," Garonar said. "We took the Mountains, and have regarded this as the extent of our dominion. I suppose we committed to using it only, and we have become desperate."

"We have tried to compromise with your people, Garonar," Alunen said. "You seem repentant now, but will your people be so content to keep to what they are given? Will they continue to steal that which is not theirs?"

"We cannot control what every person of our country does," Kuranen said.

"We will do what we can," Garonar promised, now seeming sincere. "I will assemble the people here, in the Coliseum, and address them."

"There is more you need to do," Sveraden said. "You need to restore the Vale so that the animals can return."

"That will take time, but if we can farm the Hilly Lands, I think we can do this."

"But for how long will this solve the problem?" Kuranen asked. "A few more generations? We will continue to grow in number, for the Garonites love their children..."

"Maybe it is time for some laws...." Garonar said, then barked out loudly, "Delva!"

A moment later the Sylvaian woman who had brought our meals appeared in the hall, standing before Garonar, but not making eye contact. "Yes, lord," she said.

"Send out the Falcons; send word to all of our people that we will assemble here in Hest'Vortal on the eighth day of Summertide."

"Yes, lord."

"Now, Cousins, please, stay with us until then, so that you may see that I am sincere."

Together we agreed—Norandar and Alunen, Adaashar and Sveraden, and me—that we would stay in Hest'Vortal, for indeed we did want to see that Garonar would uphold his word.

The Fall of Boris'Thirith

When invited, my brothers and sisters and I elected not to stay in the palace of our cousins, instead seeking lodging in another part of the city. Kuranen seemed to have taken offence at this, and when we did eat with Garonar in his home that evening, she did not attend. During our stay we visited all corners of this great city and marveled at how far we could see from its walls, for this plateau stood as tall as most of the mountains in the region. To the west we could see Vindras Vale, though not with any clarity; still distraught over its destruction, we were more hopeful that at least this might be resolved and corrected with time. To the south there were mountains as far as could be seen. To the east were the southern end of the Golden Valley and the mountain of Ashysin's temple, which was directly adjacent to Hest'Vortal, though the backside of the mountain faced us and we could see neither the face of the temple nor any sign of the Dragon. There too, extending from a pass below the city to the mountain from which Diras'Vorma was carved, were the remnants of a second hanging bridge much alike to Boris'Thirith. But it had become rarely traveled in recent years, as it had once extended to the façade of Ashysin's temple; now, the Garonites had lost interest in visiting Diras'Vorma.

To the north were endless mountains as well, but far away they gave way to the easternmost reaches of Mara, then to the mountains that formed the Valley of Naiad. And it was there, in the north, during the Hour of Highlight, that even from this distance and from this height we could see the far distant outline of the mountains of Skyreach, as the dark Shadows of Dragonswake fell upon us...

Still, after over three hundred years had passed since we had awakened and first experienced this sight's portentous effect, it affected us, drawing all sense of hope from inside of us, at least for a short time. Still we knew nothing about what caused it, what was beyond the lands of Sylveria, or what was hidden within the veil that might cause such an ominous event. Perhaps, I thought as I viewed it from the heights of Hest'Vortal, we would never know.

The eighth day of Summertide arrived, the day of the Garonites' assemblage, and the messenger Birds of Garonar must have gone out with swiftness, for legions of the people came in from all parts of the mountain realms. Boris'Thirith was monitored closely so that not too many were allowed to cross it at once, for the weight upon it might be too great. We watched from outside of the Coliseum as the multitudes gathered.

That morning, during the Hour of Elation, other visitors arrived by way of the air—Drovanius the Black and Verasian the Green. Upon Verasian rode our cousin, Kalenen, wife of Norgrash'nar, whom I had not seen upon my visit to Mar'Narush. Verasian took Kalenen to the ground, at the center of the arena, which was at this time empty. She dismounted and went into the palace home of her brother and sister. Each of the Dragons then perched upon the towers of the Coliseum, where they waited.

I took this opportunity to go see Kalenen, for I had not had the chance while I was in Mar'Narush, and I longed to not only see her, but to discern where she was in relation to all the things that were happening in her city. Inside the palace, Garonar and Kuranen were too preoccupied with their preparations to give her a proper greeting, and so I took it upon myself...

"Kalenen, I am pleased to see you," I said, approaching her inside the main hall of the palace.

"Alak'kiin," she said coolly. "I missed you in Mar'Narush. As did my husband. Where did you disappear to?"

"Urgent matters arose," I said. "How have you been?"

"The same as always. I serve my people and my husband. Norgrash'nar keeps me only for my status amongst them."

I frowned, for her sake. She had been the one woman chosen last amongst all of her sisters and cousins. She had been Norgrash'nar's second choice, when his yearnings for Nirvisa'nen had yielded nothing for him. He had consented to marry her only so that he might have offspring. And now, nearly three hundred years later, still nothing had changed. I had hoped that with time he would come to love her, to give her the affections she deserved, but this was simply not so, and it was apparent on her features as she spoke. Kalenen made it no secret that she was unhappy in her marriage.

"I am sorry to hear that," I said. "Truly. I wish there was something that could be done for it."

"It is alright. I love him, Alak'kiin. You know this. I always have." Her words seemed impassive, showing neither grief over the lack of her husband's affections nor solidarity on matters of her heart. "What of you, Alak'kiin? Will you ever settle down... marry?"

"I do not think it likely," I admitted. "I am content."

"Are you? Truly?" Her eyes begged the question, and I was forced to consider it.

"There is a difference between contentment and happiness, Kalenen."

"You still think of her, don't you? Nirvisa'nen?"

"At times... yes, of course I do."

"So does he. Norgrash'nar will not admit it to me. But he still thinks of her." I thought to confirm this for her, by telling her of his visit to Nirvisa'nen, but then thought better of it. Nothing would be accomplished by upsetting her. "There is a hidden chamber in our home, in Mar'Narush," she continued. "He thinks I don't know about it. There are portraits of her in there, paintings that he did himself. He disappears sometimes, and I know he goes in there to dwell upon her. He still loves her."

"That seems unhealthy," I said. "I truly am sorry that you could not have what the others could."

Kalenen chortled then, a sarcastic laugh that showed her true dejection. She said, "If only you and I had married, Alak'kiin. Had I known then what I know now, I never would have been with Norgrash'nar, no matter my feelings for him."

Confused a bit, I said, "So you would have me in your position? Married to you while you longed for another?" She glowered and shrugged. "Would you remain so obsessed over him, as he does over Nirvisa'nen?"

"I don't know," she admitted. "And that is why I cannot fault him too much. I love him, as he is."

"Kalenen, there are troubles mounting in this world. There is a growing intolerance amongst your people, and the Garonites, for those who are not like them. I have seen it in Mar'Narush, and I've seen it here. I tell you this because I know it is Norgrash'nar who is behind it. I know that because he could not have Nirvisa'nen he has become aggrieved. I truly am sorry for the hurt it causes you, but now greater and more terrible things are happening because of it. I must ask you… can you help to quell the aggressions of your people, and your husband?"

She looked at me blankly, with such indifference that I had no idea what her next response might be. Then she said, "Alak'kiin, who do you think I blame for my husband's indiscretions?"

"Who is there to blame but him?" Slowly she shook her head, and I was not entirely sure that there was not a grin playing upon her lips. "Kalenen, no one is to blame. No one has made him obsess; no one has endeared him to folly. Only Norgrash'nar is to blame."

"You are wrong, Alak'kiin. I do not blame him. He is but a man, imperfect in many ways, yet to me he is exquisite. Maybe he doesn't love me as I desire, but I love him. And it is the Sylvai who have brought grief to him. Alim'dar has tainted our bloodlines. So has Sarak'den; the Sylvai seek to eradicate us."

"Your words are absurd," I said, now surprised, for she was speaking of the same inequitable ideas as her husband.

"Absurd? I'll tell you what is absurd, Alak'kiin… It is absurd that you would side with the Sylvai. You are like them, but you are not. You have been broken by Nirvisa'nen as well. Do not think that you are untarnished."

A certain indignation was rising within me and I felt a flush of anger. "It is true that I was once hurt by Nirvisa'nen," I admitted. "But there is a difference, Kalenen... I have not become corrupted by it. I have not held on. I want more for Nirvisa'nen's happiness than my own. This is the difference between love and obsession."

"There is no difference," she said. "There is only love and enmity. I cannot have my husband's love, but I can have requital. I can bring those who have harmed him to justice. I will *not* squelch the passions and prejudices of my people, or Norgrash'nar. Not when it is all justified."

"Then we are done here," I said, and I left the chamber, furious at her words, and wondering how such debasement had permeated so many people of the world.

The harangue of Garonar was about to begin; the crowds finished flooding in and filled the Coliseum. By the Hour of Awakening most of the people had gathered. Boris'Thirith was empty again, and those who had been assigned to watch over the bridge also came into the city Coliseum as well. In no way feeling an urgency to get in the middle of the crowds, we lingered back until the way in was less congested.

Although we could, no doubt, be given special seating near Garonar, we instead found our own seats, not wanting attention drawn to us. For this, we found, to my dismay—but not surprise—that there was a certain section along the highest rows of seating that were designated for the Sylvai, Haldusians and Darians that might be present in Hest'Vortal. They were not excluded from such events, but they were kept apart. There were hundreds of Sylvai in the section, and we scaled the many steps until we were amongst them.

We were recognized there amongst our own people, and excitement filled that small area of the stadium, so much so that we had to silence them when at last Garonar began to speak.

He stood upon the dais that came out of his palace, which was raised higher than the lowest rows of seating, and through magical effects he was able to amplify his own voice, much as Norgrash'nar had done in Mar'Narush. Next to him on one side was his wife, Kuranen, and on the other Kalenen. So too were his sons and daughters there present.

It was just as he began that shadows fell upon parts of the Coliseum; we looked up and two more Dragons had just arrived—Ashysin and Merilinder—and neither looked much more pleased than they had before, in Vindras Vale. But they remained silent.

"People of Hest'Vortal, Garonites, Dragons, and all other visitors amongst us… I have called this assemblage today to announce a new direction for the people of our region. This will be followed by festivities and contests." The crowd grew silent as he spoke, for amongst the Garonites he was well respected. "There has been conflict in recent seasons with our northern neighbors, the Noranites, over the settlements in the Hilly Lands. For both our peoples have staked a claim to the region. But with negotiation I have secured our right to settle these lands, unhindered by our rivals." The Garonites cheered at this revelation.

Norandar and Alunen perked up and looked at each other, scowling at Garonar's words. So too did the Noranites amongst the Sylvai seem offended, as did Ashysin, whose scowl had not left his features since he first arrived in Vindras Vale, days earlier. Never had any of them considered the Garonites to be rivals, but in reality, these mountain people had become obsessed with competition even amongst themselves and it was unsurprising that they viewed the situation this way, regardless of its merit.

Garonar continued, "We will also hereafter cease the mining operations in Vindras Vale and all throughout the mountains. We will reseed the land to restore it to its former… glory." The Garonites seemed less enthused by this, but Ashysin and Merilinder seemed somewhat appeased, though this offering was a long way from clemency.

Then, before he continued, Kalenen, his sister, leaned over to him and whispered something into his ear. He considered her words for a moment, then nodded. He said to the people, "For it is given to me in understanding that the expansion of our people will not be tolerated by the Dragon in whose domain we dwell. To him is more precious the beasts of the fields and the Birds of the air than the people he has come to abhor!"

Cries of rage rose throughout the crowd. Ashysin flexed his wings, enraged at this accusation, snarling in distaste, for the words of Garonar were far from truth. The Dragon had always loved all of the creatures of the world equally. Only when the serenity of his natural domain had been attacked had he shown any such abhorrence.

Garonar, knowing full well that Ashysin was growing angry, said, "And so we will, for now, do as the *great* Ashysin commands us, through the mouths of his loyal followers, and perhaps someday we will find favor in his eyes once more!"

Ashysin could contain himself no more, and his voice sounded out over the whole of the crowd, "*Never have I abhorred you, Garonar, or your people. Only when you seek to destroy my domain do I grow angry. And I am angry, now, Garonar, for your mindless activities have driven the peaceful creatures of this realm away, and you have unbalanced the world!*"

"You see?" Garonar cried out to the crowd. "The Dragon wishes to squelch our progress. It is he who is to blame for ceasing our operations in Vindras Vale! And his people, the First Awakened Sylvai who are his messengers have directed me to disallow the breeding of our own people."

"Lies!" Ashysin cried out, and he leaped into the air. Merilinder knew full well what was happening here, and he followed along with Ashysin. But Drovanius and Verasian seemed confused, unaware of the intricacies of the things now transpiring. Sveraden and Adaashar, and Alunen and Norandar were also on their feet, shouting out their own outrage; the other Sylvai followed suit; for they had long been living amongst the Garonites and had been made to feel inferior.

"Lies, you say?" Garonar continued. "So is it not true that you destroyed the machines of our advancements in Vindras Vale? Is it not true that you would have us driven from the mountains?" Cries of the Nescrai rang out, furious and incensed at this perceived denigration that Garonar was falsely inspiring in the people. "And is it not also true that you have loathing in your heart for all of the Nescrai?"

Ashysin broke; he rose high above the Coliseum. Drovanius called out to him, "Remember your oath, Brother!" but he left not his perch, nor did Verasian.

"I remember our oath! I always will!" And then he let out a terrifying shriek at the Garonites, displaying his displeasure, but only inciting the people to find truth in Garonar's deceptive words. "You may stay in these mountains so long as you desire!" Ashysin said spitefully. "And if you want to leave, you may crawl through your own filth!"

The Gold Dragon circled around to the west then and disappeared from view. Merilinder was with him. But here at the highest level of the Coliseum, we could see through the openings provided between the pillars. The Dragons, with enraged purpose, soared down to the bridge of Boris'Thirith, and with each of them grasping one end of it in their giant claws, they tore it from its foundations and dropped its remnants into the chasm below. Now, the Garonites, all of those who were within the city, were trapped in Hest'Vortal, with only one way out—through the Trenches of Avaron.

The Trenches of Avaron

"That was unexpected," Adaashar said.

"I have never seen any Dragon act with such rage," Sveraden said. "I am not sure I like it."

"They were pushed to their limit," I said. "And their anger is not unrighteous. Through lies and deceit Garonar is trying to incite the people against the Dragons. And us."

"But why?"

"They have grown arrogant," Alunen said. "They feel entitled to the world around them, caring not who they take from. This was demonstrated in Southern Mara."

"And what now?" Norandar said. "Most of the Garonites are trapped here."

"They are not trapped," Sveraden said. "There are the trenches. Perhaps that will humble them...."

"There is surely only so much food in Hest'Vortal," Norandar said. "How will they eat?"

"We're stuck here too," Alunen said.

"Everything will be all right," I assured. "For all of us. See, Drovanius and Verasian look concerned, but they will figure out that they have but to bring supplies in. Ashysin did not intend to harm the people, only to ostracize them, and as Sveraden said, humble them. When the Dragons calm down, they will restore order."

"I am not so sure," Adaashar said. "They may be beyond such abilities, for the Garonites' actions are beyond reason. They will no doubt claim that men and women were on the bridge of Boris'Thirith, that they broke their oath, even though we know it not to be true. Their minds are broken, twisted in their self-importance. It is the same that is happening in Mar'Narush... the people have become unscrupulous."

"And it remains," Sveraden said. "That the Vales are in ruins and the animals without their natural habitats. Ashysin will not forgive so easily. Not now."

"And I doubt that Garonar will even honor his word to restore the Vales."

"We need to seek Kronaggas. He will have answers for us."

"It is no short path through the Trenches," Alunen said.

"And a path I don't think any of us would prefer."

"Many of the people will be leaving in the coming days," Norandar said. "If we are going to leave, we should do it soon."

Now, as we discussed these matters, the Sylvai who were in the Coliseum near us were gathering around and some were listening, for we spoke in loud tones as the roar of the crowds beyond was mighty. But I had not forgotten about them, and I said, now loud enough for them all to hear, "Are they any of you who wish to get out of Hest'Vortal?'

One man said, "This is my home. We are not treated the best here, but my family has lived here for generations."

Another said, "Everything we own is here, everything we have worked for."

A woman said, "My husband and I would like to leave, and our children. We are both tired of servitude."

"Servitude?" I said. Indeed, things here seemed much like in Mar'Narush. "You are forced into labor?"

"We are not treated terribly," she said. "At least not how you might think. But we are kept from personal ambitions by our lords. We have long sought to get out of Hest'Vortal, but we don't know where to go."

"Anywhere," Adaashar said. "Come to the south with us, or to the north with Norandar. Now would be the time, all of you. There will be much confusion in the city for many days. Follow the path of the Trenches, out of the city. There is but one way to go. They will lead you into the southern region of Mara."

"Let us get together," the woman's husband said. "We will meet and decide if we stay or go. But you are of the First Awakened... you have other matters to tend to. Do not be constrained by us."

Adaashar nodded. They were right, of course. There was urgency in our future, and we needed not to be slowed down by refugees. There were strong men amongst the Sylvai, and they would be fine.

And so we agreed that we had little choice but to leave the city by way of the Trenches of Avaron, and that the sooner we departed the better. There was nothing left to be done here in Hest'Vortal.

Most people still remained in the Coliseum. Those who had not seen the destruction of the bridges by Ashysin and Merilinder soon heard about it as word spread through the multitude. Chaos erupted, and even Garonar's augmented voice could no longer be heard. Finally he gave up and he, Kuranen and Kalenen returned to the inside of their palace. Drovanius and Verasian were left speechless as well; unsure what they could do, they remained in place as hundreds, even thousands of the Garonites cried out to them.

The Sylvai amongst us moved as a group, as a small mob pushing through the frenzied crowd, so that we might get out. They had heard of our plans to escape Hest'Vortal and to find Kronaggas the White, so as to help sort out the mess that had become of this nation in these strange times. And so with their help we were able to get out of the Coliseum and back onto the streets of the city.

The streets had yet to become congested, but I knew this would not last long. Once people realized they were stuck in the city, every lodging house in all of Hest'Vortal would be filled. Citizens would rush back to their own homes to safeguard their possessions and secure their own homes from occupation. There were others on the streets already, but not so many that the five of us were unable to move about freely.

Now, to understand why we had been hesitant to take the Trenches of Avaron, the layout and construction of Hest'Vortal must be understood.

When the Garonites first decided to settle the plateau, they had amongst them a city engineer named Avaron who had drawn up plans for it, and he had installed first, beneath what would become the city streets, culverts so that rainwater would flow out of the city, and down into a singular gorge that was to the northeast of the plateau. As the city was developed so too were added public latrines throughout, and within most structures. The sewers were washed out by a constant flow of water that was held in storage receptacles that were scattered throughout the city.

And so as it was, all of the city waste exited the city into the gorge that became known as Avaron's Trenches. Over time, the trenches created a stench that would linger in the ravine and when a north wind would arise this odor would drift up into the city. Even Ashysin had complained that the stank would sometimes drift into his temple. So they began adding lime and other absorbent stone and minerals to the trenches to keep it under control. In the beginning, wagons full of lime were dumped into the sewers from the streets, but soon this was not enough, as it frequently coalesced along the stone drain, and not enough was getting to the necessary places. The solution to this was to construct a singular roadway that went from the city to the floor of the valley. Workers then could take as much lime as necessary, and with time they brought it under control. Yet still, there was by far a difference between the stench of the sewers of the city and the lower lands which held in the filth and fetor.

At a small city gate we were able to pass through onto the roadway and down into the trenches. Now the gorge itself was far below the city and it extended far beyond where the waste was deposited. The first part of the trial of the trenches was to survive the nearly toxic fumes that permeated the floor of the valley, for in the heat of the Summer Seasons, as it was, the odors became even more pungent. We covered our faces with cloth as we delved to the end of the road and into the trench.

Many Insects inhabited the Trench, as it was their lot in life to feast upon the waste so as to aid in the natural process of keeping the world clean. The mountains were steep-sided, and so there were few places that we could step without getting into the muck, but it was not as if it were mostly fresh waste, but rather most had been dried out by the suns or by nature. Much of it had returned to the earth. But still, it was an unpleasant trek through the first part of the trench. Once we came out of this area of Avaron's Trench, we were faced with a long journey ahead, for there were nearly fifteen Marches of valley and gorge to travel before a passable place was found, just on the southeast corner of Mara.

At the dawning of the Hour of Eventide that day, we came out of the worst, though shortest, stretch of the trench and began our long and winding way back to Mara. It would be two days before we could come back out of the mountains, and another two before we could reach

Kronaggas Mountain. And even then we were unsure if we would find the Dragon there.

But at the Hour of Passions we were greeted with a most welcome surprise, for Drovanius the Black came out of Hest'Vortal in our direction and saw us, and knowing us well, he landed in the valley before us.

"Alak'kiin, Norandar, Alunen, Adaashar, Sveraden… it is good to see all of you." As always, the Dragon spoke with slow and concise words. "If only it were under better circumstances."

"And you, old friend," I said.

"You were in the Coliseum, I understand."

"Yes."

"And it was you who came with Ashysin, those whom Garonar referred to as *his people*?"

"Yes," I said, then explained. "We were with Ashysin and Merilinder in Vindras Vale, when they first arrived to see its destruction. We came to Hest'Vortal upon Kronaggas' instruction, to confront Garonar. The words he spoke, Drovanius… the things he said… his words were twisted versions of the truth."

"Of that I have no doubt," the Dragon said. "Nevertheless, I think that Ashysin's reaction was… unwarranted."

"Perhaps it was," Norandar said to him. "But what of the Garonites? They are far from innocent. Have you seen Vindras Vale?"

"I have not."

"Have you seen the Southern Reaches," Adaashar wondered. "Where the great masses of animals have been driven out of the mountains?"

"I have not."

"The world is on fire right now, Drovanius," I said. "We must get to Kronaggas to seek his counsel."

"You will not find Kronaggas in his temple," the Dragon said. "For he is occupied, I understand, with the transfer of food and grain for the beasts in the south. And who knows what terrors Ashysin and Merilinder are unleashing?"

"Terrors? You talk as if they have committed some great atrocity!"

"How is it not?" Drovanius asked. "They have destroyed the way in and out of Hest'Vortal, a bridge that I myself helped to raise for them over two hundred years ago. Do you know how long it will take for us to transport the people, until the bridges can be repaired?"

"The people will survive," Sveraden said. "Ashysin and Merilinder committed not an act of aggression, but of retribution."

"Call it what you will, but they are treading upon a very thin line and if they step off, their ancient vow will be broken."

"They would not harm the people," Alunen assured. "You know this, Drovanius."

"Perhaps. But times have changed much since you were all young, living in the Valley of Naiad, just thirteen in number. There are divisions amongst the people, of old remorse and new dissidence."

"Yes," I agreed. "The world is not so simple as it once was."

"And what are we to do for it, Alak'kiin? The suns and moon follow their courses, the Seasons turn in their cycles, and the creatures of the world go on as they always have. But the people whom Dragons first awoke have grown numerous in the land. They are not of this world; they are not capable of being one with Sylveria. And yet we love you all, for you are our children. And now we see such conflicts arising, and what are we to do? Isolate ourselves? No... we must resolve these things as best as we can, and not go tearing down bridges."

"You are not wrong, Drovanius," Norandar said. "But our children—all of them—must not disrupt the world either. We cannot allow the Garonites or anyone else to bring destruction to the lands, to upset the balance of nature. Go to Vindras Vale and see the destruction for yourself."

"I will," Drovanius promised. "And I will, in time, deal with the Garonites, for they are my children. And for now I can take you where you will go."

"Adaashar and I need to return to our lands, to tend the animals, to do what we can. Will you take us?"

"I will. I am equipped with a saddle for three. I will take you now, if you please and leave you at Sairvon Pass, and I will see Vindras Vale for myself. Then I will return for the rest of you, by Lastlight."

We spent some time then talking to Adaashar and Sveraden and saying our farewells. And then they departed to the west.

"Where will you go, Alak'kiin?" Alunen asked.

"To Kronaggas Mountain, I suppose. Perhaps I will find Kronaggas there, or perhaps he will find me upon the Plains. After that, I think it wise to go to Aranthia. Haldus'nar and Sarak'den need to know of all that has happened."

"We should return to Mara," Norandar said. "We will have the people stay clear of the Hilly Lands, so that our end of the agreement will be honored at least. Let the Garonites settle there if they can benefit more than us."

"And we will inform Alim'dar of all that is happening," Alunen said.

Late that day, before Aros disappeared into the Veil, Drovanius returned. He said to us, "The destruction in Vindras Vale is, as you said, complete. It will be many years before it can recover. Alak'kiin, Kronaggas is not in his home. He was last seen flying eastward, toward Aranthia."

"Can you take me there, then, to Eswear'Nysin?"

"I can," the Dragon said. He remained with us that night, and at Firstlight we mounted him and flew to the western edge of the Plains of Kronaggas, where I departed from my brother and sister. They traveled on by foot to the west, and I carried on to the east with the Black Dragon. My next visitation would be in the lands of Aranthia the Crimson.

JOURNEY TO ESWEAR'NYSIN

Upon the quick black wings of Drovanius I soared across the lands, over the Valley of Naiad, through Yor'Kavon Pass, through the Lowlands of Forthran, then above the forested region of Felheim, in the northernmost reaches of Verasian's Domain. Then we came to the Sea of Repose. It was this sea that held the calmest waters in all of Sylveria, for the northward currents that passed between the Horn of Aranthia and the region of Onilmar met with the east-flowing fluxes of the Dragonmere Channel. The courses of these waterways there canceled out one another, and one could sit upon a vessel there for many hours without any drift.

The day was half passed when we came back to land, over the Hills of Tiiga—so named for the second daughter of Haldus'nar and my sister, Sarak'den. There Tiiga'sin had settled long ago, when the Haldusians first moved to the domain of Aranthia. And when we passed over Varis Lake and onto the Highlands it was the Hour of Devotion. There, in the high places of this realm, stood the towering city of Eswear'Nysin, home of my beloved sister and her husband, the Nescrai man Haldus'nar, whom I considered more of a brother than a cousin.

The city was unique in all of Sylveria, for it was built upon the very heights of the Cliffs of Aranthia, which dropped down into the Vagrant Sea. From the peak of the Highlands the cliffs fell a distance of twenty Spans straight down onto fallen earth and hewn boulders that were rushed over by the ocean waters. Eswear'Nysin was, in its entirety, a singular giant tower that rose five spans above the highlands.

The construction of this city was one of the most ambitious projects ever undertaken by both Naiad and Dragon, and Aranthia the Crimson had been instrumental in the hauling of the stones from the lower lands of his island to the very peak of the Highlands. The city measured four times as wide as it was tall, and each of the levels was like a village unto itself. Amongst the Haldusians were many stoneworkers, and so both the interior and the exterior stones were expertly carved and placed so that not a single hair might pass between the square blocks. Great windows covered all faces of the cylindrical tower, granting cooling airflows that passed throughout. During the Winter Seasons these could be sealed, and so the warmth of the tower's hearth could be contained.

Lining each of the fifty levels of the city, upon the outer walls, were mantles wide enough for a man to walk comfortably along. Mounted on these ledges were carved stone statues in the likeness of imaginary creatures that seemed a cross between Dragon and Naiad. They called these *Gargoyles,* and these sculptures looked out over Aranthia and the Vagrant Sea in all directions.

The people of Eswear'Nysin had always been content living in the tower, for it was so large that they felt not confined. But not all of the Haldusians lived in this city, for in the lowlands there were many farming villages that grew gardens and held vineyards that supplied the entire domain with food and wine in exchange for the crafted tools forged in the city.

In the early years of the settlements, the Steeds of Felheim had been imported to Aranthia to serve as mounts that could traverse both the Highlands and the Lowlands. But the spirited horse-like creatures had proved difficult to tame. It was these creatures that Aisar, keeper of the Druugal in Oman'Tar, had come here some years ago to domesticate. He had been successful and a number of the Felheim could be seen in a highland field surrounding the tower city of Eswear'Nysin as we approached.

The Felheim were like horses, yet their bodies were covered in scales rather than hair; their manes were like those of a reptile—soft, caudal spikes that ran down the ridge of their spines. Their eyes were red like fire, and their hooves were large and hard; they were perfectly adaptable to the island of Aranthia and the needs of its people.

The top of the tower city was a garden unmatched by any in all of Sylveria. Trees and plants of various kinds had been brought from all corners of the world to be a part of this high landscape that served as a retreat for the citizens of Eswear'Nysin. When I arrived at the city on the back of Drovanius the Black, it was in a large clearing in this garden that we landed, for already there present was Aranthia the Crimson, who spent much of his time on these exquisite grounds.

So too were Haldus'nar and Sarak'den there, for they had been alerted to the arrival of Drovanius. When I dismounted, they approached with warm greetings and pleasantries, as was customary for the Haldusians. Sarak'den embraced me tightly, saying nothing—she didn't have to, for it was always pleasant for us both to find one another's company. Haldus'nar too clasped me genially by the shoulders.

"You have delivered Alim'dar's gift for Nirvisa'nen to him?"

"I have," I said. "He was most grateful for your fine work."

"We did not expect you to return to us so soon," Sarak'den said.

"Nor did I," I replied. It had been only two seasons since I had been here, though with all that had happened upon the Mainland, it seemed like much longer.

There must have been a look of distress on my features, for Sarak'den then said, "You look... well-traveled. Is all well in Sylveria?"

"It is not," I said. "Much has happened in Hest'Vortal. There are strange things amiss with Norgrash'nar."

"Tell us," Haldus'nar said.

As I explained everything that had occurred since we had last been together, we walked throughout the garden. So too did Drovanius and Aranthia converse with one another, for these events were matters that concerned all of the Dragons as well.

When I had finished my tale, Haldus'nar said, "Both Garonar and Norgrash'nar have grown conceited. I have seen it myself. Once, we traded extensively with the Norgrasharians, being as close as we are with just the narrow sea dividing our countries. But in recent years this has dwindled to nearly nothing."

Sarak'den added, "And we have heard rumors from our port towns that the reason for this is because they have grown to despise our people, that they look down on the Haldusians because they are neither Nescrai nor Sylvai, but a mix of both. They think this makes us inferior."

"I got the same sense when I was in Mar'Narush, and amongst the Garonites."

"I do not understand what this growing aversion is," Haldus'nar said.

"I think I know," I said. Sarak'den nodded her understanding, but the man still seemed unsure what exactly I was hinting at. I explained, "Norgrash'nar still loves Nirvisa'nen, Haldus'nar. Have you not seen this?"

"I have not considered it," he admitted. "He is still in love with her after so long? It has been nearly three hundred years since she and Alim'dar were married. He has been wed to Kalenen for just as long. Why do you think this is true?"

"He visited her recently in Nirvisa'Iinid."

"So. We have done so as well."

"He visited *only* her," I said. "And in secret. He professed his continuing love to her."

"She told you this?"

"Yes. Out of her own mouth, Haldus'nar. And Kalenen confirmed it for me when I talked to her in Hest'Vortal."

"How could this have gone on so long and it be kept from us?"

"I think it is just his way. He has moved on, at least to some measure, but still holds on to his feelings, a growing madness. Things are not right with him at all."

"His loathing of our people tells me that," Sarak'den said. "He has no reason to despise us so."

"And what does Aranthia say about this... all of it?"

"He knows something is amiss," Haldus'nar explained. "He knows that there is more going on than has been revealed, and he thinks that even Drovanius is a part of it."

"A part of it? Since when do the Dragons concern themselves so intimately with the relationships of the people?"

"Apparently since Norgrash'nar first loved Nirvisa'nen," Sarak'den said. "If all this is true then I think it reveals something else about him, maybe about all that has been happening."

"Norgrash'nar and Drovanius have become increasingly enamored with one another's acrimony," Haldus'nar said. "We have seen it. Aranthia has seen it. Before we didn't know why. Now... I don't know... Perhaps Drovanius has become immersed in Norgrash'nar's affairs, even those of his heart."

I had not before considered any of this, yet when they spoke of it, a chord was struck within me, for Drovanius' words to us in the Trenches of Avaron had seemed odd, even out of place for the character of the Dragon that I had known. For in years past, Drovanius had always been proud, but he was righteous as well. But he had seemingly defended the Garonites, or had in the least condemned Ashysin's and Merilinder's behavior.

"There is something alight in your mind, Alak'kiin," Haldus'nar said. "You know this to be true?"

"Yes, perhaps," I said, hesitant to leap to any conclusions. "He spoke of the events in Hest'Vortal as if Ashysin and Merilinder had committed the gravest of acts, as if they had nearly broken their vow never to harm any of the Naiad."

"And did they?" Sarak'den asked. "Did they harm anyone?"

"Of course not," I said. "They sought only retribution for an offense to nature."

"Yes," Haldus'nar said. "And make no mistake, what they did was not in accordance with any wrongdoing. They acted in righteousness, for to defend the world we live in is of the greatest honor.

"Do not be fooled by the wiles of Norgrash'nar or his brother. Let us make no mistake, Alak'kiin, they may no longer be the men and women whom we grew to love in those first years of our lives, in the Valley of Naiad. The world has changed; when we were awakened, something new entered into this world. Something that was not meant to be."

"What do you mean?"

"Do you not recall the words of our wedding vows? Those which were spoken first to us, and since, to all those who have been bonded together in marriage?"

"I have not considered it... It was always a mystery, what it meant."

Sarak'den then quoted the words of unity, "*Let our diminished souls be reborn, Numen. Let us be redeemed. Let us together be reunited as the purest of Amaranthi.*"

"As I said, a mystery."

"Indeed," Haldus'nar said. "For what is *Amaranthi*? This word is foreign to our tongue, and Kronaggas never would tell us what it means. Yet these very vows imply that we are not of this world—even Kronaggas said that in marriage our souls become bound to this world."

Sarak'den said, "When we were awakened in Naiad, over three hundred years ago, we were not new spirits, Alak'kiin."

"Then what were we?" I asked. "Why do we not recall anything from before?"

"That we do not know," Sarak'den admitted. "Even Aranthia is unsure. But the point is that we are creatures of great potential—to do good, or to do that which violates nature. What is natural is love and peace and harmony—things that both Norgrash'nar and Garonar have forgotten, and defiled."

"And which Ashysin and Merilinder defended," Haldus'nar added. "Their fury was virtuous. Soon, when we can be alone with Aranthia, he will explain more of this... for he has a better grasp upon the happenings of Sylveria than anyone, save perhaps Kronaggas—who is seemingly always silent on matters of greater importance."

I turned to look at the Dragons, wondering if Haldus'nar and Sarak'den might be right, that Drovanius had been taken by the rancor of Norgrash'nar, who remained embittered by his love for Nirvisa'nen. And perhaps, I considered, he had drawn his brother, Garonar into imprudent thoughts and actions as well.

Within the garden, the Dragons were, it seemed, in a heated discussion, though from the distance we had attained, I could not make out their words. Then suddenly Drovanius was airborne and took flight back to the east. Aranthia surveyed the garden, looking for us. We hurried back to him.

"Where has Drovanius gone?" I asked.

"Back to Mar'Narush," Aranthia said. "He has told me of the events at Hest'Vortal. We must make haste to resolve this situation. The Garonites are not yet all beguiled. We can save them."

"What do you mean, beguiled?"

"We have been watching the other Nescrai for some time," the Dragon explained to me. "We have seen the corruption that is seeping into them and their societies. Understand, Alak'kiin, that matters of this world are developing swiftly, even quickening. Drovanius has entertained the debasement of our children, the Nescrai. I do not know where Sharuseth, Merobassi and Verasian stand. But we must rectify this quickly, with authority and propriety. For that we will need Kronaggas."

"We must convince him," Haldus'nar said. "To reveal more to us, more of what we are, where we came from. There is a darkness that we cannot comprehend that is pervading the reason of the Nescrai."

"Let me speak with him, if I can find him," I said. "As you have found amity here with Aranthia, and others with the Dragons of their countries, I have found an affinity with Kronaggas."

"Very well, Alak'kiin," Aranthia said.

"We should go to Alim'dar and Nirvisa'nen," Sarak'den said. "We do not yet know where they stand in all of this. They may well be entrenched with the madness as well."

"That is doubtful," I said. "I was there, in Whitestone, not long ago, and I sensed none of the animosities as I did in Mar'Narush and Hest'Vortal."

"We will see," Sarak'den said.

"I will go to Hest'Vortal and do all I can to restore peace," Aranthia promised, "And to help the Garonites. They cannot exist long there as things are. There are too many of them and no source of food upon the plateau."

The following day, upon the wings of Aranthia the Crimson, I left Eswear'Nysin along with Haldus'nar and Sarak'den. Late that day, which was the tenth day of Summertide, 310, we came to land again, now upon the Plains of Kronaggas, at Kal'Taisin. We said our farewells there, and Aranthia, Haldus'nar and Sarak'den continued on to the northwest, toward the lands of Alim'dar.

Though none of us knew it then, as we departed, it would be many years before any of my siblings would see me again.

The Book of

Shadows

The Temple of Kronaggas

It was the tenth day of Summertide, 310, when Aranthia the Crimson left me upon the Plains of Kronaggas. As I walked to the northwest toward the White Dragon's Temple, I tried to gather all of my thoughts, for so much had happened over the course of the last seasons. My travels throughout this time had brought me full circle, from Mara, through Naiad, around the vast region of Verasian, across the Southern Sea, northward through the Southern Reaches, through the Mountains of Ashysin, to the Highlands of Aranthia, and now back onto the Plains between Mara and Naiad.

I was upon the plains not far from where my brothers, sisters and I had first come into contact with the Dragons, so long ago. This place was marked with a large pile of stones and was called *Kal'Taisin,* for it had been here, in this very spot, where the seven Sylvai had first met the Dragons, face-to-face. From there it was less than a March to the beginning of the Sanguine Artery, which was the crimson pathway that led up into the Mountain of Kronaggas. I covered that distance by the end of The Hour of Awakening and began my ascent into the Temple of the White Dragon.

I did not expect the Dragon to be there, for Drovanius had said he was not; still, I felt compelled to go into the temple, for it had always seemed a place of comfort to me. While the temples of the other Dragons had always been quiet and serene places, this temple had always filled me with a greater peace of spirit that I supposed rose out of the purity of Kronaggas himself. He had been the first of all Dragons and was wise and knowledgeable beyond all others.

Another Hour passed before I came to the top of the Artery and stood in front of the cavern entrance that was large enough for a Dragon to fly through. As I passed into the dark passage I walked slowly so as to give my eyes time to adjust to the light. It was not so dark as it had been long ago, when I had first come into these halls, when the other Naiad and myself had come here for the first time upon the day of the marriage of Norandar and Alunen. Since that time the once rich stone walls covered in deposits of gold and silver had been stripped and were now adorned with ornate carvings made onto the inside of the mountain. There were depictions of each of the eight Dragons, as well as each of the First Awakened Naiad, their children, and the first generations. These had been done by the stoneworkers of the family of Haldus'nar and Sarak'den upon the dedication of this mountain as Kronaggas' Temple. The Dragonfather had not at all objected, and indeed he wondered why he had not decorated before.

Within the eyes of each of the stone carvings of the Dragons were magical lights of the various colors that corresponded to the Dragon itself. These were bright enough to sufficiently light the way deeper into the temple.

Ahead was the main sanctuary where Kronaggas made his bed of shining gems and minerals and stones, and where one would always find him if he were home. I entered this cavern and there found no Dragon at all, as expected. I had known it was likely futile to waste time coming into the Temple of Kronaggas, as I felt an urgency in trying to help my siblings and the Dragons resolve the matters of these troubling times; yet I also felt a strange and unexplainable need to be here... or somewhere inside the stone mountain.

I looked around the vast chamber and I recalled that there was a multitude of passages that branched off from the main entrance hall and this main hollow. I had rarely ventured into any of them, as there had never been any need to do so. So too did there now seem little reason to explore... but even as this thought touched my mind did I notice that to the far side of the room was a glowing fissure in the wall—one that I had never ventured into. Why it should be glowing I did not know, and I found it most curious.

Then I realized, as I found myself drawing nearer to it, that it was not a glow of any natural or typically magical accord, but rather it was an aura. This was a kind of magic that I had been touched with only on rare occasions in the past, the first being long ago upon the night that I pursued the Nescrai across the Hills of Nightrun. Then, I had been able to see a faint glow about the hills, and about all things natural in the world around me. Then, it had been a magic that had awakened my awareness so that I could accomplish something I desired.

The light coming from the passage in Kronaggas' chamber was the same—a faint blue—yet it was not like before when it had illuminated and traced the outline of all things. Instead, it lit only this one passage. It was the same—yet it was different, because by no will of my own did this light show itself. It was not my magic at all, but something else...

It drew me closer; I moved slowly, not with caution but with prolonged anticipation. At the entrance into the passage I stopped, peering down the unadorned passage that disappeared around a bend just ahead. I knew that whatever was in there was something I was supposed to find, something I was supposed to see...

I stepped into the light, and I was filled with a warmth unlike anything I had felt before. Whenever Aros shined its light upon me, I was warmed by its energy. Whenever I bathed in the hot springs in Whitestone, I was filled with a comforting and soothing heat. And whenever I was with my dearest of friends, I was consumed with a kind of warmth of spirit... But this was different than it all; it was something new, something good, and something that permeated the whole of my existence. It was love, peace, absolute tranquility of mind and soul—it was divine.

I moved deeper into the passage and came around the corner, where the light continued, compelling me onward, down a path that seemed far away but welcoming. My heart began to race with delight, though I could not understand why... for what could be at the end of this course that would inspire such mounting elation?

The further in I walked the more intense the radiance became, the more absolute. I was filled with an intense longing to understand what was happening, what was ahead, what was the light...

And then it came into view—just ahead—a figure, a stranger. It was a man unlike any I had seen before. He was different than me, different than the Naiad, either Sylvai or Nescrai. He was short in stature and he appeared... strange, for his skin was wrinkled, his hair gray, his stance slouched. But his eyes stared into mine.

"Alak'kiin," he said. His voice was warmer even than the surrounding light. "It is good to see you, again."

I was perplexed by his words, for though I was not certain of many things at that moment, I was entirely sure that I had never met this man. "Who are you?" I asked.

"You know who I am. Or you will."

"I don't understand."

"Then listen, and you will. For you, this world is just beginning. For me, all things are at their end. But this is not cause for alarm. What will be will be."

"Who are you?"

"I have been called by many names, but know this, Alak'kiin... I am the Light. And you will soon learn what this means... I have called you here, to this time and place, so that you may be given a seed of understanding."

"But I don't understand...."

"A tree does not spring into existence fully grown, but is started as a seed that develops. It grows with time and with nourishment. So is the order of creation. You too will grow, your understanding ever increasing. And you will be a light to this world."

"What are you talking about?"

The stranger laughed, humored, I supposed, by his own enigmatic words. Either that or he was touched with madness... "Alak'kiin, you are not meant to understand all things. Not yet. But you will. Have patience. Kronaggas will enlighten you further... soon."

"What more can you tell me?" I asked, thinking then that the stranger was about to draw this visitation to an end.

"I can say no more."

"I have learned nothing. Why did you draw me here? Only to add confusion to my mind? There are things happening in the world, and I don't know where this will all lead. Have you come here to help or to do something else?"

"I have come because I have missed you... but also so that you may be touched by the Light... You are chosen, Alak'kiin."

"Chosen? For what and by whom?"

"Chosen by chance, perhaps. Or chosen by your own choices... It does not matter. But you must accept this. You must commit to the Light if you will."

"What does that mean?"

"The Light transcends all things. The Light is righteousness, goodness, and rightness. You must become a Servant of the Light if you are to uncover your destiny."

"Destiny? I do not understand this word."

"You will. The Dragon will make it known to you."

"I *do not understand*—"

"Alak'kiin," the stranger said. His voice was soft and consoling. "Come toward me, if you will."

There was no question in my mind that I would do as he said. I was compelled not by his words but by my curiosity, my own longing to be nearer to the Light... I stepped toward him; his head came only to my chest, and he looked up at me with such love and compassion in his eyes that I did not at that moment doubt that he was a force of goodness. Then the stranger winked at me, and he reached out and placed the palm of his hand on my chest. A power beyond comprehension surged through me, as though I had been struck by all of the light and energy of the heavenly bodies all in one instant. It overwhelmed me, and I fell to the stony ground, rendered speechless, blinded, even incapable of moving.

Then I felt something I had felt only once before, three hundred and ten years earlier, just before I had first awakened inside of a cave—I felt disembodied. I was not in the Temple of Kronaggas any longer, wasn't even upon Sylveria. And I was certain that I had reached an abrupt and swift end.

But my eyes cleared and after a moment I could see a man standing before me. It was the short man I had met in the mountain passage, but he was different here. He was made of the purest light that penetrated all darkness. He said to me, "Alak'kiin, there are things that you need to know, things you must see, and come to understand. But I will show them to you only if you accept."

"Accept what?"

"That you are a servant of the Light, a child of creation. You must decide that this will be your fate."

I did not understand what he meant, knew that I couldn't, but without hesitation I said, "I will accept."

This man, this being of light, looked at me then, seeming surprised, and he said, "Just like that? No thought, no consideration, no question?"

"None."

"Do you not want to know what it entails, first?"

"No. I know that you—whatever you are—are the Light of the world, the creator of all things. You are Numen, are you not?"

"I am."

"Then for this, Numen, I will be a servant of the Light. I will do as you tell me, for what else has been given unto me in life but solitude? For three hundred years I have walked Sylveria, never finding a home, never finding a purpose, and now you tell me that I may serve he who created all things? No, I do not hesitate to consent."

"The way forward will be trying, Alak'kiin. Dark things are awakening in Sylveria. Yours will be no easy task."

"Then I will be tested in the fires of this fate," I said.

"Very well," Numen said. "I will show you things beyond anything you have seen, things beyond your imagination, and you will understand."

"If you will give me understanding, I will make a vow before you, Numen; that never will I harm another creature of Sylveria, in times of peace or in *war*, for I feel in your very essence that you are love, and peace, and perfection."

"Be careful of the vows you make, Alak'kiin. For you have not yet seen the tribulations ahead. But for your righteousness, I grant you protection, so long as you hold to your word. No harm can come upon you; you will not see death so long as you keep this covenant. But know this: you will always be loved of the Light."

"Then show me, Numen, what it is that I must see, so that I can understand...."

And indeed, understanding did come to me that day. Visions came to my mind, scenes of things never before known to anyone in all of Sylveria, conceptions of cosmic events that happened long before this world even existed. These were the things shown to me...

In the beginning, there was the Numen.

This was in the time before time, before the ages of the world began, before either Dragon or Naiad had first taken breath. It was in the time before the seas filled the depths of the earth, before any wind had moved across the surface of the lands, and before any world had yet been inscribed. In those times there was only the Numen, who was to become the creator of all things.

Then the Numen made a wish that a great and good creation would come to be. This wish became a dream, and the dream became manifest. A vast space erupted and it was stretched out over a vast landscape of the elements, and many unfathomable worlds were etched into this creation. In places deep, the power of the Numen's wish awakened beings that he could love, creatures born of the light of conception. These entities were known as the Amaranthi.

Upon the face of many worlds the Amaranthi dwelled, serving their god by their mere existence, but all of their endeavors were only of the Numen's will. In this the god realized that these souls were immersed in vacuity, for there was no true choice of their own present, and they existed only for the Numen's sake, always obedient to his resolve.

This displeased the Numen, for he had desired beings who could love him in return and appreciate the beautiful things he had made. Instead, he had awakened mere constructs that were bound to a restrictive disposition that was naught but a reflection of his own.

And so in order that his creation might have meaning, the Numen imagined a gift that he could give to the cosmos, and this gift was Freewill. He declared that all creatures should possess the ability to choose whether they would regard creation with love, or revile it; only in this could there be individual purpose for the children of the cosmos. Therefore, the Numen spoke the Word of Law, and the force of Law came into being as the lord over Freewill, to make sure that this gift was both given and maintained.

When it came to be that the Law granted Freewill to the children of the cosmos, some of the Amaranthi praised the Numen for the gift they had been given, but others abused it, charging now that they could become alike to gods, for there was power in their souls, and power in their words.

Although the Numen was afflicted by this betrayal, he knew it was the price that had to be paid so that all individuals would have the right to choose what they would do with their time, and so that existence could have both purpose and meaning.

Across the reaches of creation great wars erupted as those Amaranthi who turned aside from the Numen sought to display their power and oppress those who did not. Many worlds were destroyed in these cosmic battles, and neither one side nor the other ever reigned supreme.

In order that his creation might not be completely destroyed in these senseless wars, the Numen then set creation in motion, ever-expanding into an infinite plane so that it could continually revitalize itself, and for each world that was obliterated, others formed elsewhere, far and deep across the endless expanse of creation.

When untold epochs had passed, the Numen grew apathetic because of the continual wars of the Amaranthi, and he longed to have companions with whom he could converse, souls who would not become immersed in the cosmic conflicts.

So it came to be that at the center of creation, where the beacons of the dreams had first been instituted by the god's wish, the world of Patralgia was formed, and it was far removed from the wars that had spread to the distant reaches of the infinite plane. In its beginning, it was an unrefined world, existing only of the raw elements, for the Numen intended the shaping of the lands to be to the desire of he who was soon to awaken...

Born then of the Light and the goodness of the Numen, the first to awaken in Patralgia was a great and marvelous creature who called himself a Dragon. The great winged beast was covered in scales of the purest white and he radiated the holiness of the Numen. He took the name Kronaggas, which meant—in the tongue of Dragons—*First of All*. The Numen then suggested that the Dragon shape one-half of the world to his own liking, and Kronaggas took this to heart.

For a thousand eons Kronaggas worked the elements using the great magic that was within him, which was the essence of creation. Dry land came forth by the will of the Dragon and it quaked at his command. The seas rose and obeyed his word. Forests and vegetation sprang to life and rivers flowed wherever Kronaggas declared. Then, by the righteous love of this creature, great animals came to be, and they began filling the seas and the skies and the lands. By the workings of Kronaggas everything was made splendid, and he called his creation Sylveria, which meant *Beautiful Land*.

Now, when Freewill was granted at the behest of the Numen, the Law became a force unto itself, reasoning of its own accord and determining how this gift would be maintained. And it deduced that in order for Freewill to be, there must exist the requirement that all beings be presented with an alternative to following the ways of the Light. Although the Numen had set Patralgia apart from the cosmic wars of the Amaranthi the edicts of the Law still fell upon this isolated world.

And so on the opposing side of the world of Patralgia, opposite Sylveria, the Dark manifested in the form of an abomination to the Light—a great fiery beast of the shadow, in the likeness of Kronaggas. This wicked Dragon was called Vorgrannas, which meant *Desolate Soul*, and he was all-seeing. Like his brother, Vorgrannas shaped his half of the world to his own liking, and he called the dark lands Nefaria.

Although the Numen was the pure essence of the Light, he would not charge the Dark with destruction, for by the Law of Freewill, all beings had to be given the choice whether they would follow in the will of this god or turn it aside to be born again of the Dark. In the absence of choice there would be no Freewill. And so the existence of evil was maintained so that the value of the gift of the Numen would be everlasting.

As the Law observed the two great forces upon Patralgia, it came to understand that the Light would ultimately be devastated, for the hatred of evil was far mightier than the passive innocence of goodness. In this there would be no enduring balance between the Light and the Dark. Evil would eventually obliterate all in its wake, never ceasing until all goodness was gone from the world. And this would be a violation of the original intent of the Numen—for if evil were to exist, good must also.

So the Law declared that something must be done to ensure that the will of the Numen would be maintained. For this it established a law unto itself—the Law of Balance—so that neither the force of Light nor the force of Dark would ever become discrepant. The Law's purpose then became the sustaining of equality between them, taking neither side against the other, but always seeking balance.

There is power in words, and the following are the words that the Law proclaimed should always be kept so long as it held authority over such matters:

"The Dark has awakened of imperative accord, for in the creation of all things and the declaration of Freewill, it has become necessary that out of the freedom of the Light must come adversity—the awakening of all evil.

And now, if the Dark ever seeks to extinguish the Light, as it so desires, the Light must be empowered against it, for the Dark will not rest until its transgressions are complete. To do otherwise—to allow wickedness to annihilate righteousness—would be arbitrary to reasonable justice, for the Light has done no wrong. And although it will be reborn again to reestablish balance, let the Dark for now be obliterated. Then perhaps in its rebirth it will find compliance with the Law.

And if the Light is ever to interfere in the affairs of the Dark, it will have become evil in itself, for only the wicked make dealings with evil; the Light will have become corrupted and still darkness might consume all of creation. For this, what was the Light—but which has become infiltrated with confusion—must be destroyed. Until it is, it cannot reawaken in balance with the Dark.

So let these words serve as the Law that both the Light and the Dark obey, lest its own destruction be its judgment: The Dark must never attempt to extinguish the Light; likewise, the Light is never to interfere in the affairs of the Dark. If either breaks this decree, let the destruction of the offender be forthcoming."

The Council of Dragons

After this, I saw many things—all things that had happened before I saw again through the eyes of my spiritual insight. They were shown to me so that I would remember...

In this vision, I saw as the Dragons Ashysin, Merilinder and Sharuseth came together in the Valley of Naiad and cast a spell upon a stone boulder; yet nothing happened, so far as they could tell. For this, they left that

place; yet in truth their spell had awakened seven beings into Sylveria...
These were my brothers and sisters and me. Yet from this perspective I
could see that we were not simply new creations, but spirits drawn from
elsewhere—from somewhere far away, beyond Sylveria, beyond our
world...

Upon the next evening, we, the Sylvai, had our first encounter with the
seven Dragons, and then, after we had been placed into a magical slumber,
Drovanius, Merobassi, Verasian and Aranthia had performed a spell that
was just like the other. And in the Valley of Naiad, in the forest of
Sternwood, the Nescrai awoke, six in number. They too had been drawn
from somewhere else.

Yet far away, for reasons unknown, in a land that I did not recognize,
another alike to them awoke... But this vision was a mystery to me, for I
had no previous knowledge of this being, and would not learn of it for a
very long time.

Time quickened in my visions then: as a people, the Naiad settled
within the Hills of Nightrun and began the learning of all things they
desired, their crafts, their professions and their passions. They soon
married one another and children were born to them. The innovations of
these first people of Sylveria gave rise to civilizations that spread across
the world.

Then conflicts arose amongst them, for the First Awakened Son,
Norgrash'nar, had grown bitter over the loss of Nirvisa'nen's affections
and marriage to Alim'dar. Drovanius the Black had sympathy for his son,
and in his misguided compassion, he too became resentful. So too did the
Garonites grow to despise both the Sylvai and the mix-blooded people of
Haldus'nar and Sarak'den, and Alim'dar and Nirvisa'nen. And it came to
be that a plot was construed by all of them, for the conquest of the world of
Sylveria.

But even in this, the Law of Balance remained unbroken, for all of the
Dragons and all of the Naiad were Children of the Light, and they meddled
only in their own affairs.

Then, as the conflicts arose during the year 310, I saw again all of the
events that had occurred during the Seasons of Summer. The Garonites
raided the farms of the Noranites, who resisted them. Norgrash'nar and his
people lorded over the Sylvai in the eastern regions, and discriminated
against them in all manners. Vindras Vale and the many areas of
Ashysin's Mountains were devastated by the machines of progress and the
animals of the wilds were driven out of their homes. And finally, for their
righteous retribution, Ashysin and Merilinder tore the bridge asunder at
Hest'Vortal, cutting the Garonites off from the rest of the world.

And I saw as I was taken from the Plains of Kronaggas to Aranthia on
the back of Drovanius, as I walked atop Eswear'Nysin, talking to

Haldus'nar and Sarak'den. Soon thereafter, I was taken back, near to the Temple of Kronaggas, where I saw myself disappear into the darkness.

All of these things were visions shown to me so that I would be reminded of all that had been.

Then, new things occurred.

The Dragons, all of them, came together upon the Goren'Tong Plateau, and there held a council.

Kronaggas the Dragonfather said to the others, "These people you have awakened have become numerous, and you say they have become too crowded, and that this is what has given rise to their conflicts... yet the lands of Drovanius have not even been occupied; neither are the lands of Merobassi settled."

Drovanius the Black was there present and he replied, "It is true that my lands are unoccupied and I now offer them to the Nescrai, but neither will any Sylvai nor those of mixed blood be permitted to dwell in my lands; for if they were, we too would become crowded and I would not have enough room for myself. I have kept my domain set apart for my own, and if I allow only my own children to come, then all of the Nescrai will always have a place to go. But if I were to allow the Sylvai in, we too would become overcrowded."

Also in attendance was Merilinder the Silver, and he said, "In recent times I, and my brother Ashysin, may have acted rashly against the Garonites. But these people have violated natural arrangements and must not be allowed to do so any longer."

Then Ashysin said, "I do not regret the retribution which I have sought against the Garonites. But I am not without the capacity to forgive. For long I have loved these people and welcomed them into my domain. But they must be held accountable, and a reasonable resolution to this matter must come."

Drovanius said, "You have condemned my people to suffering by your actions. Hest'Vortal cannot support so large a population."

"Still your anger, Drovanius," Kronaggas said. "For the people will be fed, as will the animals that have fled to your lands, Merilinder. We will rebuild a bridge so that the Garonites can return to their homes, and the region will stabilize."

Sharuseth the Copper then said, "The Garonites have also incited inequity amongst the Noranites, in the Hilly Lands of the south. Though my people have not handled the situations with perfect integrity, the thievery of their labors is not acceptable."

"I will deal with the Garonites," Drovanius promised. "Help me to rebuild Hest'Vortal and we will correct this wrong."

Sharuseth nodded and said, "Though my lands are vast, my people have multiplied quickly. Some of the people of Alim'dar have begun to settle in the northern region, south of their own. But there is no conflict with them. My lands are growing full, and though the Goab'lin Plateau is entirely unsettled, it is a region of wild creatures that are best left in their untamed habitat. Yet I am not without suggestion, for is there not an island to the east of Sylveria that remains uninhabited? I will offer my wings to any who wish to migrate there."

Verasian the green then claimed, "Though my lands are plentiful and not yet full, we must preserve what remains for farms, for it is fertile land. My people have been feeding both themselves and the Sylvai for many years, and what have they been given in return? Enchanted wood from the Noranites, baskets from the Adaasharians, carved stones from the Darians, and inks and parchment from the Haldusians... Useless trinkets all of them! If we give up farmland for more cities, there will not be enough food for ourselves, much less the Sylvai!"

Then the noble Aranthia the Crimson replied, "As it has been said, there is indeed a land to the east that is unsettled; I have claimed it as part of my domain, and I have reserved it for the future, for when others need a place to settle. The Haldusians are growing crowded upon the mainland, but they are getting along. Any who wish to settle within the minor land are welcome to do so. Likewise, any who find no comfort elsewhere may come to our cities, to the land of Haldus'nar and Sarak'den, for we welcome everyone, whether Nescrai or Sylvai. Not one is better than the other." This he said because he knew well of Drovanius' and Verasian's growing disdain of the Sylvai.

And at last Merobassi the Blue offered his thoughts, saying, "My lands are largely unoccupied. I have few people of my own. The mountains and plains and forests are cold—perhaps too much so for any of the Naiad. Only one tribe of people lives there. They call themselves the Arkanites, for they are descendants of Arkan'ar, who is the grandson of Haldus'nar. But even they rarely visit me in Luen'Aril anymore. They have become reclusive and I do not think they even commune with their brothers and sisters and cousins from across the seas. I do not know how they survive, for my lands will not grow crops. Still, any who wish to come and settle there are welcome, but I fear none will heed my invitation...

"Yet today I have witnessed as you have all offered your solutions and what are they but temporary answers? Will the Naiad not continue to grow until they are so numerous that they cannot stand side by side across the whole of Sylveria? What then, wise Dragons, will we do? Now, before you answer, allow me to propose a solution that will resolve this quandary.

"Behold! I have flown northward beyond the Skyreach Mountains. Indeed, I have braved the fierce icy storms and treacherous winds just to see what was on the other side. And it was there that I found the answer to our problem; for beyond my lands, across the northernmost ocean, where the world turns upon itself, there is yet another land that is at least as big as the whole of Sylveria. I know little of this land because I saw it only from a distance. It appeared dark and empty, for it lies within the Veil. So let us explore this place and settle the lands, and there will be enough room for both the Sylvai and the Nescrai for at least another hundred generations."

Then Kronaggas who had patiently listened to his children's discourses, became suddenly angry, saying to Merobassi, "Imprudent creature that you are, you do not know what you have done! For until this time none but I knew of what dwells on the other side of this world. Now you have opened a door to darkness and I do not know what the consequence will be. But know this: those lands are not empty and it was deemed long ago that none but I should know of the evil that dwells there. I tell you now, be wary of the knowledge you have gained, for those lands are called Nefaria. It is an abominable place filled with things that would seek to destroy us all."

"But then what are we to do about the Naiad?" Verasian cried. "For the lands are truly growing smaller, and if not Nefaria, where will the people go?"

"Today," Kronaggas said remorsefully. "I fear you have solved the problem brought before me. Though these words are a mystery to you now, soon no more will the Naiad need to worry about finding places of comfort, for the Dark will surely enter through the gateway that has been opened, and if this is so, then the luxuries of peace will be no more and your children will perish."

But the other Dragons did not know what it meant to perish, for none of them had ever seen death; Sylveria had been created in perfection, and death beforehand was not a part of life.

Thereafter, Merilinder invited any of the Naiad who desired peace to come into his domain to live with the Adaasharians. Many of the Garonites went there after leaving Hest'Vortal, but they found that the air was too hot for their liking and they had grown to prefer a cooler climate. So all of them left and went to the lands of Drovanius. It was there that they founded a great city that they called *Nescropolis*. This dark city was built within the cusp of the three mountains beneath Drovanius' den, near the Arge'Kort Mountains of the northeastern realm.

The small island of Aranthia Minor was settled by people of both Sylvaian and Nescraian descent, but isolated as these people were in the forests and mountains of that land, there was little contact with the outside world thereafter.

In the Mountains of Ashysin, the Garonites continued to develop their technologies and build what cities and farms they could, but they did so with greater respect for the land—or perhaps with greater respect for Ashysin. In those times, the Garonites became even closer to their brothers, the Norgrasharians, who also continued to advance in their technologies, creating great wonders.

And so the world remained balanced upon a fragile peace, and the population continued to grow.

Thereafter, I kept on watching, and as another five generations passed, more children were born to the Naiad, and the lands became even fuller. It was one hundred years after the Council of Dragons when Drovanius went to Merobassi and said, "Look, the lands are becoming even more crowded and I am growing uneasy. Show me the lands you have seen far to the north, beyond your domain, where the world turns upon itself."

So Merobassi obeyed his brother and showed Drovanius the way through the frozen mountains of the north, over the icy crags that separated the light from the darkness, and beyond the furthest reaches of Sylveria. And when they had done this, they saw the distant shore of Nefaria, and they went into the freezing waters and there floated as they observed.

"I have gone no further than this," Merobassi said. "For to go onward is to enter the Veil that swallows the suns and the moon."

"And you have seen this, the vanquishing of Aros and Imrakul?"

"I have, but only from a distance. Once they enter, their light becomes faint and then vanishes altogether."

"How do we know that we will not be vanquished if we go into the darkness?"

"Do not the suns and moon reemerge at their appointed time, when they have completed their cycle and are returned to light the world?"

"They do," the Black Dragon said. "The ending of their light upon Sylveria is only temporary..." Drovanius was somber and thoughtful, for to him his considerations were on things more profound than the cycles of the suns, and while Merobassi believed they were talking about the heavenly bodies, Drovanius was in actuality thinking about them—the Dragons. "Even if they fail, may they return unto the Light..."

"Indeed, for we see this every day. The Aros that leaves in the west is the same that returns in the east. All things begin anew. This is the nature of existence."

"Very well, then. Let us go into the dark Veil, into this land of shadows and see what is there."

So they again took flight, and without further reluctance they flew into the Veil.

THE SHADOWS OF DRAGONSWAKE

When they went unto the other side of the world, the things they saw there were darkly astounding, for as it was, it was the Hour of Highlight in Sylveria, the hour when the Shadows of Dragonswake flooded over the realms—that strange event that none ever had understood. But here and now, what the Dragons saw explained it all.

For straight ahead did the green moon Imrakul shine as fiercely upon Nefaria as did Aros shine upon Sylveria. But all things were reversed, for whereas Aros gave light to the darkness, Imrakul here gave darkness to the light, shining in a bleak and vacant obscurity that drove the light away, leaving only a trace of radiance upon the dark lands.

And it was this opposition to the light that shone forth at this time of day, piercing the Veil, striking the mountains of Dragonswake and casting its oblivious shadow to fall upon the lands of Sylveria.

They looked upon the world of Nefaria, and from all they could see it was a vacant desert, void of life, and it was ready, in Merobassi's estimation, to become the home of their children.

"Indeed these lands are as vast as you claimed," Drovanius said. "Yet they are dark and cold. None amongst the Sylvai would be content in this place, and it might be even too cold for our own children. I see no sign of the dark entities spoken of by Kronaggas, but perhaps further on, beyond our sight and the horizon of this land there will be warmer places that might suffice. If so, the Nescrai could inhabit these lands and leave Sylveria to the Sylvai and the mix-blooded breeds."

In the soul of Drovanius I could see a struggle, for he had been seduced by Norgrash'nar's devices, and yet still he remained a creation of the Light. He sought, in those moments, to find reconciliation for the troubles in the world, and in his heart.

"Though your intentions are pure, and your thoughts wise," Merobassi said. "I do not think the Nescrai will abandon Sylveria entirely. They have always known those lands, and it is theirs by right, for we have given it unto them. Since the First Awakened and the Firstborn left the Valley of Naiad, the lands have been in their possession."

"Indeed, you speak truly, Brother, but some may still be content to leave for new lands, for it is they who have been most outspoken about their discomfort. Better still, perhaps the Sylvai could come here and leave Sylveria to us... Let us return to our world and discuss this with our brothers, and perhaps we can explore these dark lands, and we will see that Kronaggas has misrepresented this world, for is there not a dark comfort that even you feel here, a reprieve from the demands of the Light?"

So Merobassi and Drovanius returned to Sylveria, and they called a council with Verasian and Aranthia. The others were not summoned, for the Black Dragon thought them too void of reason in these troubling times.

Then I saw again as time was carried forward. The Garonites fell back into their destructive ways as their technologies became a compulsion to the people, overshadowing their lives and the trueness of their spirits. So too did the Norgrasharians become reliant on their workings, becoming obsessed with the comforts of their existence and the trifles of their technologies. And in both of these realms, the animosity toward the Sylvai and the mix-blooded children became ever greater, coming even unto hatred.

The Entities of Nefaria

Now, while all of these things had happened in Sylveria—from the time of the awakening of the Naiad until now—far away in the dark lands of Nefaria, many things had transpired in accordance with the Law. Great beasts awoke in the dark places, creatures born of the elements. These were the children of Vorgrannas, and they were called *Drakes*. The Drakes were great wingless Dragons who, like their father, were without souls. These were the names of the Drakes and the entities that rose to be their subservients:

Talentaran was known as the Fire Drake, for flame fell over his entire body as if to consume him, though it did not. He was the creator of the Giants—the Trolls and Ogres who possessed renowned strength and cruelty.

Valanaryn was known as the Smoke Drake, for a cloud of smog always lingered around him, so that none could see his true self. He was the father of the *Wanderers*—those vicious entities that could shift between spirit and flesh.

Mananaran was known as the Adamant Drake, for his scales were harder than steel and no weapon forged could pierce him. He was the father of the Golems—those wicked servants indestructible.

Elbannoran was known as the Silt Drake, for his scales were covered in rot and maggot. He was the begetter of the undead—creatures of all kinds raised from the dead of war and given new life to serve him.

From the very moment of their awakening, each of the Drakes, along with their scions, were at odds with one another, and if not for the lawful nature of Vorgrannas, they may well have destroyed one another. Imbued with the chaos of their fathers, some of the lesser races later mutated into entities that were further abominations of the Light.

THE DISCORD OF DRAGONS

For another hundred years the four Dragons—Drovanius, Merobassi, Verasian and Aranthia—made flights over every corner of Nefaria, and there they witnessed the truth of all Kronaggas had said—the wicked creations and foul deeds in those lands. It was there that they first saw death, for the servants of the Drakes fought vicious wars, killing one another with strange and destructive weapons, fire and dark magic. And in this the Dragons determined that Nefaria was not a land fit for any of the Naiad.

But Drovanius was not content with this, for he desired a way in which to separate his own people from the Sylvai, and along with his favored sons, Norgrash'nar and Garonar, he began to form a plan that would ensure enough land for the Nescrai regardless; his concern was with them alone, not the Sylvai or the mixed children, whom Norgrash'nar had convinced him to despise.

Two hundred years had passed since the Council of Dragons and the population of the Naiad had grown ever more so. They filled the lands of Merilinder, the forests of Sharuseth, the Mountains of Ashysin, and the island of Drovanius.

Then it came to be that both Merobassi and Verasian agreed with all Drovanius said, and they counted the mixed Naiad of the Haldusians and the Darians amongst the Sylvai; for to them, their blood was defiled. But Aranthia the Crimson did not agree, and he did not share in their odium, for his brothers now perceived that the Sylvai had taken advantage since the very beginning and claimed the most resourceful lands for themselves, relying on the Norgrasharians for their food.

"So what will you do?" Aranthia inquired harshly of Drovanius. "Will you push the Sylvai into the Western Sea, or perhaps slay them as the Nefarians would do? Never should we have gone to those wicked lands; we should now heed the warnings of Kronaggas and repent of our curiosity. But I fear your minds have been defiled and you will not listen. Perhaps it is too late for you..."

Drovanius said to the others, "Too long have we let the Sylvai and the other Dragons claim more of Sylveria than we. Now I will tell you of something that I have long kept within my own thoughts; I have seen a truth that eludes even the great Kronaggas and the Law and the Numen himself. Let me tell you about the illusion of Freewill… The Law says that all have Freewill, and for this to be so we must be given choice. Yet what choice have we had when the truth of Nefaria has been kept from us?"

"Indeed," Merobassi concurred. "Until my eyes fell upon Nefaria I was not free, but a slave to innocence and I was bound to goodness, to the strictness of the Law, and under the word of Kronaggas. But now my curiosity has led me to open my eyes and I have seen that there is a war raging beyond this world, between the Light and the Dark. What lurks in Nefaria is a manifestation wrought of this cosmic war, and here in Sylveria is the essence of the Light. We are but pawns… How long can we remain slaves of the Light while that very force disgraces our children?"

And Verasian also agreed, saying, "We have been slaves to Kronaggas, all of us, Dragon and Nescrai; for as we were assured that Freewill was ours, the truth was concealed, and we knew nothing of the true choices we had. We were told to do as we please and to hold domain over our lands, yet we had no knowledge of the whole truth. So what is Freewill if we know not of the true choices we have? I say that we have been deceived by the Law, by the Numen, and by Kronaggas, and if they are of the Light, then perhaps justice lies with the Dark."

Aranthia had remained silent, considering all that his brothers said, but still he did not agree. Now he spoke, saying, "Brothers, your words are prideful and will lead to destruction. Consider that Kronaggas did indeed keep a greater truth from us, but perhaps it was for the good of all, both Dragon and Naiad. You say there was no choice without knowledge, yet at any time could not any of us have razed an entire city to destruction? Our powers are great and we are indeed free to use them as we choose. Our days have been fulfilled by our choices and our actions and if we did not have Freewill we could not even have journeyed to Nefaria. This alone is evidence of the truth of the Law.

"And did all of your pride, great Drovanius, come only after you learned of Nefaria? I say it did not! For over three thousand years you have been proud because of your great size and it has made you arrogant and has led you to reject reason and to reject the Sylvai, and to be seduced by the Dark."

"You accuse me of pride, Aranthia," the Black Dragon argued. "But let us consider those things shaping your mind and your words. You alone have let you lands become poisoned by the blood of the Sylvai. For this you have sympathy with those who have claimed three fifths of the Mainland for their own. You are a traitor to your own children, and though your scales are shaded of chrome and not metal, your thoughts are like the

Metallic Dragons' and your heart is bewitched!

"From this council I expel you, and I command you not to return. Go if you will and tell Kronaggas of our workings, but know that your loathsome people are trapped between the lands of Merobassi, Verasian, and my own, and there will be none to witness what we will do to them if you betray us to our enemies."

"You have taken a vow to never harm even one of them!" Aranthia condemned. "Do you think there will be no penalty for breaking such a vow?"

"The Law is an anomaly of itself!" Drovanius asserted. "For in one breath it both gives and takes away Freewill. If this is the Law we are to follow, and the Law by which we took our oaths, then from our vows we are released!"

"You have become foolish, Drovanius. You cannot absolve yourself of such a vow! There will be consequence."

But so taken by corruption had Drovanius become that he would not listen, and he again cast Aranthia out, refusing now to even reason with him. So the Crimson Dragon left their council and for a time he remained silent, for he loved the Haldusians and did not want harm to come to them.

The Law of Balance Broken

Drovanius and Verasian began making frequent flights to Nefaria, for they had become fascinated with the evil of those lands, and they learned more of the dark entities that dwelled there. While they did this, Merobassi was left in Sylveria to keep watch upon the Metallic Dragons and Aranthia, whom they no longer trusted.

Then it was in Nefaria that Drovanius met the Fire Drake, who was named Talentaran, and with him began relations, for the Drake was at war with the others, and had devised great weaponry with which to slay his enemies.

"I fight three armies on every front, each as strong as my own," Talentaran told Drovanius. "To have you as an ally would be most beneficial. Still, there is little I can do, for I am bound by the Law to not interfere in the Light's affairs."

"Is that really what the Law says?" Drovanius asked. "Or does it say that you may not seek its destruction?"

"Your words seek to deceive me, Drovanius."

"I do not. Even knowing of the Law, I stand here upon your lands without fear of repercussion, for I believe the Law is entirely without merit. Let us suppose that I am wrong, and that every word of the Law that is written would be fulfilled. The Law says that the Dark must not seek to extinguish the Light. Now, what I would propose would be of no risk to you, Talentaran, for unless you strictly seek our destruction, then you are protected by the Law itself."

"And what is it that you propose?" the Drake asked, his curiosity peaked, for he comprehended the reason of the Dragon's words.

"Tell me, what is it you need most of all to continue in your war with your brothers, the other Drakes?"

"I have drained these lands of its resources," Talentaran said. "The ore from which my children have made our weapons is depleted. Without it we cannot continue, and we may fall to defeat against our enemies. We have strength, but they have vast numbers as their advantage."

"This ore you need is plentiful in the Mountains of Ashysin. My children, the Garonites have harnessed it. They have machines that can tear a mountain down in a day, if only they were allowed... the ore would be abundant, and if I bring it to you, then you may continue your war. And what threat is there in this to you? You would not at all be seeking the destruction of the Light."

"But what of you?" the Drake asked. "In this you would be interfering in our affairs and this is a clear violation of the Law of Balance."

"Let the whole of the Law's penalty fall upon me," Drovanius said firmly. "So sure am I of its fallacy that I will let all punishment come upon myself, if it is true. You will not be judged guilty."

"It is true that I do not seek the destruction of the Light," Talentaran said. "For my father, Vorgrannas, is subservient to the Law and will not allow it. Yet if you are willing to risk your own chastisement and bring me the ore I require I will give you whatever you ask, if it is within my power. What is it that you would desire?"

"My children are untrained in warfare. We have had only minor conflicts with one another anywhere upon Sylveria. They have no weapons or the plates of steel that your children wear upon their flesh. If you could supply these to us, then we would learn to use them, so that we can destroy our own enemies."

"The swords and armors and all tools of warfare are forged of the very ore you claim you will bring. If you will do this then I will teach you of war, and you can take this knowledge to your own children, and do with it as you will. But I will be free of culpability, for you are in violation of the Law, not I."

So Drovanius had convinced Talentaran that in making arrangement with him he alone would take the retribution of the Law upon himself, if there was to be any at all. And they made a pact that day that the precious ore of Sylveria would be traded to the Nefarians for weaponry fit for the Nescraian people and for the knowledge of war.

It was at that moment that the Law of Balance was broken, for Drovanius had conspired with the Dark and thought himself above the Law. The prideful thoughts of the Black Dragon had led him to deny wisdom and to seek his own path, for he had become consumed with the anguished love lost for his son, Norgrash'nar, who remained bitter to this day.

And so it was not the Dark that violated the Law, as Kronaggas had feared, but a child of the Light, and it was then that true evil first entered into Sylveria through the heart and betrayal of Drovanius. Though they did not know it yet, both Dragon and Naiad began to die.

THE CITIES OF KOR'MAGAILIN

Drovanius, Verasian and Merobassi began scheming in how they would attain the ore that the Nefarian Drake required to forge weapons and armor, so that they could learn how to make war from Talentaran and drive the Sylvai out of the lands. After much conspiring and dialogue with Garonar, Norgrash'nar, and their wives, a plot was construed, for all of them had become corrupted by their desideration.

Beforehand, Ashysin had prohibited the Garonites from using their massive machines that could excavate the mountains in Vindras Vale, but they were convinced that with new proclivity even this could be changed, for the entire success of their strategy depended upon it.

They called together all of the Dragons, all of the First Awakened Sons and Daughters, and all of the Firstborn Children of the Naiad. Everyone was there present except for two... for Aranthia the Crimson was indisposed and could not attend, and I remained asleep somewhere in the depths of Kronaggas Mountain, still having these visions.

This assembly took place in the great Coliseum of Hest'Vortal, which had long since had its bridge of Boris'Thirith repaired and which had become a thriving city once again amongst the Garonites. There had been a relative peace amongst the people of Sylveria, even throughout the last two hundred years. Even as tensions grew and the Nescrai learned to despise their cousins even more, peace was somehow maintained by the Dragons. But this uneasy peace, they knew, would not last forever.

It was Norgrash'nar who spoke first that day, which was the last day of Winterfel, in the year 512 of the 1st Age of Sylveria.

"People and Dragons of Sylveria, we have called all of you together today so that we might entertain new notions of peace and prosperity for all of us. For in years past, there has been great animosity arising amongst the Naiad. Peace has only been kept amongst us by fragile alliances, and by the charges of our fathers, the Dragons.

"And what have these conflicts been over, if not for the growing scarcity of land and resources in this world? We have grown too numerous to count, and our needs are increasing to an unsustainable level. Yet we are here gathered to announce a new technology that may well preserve our way of life as we continue to grow.

"For since first the Norgrasharians set foot in the domain of Verasian, we have been innovators. Our engineers have created transports that traverse the surface of the land, towers that collect the energy of the suns, methods of communication that allow people to speak from one city to another, and methods of farming that have kept all people of Sylveria fed. We have adapted to the needs of the times, and now, as we face new troubles, we have together created the solution to our overpopulation."

The children of Norgrash'nar and Kalenen, and Garonar and Kuranen, seemed exhilarated by his words, while the rest of the people did not. Nor did Kronaggas or the Metallic Dragons consider his words anything more than pretentious self-importance.

"By the consent of Verasian," Norgrash'nar continued. "We will, with the blessing of this entire council, build twelve of the greatest cities ever known. Built upon the Onilmar Plateau, these will be cities that reach for the heavens, so tall will they rise above the plains."

Kalenen then stood with her husband and explained, "We have the designs for these cities which will be provided to all of you. But know this now, each of them will support an entire generation of the populace of all of Sylveria. And we are not constrained to the twelve cities planned."

"And who will dwell in these great cities?" Ashysin asked. "Would you force the Sylvai to live in them, abandoning their lands and leaving them to your own children? In times past you have shown disdain for our children. Or perhaps these cities will be so grand that you will allow the Nescrai to rule over the Sylvai, to lord over us all from the heights of great cities."

Drovanius replied, "It is true that I have shown preference in my dealings with my own children. But I tell you now that both Sylvai and Nescrai as well as the Haldusians and Darians may dwell in the cities of Kor'Magailin. And to demonstrate my sincerity, I will henceforth allow all Naiad—even Sylvai and the Mixed-Bloods—to settle in my lands. Verasian has agreed to the same. No more will your children come to our lands and labor for us."

Sharuseth then said, "And yet all of these cities will reside in Verasian's domain, in Onilmar?"

"Yes," Norgrash'nar said. "But only for a time... even this is not permanent, for we have yet to reveal the true glory of the cities of Kor'Magailin. Kalenen," he said, turning to his wife. "Show our demonstration..."

Kalenen then stepped forward, raised her hands and closed her eyes. Words of magic came from her mouth, an incantation to form an illusionary image before the whole of the people. And there, filling the Coliseum was a translucent rendering of the Onilmar Plateau. Upon it stood twelve towering cities that dwarfed even the Haldusian city of Eswear'Nysin. Level upon level surrounded the cities that were more akin to mountains, for they were made of stone and steel and covered in the likeness of the solar collectors that made the spires of Mar'Narush. Great trees grew from vast gardens that were upon the various planes; water flowed from caves in the peaks, watering the entirety of the cities. And great masses of people, happy and content, were shown in this representation of the future.

Then, the cities began to rise... out of the surface of the plateau, into the air, with nothing to support them. All that was seen on the underside were a multitude of turbine engines that thrust the cities into the higher places of the world. The cities lingered there not long, and they began to move about, guided by the magic of technology, and they spread throughout all of the lands of Sylveria. Then the magical vision faded, and Kalenen resumed her seat.

Those present were astounded, for if such a feat of technology was possible then the Norgrasharians may well have solved the problems of overpopulation as they had claimed. The people and the Dragons were silent for long moments as they considered all of this.

Now, above the other Dragons, Ashysin the Gold was most enticed by the prospect of the sky cities, for perhaps if the Garonites were to move into these cities, they would leave his domain alone. But he was not unwise and he knew there would be a cost. He said, "This technology is impressive, but I must ask from where the resources for the construction of these cities will come. For I see these are cities of stone."

"They are cities of stone and brick and steel," Norgrash'nar said. "But take no concerns upon yourself, Ashysin, for the stone we need will be drawn from Skyreach—Merobassi has consented to this already. Vindras Vale has been restored to its former beauty and we will not touch it. But there are, I'm afraid, great amounts of steel required, and the ore that is needed for the forging of it is found only deep within your mountains."

Ashysin glowered, but said nothing, for still he was allured by the prospect of having the Garonites out of his domain. "How much of the mountains must you destroy?"

"Not so much as you might fear," Garonar now said. "For we have perfected our machines and no longer need to tear down the mountains. We have developed giant drilling machines that can tunnel under the mountains, into the deep places, where the landscapes will be untouched on the surface. There are incredible amounts of ore beneath. Still, we will do none of this without your consent, for in times past we took advantage of your kindness and did as we pleased, not considering the effect of our undertakings upon you or the creatures of the world. In this you sought your just retribution upon us, and we now repent, if only you will allow us to delve beneath your domain. Then, everyone may benefit."

"To accomplish all that we have shown you," Norgrash'nar then said. "We will need but the cooperation of all, and a span of forty years. Then, we can become races of men and women amongst the most high."

Kronaggas then spoke, addressing Drovanius directly, and he said, "Upon the surface these things your children propose would seem prolific, and I too am drawn to these concepts. I have seen the wondrous inventions of the Norgrasharians and I have no doubt that such a feat as these sky cities can be developed. Yet you must understand that I have misgivings… in years past you have all shown disdain for the natural order of this world, and you have shown hatred for some of the Children of Dragons. However, I suppose now in your repentance that you work for the betterment of the world. If all of the things that have been said this day be true, and no more harm will come to this world for your actions, we will consider your proposal. But first I ask you simply, Drovanius—speak to me words that cannot be broken."

This Kronaggas said because although it was little known amongst the Naiad, a Dragon's word when spoken to another is binding. It is unlike an oath given to the Law, or even a god. But what the Dragon promises is, by its nature, given to happen.

And Drovanius, understanding that the entire proposal hinged upon his words that followed, spoke carefully and without deceit in his tone, for he was crafty…

"It is my word to you, Kronaggas, and to all Dragons, that the Sky Cities of Kor'Magailin will be inhabited by the children of all Dragons—both Sylvai and Nescrai and in proportion the children of Haldus'nar and Sarak'den, and Alim'dar and Nirvisa'nen. So too will we not allow the over-world of Sylveria to be destroyed by the machines of progress; only in the deep places of the world will we mine for ore. And lastly, all Sylvai who live in the lands of Sylveria will be given unto complete freedom, to not serve any other against their will so long as the oath of Dragons remains intact, to never harm even one of the Naiad."

Upon hearing these words, Kronaggas and the Metallic Dragons spoke in private with the First Awakened Sylvai and with Haldus'nar and Nirvisa'nen—who were the Nescrai who had not given in to dark temptations. By consensus they all agreed that the Sky Cities of Kor'Magailin were the progress that Sylveria needed, so that the people could persist.

"There is but one stipulation," Kronaggas said when they returned to the council. "And that is that the great undertaking of building these cities must be shared in by all—Chromatic and Metallic Dragon, and the Naiad of every shade."

Drovanius agreed to this, the council was dispelled, and the great undertaking was started.

So the mining of the Mountains of Ashysin began; in a place that came to be called Undermountain that was between the Mountains of Ashysin and the Hilly Lands of Southern Mara. Deep into the underworld the Garonites drilled, pulling forth the rich resources that were needed for the construction of Kor'Magailin. But this was done under the supervision of Verasian, and only two-thirds of the vast amounts of ore taken went to the building of the Sky Cities; the remainder was secretly taken to Nefaria, to Talentaran, where also began the teaching of the art of warfare to the Nescrai.

As well, in secret, there was a great undertaking achieved by delving northward beneath the Plains of Kronaggas, and great caverns were made thereat. In this, there was no more destruction to the Mountains of Ashysin than was necessary, yet the Garonites were able to acquire far more ore than the Metallic Dragons or the Sylvai were aware.

As these discrete plans were employed, both Nescrai and the Chromatic Dragons—less Aranthia—cooperated with the Sylvai and the Metallic Dragons to build the great cities, and all the while the Light remained unsuspicious, for the concurrence of all seemed most eminent.

Great masses of stones were cut from the Skyreach Mountains and carried by the Dragons to the Onilmar Plateau, which were to serve as the foundations of the cities. The Norgrasharians installed their turbine engines and their solar panels. The Haldusians carved and shaped the stone of the cities. The Noranites tended to the planting of the gardens. And the Adaasharians provided food and services to all of the needs of the other workers. And when thirty-eight years had passed, eleven of the great Sky Cities of Kor'Magailin were raised from the earth to hover over the lands of Sylveria. Twelve had been planned, but one had been rendered useless by a fracture in the stone foundation. That city, which was called Dan, remained upon the Plateau, never rising into the air.

Only absent from all of these endeavors was Aranthia the Crimson, for he had gone into a deep state of meditation, torn as he was between the threats of his Chromatic brothers and knowing of what he should do.

But he was not to remain dormant forever, and in the year 550, when he first saw the citadels lingering over the lands to the west, he was certain that his brothers were not working for the good of all people, for if they had truly turned away from their prejudice and wickedness they would have come to him in repentance.

And so knowing of the place at which the three Chromatic Dragons often met, Aranthia used magic of transfiguration and took on the form of a mole, and he burrowed his way through the dirt and into Verasian's Cave, which was within the region of Etharg'Heron, near the lone mountain in that realm. There, as he kept watch upon them, his suspicions were confirmed. The Chromatic Dragons, along with the Garonites and Norgrasharians, were plotting the usurpation and extermination of the Sylvai and the mix-blooded Naiad.

Although he feared what might happen to his children, the Haldusians, as a result, Aranthia then began forging his own plans to thwart the dark workings of the others.

Aranthia then sought audience with Kronaggas, Ashysin, Merilinder and Sharuseth, and he met with them in Naiad. He said to them, "I have seen a truth that has eluded all of you, but I say this with no condemnation, for the workings of the Dark are deceitful, and its depravity knows no limit. See, I have flown to Nefaria with my dark brothers, and we there have seen horrible, foul things... And I now seek exoneration for my sins—for in knowing that you forbade it, Kronaggas, I nevertheless was drawn away, and I did follow Drovanius, Merobassi and Verasian to those wicked places.

"And I then tried to convince my brothers that no good would come of dealings with the Dark, but they did not listen, and they threatened the children of Haldus'nar and Sarak'den, if I were to tell you of their workings. I then went into reclusion, for I have feared what might come upon my people. When I saw the floating cities I was brought to awareness, and I saw them as dark portents.

"It was then that I went into a hidden assembly of my brothers, and there learned that they are not repentant. They have not changed their ways, and they have in fact made pact with the Nefarians."

"What evidence have you of this?" Sharuseth asked. "For while you were in seclusion, all of the people and Dragons of Sylveria worked together for the future of the world in the raising of Kor'Magailin. And now you tell us that it was subterfuge? Yet everywhere we look in all of Sylveria, the people are at peace. After two hundred years of tensions, there are no more conflicts."

"Believe as you will," Aranthia said. "But I tell you now that if we do nothing the war will already have been won by Drovanius!"

"War?" Ashysin said. "You speak of something that has never been. We Dragons—even Drovanius, Merobassi, and Verasian—have worked to keep peace amongst the nations, and we will continue to do so."

"It is too late!" Aranthia cried. "We must act!"

"What would you have us do?" Merilinder asked.

"We must arm the people. Prepare them for the coming war, or they will be taken unaware. Give to them the means to make weapons. Let us too learn of warfare, as have the Nescrai! If we do not, they will drive everyone from the lands and into the sea."

"Your words are reckless and absurd," Sharuseth said.

"You will not think so when the Noranites are lying dead within your lands. Behold, I have seen death at the hands of the Nefarians, and it is not something we would desire here. Please, Brothers, heed my warning."

"Death in Sylveria?" Kronaggas said. It was a concept he understood, but had not considered, for since his own awakening long ago, this world had not been touched by its dominion.

"Yes, death!"

"The only way this could happen," the White Dragon said. "Is if the Law of Balance has been broken—if we have been betrayed by our own..."

"That is what I am telling you, Kronaggas! All of you. Drovanius has broken the Law. He has interfered in the affairs of the Dark, in Nefaria. Death is coming to us all..."

"I do not believe it," Ashysin said. "For he has shown repentance for his actions, and the world has since turned for the better."

"This is the way of the Dark," Kronaggas said. "It deceives. It seeks to appear good, hiding within integrity and virtue. And it rises from good intent, showing itself only when its corruption is complete."

"You have come to agree with Aranthia?" Merilinder said.

"We must consider it."

"What is there to consider?" Merilinder asked, now himself wondering if there was merit to Aranthia's words. "If it is true, that Drovanius has been taken by the Dark, and the others, then how would we know?"

In careful consideration, Kronaggas then said, "Always I wondered if the Dark would break the Law of Balance and come here to Sylveria to continue its wars, for evil and destruction are its nature. Many years ago I warned that a door had been opened, and those were words spoken out of the fear that the Nefarians would enter in through it. But never did I consider that it would be one of our own—a child of the Light—that would bring wickedness to our lands. If this is true, there will be consequences for the violations of Drovanius, and great malady will come to us all.

"And I find now that we are constrained from action, for if the others are now servants of the Dark, and if we arm ourselves and fight them, are we not interfering in their affairs, as we have been commanded not to do? If we fight them, we ourselves will become breakers of the Law and shall surely be smitten for it. Yet if we do nothing, the beloved sons and daughters of Dragons will die. Either way it seems our destruction is forthcoming. We will suffer for the atrocities of Drovanius, for the Law cannot be broken without penalty. Though we may repent of this offence, only Drovanius may have the power to change all that will result. But if his heart has become like the soulless Nefarians, and he has been taken by the Dark, there may be nothing that can be done at all.

"Still, the Numen is almighty, righteous and just. I will commune with him, for harrowing days are certainly ahead. For now, children, do nothing. Do not arm your people, for in doing so we are acting as the Nefarians do, and this may be an unforgivable offence."

"How will we know if the Law has indeed been broken?" Ashysin asked. "And if war is coming?"

"Look for a sign," Kronaggas said. "All will be made clear. If death comes to Sylveria, even to one, you will know."

Ashysin, Merilinder and Sharuseth heeded the words of Kronaggas and did not make preparations for war. But Aranthia did not, for he had seen more than the others; he already knew what was coming, and he was not content to let his children, or any of the Sylvai, perish for the wickedness of Drovanius. And so he went then to the Haldusians, and to the Darians, who were the mix-blooded Naiad, and he told them what was happening. And these people agreed that it was time to take up arms, to defend themselves, their children, and their lands from the evil that was awakening; for of all the good people of Sylveria, none had been so discriminated against as them.

Into the ranks of the Nescraians Aranthia sent spies, and from the fallen people he learned of the methods of warfare that they were acquiring from the Nefarians, and he began teaching it to all of the children of Haldus'nar and Sarak'den, and Alim'dar and Nirvisa'nen.

In those days, the shadows of the Dark were lingering over the face of the world, for war was coming; and it was time for me to return.

THE BOOK OF

INCITEMENT

THE RETURN OF ALAK'KIIN

When my visions subsided I was drawn back into the present time, though I was entirely uncertain if all of the things shown to me had already happened, or if they had been a prescient showing of what was to come. Had I simply envisioned these things and been away from my body for but a few moments? Or had more than two hundred years passed me by while I slept and all these things occurred?

As I awoke there remained a faint trace of the light that had encompassed me when I had come into the chamber in Kronaggas Mountain, but it was quickly fading away. I was disoriented and then complete darkness surrounded me. I was upon the stone floor of the chamber.

My thoughts lingered on all that I had seen, the terrible things that had come upon Sylveria... or would soon come. The betrayal of Drovanius... the falling of the Nescrai to the Dark... the breaking of the Law... coming war... Could all of these things become a reality? Had they already? When I went back out into the world of Sylveria would I find it wartorn and desolate, or was there still time?

Hope told me that the visions had been a forewarning of things to come, but my heart told me that they had already happened, all while I slept in some provident, mystical sleep. But why would the Numen have kept me away from the world? Perhaps I could have changed things, and perhaps that was his intent, if by chance these were foresights.

Regardless, I had gained a knowledge that none had ever been shown, save perhaps Kronaggas himself. With this was a deeper understanding of the past, even the times before the Dragons had awakened the people of the world, and in places deep beyond our world.

When we had first awakened we had suspected that there was something more to us, something before. I myself had heard strange words in the first moments of my existence, words I still could not comprehend, residual thoughts or emotions... Even now after my given visions, I could not truly understand everything that had been in the distant past, before our world was even forged. These were all things of mystery, and only time might reveal more.

Likewise, there was nothing I could do for what had come before, whether in the cosmos or in the lands of Sylveria. I could only look to the future and try to move forward, and I could not do this while sitting on the floor of the chamber in the darkness of Kronaggas' mountain temple.

I felt around in the darkness, into my pockets, and I found the lightstone given to me by Alunen long ago, and I used it to light the chamber. It was now, without the presence of the Numen, quite ordinary—just a tunnel cut through the stone of the mountain that was never carved into anything remarkable.

I rose from the stone floor and looked about. The passage ran from where I had come and continued on deeper into the mountain. Though I wondered what might be deeper still, I wanted to get out of the caves and into the light of the world, so that I might discern at what point in time I now existed. So I walked back the way I had come before—whether moments or centuries ago, I did not know. When I came again into the sanctuary of Kronaggas I still could not tell, for it looked the same as it had before. But it felt different.

Through the heart of the temple I went, then through the passage decorated with carved stone and toward the entryway through which I had entered before. And when I stepped out into the light of Sylveria, I knew that at least some time had passed, for Winterfel had come. When I had gone into the mountain it had been Summertide.

A blanket of snow covered the Plains of Kronaggas. Cold winds swept over the withered grasses, and I found myself chilled, for I had not come here dressed for this season. I looked to the skies; by the heavenly realm I was able to discern that it was the sixth day of the season. For the blue light of Vespa was melding with that of Aros in the near eastern sky. It was the Hour of Meeting. But of what year it might be was unknown, for there were no heavenly indications that marked the longer cycles of Sylveria.

Across the plains I saw no sign of life—no Dragons or people, and no animals. But this was not uncommon, for in the Winter Seasons, the creatures of the world often were in hibernation or had migrated southward, seeking somewhat warmer climate.

But then he came, a glistening beacon that was at first imperceptible, for he blended in with the snow. Kronaggas the White soared low over the plains and soon came to stand before me as I emerged from his temple. He stared at me with wonder and pleasure, for it had been long since he had seen my face.

"Alak'kiin... Is it truly you?"

"It is."

"You have been gone so long... where have you been?"

"I have been here, inside your temple, in one of the dark passages, asleep, envisioning, seeing all that has been... or will be... tell me, what year is this, for when I entered it was 310."

"Two hundred and forty-two years have passed since you faded from the world, Alak'kiin. The last who saw you were Aranthia, Haldus'nar and your sister, Sarak'den. They say they left you upon these plains, and you have not been seen since."

"The year is 552?" I asked astounded. Though I had seen these years pass in my visions, it seemed now impossible that I could have been away for so long... "Then all of the things I saw are true... Drovanius has broken the Law... The Nescrai now prepare for war... the coming onslaught will be vicious, Kronaggas."

"That is why I have come here, Alak'kiin, to consult with the Numen. I must understand what is happening..."

"The Numen..." I said, recalling my visitation with him.

"The Numen is the god of all creation, Alak'kiin."

"Yes. I met him, Kronaggas, deep inside your mountain, he came to me, over two hundred years ago. It was he who showed me all things."

"If this is true," the Dragon said. "Then Aranthia is not wrong. The Dark has been fully awakened in Sylveria." He was deeply troubled, as was I, for the things that were happening would bring naught but destruction to the beautiful lands of Sylveria. "I must go inside, Alak'kiin. I must talk with the Numen. Join me, if you will..."

THE PROPHECY OF THE NUMEN

Inside the sanctuary of his temple, Kronaggas lay himself to rest upon his bed of treasures. He said, "Stay with me, Alak'kiin. For what comes next may be knowledge that must be carried on by you."

I sat upon a stone bench, one of many that had been brought here long ago to seat the visitors of the White Dragon, and then I waited in silence. He settled in and closed his eyes. Words issued forth from his mouth, words unknown to me, for they were not even of the tongue of Dragons. They were whispers of magic, or words of gods, powerful and exquisite. Then Kronaggas spoke, not to me, but to the Numen.

"Great awakener of the world, and creator of all things, I come to you in sorrow, for the Law of Balance may well have been violated by one of my own. I understand the consequences of this, but my heart is distraught, for there are countless children of the Awakened Dragons, and my love for them is unending. Are all to perish for the corruption of Drovanius?"

And then he was silent. But the Numen's words to him were not held only within the Dragon's mind, but were ever present here in the sanctuary, and I could hear them as well.

"It is true that the Law which has been established has been violated by the Light. Yet this does not mean that my own love has diminished. The Dragons are my children as well as yours, and the Naiad are their children, and I have come to love them all. But the Law has become unforgiving and a god unto itself. It is vacant of love and justice, for it seeks only to balance itself. And now, for the transgression of Drovanius, many will die for millennia, and there is naught that can be done for this; yet I now offer unto the world this: penance may be paid. Redemption demands sacrifice. Hear now my words and know that all things may come unto justice.

"There are four spirits in the whole of creation, each of them pure— Faith, Hope, Love, and Understanding. Throughout the ages these spirits will suffer, but they will also endure, and they will find embodiment in the souls of heroes when the fourth awakening is soon to come. It is they who may bring about the redemption of the world. Now hear my words... A single light shining from the east and the west, the chosen Keepers may come to find their way. The spirits will be awakened with them, and they must strive to redeem the Law.

"These words remain a mystery to you now, and shall be such for all during the ages to come, but those who are wise will hear the whispers of my calling."

Then the Numen was silent, at least to my ears, yet Kronaggas remained in his trance, and I thought that Numen must be speaking to him in words not meant for me. When Kronaggas returned, he looked to me and said, "Numen's words are wise, Alak'kiin. The others will not believe that trouble is coming until they see death staring them in the face. They cannot remain in doubt. There is much work to be done, Alak'kiin. Bring the others to me, those most loyal."

"How will I find them?"

"Much has changed since you were amongst us. Magic has awakened moreso than ever. Use the magic of your heart to converse with them. For now, I must rest."

Kronaggas laid his giant head down upon the sanctuary floor, and as he closed his eyes I could not help but notice how sorrowful his demeanor seemed, for terrible things were indeed coming to Sylveria.

I left the temple so as to give Kronaggas the rest he needed. Standing again at the top of the Sanguine Artery, I stared absently out over the snowy plains. Sorrow was in my heart too, for dark things were coming. Hope for peace was waning, for by the words of the Numen, a price had to be paid. *Redemption demands sacrifice...* It was the transgression of Drovanius that was bringing immanent destruction upon us, and so it was he who must atone.

Yet Drovanius was filled with every kind of destructive evil, for he was willing to cast off his vow, declare the Law fallacious, and lead half of the children of Dragons into war with the other. One such as he was surely not in a repentant disposition, for the Light within him had become dark.

And only one thing was certain—war was coming.

I heeded Kronaggas' words then, and I focused the intent of my will, which was the source of all magic; as I opened my heart, I was able to open up a channel that transcended space, for my desire was to contact my brothers and sisters, and Haldus'nar and Nirvisa'nen. And for this I was able to call a meeting together that was to be held at Kronaggas' Temple in four days' time.

THE WILL OF KRONAGGAS

By the Hour of Attrition on the fourth day, which was the tenth of Winterfel, all of my siblings, and also Haldus'nar and Nirvisa'nen had arrived at Kronaggas Mountain. I greeted each of them outside, for to them it had been more than two hundred years since they had seen me.

"Alak'kiin, it is so good to see you," Adaashar said, clasping my shoulder as Sveraden embraced me, wordless and with tears in her eyes.

"Where have you been all these years?" Alunen asked when she and Norandar arrived; they were both tearful as well.

"It is a story for a later time, when all of us have gathered."

Haldus'nar and Sarak'den arrived next, and he said, "You have been missed greatly, Alak'kiin. I feel more hope now than I did before I received your calling."

"Dear Brother," Sarak'den said. "You cannot just disappear like that!"

And lastly, Alim'dar and Nirvisa'nen arrived. Although he was as stoic as ever, my brother could not hide his own emotions, and he embraced me tightly. "This world needs you, Alak'kiin."

Then lastly Nirvisa'nen hugged me but did not long linger there; still, she said, "We searched for you, all of us. But it was as if you were gone from this world."

"I was," I said, and then I proceeded to explain, now that all of them were present, where I had been for the last two hundred and forty-two years. When I was finished, each of them was amazed, for I was the only one amongst them who had ever been blessed to hear the words of a god.

"It is Kronaggas who has called us all here," I said. "Let us sleep until Firstlight, then we will awaken him."

In the morning when we were all awake we entered into Kronaggas' Temple, and there in the sanctuary we found that he had already risen.

"My children, my servants of the Light, welcome," he said. "For you are they who have not fallen to the ways of the Dark. You have remained true… for this you are all blessed. There are some things we need before we proceed."

"Proceed with what?" Alim'dar asked.

"With what must be done." Still Kronaggas seemed pensive, his thoughts distant. "I need a stone tablet, one that measures five lengths by four. I need an altar of polished stone on which I can make inscriptions. And from you, Norandar, we need a hammer large and powerful enough to shatter stone. Can you get these things for me?"

"We can," I said. "You likely have the things necessary here in your trove. We will search."

We dug through the hoard of treasure, all of which had been brought here by the followers of the Dragon in times past, given as offerings. There amongst the paragons of wealth we found an ornate hammer made of a solid stone that was attached to a firm handle cut from the Sternwood Forest of Naiad. So too did we find a marble slate that was not etched upon. Showing these to Kronaggas, he approved of them, but said, "We still need an altar…."

"Will the marriage fountain suffice?" Alunen asked. This was the place at which she and Norandar had been cleansed, so long ago, just before the first wedding of all of the Naiad.

"Don't the Naiad still come here to be cleansed and bound together?" Sveraden asked.

"They do," Kronaggas said. "But this must change from here forward. The Temple must be sealed and entered only by you hereafter. You must teach your own people how to perform the bonding ritual. You will be priests of my following."

"But what of the fountain of cleansing?" Alunen asked. "We were told to bathe before you performed the bonding ritual… Is this not necessary?"

Kronaggas swung his head side to side, and through the gloomy demeanor that now surrounded him, the faintest of smiles touched his giant mouth as he said, "No. It never was needed. You smelled of Dain when you arrived that day. The words are what matter. Remember the words."

"We can seal the fountain with magic," Norandar said.

"It will need a stone to cover it," the Dragon said. "But that can come later. Now, lay the tablet out before me."

"Alim'dar took the marble slate and placed it on the stone floor before the Dragon.

Kronaggas raised one giant claw to his chest and covered his heart. He whispered words inaudible and a faint white light emanated from within and formed into a sphere that he held in his hand. And he took this light from within himself and placed it above the slate; then with further words of magic, the stone absorbed it all. Upon the face of the marble were now symbols unfamiliar, words perhaps in the language of the Numen.

"You are to take this tablet in five days' time, at the Hour of Elation, on the fourth day of Wintertide, and Norandar, you are to strike it with the hammer you have taken from my hoard. It will break into four even pieces, and this will be a sign that you have done all as instructed. Place one piece of this stone tablet into the altar here and seal it, and take each of the others to the temples of Diras'Vorma, Norad'Taun, and Nysin'Sumuni. When the tablets are properly sealed within their own altars, words of magic, images and emblems will be etched into them by the hand of the Numen. Only those destined to find what is inside will have the power to unseal them. They are to remain hidden there, their existence known only unto you, my favored children, for all time. This tablet is the seed of the future. This is my command to you."

Each of us together concurred, and Kronaggas continued, saying, "Amongst all of the Naiad you have been the most loyal and loving. My time to leave this world has come; it is time for me to fall asleep, so that perhaps someday I may reawaken in a time when the Light is nearly gone. Your eyes will never fall upon me again as I am, but my spirit will reside with you and will keep your love true until it is time for you to sleep as well. Times ahead will be trying, and although Drovanius is the cause of these coming tribulations, know that he is still loved of the Light, for he has but lost his way, and it is through him that the world might be saved. He is not beyond redemption.

"Speak these words to the people so that this message will find its way to the ears of the Nescrai, and then to Drovanius himself, and the Dark might not prevail. My gift to the world has been given into your hands, though like the seed of a tree its fruits will not be revealed for a long time to come.

"Now, to the Dragons Ashysin, Merilinder, Sharuseth and Aranthia, give this message: you are to follow your hearts and do what you think is right, for the Numen will consider all things and is understanding of the heart.

"To the good people—the Sylvai, the Haldusians, and the Darians—say this: I, the father of Dragons, have had many children and I have loved them all, for they are children of the Light. If you choose, the Light will remain with you until your final breath. To those who endure will come a glory and honor that will remain for all times in the hearts of future generations.

"And finally, to the Nescrai, say this: you have become filled with the evil of your fathers, and you have abandoned all reason for your lusts. Turn your backs upon the Dark, and the Numen will return you to his heart, for his love is everlasting. Maintain this folly and your minds and flesh will be twisted, and you will become fouler than the creatures of Nefaria, if it were possible. Your spirits will become as phantoms, mere shadows of what they once were, and your souls will perish. Repent of your madness and you will be released from this fate; do it not and you will become the bane of all righteousness."

Alunen promised, "We will do all the things that you ask, and we will protect your secret tablet. But tell us what you mean... where are you going?"

"I am doing only what I must. You will not understand at first, but with time you will come to see."

"You cannot leave us now," Sarak'den cried. "With war coming, we need you more than ever. Who will guide us?"

"Your hearts will guide you. You already have within you the wisdom to discern all things. Your hearts are pure."

Nirvisa'nen said, "Though I am Nescrai and I am few amongst my kind, I promise you that I will not be consumed by the Dark." Haldus'nar concurred, making the same pledge.

"There are still some amongst your kind that have not been enticed with the darkness," Kronaggas said. "Seek them out, and save them if you can."

Sveraden said nothing, but she walked up to the Dragon, who lowered his mighty head to her, and she placed her arms as wide as she could across his great snout.

When she withdrew, he said, "Your love for the creatures of this world is unmatched in all of Sylveria. You, daughter of Dragons, are a beacon of love and creation."

Tears overwhelmed the women amongst us, and for this they retreated from the sanctuary. Then, Kronaggas, the greatest of all Dragons, looked fiercely at the remainder of us and he said with passionate words, "When the time comes and the Nescrai bring this war upon Sylveria, destroy every last one of them that will not swear allegiance to the Light. Let there be no exceptions. No man or woman or child can remain alive who has become inundated with the Dark."

Though utterly surprised by the viciousness of Kronaggas' words, it was this intensity that compelled us to take heed of this command.

Then, as the men prepared to rejoin with the women, Kronaggas said, "Alak'kiin, I would like you to accompany me to the south, to Oman'Tar. Will you do this?"

"Of course I will."

And so with final farewells, and tears of sorrow, Kronaggas the White went to the south, with me as his rider, destined to be the witness to the glory of his end.

The Transfiguration of Kronaggas

As I soared the skies this one final time with Kronaggas the White, he said to me, "You know what I am soon to do, do you not?"

"I do."

"And do you understand that it is necessary?"

"If only there was another way...."

"There is not. Death will come to everyone if I do not. This, Alak'kiin, will bring the others into preparation. Redemption demands sacrifice."

"But it is not you who needs redemption."

"It matters not, Alak'kiin. Until they see they will not believe."

"But how will this change anything at all?" I asked. "For war will come regardless."

"Indeed it will," the Dragon said. "But when they see that I have fallen, they will know that death has come unto Sylveria. They will understand that no longer is life eternal. They will see that everything Aranthia has said is true, that the Law of Balance has been broken, and for it, there is no turning back the tide of war."

"They will lose hope, I fear."

"Perhaps for a time. But they will find it in the end. They will be awakened to their own true power power that comes to those who are called Champions of the Light."

"There is no changing your mind, then?"

"I cannot undo what has been started, Alak'kiin. Nor would I, though the sorrow of leaving this world is greater than I can express."

"You too will be missed, my dear friend."

On the fourth day of Wintertide we arrived in Oman'Tar, during the latter part of the Hour of Firstlight. It was the beginning of a new day, but it was the eve of war, and as it was, we were not alone in the skies over the city.

The cities of Kor'Magailin had risen two years ago, from the Plateau of Onilmar and into the skies of Sylveria. The war had not yet broken, and still many of the people were unaware of what was coming. Though rumor had spread throughout the lands that war was upon us, and death with it, most did not comprehend what this meant. Even those who did believed it not, for death had never been a part of our existence.

Now, on this day, it so happened that the Sky Cities had come unto the Southern Reaches, each of them upon an excursion around the world, so that all people would see the majesty of this advanced technology. This, I knew was but a pretense, for Norgrash'nar surely did his circuit over the lands so as to display his power, and when the war did start, his enemies would be overwhelmed by his might.

Although the Dragons Ashysin, Merilinder and Sharuseth had been unconvinced that the Dark was awakening in the lands and that death was to become a reality, they were not foolish, and they had kept watch upon Norgrash'nar, the Garonites and the Cities of Kor'Magailin, for they had each considered the possibility that Aranthia had been right, for even Kronaggas had given merit to the claim. So, these three Dragons were there present in the skies over Oman'Tar as well, circling between the citadels.

Now, Ashysin had before asked, *How will we know if the Law has indeed been broken? And if war is coming?"*

And to this Kronaggas had replied, *"Look for a sign. All will be made clear. If death comes to Sylveria, you will know it."*

Whether fate or chance I did not know, but something had brought the Dragons here this day, at this place, and at the time ordained by Kronaggas that Norandar should strike the magically imbued tablet in his temple. Although I knew what was soon to happen, I did not know how, nor did I have full understanding of the reasons.

"The time has come, Alak'kiin," Kronaggas said, and he landed upon the peak of the Temple of Nysin'Sumuni, where I dismounted. "The hour of my revelation approaches. It is time that I bid farewell to you, my old friend. Never forget that you are favored of the Light."

I said nothing at first, but hung my head in mourning, for I knew Kronaggas had reached his end. Then I nodded, and whispered, "You will not be forgotten, Kronaggas the White."

With that, the Dragon took a leap into the air, and flew out a short distance over the Southern Sea, hovering there amidst the Sky Cities and the Dragons, where all could see, his wings spread open, facing skyward, and looking nowhere but to the heavens.

And when Firstlight gave way to the Hour of Elation, far to the north, Norandar struck the stone tablet with the hammer. At that moment a dazzling and beaming white light burst forth from the White Dragon, and his true self was shown—His appearance was the same, but in that instant he no longer seemed physical, for all who saw him were witness to the pure soul of a Dragon. His spirit was golden and shown with the same brilliance as had the light I had seen in the world beyond Sylveria, when the Numen had taken me away...

Then, in another instant, the spirit of Kronaggas was soaring upward, swiftly out of sight, but his physical body remained—now broken, now even lifeless, and it fell into the sea below, just south of Oman'Tar. Remnants of the body of the Dragonfather remain to this day in the sea south of Oman'Tar —blood and bone, scale and flesh, never decaying, for this was the broken body of the first of all Dragons, divine of the Numen.

The first death had come to Sylveria, and a great ripple was felt throughout all of the world, for the greatest of Dragons had perished. The whole of creation wept for this loss.

When Ashysin, Merilinder and Sharuseth witnessed the death of their father, they knew that they had received their sign, and they were filled with sorrow, for they had not believed him, and perhaps if they had, he would not have had to perish.

When the Sylvai, the mixed-blooded children of Haldus'nar and Sarak'den, and Alim'dar and Nirvisa'nen learned what had happened, they were incited in their rage, for though they were the good people of the world, they had, for too long, been scorned and maltreated. And it was not as if the people were ignorant of the affairs of Dragons, and they had little doubt about who was behind the death of Kronaggas, for in all things the Nescrai and the Chromatic Dragons had become malicious.

For the foresight of Aranthia, the Haldusians and the Darians had, for two years now, been preparing for war, learning of its tactics and forging weapons of steel and armor, all of it in secret. But now, inspired as they were, they began arming the Sylvai, transforming them in a short time into a militia that could stand against the Nescrai.

THE SECOND DRAGON COUNCIL

With the death of Kronaggas, all those who had not yet been beguiled by the Dark lamented the loss of the Dragonfather. For seven days the servants of the Light mourned, but the Nescrai were publicly silent on the matter—although they were secretly joyful, so far had their moral character declined.

Drovanius, Verasian and Merobassi were distressed and in part even sorrowful, but so too were they corrupted to an extent that allotted them some rejoicing, for now their greatest opposition was gone.

When the seven days had passed, Drovanius called together all of the Dragons and he said to Aranthia, Ashysin, Merilinder and Sharuseth, "Kronaggas has now passed on; he is the first casualty of this war. We have given you time to grieve your loss, and now I reveal to you a dark secret: war is coming, and my people have been made strong, and we will soon overpower the Sylvai and the filth that are the children of Alim'dar, and of Sarak'den, and we will drive them from this land. You are our brothers, and as such, we offer you this: follow with us as we take Sylveria for our children, or perish with your own."

Ashysin said, "Brothers we are not! For we are children of the Light and you have become attendants of the Dark. We know your workings, for Aranthia has done right and has told us of your union with wickedness. Kronaggas has left us with final instructions, to do what we know is right, and it is this that we will do!"

"Kronaggas' last words," Verasian said. "Were the words of a desperate fool who knew his end had come. He could not face the truth of what was coming, and he abandoned you and your children!"

"We do not know the full scale of Kronaggas' sacrifice," Merilinder said. "But we have faith, for there are powers greater than any Dragon at work here in Sylveria. And if we were to go to war against you and the Nescrai, we would be breaking our vows. There is agreement amongst the three of us, that we will uphold our vows and not harm any of the Nescrai, for then their blood would be upon us, and we would be condemned by the Law, just as you will be foredoomed if you persist in this madness. Heed the final words of Kronaggas and turn back from your delusions!"

"We will not," Merobassi said. "For the truth of all things has been revealed to us. The Law is fallacious, and the Light that Kronaggas alleged to be the way is deceiving! We will, for this, drive the Light from these lands, so that our own pure children will prosper!"

"Why do you desire such wicked things?" Sharuseth asked.

"We desire only that the lands of Sylveria belong to the Nescrai," Drovanius said. "For the Sylvai and the *toron* have dominated too long, taking advantage of the Nescraian farms, devouring the fruits of the eastern lands in exchange for foolish baubles and gems and carved stones. They have tainted some of our own children with their foul blood. For this, the world is ours by right. If you desire to save their miserable lives, then take them where you will, so long as it is nowhere in Sylveria."

Aranthia the Crimson then said, "And where would you have us take them? Shall they go to the loathsome lands of Nefaria to die at the hands of the abominations that dwell there? Or shall they dive into the sea and hope for salvation in the depths of the oceans?"

"I care not where they go," Drovanius said coarsely. "But if they do not leave, every one of them will perish at the hands of their stronger cousins."

Merilinder said, "How can you sentence any of the children of Dragons to death? Did you not, five hundred and fifty-two years ago swear a vow unto the Law that you would never harm even one of them, either Nescrai or Sylvai?"

"I did. As did we all. But times have changed and I have seen the falsity and deception that is in the Law by which our oaths were sworn. I have absolved myself from any consequence on these grounds."

"Gaumless brute!" Ashysin roared. "You *cannot* release yourself from such a vow! By no authority can you dissolve your own word, for if this were possible, the value of a promise would be meaningless to begin with!"

Drovanius did not respond. But in some small part of his mind, in the fragment of his soul, there remained a sliver of the Light, for when Merilinder spoke next, the Black Dragon listened.

"I implore you, Drovanius, if you must persist, then allow my people and the Haldusians and the Darians to move out of their lands and into my own domain, far to the south. The Nescrai do not like that region, for it is too hot. Our people would be crowded there, but surely it is better than death."

Ashysin agreed to this, saying, "I too will forfeit my claim upon the mountains if it will save our children, and leave them to you and the Garonites, and they may do with them as they please. Only our children and the Darians and the Haldusians must not be harmed. We will keep the Law and never interfere in your affairs, for you have become of the Dark."

And Sharuseth agreed as well, declaring, "And I too will give over to you my claim upon the region of Mara and the Hilly Lands of the south, if only you will spare our children."

After consorting with Verasian and Merobassi, Drovanius returned to the Metallic Dragons and said, "These are terms we will accept, though with exception, for it is true that the Nescrai do not like the blistering prairie heat in the Summer Seasons. The mountains will serve as a boundary between our peoples, and any of yours who cross into them will be slain by the Garonites for their intrusion. However, neither the Haldusians nor the Darians will go with you to the south, but they will be wiped from the memory of the world, for they are abominations."

"They are our children too!" Merilinder cried. "And yours as well! If you will not consider them amongst your own, then let us keep them with ours!"

But Drovanius would not accept this, for he despised the tainted blood of these people, and he desired that even Haldus'nar and Nirvisa'nen be slain, for though they were his son and daughter, they had defiled themselves by marrying Sylvai. And so the seed planted long ago by the bitter loss of Norgrash'nar had grown into fruition, and the Black Dragon's heart had been consumed.

The Metallic Dragons were distraught, for the destruction of these people would be a great atrocity, but what could they do, save break their sacred vows and lead the people unto their own destruction in a war against the Dark?

Aranthia the Crimson then spoke, saying, "I know that you despise my people, Drovanius—the Haldusians—and the Darians, for in your eyes they are reviling, and I know you count them not worthy to live. Today I tell you that these mixed children will neither leave their lands to you nor die without a fight, for what was given to them in the times when the world was awakening was given to them eternally. I shall perish before I allow even a single one of them, or any of the Sylvai, to have taken away what is theirs!"

Then he turned to the Metallic Dragons and said, "Ashysin, Merilinder and Sharuseth, I pray you consider me your brother though my scales are not like yours. I have seen the wrongness of the others' ploys, and now I urge you not to flee to the Southern Reaches, but to stay and fight! For how long will it be before the corrupting evil overtakes our enemies completely and they decide there is no place in the world, even in the lands of Merilinder, for the Sylvai? Behold! I have been preparing the dark children of Alim'dar and Haldus'nar for war, under the very nose of our enemies, and they are prepared to fight and die for the freedom of all people. These lands were given by right and *we* will fight for them!"

"Dear Aranthia," Sharuseth said remorsefully. "We count you as our brother, for you have not been seduced by the Dark. But in this resistance you propose, will your own vow not be broken? Will you cast it off as Drovanius, Merobassi and Verasian have? If you cannot retain your word, then how far are you from them, from becoming wicked yourself? Do you think there will not be consequence?"

"There is always consequence," Aranthia said firmly. "There is always a price to be paid for doing what is right. And on the day that the Darians and the Haldusians raise their swords in defense of Sylveria, my claws will be drawn and my teeth bared, and I *will* break my ancient vow, for it was taken in another time, when the world was at peace, when the Dark had not yet seeped into every crevice of the souls who are now infected. I will neither let my own people perish for the crimes of Drovanius, nor will I let yours."

But still the Metallic Dragons denied Aranthia's bid, for they feared the retribution of the Law and they thought that their Crimson brother would be drawn unto the same fate as Drovanius.

"I will not try to change your mind, Aranthia," Ashysin said to him. But let me say this... in the time when the people of Garonar were destroying Vindras Vale, I reacted according to my emotions, my rage, and my fear. I trod a fine line that day, when I destroyed the bridges of the city. It is a narrow path that leads from the Light to the Dark, and I fear you are upon it. And now I implore you to allow the Darians and the

Haldusians to make their own choice, whether they will fight or flee."

"They have made their decision already," Aranthia said. "And they are in agreement that not one of them will live in peace so long as there is insurgency against the Light. Flee if you must to the south, and take those with you who desire to live and not die, and I will hold no ill will toward you or them. But let those who wish otherwise to stand with us."

Merobassi, who had, amongst his brothers, been listening to the exchange between Aranthia and the Metallic Dragons, was stirred to speak then, and he said, "Go then, all of you. Hide your people, or watch them perish. We will come into your domains and your cities and your homes and crush all who do not flee to the south. Your people are weak, and ours strong. And woe to the Haldusians and the Darians, for they will be carried away and dropped into the seas, for their sins are beyond reparation."

The council dispelled then, and the Dragons went their separate ways—the Chromatics to prepare for the annihilation of their enemies, the Metallics to evacuate the people from the lands, and Aranthia to set the people upon a course for war.

Ashysin and Sharuseth went to the people of Mara, to tell them that they must leave their homes and their lands, and seek refuge in the south, or they would perish. Likewise, Merilinder went to the Adaasharians and informed them that the Noranites would be joining them in the Southern Reaches, and that also any of the Haldusians or Darians who could escape would come as well and be put into hiding.

But amongst the Noranites, not one of them was prepared to accept this, and they denied the Dragons, saying, "We will not leave our homes, no matter the cost. We have seen the sacrifice of Kronaggas, and we understand the consequence of our decision—if we are to die, then we will die. But we will not succumb to their desire of exile."

And the Adaasharians said to Merilinder, "We would gladly welcome our brothers and our cousins, but we will not stand for the intrusion of the Dark into the world. We will not abandon our brothers, and we will march northward and face the Garonites, and when we have crushed them, we will fight alongside our brethren in Mara."

Aranthia went to the Darians and the Haldusians and told them that the time had arrived. And in the days that followed, they sent weapons and armors and shields and tools of warfare to the Noranites by land, and to the Adaasharians by way of the Etakos Rapids. Although neither the Sylvai nor the mixed-blooded children were as well trained in combat as the Nescrai, they were determined as a whole to fight for what they knew to be right.

Still, Ashysin, Merilinder and Sharuseth remembered the oath they had taken, and they remained morally bound to it, refusing for the sake of the Light to prepare for war. And in this they even tried to discourage the people. But they now rebuked the Dragons, saying "Though you are our fathers, whom we love, and you are even alike to our gods, who love us, we will not run from the threat of war, or of pain, or of suffering, or even death. We will not remain bound to your vows, even if you must. Even the commands of gods should be ignored if they are in conflict with justice."

Suffering the reproach of their own children, the Metallic Dragons became ashamed, and they fled into the southern arm of the Golden Valley, near Ashysin's temple. And as the people prepared for the war that was soon to break, they wept the first tears that had ever fallen from the eyes of a Dragon for what was soon to happen to all of Sylveria. It was then that the Golden Valley became known as the Valley of Tears.

And in all of Sylveria, the people of every nation were incited—the Nescrai determined to obliterate their enemies; the Sylvai, Haldusians and Darians provoked to a point beyond return. Now, there was no avoiding war.

THE BOOK OF

CARNAGE

PROLOGUE TO WAR

In the seasons that followed I often wondered how all things had come to such destruction—how it was that men and women had gone from being brothers and sisters, cousins and friends to killing one another, for we had, all of us, grown in a beautiful and peaceful world. For although we had all known of the death of Kronaggas, in hindsight it seemed that such violence as was to follow came too easily.

But with time I came to understand it... for it was that because the people had no previous experience of death, they also had no real understanding of the finality of it. They had no understanding of what it meant to perish, and it was this that indeed made it easier for the carnage that followed, for in not understanding death, it seemed to them not so terrible of a matter.

It was the fourth day of Wintertide, in the year 552 of the 1st Age, when Kronaggas the White sacrificed himself to the Light so that the good people of the world might be incited to rise up in their own defense. There were seven days of mourning, followed by an additional day upon which the Second Council of Dragons took place. And it was on the first day of Wintermelt of that year when the war officially began.

The Metallic Dragons Ashysin, Merilinder and Sharuseth remained in the Golden Valley, distraught and ashamed, for they knew not what to do. There was no way to protect their children without violating their vow to the Law.

The Garonites cried out from the city of Hest'Vortal, sounding drums of war and blasting on horns of triumph as they marched from their mountain city into the Trenches of Avaron, a path that would take them into the realm of the Noranites, in Mara. The echoes of war sounded out to the east, into the Golden Valley and reached the ears of the Metallic Dragons. In this they were tormented even further, for it was the resonance of the coming destruction of their people.

I was with the Dragons there, that day, for I too had made a vow to the Numen that I would not harm another living creature of Sylveria. Together we mourned, for that which was soon to happen had never before been witnessed by any of us. The hours passed slowly as we waited, tormented, wondering if we were being complacent in the holding of our oaths. Truly, for all of our fears and efforts to avoid war, the true horrors of it were at that time beyond our capacity to comprehend. And this lack of understanding made it easier to hold to our promises, for in righteousness we desired to be servants to the greater good, and to have hope and faith in powers greater than ourselves.

But on the third day of Wintermelt the Garonites breached the mountains and came unto the region of Mara, where the outer villages of the Noranites had yet to be armed. The people were there slaughtered without mercy, and the cries of the dead echoed throughout the silenced lands of Sylveria, through the mountains, and into the ears of we who had remained idle in the Golden Valley. And the torment that these cries brought to the Dragons was insurmountable, for the first of their children had perished viciously. The intensity of the anguish was so great that the Dragons sweat blood from beneath their scales and it ran out into the valley, and yet their restraint remained, and they did nothing.

Then, from out of nowhere there appeared a man—one familiar to me, for I had seen him once before, in the Temple of Kronaggas. He was shorter than the Naiad, his ears rounded rather than pointed, and a thick beard covered his face. Yet he appeared to me not of such age as he had been before.

"I know you..." I said.

He looked to me and said, "I have known of *you* since you were awakened. But of how you would know me I am unaware." Then he turned to Ashysin, Merilinder and Sharuseth, and he said, "Why are you hiding here, while your children perish? Do you not know that they are being slain?"

Ashysin replied, "Who are you and of what creation? For we have never seen your likes..."

"I am not of your time," the man said. "But you must not remain here. You must go to the battle and save your children!"

"But we cannot," Merilinder cried. "For we made a vow long ago to never harm even one of them, any of the children of Dragons. And if we go to war, our vow will be broken."

"If you do not," the man said. "How many of them will die for it?"

"If we do," Sharuseth said. "We will be violating the Law, and destruction will come upon us all."

"Destruction will come regardless, for I have seen what the Nescrai and those evil Dragons are doing to the Sylvai. You must go to them. You are their only hope!"

"Ashysin replied, "Are not our vows and promises to be kept eternally? For if we cast them off and do as we please would we remain any different than our enemies?"

The man, after consideration, said, "That is, I think, dependent on your reasoning. In what state was the world when you made your vows? Was it under the shadow of darkness and war, as it is now? Or was it in a time of peace, when none even knew the meaning of suffering or death? Time and circumstance have relieved you of your vows."

The Dragons considered the small man's words, and as they did so, so too did more of the screams of their dying children echo through the valley, as the onslaught continued. And the words spoken to them by the strange man compelled them to action, and for this provision, the Dragons' hearts suddenly erupted into chaos, and their pain became their fury, filling their souls—a rage that surpassed the loyalty to their oath. Fire filled their eyes and their mouths, and in those moments they were transformed into vicious creatures—though not of the Dark, but rather as Champions of the Light, now bent upon executing all virtues of justice within. In their rage they took flight, toward the battles, unable to allow the suffering of their children now that doom was upon them. And when they saw what was happening as the Nescrai overpowered the Sylvai their fury took hold and they focused the whole of the magic that was within them and it became a powerful and deadly weapon that issued forth from their mouths and soon fire rained down upon the enemy. The scales of battle would now be balanced.

As the Dragons took flight, each in their own direction, I was left behind in the Valley of Tears with the man; my own vow remained unbroken. So I said to him, whom I knew to be the essence of the Numen, for I had visited with him before, "What should I do, Numen? I have thus far held to my promise, but I too would like to help them."

"I do not know why you call me *Numen*, Alak'kiin, but if *you* have made a vow, it is for you to decide if you will keep it or deny it. You are but one man, and not a significant force... perhaps you would best serve as an advisor, a recorder of the events of this age. Your abilities lend you well to this, do they not?"

As I considered this, looking to the man, he began to dematerialize before me, and I wondered what could be happening, for he had not seemed to understand why I called him Numen... Something more was happening here that I could not discern. And as he faded away he left me with the final words, "Do what you know to be best, Alak'kiin." Then he was gone, and I was left alone in the valley.

Across the lands of Sylveria the war erupted, and as it was, I could be in only one place at a given time, and did not bear witness to all aspects, battles, or proceedings. Yet for the sake of inclusiveness, the following chapters are derived from the accounts of my brethren as witnessed by them during the stages of the First Dragonwar. In truth, I played but a small role in the greater extent of the events that followed.

The Battle of Eswear'Nysin

For the Haldusians and Aranthia the Crimson, the war began on the first day of Wintermelt, 552, during the Hour of Lastlight. The Sky City known as Vainus appeared to the west, seeming upon a course set for Eswear'Nysin. Encircling the massive hovering structure was Drovanius the Black.

Haldus'nar and Sarak'den were in the city, for they had known that war was coming, and they had been preparing their people for this very day. Aranthia too was ready, though he was perched upon the causeway of his temple, three Marches to the South of Eswear'Nysin, keeping watch upon the lowlands, for they knew not where the enemy's assaults would begin. Fire filled the Dragon's eyes—though not his mouth—for unlike Ashysin, Merilinder, and Sharuseth, Aranthia had not suffered the transformation; magic was still this Dragon's weapon.

The hour of the assault of Vainus was well planned, for it coincided with the failing light of Aros, far to the west, and the Sky City came against Eswear'Nysin into an almost direct position between the sun and the Haldusian city, so that the intense light cascaded over the top of the city. And so the Haldusians were blinded by the light, making the exact discernment of the Nescrai's tactics difficult.

The enemy then came out of the apertures and gates of the flying city—a thousand strong—Nescrai men and women upon winged contraptions that were called Sailplanes. These were but simple designs that strapped onto the backs of the people and allowed them to glide from high above to places below. Blocked as they were by the light of the sun, they were practically unseen until they were upon the top tower wall of Eswear'Nysin, and upon the outer mantles. While most of them came to land upon the highest places in the city, in the garden atop the tower, others missed their mark entirely and sailed past and below the ledges of the cliffs of Aranthia. Others still struck stone as they had not the height to clear the top of the city. And one unfortunate Nescrai lost control of the Sailplane and was propelled directly into the giant arrow of one of the Haldusian ballistas, which had not yet been fired. This was the first blood spilled in the Battle of Eswear'Nysin.

The ballistas had not yet been fired, for Vainus was out of range and even if the operators had seen the coming of the Sailplanes they could not have taken aim, for they were too slow to align themselves with a fast-moving target. Yet archers were atop the tower, and once the assault began, there was little time to draw arrow, and they were forced into melee with the intruders.

Soon after the first assault was launched, a second wave of Sailplanes departed from Vainus, this one larger, perhaps two thousand, these aiming themselves to the ground below, upon the Highlands, at the outer base of Eswear'Nysin. Many more of these arrived at their intended destination, and shedding their wings, they engaged the Haldusians who guarded the city gates. With forged steel the cousin peoples clashed for the first time in history, sealing the animus between them forever.

About three thousand of the Nescrai then planned to engage the citizens and soldiers of the city, and the Haldusians wondered why so few, for the entire population of Vainus was at least ten times this number. They considered that either the Nescrai thought highly enough of their own skills and that it would be enough, or that maybe such arrogance was warranted, and they *were* skilled enough. Neither of these proved to be true…

Upon the city top, five Spans above, Haldus'nar and Sarak'den both fought amongst their people, he with a longsword, she with a dagger and an elegant, magic sword. Though it was true that the lords of this city were not so well trained as the Nescrai, for they had far less time in preparation, they evened this with their use and understanding of magic, for they were able to will their spells upon both the weapons of their fellows, and upon the people themselves. These were spells causing their weapons to pierce deeper, to strike harder, to slow down their enemies while they were increased.

There were perhaps two hundred of the Haldusians upon the tower top, coming against nearly a thousand of the Nescrai… In this battle the Nescrai were highly favored.

"Retreat to the ingress!" Haldus'nar roared, and the Haldusians followed his command, backing away into a formation that surrounded the one entrance into the tower, which was a stone top that covered the stairwell into the city. This stone could be moved by means of a mechanical contraption that pulled the carved masonry top into or out of place.

When the battle seemed even more dire for the Haldusians, he commanded them, "Get below! You too, Sarak'den!" And all but his wife listened.

"If we are to keep them out of the city," Sarak'den cried over the rageful cries of the Nescrai, "It will take both of us."

Haldus'nar nodded and said, "Blind them!" And as the Haldusians moved below, both he and his wife together willed into being a great burst of light that blinded, for the moment, all of the surrounding Nescrai.

Expected as it was, the Lord and Lady of Aranthia were unaffected, as they closed their own eyes to protect their vision. "Seal the city!" Haldus'nar commanded.

The stone soon began shifting into place, and there remained only a short window for Haldus'nar and Sarak'den to enter. Swinging wide his sword, he told his wife to get below, and she listened, knowing that he would be right behind.

But Haldus'nar became entangled, for the fallen Nescrai still had upon them the mechanical contraptions that were the Sailplanes, or what was left of them, and he became snared in the cables of one of them. Only Sarak'den made it into the city before the door sealed, and Haldus'nar was left alone in the trampled garden atop the city of Eswear'Nysin.

Upon the ground, the two thousand Nescrai came to rest after their trek through the air, and they were there engaged by the larger force of the Haldusians, who came out of the city gates against them.

By this time, Aranthia the Crimson had arrived, for from the temple in the south he had seen the assault of the Sky City. He had before waited at Atim'Unduri, keeping watch for any assault that might come by way of the sea. But he had not seen any sign and thought maybe the Nescrai were dull enough to have attacked only by air. And when he saw that Drovanius was present at Vainus, he thought it best to engage his brother, for the power of a Dragon might prove devastating to the people. Never had one of his kind come up against an army, though, and he was wise enough to know that the weaponry devised in Nefaria and adapted to both sides in this war could be deadly to a Dragon. The great ballistas could severely pierce or wound a Dragon and its wings.

When Aranthia arrived at Eswear'Nysin, Drovanius had yet to notice him, and was occupied near Vainus. Seeing Haldus'nar alone atop the city, he soared as quickly as possible to the aid of his favored son. It was just as Haldus'nar was nearly overwhelmed that Aranthia's magic fell upon the Nescrai. Now, although it is drawn from the same source—the will of the caster—a Dragon's magic is much different than that used by the Naiad, and it is with spoken word or the drawing of a breath that the great beasts issued their mystical commands. They were words not even of the Dragons' tongue, but words from beyond this world. And when Aranthia spoke them, storm clouds swarmed in from all directions in an instant, and bolts of lightning struck fiercely in a circle all around Haldus'nar, scorching all of the Nescrai in their path; fifty perhaps fell in this first strike. And Aranthia felt no remorse in that instant, for all around him he saw the slain corpses of many of his children, and those whom he had killed were children of corruption, and in this he disavowed his kinship with the Nescrai.

This gave Haldus'nar time to recover and untangle himself. There he willed his own commands, and his sword became like a whip of light that lashed out at further enemies as they approached, coming over the corpses of their own kind. The whip cut through the armor of the attackers, lacerating their flesh and causing severe pain that took them out of combat. Further lashes and further strikes of lightning kept the Nescrai held back, but it would not be enough to stop them all. For then, coming out of Vainus were thousands more upon their Sailplanes, some to the tower top, but most to the lands below.

Then Aranthia looked and he saw that just as Vainus was drawing closer to Eswear'Nysin, so too was Drovanius coming toward them, for the magical bolts of electricity had drawn his attention, and he knew it was time to confront his brother.

"Drovanius!" he cried out. "Stop this madness before more die!"

"I did not force this war upon you," the Black Dragon roared, soaring closer. "You have done this with your idleness. For had you done what was right and not compelled the Haldusians to action, they would soon be buried by our might!"

And in Drovanius' words, Aranthia saw the complete decline of reason, for the Black Dragon had in his madness assumed that even his Crimson brother was crying out in sorrow for the deaths of the Nescrai, for largely, thus far, it had been they who were falling in battle.

"You are beyond reckoning, Drovanius!" Aranthia cried, and he began reciting the words that would bring even more death down upon the wicked Nescrai, for his tolerance of evil had come to its end.

But he was cut off, not by Drovanius, but by Haldus'nar, who said, "Take care of Drovanius! I will get myself off these walls!" And trusting his beloved son in his own wisdom, Aranthia instead unleashed the spell of lightning upon his brother.

Drovanius shrieked with pain, but so mighty was he that little real harm came to him. Yet he retaliated with mystical words of his own, and a great and thunderous blast sounded throughout the Highlands, and Aranthia was thrown backward through the air by an unseen force. Upon the top of Eswear'Nysin, even the Nescrai and Haldus'nar were knocked to the ground, even as Aranthia recovered. Likewise, little harm was done to him by Drovanius' magic. It became clear to both of them that this battle would be settled by tooth and claw and not by magic.

As soon as Haldus'nar saw that the Nescrai had been thrown to the ground, just as he had, he took the opportunity of confusion to run toward the nearest edge, where he found upon the blood-stained stone a fallen Nescrai still strapped into the Sailplane gear. Quickly he removed it, and he struggled to attach it to himself even as the Nescrai came for him. Though he was unskilled in the operation of such a device, Haldus'nar nevertheless took a leap of faith off the side of the city just as he finished strapping himself in.

He toppled through the air at first, but soon found that the winged sails were designed to right themselves and he began slowly gliding to the lands below, where another battle raged. He looked up and saw that many of the Nescrai had also taken the dive and were pursuing him to the ground. So too were others joining them, the most recent sailors from Vainus.

In the air, Drovanius and Aranthia clashed, their massive bodies striking one another, claws lashing out, teeth gnashing, in what was the first physical altercation between the Dragons of Sylveria. It was unclear who would win in this quarrel.

When Haldus'nar had been left behind atop the tower city of Eswear'Nysin, and Sarak'den realized it, she commanded that the Haldusians open it back up. But following a protocol that had before been established, they refused, and explained to her that the Nescrai would breach the city if they did. She knew them to be right, and instead she began the long run down the many flights of stairs that would lead to the battlefield below. The others followed, gathering all of the available soldiers and citizens who would fight along the way.

At the base of the city, two thousand Norgrasharians engaged the larger force of the Haldusians, and despite the greater numbers, the Nescrai were overpowering them with their superior combat skills. The Nescrai, empowered by over two hundred years of developing hatred for the mix-blooded people of Aranthia, fought with vicious strikes that left their enemies split open, crushed, and defeated. And coming from above were the many reinforcements in pursuit of Haldus'nar, and they were nearing the ground.

Still, Drovanius and Aranthia tore at one another in the sky, and Vainus grew ever closer to Eswear'Nysin.

When Sarak'den and her forces reached the outer gate of the city, the Haldusians' own reinforcements arrived, for with them was the greater portion of the city's combatants. And in addition to this arriving ground force, the archers of the city came out upon the lower mantles; half of them began raining arrows down upon the Nescrai, while the others targeted the downward sailing enemy. When a sufficient number of them had fallen, the ground force flooded out, now including a great number of the people of Eswear'Nysin. This force now was four times the number of remaining Nescrai, and this made for a more even fight.

As Haldus'nar came down upon the battlefield, Sarak'den joined him, swiftly helping him to remove the Sailplane gear so that they could fight side by side. She said, "How did you survive up there?"

"Only with Aranthia's help."

Above, the Dragons' fight had brought them closer to the city and the ground, and when Aranthia glanced and saw that so many of the Haldusians had come to their end, rage filled him, and he struck viciously at Drovanius. One of his claws tore through the membrane of the Black Dragon's wing; he shrieked in agony and took a dive away from Aranthia and toward the ground.

Now all of the sky forces of the Nescrai had joined the fray upon the ground. By the dozens both Nescrai and Haldusians fell to deadly wounds and the scene was littered with blood, severed limbs, and broken bodies. All present were in a state of shock and had it not been for the rush of battle, they might all have collapsed for their own fear, for so great was the carnage of the battle, and none of them had before seen such a sight.

Drovanius recovered slightly, still able to fly but not so well as before, and he thought that he would no longer be a match for Aranthia, who was propelled onward by his own conviction. And he flew not back into the struggle, but retreated instead toward Vainus, which was drawing ever closer to the tower city, perhaps now only twenty spans away.

And Aranthia saw then why it was coming so close, for mounted upon the floating city were ballistas of a similar design to those still unused upon the top of Eswear'Nysin. And the Nescrai there began firing, not only at the high walls of the tower, but at Aranthia as well. The Crimson Dragon had little difficulty in dodging the bolts, but was distracted by this assault.

Then Drovanius came to land upon the outer wall of the Sky City and he barked out a command to the people there. Immediately they ceased in the cranking and releasing of the projectiles, and instead began strapping themselves into Sailplanes.

Although the battle below on the highlands was turning in the favor of the Haldusians, Aranthia saw that this would be only further reinforcements for the Nescrai, and that all of his people here might be slain. But this was not the intent of the Nescrai who leaped from the city, for they did not glide toward the battlefield, but instead to the west and south, away from the battle, thousands of the last Nescraian occupants of the city. Drovanius soon followed, and they together sailed down toward the western shore of Varis Lake. They were abandoning Vainus.

Upon the ground Haldus'nar and Sarak'den survived the battle, and when nearly all of the Nescrai had been slain, the remainder surrendered reluctantly, for they had been defeated by their loathed enemies, and because they knew what was coming next...

Then they heard in a voice that was deeper, louder and more penetrating than any they had ever heard, the cry of Aranthia, "Get out of the city!" He was hovering between Eswear'Nysin and the Sky City of

Vainus, in a gap that was quickly narrowing.

Sarak'den knew then what was happening and she cried out to the people, "Get away from the walls, as far as you can!" And the Haldusians ran.

"Aranthia!" Haldus'nar screamed. "Get out of there!"

And just in time, the Crimson Dragon took flight upward and over the city. A moment later, Vainus collided with the tower just as a great crash was heard of stone on stone; so too were there heard the terrified cries of countless people who were trapped in the Sky City. These, they could only assume, were the Sylvai who had occupied the city, for not one of them had been seen evacuating.

The entirety of Vainus came upon Eswear'Nysin that evening, just as the last light of Aros fell upon the land. The tower collapsed under the falling weight of itself, just as Vainus, now unable to retain its own flight, was deflected back to the west and to the south, where it fell into the Gaping Sea.

Thousands had died at Eswear'Nysin, and thousands of the Sylvai had occupied Vainus and were drowned in the sea. Drovanius had used this one Sky City as a sacrifice to guarantee the destruction of the greatest city of the Haldusians. Though he had been injured and many of his own people had perished, it was clear who had won this battle, for the beacon city of an entire civilization had crumbled.

Those of the Haldusians who survived gathered together upon the Aranthian Highlands south of where their great city had fallen. Throughout the night and into the next day they searched the wreckage for any survivors, but few were found.

To the west of Varis Lake, Aranthia watched as the wounded Drovanius and the surviving Nescrai fled to the shoreline of the Gaping Sea. There, the people remained with nowhere else to go. For now, they were not a threat. His heart torn, Aranthia resumed watch over his lands, for he was certain that the Nescrai were not finished.

Assault by Sea

The loss of Vainus was an intentional and acceptable loss to Drovanius and the Nescrai, for this had not been the entirety of their plan against the island of Aranthia. And when the Hour of Feltide came, on the second day of Wintermelt, so too did the ground assault begin...

Although Aranthia had been watching for this very thing he had not anticipated the tactics of the Norgrasharians. For when he looked out over the shoreline to the south and west, the Dragon saw no sign of the

Nescrai's approach by sea, and he thought that they must have kept all of their forces upon the mainland, save for those who had invaded from Vainus.

But the Dragon was wrong, and as the surging tides came in, so too were the ships of the Norgrasharians drawn in from far out to sea, outside of the Dragon's range of vision. They came from the south, from where they would also be unseen by the watchmen upon the Horn of Aranthia, and onto the shores of the Shallow Lands. Here, at the Hour of Feltide, the ocean dragged the Nescraian ships far inland, where they crashed upon the lowlands of Aranthia, exactly where they wanted to be. A hundred of the ships there were, each holding an army of a hundred of the trained fighters, armed with sword and spear, mace and axe, and armored in Nefarian steel.

But it was not only the Haldusians of Eswear'Nysin that had been trained in combat and armed with weapons similarly forged to those of the Nescrai, for all across Aranthia the people had settled and in every city, village, homestead and farm there were found those who could fight. When word reached them that Eswear'Nysin had fallen and that a new threat was coming upon them, they rallied and together moved toward two positions along the lowlands. The first was north and west of the Shallow Lands, and the other was to the northeast, across the Lord's River that came down from the Highlands.

There were but two easy pathways from these lowlands onto the highlands, and the Nescrai anticipated that the enemy would guard both of these ways; and this was confirmed for them by the two places of gathering of the armed Haldusians, for the group to the east of the river stood before one, and those to the west guarded the other. But now that the capitol city of Eswear'Nysin had fallen, they saw no reason to even mount the Highlands—at least not until they had destroyed the Haldusians who guarded the lowlands.

Norgrash'nar was amongst those Nescrai who had come ashore, and it was he who decided it best to divide his own forces, one to engage each of the Haldusian divisions. So while he sent his firstborn son, Rhinusor to lead their eastern party, he himself led to the west.

In the east, which was the region of the Bolaias Farms, the opposing armies were evenly matched in number, for the smaller division led by Rhinusor had gone over the river; thus, it was here that Aranthia went to aid, for, again, the Nescrai were more well suited for combat than the farmers and villagers of those places. But by the time he arrived, the battlefield was too comingled for his spells of lightning to be used, for his aim was too uncertain. And instead, the Crimson Dragon landed amongst the conflicting Naiad, and he culled the Nescrai with his giant claws, and struck at them with his mighty tail, crushing those who were the descendants of some of his own children. Though it grieved him to do this, so too did he recall that the Norgrasharians had long ago followed their father into darkness, and by consequence they were, in his mind, justified for death, and the Haldusians, having been the noble occupants of his lands for many long years, had become his true children, those he loved more than any.

So fearsome and frightful was the Dragon's slaughter of the Nescrai, that the Haldusians withdrew, clearing a path for Aranthia's destruction. Hundreds came against him all at once, and each billow of the Nescrai was ended that day by Aranthia. Though he suffered wounds himself—piercings under his scales, shattered claws and broken teeth, he would not be stopped, for the Nescrai had crossed a line and Aranthia would not allow them to prevail. And those who survived the battle that day knew it would never again be wise to nettle a Dragon enraged.

The first son of Norgrash'nar, Rhinusor, was slain that day by Aranthia the Crimson, and the Dragon regretted it not, for the atrocities of the Nescrai warranted their slaughter.

In the west, upon the Plains of Dinis, the Haldusians outnumbered the Nescrai two to one; in this was perhaps an even match. Regardless, the Haldusians did not face off against them, but rather, when the enemy led by the First Awakened Son Norgrash'nar ordered the advancement of his army the Haldusians retreated to the north, up the Lord's Way, which was the steep incline that led onto the Highlands.

Norgrash'nar, considering them frightened and weak, ordered the pursuit up to the higher grounds. But knowing their own lands, and having prepared for such an event, the Haldusians had long ago built a gate that crossed the top of this way, and they sealed it behind them, so that the Norgrasharians would be slowed. The Lord's Gate was constructed of thick wood brought from the forests of the lowlands, and reinforced with steel.

It was then, as Norgrash'nar stood at the gate, that Drovanius rejoined the fight, for he had recovered enough from his injury to do so. He landed beside his son, saying, "Take your people back, Norgrash'nar. I will tear this gate from its stone mounts and we will have victory today!" He drove his giant claws into the wooden planks of the gate, and though they were as thick as trees, the wood shattered and showered the Haldusians with splinters forcefully enough to penetrate thin armor and flesh. Then the Dragon grasped the steel beams that framed the gates and he pulled with all of his might. The stalwart frame held, but rattled the stone foundations onto which they were affixed. He pulled again and the stone began to crumble. And then, the Haldusians struck...

For hidden there, all along the knolls along the southern edge of the highland plains they had dug out many Spans of open underpasses and covered them with moss and vines and other vegetation so that enemy Dragons passing overhead would not be aware of their presence. And within these vestibules were waiting a cavalry of men and women upon the backs of the Felheim. These steeds were those like horses, but covered in black scales, spikes of hardened integuments that ran down their spines, and with fire in their eyes. The riders of the Felheim then lined up all across the broken gateway that spanned the top of the pass; then they waited...

For so too had the Haldusians moved into position, hidden from an overhead view by the wide frame of the gates, fifty of their ballistas, these fitted to shoot large stones that had been worked into spheres. And as soon as Drovanius broke through the steel frames of the gate, each of them fired. Three of them struck the Dragon with such force that bone cracked, scales crumbled and he cried out with pain. The remainder of the boulders began their journey down the slopes, rolling over and crushing many of the Nescrai.

As the ballista operators reloaded, the Felheim charged, leaping over the lower frame of the gate and charging down the slopes. As they passed Drovanius by, they missed not the opportunity to lash out at with him with sword and lance and he suffered many more wounds, many of them to his wings, intended so that the Dragon might not fly away. The cavalry continued downward then, into the masses of Nescrai.

By this time, which was approaching the Hour of Devotion on this, the second day of Wintermelt, Haldus'nar, Sarak'den, and many of the surviving Haldusians from Eswear'Nysin arrived to join the fight just as the Felheim were galloping from the gate. And they came through to face Drovanius, who now was battered, torn and weakened.

"It is not too late, Drovanius," Sarak'den said. "We do not want your destruction, or that of your people. End this now."

The Dragon spoke not, only panted in strained breaths, but the hatred in his eyes was apparent. But another did speak, for coming from behind the Dragon, still unscathed, was Norgrash'nar. Calmly he said, "You will not win this battle, or this war, Brother."

"Norgrash'nar," Haldus'nar said. "So many lives have been lost this day... Can we not just end this peacefully? Return to your lands, and leave us, so that the bloodshed might end."

"Not until the last of your children are removed from these lands, and all of Sylveria."

"What has brought you to such complete iniquity?" Sarak'den asked. "For five hundred years we always found a way to—"

"The time for debate has ended. The war *is* here and it will not end until we have slain the last of your foul children."

The ballistas were reloaded now, and Haldus'nar lowered his head regretfully and ordered the unleashing of another bombardment, for from far below, a horn had just sounded, signaling that the cavalry had reached the end of the line of the enemy and that they were clear. Now six of the boulders assailed Drovanius, and he cried out with such agony that Sarak'den cringed for his sake. The rest of the stones plummeted down the slopes, cutting through the Nescrai who were just now recovered from the previous round, and from the assault of the Felheim and their riders.

Norgrash'nar was unharmed, and just as Haldus'nar and Sarak'den were together about to cast a binding spell upon him, he willed his own protection and instead of engaging them, he mounted the dilapidated Dragon. Drovanius then took off from the ground, a clumsy and crooked affair, and with his son Norgrash'nar, limped through the air to the west, away from the fight, abandoning the remainder of the Nescrai to their demise at the hands of the Haldusians, for despite their haughty words, they knew the battle was lost.

The battles for Aranthia had been won—if a victory could even be considered in such circumstances, for tens of thousands of the Haldusians and Nescrai had been killed in just two days of warfare.

"We cannot let them escape," Sarak'den said remorsefully.

"We will wait for Aranthia then," Haldus'nar said. "Let our children see to the capture of the Nescrai who remain at Varis, and here."

"We will take their survivors into custody. We cannot release them so long as this war continues on the Mainland."

"And when this is done, let our men and women go across the sea, into Verasian, so that we can continue the fight for our true brothers and sisters, the Sylvai, and for Alim'dar and his children."

Orders then were given to the commanders of the Haldusian forces. The survivors of battle on both of the southern fronts gathered together and Haldus'nar and Sarak'den were reunited with Aranthia. Together they decided to pursue Drovanius and Norgrash'nar into his own lands, so that they might find a way to end this war—so that perhaps the bloodshed that had fallen on their lands would not have to come to all of Sylveria.

Several days later, on the fourth day of Wintermelt, Drovanius the Black was seen flying south of Aranthia, to the east, presumably back to his own lands, defeated and no longer a threat. But this was not so, for the vengeance, impetuosity and the madness of this Dragon was more than anyone had imagined, and he went far beyond the reaches of his own domain, and returned unto the dark lands of Nefaria.

Retreat to Mara

It was on the third day of Wintermelt, 552, one day after Drovanius and Norgrash'nar had come against Aranthia and the Haldusians, when the first fight of the war came upon Mara. The Sylvai who had settled in the region to the east of the Hilly Lands—which had once been disputed territory between the Garonites and the Noranites—had been existing for some time in a state of worry, for as rumors of coming war swept over the lands, they worried that it was they who would be the first victims if Garonar ordered an army to attack Mara. The most direct route to Mara from Hest'Vortal—the center of the Garonite population—passed through the Trenches of Avaron. But so too did many Garonites dwell in the mountains and in Vindras Vale, and they came through the Tybor River Valley Pass and these two forces came together to assault the peaceful villages of eastern Mara.

When word spread across the land that the war was indubitably coming, the people prepared as best as they could, arming themselves with the few weapons that had been distributed thus far from Alim'dar and with the tools of their trade, which were pitchforks, axes and scythes. The citizens of this land were farmers by trade, for this far to the east the land had been cultivated where the forests of the Baobab Trees had yet to spread.

Alunen herself had brought word and weapon to these people in the days leading up to the war. She promised these farmers that reinforcements would come as soon as possible, as Norandar himself was organizing the trained fighters of Mara. But even with the reassurance of their Mother, the people were wracked with fear, for they knew not the true implications of war—they had heard of course of death and suffering, but having never seen it they had little understanding, and this stood in their minds as overwhelming consternation.

On this day, when the war began, at the Hour of Eventide, horns blasted from the mountains to the southeast, signaling the coming armies. Soon, the distant throbbing of drums arrived—a tactic meant to bring fear into the hearts of the victims of the coming attack. And in this it was quite effective.

Erring on the side of caution and seeing the great trepidation that was falling on the farmers and villagers of the Eastern Settlements, Alunen ordered that they immediately retreat, back to the northwest, through the High Hills of Imara, and toward the forests of Mara, where they would be safer. But while most quickly gathered their necessities into wagons and upon horseback, there were those who chose instead to stay and fight. Many of these were those who had been quickly trained in the basics of combat and who were considered to be elites (though in comparison to their enemies, their skills were quite unmatched). So too did many offer to stay so that they might slow down the march of the enemy and give more time for their children to escape.

It was these men and women's cries of slaughter that echoed throughout the region and into the Valley of Tears, where Ashysin, Merilinder and Sharuseth were transformed into the champions they became. For as the Garonites arrived in the Eastern Settlements, they came from their two routes. These two armies met at the Hills of Imara, where those who had remained were trapped between the southern branch of the Iidin River that came out of Naiad, the mountains, and the hills from which the Garonites came. In but a short time they were slain, and not one was able to get out to tell the Noranites that the numbers that came against them were far greater than they had anticipated.

West of the High Hills of Imara were the southern forests of Mara; it was to this region that Alunen led the people from the east on the fifth day of Wintermelt, for she thought they would be best concealed in the forests. They would fight better there, amongst the trees. But upon arrival, two of the Sky Cities of Kor'Magailin came into view, hovering over the lands— Mishran to the south, Dian to the north—and Alunen knew not what the state of the cities was. For in years past, Kor'Magailin had been occupied by the Sylvai as well as the Nescrai. Still, it was thought, as the rumors of war grew, that being of Nescraian design, the cities would likely be controlled by their enemies.

This in fact proved to be true as Alunen led the people to the northwest, for when they were seen from above, the Nescrai dropped to the ground from Mishran upon Sailplanes, just as they had in the lands of Aranthia. But here, the thick branches of the trees became a kind of netting, trapping many of the Nescrai's contraptions within, stranding them many Heights above the ground below. Knowing that her people had been viciously killed in the east—for their cries had come even this far to the west—Alunen ordered those armed with bows to eliminate the Nescrai who were bound above. Though some of the Nescrai made it through to the forest floor, most were killed in the higher realm of the forest. Those who did come upon the ground did so in numbers small enough that the Noranites could eradicate them without much effort.

And so they were left fleeing only the pursuing Garonites who came from the Hilly Lands and from the Eastern Settlements, who were still at least several Marches behind. This gave them a window of opportunity to escape across the Southern Divide. But this would be risky, for just east of there was the place where Dian hovered high overhead.

And as with Mishran, by the thousands the Nescrai soared to the ground upon their Sailplanes. Here too did many get entangled, but these were better equipped, for as they hung from the high places in the trees, they fired arrows down upon the Sylvai, and many were pierced as they fled the onslaught from above. Those that came upon the ground were also better prepared, and in greater numbers as they had directed their flights to bring them together, so that they could stand as a unit against Alunen and her people.

It was at the Hour of Elation when the well-armed Nescrai came upon the ground against them, and when Sylvaian reinforcements arrived—for coming across the Southern Divide, Norandar had come with an army sufficient enough to handle the sky-fallen enemy; and from the northeast did come another powerful ally—Sharuseth the Copper, enflamed now by the transformation that had brought him into the war. Seeing the Nescrai hanging from the high places in his forested land, Sharuseth unleashed his fiery breath, which was now the essence of his magic, and set both leaf and branch ablaze, scorching to death those Nescrai who had not yet died, both in the trees and upon the ground.

Norandar's army, consisting of ten thousand men and women, came across the Southern Divide just as Sharuseth was raining fire upon the remnants of those who had come from above. Yet still these were but the invaders from the Sky Cities, and the great force of the Garonites that had come from the hills and the mountains still remained. According to Sharuseth, their numbers were twice that of the Noranites here present. And so too, he explained, "To the north, coming out of the Valley of Naiad, there is a legion of the Norgrasharians, marching from the northern region of Verasian. There is no Dragon amongst them, but their force is mighty. Ashysin has gone to slow their advance."

"This is but a division of our own forces," Norandar said. "We have companies to the east, near the Plains of Kronaggas, ready for them. And Alim'dar has already sent word that his army will soon be marching to our aid. Where is Merilinder?"

"I know not for sure. Probably to the south, with his own people. We each have gone upon our own way, each of us ready at last to redeem our children. With my last breath I will defend you and your people... our people."

"How far will you go?" Alunen asked, looking off to the east, through the forest, which the Garonites would soon breach. Fear was upon her, upon everyone. In so short a time there had been too much death. "How far will you go to save us?"

Sharuseth understood by the tone in her voice, by the look in her eyes, and the regret upon her features, what it was that she was suggesting. "I love my forests," he said. "But I love our people more."

Norandar and Alunen, now reunited, led the people and their army back across the Southern Divide to the north, and there set up the place where they would make their stand.

In the planning of the war, in the seasons leading up to it, when Drovanius, Norgrash'nar and Garonar, and their wives and children planned how the campaign of extermination would unfold, they had not counted on the intervention of the Metallic Dragons, and did not even count Aranthia as a certainty. So when the Garonites came out of the hills and out of the Eastern Settlements into Southern Mara, they expected to either overpower their enemies, or to drive them to retreat. And when they came into the woodlands where their Nescrai kin had sailed from the sky and been burned alive in the trees and upon the ground, they thought still that it was just a desperate tactic of the Noranites, enacted as they fled from the coming army.

The two companies of the Garonites joined together late on that day, just to the east of Imara, outside of the forests of Sharuseth. There they made camp, for they had a full day of slaughter awaiting them upon the next.

Neither Garonar nor Kuranen were present amongst these companies; there still was a multitude that was held back in Hest'Vortal, for they knew that they still had the Adaasharians to contend with, if they were to enter into the war. This company, unused for now, was comprised of the most elite of the fighters and warriors of the Garonites, for they had in times past participated in the games of the Coliseum, which had grown to become contests of strength and skillful abilities in the years since their training in Nefarian warfare had begun. And in the first days of the war, while even their own brothers were dying, the Garonites continued their games, though they remained on constant watch for an intrusion into the mountains by the Adaasharians.

In Southern Mara, where the Garonites had made camp, at the Hour of Attrition when most of them slept, Sharuseth struck. He started first at the mouth of the South Umonar River, and he traced a line of fire across the eastern reaches of this region all the way to the edge of the Hilly Lands, then back again to the eastern side of the High Hills of Imara, where the enemy was camped, so that the Garonites had little place to retreat.

It was the season of Wintermelt and only a light covering of snow remained, clothing the fallen leaves below; the high places of the Baobab trees were dry and burned with great ferocity. It was not until the Hour of Midnight, when Sharuseth had finished his blazing trail that the Garonites awoke and realized the peril of the tactic, for they were caught unaware by the heat and light coming from the east.

The fire spread quickly from Imara, westward, driving the unsuspecting army of the Garonites to quickly press onward, in the darkness of night, with only the faint light of Imrakul to ease the way. But as they moved away from the close blazes of the forest fire, they were met with another more searing wall of flame, for here the trees had burned longer. Trapped as they seemed, they saw but one way out—to the north, across the Varin'soth River. Though they wished not to brave its rapids, they saw this as their only escape, for the burning Baobabs created an impenetrable wall of flame nearly a Span tall that was closing in.

The Garonites moved northward, and in doing so were forced to abandon much of their gear—their instruments of war, their carts of supplies and even their weapons and armor. Most escaped that night with their lives, but with little else. And they were—as Sharuseth and the Noranites hoped—left with a choice. They could go to the west across the Southern Plains of Kronaggas and resume their campaign with only weapons they could devise from the land, they could turn back and retreat to the mountains across Eastern Mara, or they could remain where they were and hope for reinforcements to arrive from either Hest'Vortal or from the Norgrasharians, whom they knew were coming out of Naiad, six Marches to the northeast. Tired from their retreat across the river and having had little rest the night before, the Garonites elected to stay where they were for now.

And although this was a victory for the Noranites and Sharuseth that early morning of the fifth day of Wintermelt, there would be retaliation, and it would come swiftly upon them.

When Aros emerged from the Veil the next morning, the Nescrai who controlled the Sky City of Dian saw the still burning forest below, and they knew that their brothers had been defeated, if not entirely wiped out, for the Noranites had not moved from their positions to the west. So they moved their city from just to the east of where the Noranites had set their own army, so that it would hover directly over Aisper Hill. Though they knew that they had not enough of a force to send to the ground to defeat the Noranites, the Nescrai there in Dian had other plans, for the Sky Cities had been designed to not only be cities of occupation, but also machines of war—though the designs of warfare had been hidden well within the understanding of the mechanics that kept the cities afloat. And this knowledge was held exclusively by the Norgrasharians and the Garonites.

Dian hovered over the entirety of the Noranite army that was there present, and turning off some of the engines that kept it airborne, it began sinking toward the earth, lower still as the moments passed on, and Alunen and Norandar wondered if their people might be crushed if it persisted. Soon, winds were stirred by the exhaust of the turbines, torrents of hot air that made it difficult to breathe. In a panic, the Noranites began fleeing the scene to the north.

Although they tried to organize and calm the people, Alunen and Norandar were ineffective, as their commands could not be heard over the whining and grinding of the ever-nearing engines. Sharuseth was exhausted from the expelling of the whole of his fire upon the forests the night before, and was little help in anything other than getting himself to safety so that he might recover, and so he retreated as well, to the north, with the greater number of the Noranites.

As Dian neared collision with Aisper Hill, it came to a stop in its declination, and there unleashed the fullness of its wrath. For not only did the engines exhaust the hot air, but so too was there the design to expel the oily lubricants and waste that served the mechanics of the Sky Cities. And here they were released, spraying out over a great area that soaked the land and the Noranites in a viscous sludge that they thought would catch fire. For then came upon the edges of the city the Nescrai, who dropped barrels of burning oil which they hoped would ignite the whole of the forest below.

But to the fortune of the Noranites, the sludge burned not with flame that scorched them, but only created thick clouds of smoke that covered the land, and covered them from the view of the Nescrai above. Thereafter, many of the Noranites fell ill with dyspnea from inhaling the fumes, but as a whole they escaped to the north, out of the current range of the Sky City of Dian.

Once they had come out of the smog, the Noranites took time to recover in the Cusp of Ayron, just east of Lake Abai. Though they did not know how long they might have before the Norgrasharians came into Mara, Alunen and Norandar counted it as a necessity to rest.

From amongst those least affected by the past days' events, they sent scouts to the east to keep watch upon the Plains of Kronaggas, to the southeast to observe the Garonites who were themselves recovering, and to the north, to wait for the arrival of Alim'dar and his better-trained forces. For now, if they could hold off any enemy assaults they would save the lives of those not so equipped to fight.

On the eighth day of Wintermelt, when they had been at camp for two days, scouts reported that the Sky City of Dian had fallen and crashed upon Aisper Hill. Whether this had been a result of its tactics in the past days, or from some other cause, they did not know, but at least for now, one of the Sky Cities was removed from the war.

THE SIEGE OF HEST'VORTAL

As soon as the broken body of Kronaggas the White fell into the sea just south of Oman'Tar, the people of the Southern Reaches began preparing for war. Supplies had arrived to their lands from the north, from the lands of Alim'dar in Whitestone—loads of weapons and armor that had been forged, and men and women who could train them. These things arrived not by ship, but by way of the Etakos Rapids.

These were the waters that flowed from the north to the south, between the two ranges of the Etakos Mountains that ran all the way from the lands of Alim'dar, past northern Mara, beside Goab'lin, and then fell into the Sea of Telder, flowing nearly thirty Marches along its path. These waters had long been used by the Darians to quickly get trade goods to the Adaasharians, far to the south. For as it was all goods were sealed inside of wooden barrels that were made by the Noranites and carried up the rises of the Westward Steeps and deposited into the river that came down from the Springs of Iilan. From there, the barrels would go upon the course of the river, passing through the narrow mountain valley and eventually fall into the Sea of Telder. Thereafter, the ocean currents would draw the barrels southward, to the Tidelands of Somoran, where they were captured between converging currents in the seas, and held there long enough for the Hour of Feltide, when the waves would push the barrels ashore.

On occasion, a portion of the barrels would be lost at sea or would become hung up on the rocky shores of Etakos, but more often than not the shipments arrived where they could be carried away by the Adaasharians. The loss was counted worthwhile with as much time as was saved in transporting goods, and in this case, armaments, to the Southern Reaches.

Now in these troubling times, the Darians had thought to send men and women capable of training the Adaasharians in combat along this same route, but in broader barrels that floated upright instead and could be steered by oars. So too could they optimize the success of the shipments. And so the vast majority of weaponry sent out arrived effectively in the south.

After the sacrifice of Kronaggas, Merilinder had found Adaashar and Sveraden upon the Dragonfather's Plains and returned them to Oman'Tar; then he had left and gone to the Valley of Tears to mourn with his brothers.

So it was that on the first day of Wintermelt Adaashar and Sveraden were both amongst their people, all the way to the south of where they truly wanted to be, for here, the war seemed not as likely to come with as much efficacy. Together, Adaashar and Sveraden left Oman'Tar with all of the people who would fight against the enemies of the Sylvai. As they crossed the plains and prairies, they gathered with them all of the nomadic people they could, as well as enlisting the help of the Druugal, who were always willing to assist.

They were joined on that day by the men and women who had gathered the weaponry from Alim'dar's shipment, as well as the few Darians who had come along as trainers. And so even as they traveled the Adaasharians were made more efficient in combat.

Two of the Sky Cities had come to rest over the Southern Reaches. These were Dol and Set. Even as Sveraden and Adaashar began their northward march, Set, which hovered just north of Oman'Tar, held its position, and they knew not what this meant—for the Sky Cities of Kor'Magailin had been home to many of all of the races of Sylveria, and what might be happening there in high places was unknown.

As they moved northward Dol came into view, floating above the western plains. As nomads from that region arrived to join with their mother and father, they reported that the Nescrai had invaded from above upon winged devices that let them glide down to the plains. But upon the command of the people, these had been quickly eliminated by the Druugal and the fighters of the tribes. Thereafter, whatever enemy forces might be in Dol remained there and the city seemed little threat.

Though it was a long march, the Adaasharians reached the mountains at Sairvon Pass late that night and with them were a hundred of the Plains Serpents, and fifty thousand of the tribesmen of the Southern Reaches.

The next day, the second of Wintermelt, they were greeted by the arrival of Merilinder the Silver, who had now joined them after the awakening of his fury in the Valley of Tears and after a brief detour that took him over the city of Hest'Vortal. There he had done nothing but gain information on the enemy, counting their numbers and seeing what they might be planning. But to him, he had seen only that while a great number of the Garonites had departed for the north to go to war, an even greater number had remained behind—and it seemed to Merilinder as if life in Hest'Vortal was continuing on as normal.

Joined together now, the Adaasharians and Merilinder marched through Sairvon Pass and into Vindras Vale, where they fully expected to be met by the Garonites.

But to their astonishment, the Nescrai were nowhere to be found. Now, their intention was to fight their way through the Vale and then the Tybor River Valley where they would go to the aid of their brothers and sisters, the Noranites. But when they had crossed the whole of the Vale, they found not a single sign of the Garonites. And they wondered if the whole of them had already gone into Mara. If this were the case, they felt a great urgency in getting there, for the whole of the Garonite army might well be enough to destroy all of the Noranites. So at the Hour of

Darkening, on the third day of the season, they began their march through the river valley.

While the army pressed through into the river valley, hoping to come through by Lastlight, Adaashar and Sveraden rode upon the back of Merilinder, scoping the landscape of the vale for any sign of the enemy, but still they saw them not. Once they were satisfied that the vale was vacant and that the Adaasharians would not be attacked from behind, they circled ahead, over the Tybor Mountains in which much of the southern army had come. And here they realized their mistake—one that would cost them the lives of thousands of their people.

For upon the high ledges and cliffs of the valley had been moved the terrible mining machines, and when half of the Adaasharians had marched within, the Garonites started them, and with great force they used them to send boulders and earth and entire mountain tops falling down upon their enemies.

Merilinder reacted as swiftly as he could, pulling their machines from the mountains with his giant claws and casting them away to the east. But still, for each of those he destroyed, a thousand of the people had already been crushed below. The cries of the dying and injured surged through the valley, and the Adaasharians never made it through the Tybor River Valley, for then it came—a great and thundering sound unlike anything anyone had heard. A violent and earsplitting discharge rattled the air and stone and what remained of the mountain tops were thrown out of place, and a great avalanche of stone and earth fell down, burying the remnants of those who had gone into the valley. Another of the Garonites' inventions had been unleashed with the first use of explosives known upon Sylveria.

For this horrible slaughter, Merilinder scorched the mountains, hoping only to destroy any of the Nescrai who might remain. From the north to the south ends, he unleashed fire upon the broken stone faces of the east and west ranges of Tybor.

Only those Adaasharians who had yet to go into the Tybor River Valley survived that day. Thereafter, The Tybor River Valley was forever sealed, the way from the south to the north cut off, except by way of Hest'Vortal and the Trenches of Avaron.

Now, the fire of a Dragon enraged is powerful, for it is the full essence of the magic it once held, now converted into elemental form. So strong had it become in the Metallic Dragons that Sharuseth had been able to set ablaze the span of the north to south ends of Southern Mara. So too had Merilinder now unleashed his blazes upon all of the Mountains of Tybor where not one of the Nescrai survived. But for such an unleashing, their energy was depleted and they were unable to use it again until they had recovered. And so after the vicious slaughter of the Adaasharians, which killed half of them who had come from the Southern Reaches, Merobassi the Blue then arrived from the east, and the broken people thought all was lost, for this Dragon, aligned with the Dark, could not be stopped by the exhausted Merilinder.

Merobassi landed upon the fields of the Vale, just south of the collapsed valley, and there faced the remaining Adaasharians. Yet he did not immediately summon his own magic to assault them, but instead engaged Adaashar and Sveraden with words.

"As it is," the Blue Dragon said. "Garonar does not seek your destruction. We made agreement before that any who breach the mountains from the south would be slain as intruders, and that your lands would be a haven for the Sylvai. Yet though you have violated this today, your losses have been great and the savagery of the Garonites has astounded even me. I offer you this... turn back to your lands and do not return, and no more of your people need to die this day."

Rage filled Adaashar, Sveraden and all of those present, and in Merobassi's attempt at appeasing those who had just lost so many kinsmen, he only served to enflame the wrath of the Adaasharians for their cousins, and they considered not turning back, but marching on to Hest'Vortal and leveling the city. But first they would have to get past Merobassi, and defeating a Dragon they knew would not be an easy task.

But before either of the First Awakened could respond, before even Merobassi had considered it a possibility, the Druugal that remained amongst the Adaasharians who had not also died in the avalanches, rose up without any given command and struck at the Dragon. Thirty-two of them lashed, and with their giant fangs that had before been intended for piercing the thick egg shells that were their food, now punctured the softer places upon Merobassi—wings were impaled and torn, scales cracked and broken, and in a frenzy, the Dragon could not at first even summon the words he needed to cast spells that might defend him, so taken aback was he. Rather, he leaped into the air, trying to escape, but the Druugal hung on, writhing and wrapping around the greater creature even as he took flight, still biting.

Once airborne, Merobassi spoke his words and a burst of freezing air issued forth from all about him, disabling, for a moment, the strikes of the Druugal. Half of the Serpents fell to the ground, and another burst of cold froze the others to such a point that when Merobassi slammed himself against a mountain, they crumbled into pieces that fell to the ground below.

Wounded and exhausted, Merobassi then came to land upon the mountain he had struck and with fury in his voice he said, "I gave you a chance to live today, but now I rescind that offer. Go if you will to the north, but you will have to go through Hest'Vortal, and you will not survive what the Garonites have planned for you there." Then, unable to fly any longer, the Dragon climbed down to the other side of the peak and disappeared.

That night, as the Adaasharians mourned, so too did their leaders, Adaashar and Sveraden, for not only had so many of their people died that day, so too did their three youngest children, who were Barvan'nar, Riiska'nar, and Aisaven. What remained of the mountains of Tybor thereafter stood as markers of the graves of the first slain of the Adaasharians.

But despite their loss, the Adaasharians vowed to continue on, and to tear Hest'Vortal from its foundations, whatever it took, and then to move on into Mara, to go to the aid of their brothers and sisters.

Merilinder was too weakened by the battle to continue on, his fire expelled and his will drained by the devastation of his people at Tybor, yet he promised Sveraden and Adaashar that if they marched on ahead to Hest'Vortal, he would join them as soon as he was able.

The Adaasharians took the only path to the old city, which was Gnok'Gerthorn Pass, that went over the mountains and would lead to the mountain home of Garonar and Kuranen.

As soon as the remnants of the army had mounted the first peak of the pass, the Sky City of Dinmolar came into view, hovering east of Hest'Vortal, and they feared an assault from above, as their army had already been so weakened. None of the Nescrai dared, however, to use their Sailplanes to try to reach the ground, for the mountain pass was high and the contraptions too imprecise. When the occupants of Dinmolar saw the Adaasharians, they began taking the city southeast, seeming to follow along as they approached Hest'Vortal, and making Sveraden and Adaashar extremely uneasy.

To them, it was a fortunate thing that long ago, when they had once visited Hest'Vortal, Ashysin and Merilinder had torn down the old bridge of Boris'Thirith, for in the years that followed, with the help of Dragons, a new bridge had been erected, one of stone foundations. But even this they feared, for with what they had seen at Tybor, with the explosives and collapse of entire mountains, it would take even less to do the same with this bridge, and if the Garonites minded not shutting themselves off with only the Trenches of Avaron into or out of the city, they might well destroy Boris'Thirith just to wipe out the remnants of the Adaasharians.

At the lead, Adaashar and Sveraden stopped just before the bridge, calling a stop to the long precession across the pass.

"We can't risk losing the rest of our people," Sveraden said to her husband. "So many have already...."

"We are already risking them," Adaashar said. "As soon as we agreed to fight all of our lives were forfeit for the cause."

"The bridge is too narrow... We need Merilinder to clear the way across. Otherwise we will be picked off by their archers as we cross."

"I agree. But every day we wait is a day that the Noranites are without our assistance."

"We don't know the state of Mara," Sveraden said. "Though I too wish we were amongst them in the forests rather than high in these mountains, we can only worry about our own people. I say we must wait for the Dragon to recover."

"Whatever they are planning, the Garonites, it was intended that we be drawn here, to Hest'Vortal. It seems that if even if we can safely cross Boris'Thirith, we will be falling into their trap. What else can we do but wait for Merilinder?"

And so the Adaasharians waited there that day, and camped that night in the mountains. Still, Dinmolar hovered not far away, waiting, it seemed, to see what the Adaasharians would do. It was not until morning that Merilinder arrived; he was not fully recovered, but had a plan of his own.

"I will fly ahead and see what is happening in the city," he said. "How many of the Garonites there remain, and what they are doing—if they are preparing to destroy the bridge with all of our people upon it."

"You cannot go into the city, even from above," Sveraden said. "They will surely have arrows and arbalests to defend against you."

The Dragon considered this and nodded, then said, "If only we could get you across, all of you at once."

Then, to the north, sounding out from Dinmolar, there was a sudden grinding sound, and the whirring of the engines intensified and the city began moving toward them, clumsily tilting as it did so, and they wondered if the city might not fall into the chasm beneath Boris'Thirith, or strike the bridge itself, cutting them off from Hest'Vortal. But neither of these happened and it soon righted itself and came to hover instead directly over the stone bridge.

"I think our best option is to have you, Merilinder, scorch the bridge ahead of us," Adaashar said. "Perhaps if they have there planted explosives, your fire will ignite it and we will know that they planned our destruction in this way."

"But the bridge will be destroyed and there will be no way into the city," Sveraden said. "And we will be cut off from the only path to the north."

"What choice do we have?" Merilinder asked.

"But perhaps... well, I don't think they would destroy the bridge," Sveraden said. "Or their own way into Vindras Vale would again be severed."

"Then I must risk flying into the city, at least the western district, to take out their archers, and those who would come against us first."

"You cannot fly well yet, can you? We cannot risk you any more than our people," Sveraden said, tears welling in her eyes.

"I told you," Adaashar said. "We have already risked everyone. We must either continue or turn back."

Then a thump sounded, just ahead at the edge of the stone bridge, where it met with a mountain . They looked, and there upon it was a body, broken.

"It fell from the Sky City!" one of the men close by said.

"It is Nescrai," another said.

Then another struck the ground, and another... seven in all came to strike the ground near the bridge, and three others fell from the sky and down into the chasm below.

"What is going on?" Sveraden asked.

Adaashar rushed over to examine the other bodies. All of them were Nescrai. "They have been slain, not by the fall, but by sword. And look!" He held up a scrolled parchment that had been tucked into the tunic of the man. Unrolling and reading it he held it up for the others to see.

Upon it was writin the simple words, *We have taken the city. Wait for us.*

"If Dinmolar has been taken from the Nescrai, this changes everything!" Adaashar said. "We must coordinate a plan...."

But as he said this, the engines hummed and whirred again, and slowly the city began moving again, now toward Hest'Vortal.

"What will they do?" Sveraden said.

"It seems to me that they have a plan," Merilinder said. "So let us do as they said and wait."

And so the Adaasharians did nothing as Dinmolar moved over the bridge and chasm of Boris'Thirith, where it came to a stop over Hest'Vortal.

From up on the ledges and walls and out of the apertures of the Sky City came a rain upon the Garonites in Hest'Vortal that day, for Dinmolar had indeed been taken over by the Sylvai who had inhabited it, and they had slain their Nescraian captors thereupon. And now, the rain that fell upon the streets below was not of water, but of bodies—the thousands that had been taken in the battle in the air. The falling bodies of the Nescrai were not intended as weapons to cause damage to the buildings of Hest'Vortal, but rather as instruments of demoralization, and as the Garonites saw their kin above defeated and dropped down upon them, they thought the Sylvai vicious and even became alarmed, for now an entire city was coming against them when they had expected only the remnants of the Adaasharian army. And disconcertment filled them.

Many abandoned their posts and went into hiding, for this was to them a tragedy, and they had thought the Sylvai too brutal for such an act, even knowing what their own people had done to the Adaasharians. Rather than be enflamed with war-lust, this dispirited them to such a measure that the common citizens laid down their arms and fled into their homes and basements. Still, the battle was not won by this simple disconcerting tactic by the Sylvai of Dinmolar, for there remained those soldiers more trained than any of the Garonite citizens, and as they scattered about the city, the elite soldiers of Hest'Vortal tried to organize.

When a horn sounded from Dinmolar, Merilinder took it as a sign to do his part, and knowing that the Adaasharians could not cross Boris'Thirith until they were certain it would not drop them into the gorge below, he took clumsy flight over the bridge, pouring fire down upon it, so that any explosives there would be ignited. But Sveraden had been right, and the stone had not been rigged with any charges as had been the Mountains of Tybor. And so they presumed that the intent had been to simply draw the Adaasharians into Hest'Vortal and assault them there, as they crossed the bridge.

"The way is clear," Merilinder said when he arrived back to the western side of the bridge. "Still I will lead the way, though I am already weakening once more. I have it in me to do this one last thing."

The march across Boris'Thirith began, Adaashar and Sveraden leading the way, just behind the Silver Dragon. To the relief of the Adaasharians, the elite soldiers of Hest'Vortal had yet to come together, and the path all the way into the city was clear.

Then, as the Nescrai had done in Aranthia and in Southern Mara, now the Sylvai from Dinmolar came down from above in Sailplanes to assist their people in the taking of Hest'Vortal.

There on the streets of the city, the Adaasharians began engaging any of the Garonites who elected to fight, and the number of them was not few, for even as many had been demoralized, they now came out of their homes to fight, for their hatred of the Sylvai was now at its peak.

The stone streets of Hest'Vortal flowed with blood as the Adaasharians and the other Sylvai spread out over the city, engaging the enemy, and as they did this, so too did Merilinder continue fighting with tooth and claw rather than magic or fire. And the Garonites he encountered were no match for him. The Dragon suffered many wounds before the battle was over, but he survived, however weakened.

Now, while all of this was happening in the city, Adaashar and Sveraden, along with a dozen others, fought through into the Coliseum, for they were certain they would find the leaders of their enemy here— Garonar and Kuranen.

The Coliseum was empty save for the palace guard, who, when

approached by the Adaasharians, raised their swords and lances and thought only to bar the entrance into the home of Garonar.

"You cannot pass," one of the guards said.

"You are outnumbered," Adaashar said. "If you do not wish to die, then move out of the way. Garonar must once again answer for what he has done."

The guards looked to one another, and hearing the dying cries of their people outside of the Coliseum, threw their weapons to the ground, and stepped aside. The Sylvai bound the guards to pillars of stone, so that they might not change their minds and follow them into the palace.

"Garonar! Kuranen! Show yourselves!" Adaashar shouted fiercely as they entered into the palace.

He and Sveraden half expected that when their cousins came out that they would be dressed in their fancy robes, entirely unaware of the threat that came upon the city, for in times past they had shown themselves to be idle and careless in most matters that did not involve the festivities of their pleasures.

But they were met with a much different sight, for both Garonar and Kuranen were clad in plate armor and wielded jagged-edged swords meant to pierce and then tear their enemies from within.

"You have reached your end," Sveraden said. "You cannot win this battle."

Kuranen stepped forward, just out of sword's reach from Sveraden and said, "Your people are diminished, plainswoman. Even if you win Hest'Vortal, there are two companies that march on Mara, and when they finish the Noranites and kill your dear sister, Alunen, they will return for you."

Adaashar said, "Signal a surrender now, and you may live—"

But Sveraden did not allow her husband the opportunity to negotiate, for upon hearing the threat made to Alunen, she lunged forward, driving her own blade into the chest of Kuranen; though it did not pierce the plate of steel, it did strike her off her guard, and Sveraden followed her surprise with the jab of a dagger that found its way into Kuranen's throat. And there fell the first of all of the First Awakened children of Dragons.

Both Garonar and Adaashar were stunned, for they had not expected such an assault, which was, in her own defense, exactly why she had done it.

Garonar saw his wife fall, and he was filled with rage. But before he could react, Adaashar had come forward and the blade of his own sword was at the throat of the Nescraian lord.

"You have—" Garonar began, but in that instant, Adaashar was seized with the images of the thousands who had been crushed at Tybor, including his own children, and his mercy left him. Garonar choked on his own words, his own blood, and then fell limp to the ground as the blade nearly severed his spine.

They wiped the blood of their enemies upon their own bodies and together with the others who had come with them, conspired as to how they would further demoralize the Garonites, who still outnumbered them in Hest'Vortal and who were by now likely more organized.

They dragged the bodies of Garonar and Kuranen out of the palace and across the Coliseum, then up to the highest level of the stadium's outer walls. And there they took the banners that had flown here before and tied them about the necks of their cousins, and they hung them there, facing the outside of the Coliseum and into the streets of Hest'Vortal. Yet for the deep wound that was upon Garonar's neck, he became fully decapitated as it hung and his body fell to the ground below for all of his people to see.

It was not long before the Garonites saw the bodies of their beloved leaders—one still hanging and the other sundered—and word of it quickly spread across the city. Many of them then surrendered, hoping their own lives might be spared and that they would not suffer the same fate as their mother and father. Though some of the Adaasharian showed them mercy and bound them as prisoners, others executed their own captives, for the brutal loss of their brothers and sisters at Tybor was still too fresh in their minds.

The battle consummated at the Hour of Concession on the fourth of Wintermelt, and despite their great losses, victory belonged to the Adaasharians.

Merilinder recognized that his people had become incited to slaughter their enemies with the same viciousness that had caused the uprising of his own fury, and he felt justified in the destruction of their enemies. Yet still, deep within his soul he knew that to continue on in vengeance would be a surrender to the darkness that was now awakened in Sylveria. So he convinced Adaashar and Sveraden to let the remainder of the Garonites live.

From above, the Sylvai of Dinmolar came down into the city once victory was achieved in Hest'Vortal, and they explained all that had happened there. Upon the start of the war, the Nescrai had made prisoners of all the Sylvai who inhabited the Sky City, locking them inside of their own chambers. And slowly the Nescrai were killing them, man woman and child, even as the city kept watch over the world below. But an attempt at an uprising was successful, and while the enemy was focused on the progression of the Adaasharians below, the Sylvai struck, overpowering them only through opportunity afforded to them by circumstance. They had slain all of the Nescrai in Dinmolar who were armed and who had the will to fight, but imprisoned the others and the children in the same way they had been held.

So too did the Sylvai tell the Adaasharians that there were uprisings within some of the other Sky Cities, for there was within them a magical or technological means of communication between them.

Together then, the Adaasharians, the Sylvai of Dinmolar, and Merilinder offered the surviving Garonites an option. They could be taken to the Sky City as prisoners of war, or they could be left behind in Hest'Vortal, which would be cut off from the rest of the world. Most chose to stay in their city, not understanding the consequence of what was proposed.

For on that night, the Adaasharians found the supplies of the explosives of the Garonites, and with it did what none of them had before wanted done... they blasted the bridge of Boris'Thirith, where it fell deep into the gorge below, never to be raised again. There was then but one way out of Hest'Vortal, and that was by way of the Trenches of Avaron.

During the Hour of Elation on the fifth day of Wintermelt the Adaasharians left by way of the Trenches, leaving the enemy behind to their own demise, for so too did they, when all of their people had gone farther to the north, blast the roadway that led from the city to the gorges below. Hest'Vortal was now sealed off from the rest of the world, with no means by ground of getting off the Plateau.

After this, the remnants of the Adaasharians, as well as Merilinder, trudged on through the Trenches of Avaron, where they would come eventually to the Eastern Settlements of Mara. Dinmolar, still under the control of the Sylvai, remained there hovering over Hest'Vortal, keeping a watchful eye upon the Garonites, so that they could do no further harm throughout the rest of the war.

It was in the latter part of the sixth day of Wintermelt when the Adaasharians came out of the mountains, crossed the Southland River and came into the Eastern Settlements. There they rested, for the warfare waged in days past had been fatiguing and they had yet to have time to fully mourn their losses at Tybor.

They remained there until the morning of the seventh day of Wintermelt.

THE PRIDE OF DROVANIUS

Early in the morning, during the Hour of Gathering on the fourth day of Wintermelt, Drovanius the Black, still battered and torn from the humiliating defeat in Aranthia, left the city of Mar'Narush, where he had left Norgrash'nar.

He spoke not a word to his First Awakened Son, for though Norgrash'nar had also failed in achieving absolute victory in Aranthia, Drovanius felt as though he had disappointed his son. He had for many years become most fond of this man and his offspring, and whether it was for love or sympathy, or some sense of loyalty, the Dragon did not know. He knew only that what this son wanted, what he felt, was of the utmost importance in his own purposes.

In his mind he knew that he had fallen far away from his brothers—even Merobassi and Verasian—for while they had fallen in line behind him, they held not the absolute darkness within them that he knew was now awakened within himself. For it had not been they who first denied the Law of Balance, even broke it; it had been his own alliance with the Drake Talentaran that had done this. Yet now there had been no seeming consequence to this—as he had proclaimed before—and the Blue and Green Dragons had become even more convinced by this that they were doing what the Law intended. In their minds they were doing right. But Drovanius knew better, for he could feel the darkness within, and he could not fight it. He had fallen too far.

In spite of this, so too did Drovanius hold to Norgrash'nar's ideals that the Haldusians and the Darians deserved destruction, for they had mixed the bloodlines, creating a race of men and women that were an abomination. Yet he would not admit the truth even to himself, which was that the source of animosity toward the mix-blooded was only derived from Norgrash'nar's loss, long ago, of the affection of Nirvisa'nen. So far had his son taken his grief that it had grown into absolute acerbity. And Drovanius had conceded to this same indignation.

And so it was on this day, as far away in Hest'Vortal the Adaasharians were about to slay Drovanius' other son, Garonar, that the Black Dragon soared across the far eastern sea toward the lands of Nefaria. When he entered the Veil, the Hour mattered not, for he was here under the dark influence of Imrakul, which showed its darkness and drove away the light.

Although this was the longest route, it was the safest, for he did not want to be seen by either his enemies or his brothers, and he knew not where Merobassi or Verasian were. His mission now, his intent, was a dark act that he didn't want to bring upon them.

When he crossed into the Veil he turned back to his left, not knowing which direction was which, for the workings of Nefaria were bewildering. He flew over the outer lands of Nefaria, which was the domain of a different Drake, and then to the head of the realm where he had first met Talentaran. There, upon a battlefield littered with the remains of countless repulsive and unnatural entities, Drovanius found the Drake, and he came to land near him.

But the servants of Talentaran would not let the Dragon close. These were the horrid Trolls and Ogres of Nefaria, who were feasting upon the corpses of creatures unknown to Drovanius.

The Dragon's magic did not work here in Nefaria, for his abilities were drawn from the lands of Sylveria, and he was here left defenseless as the Giants came for him, wielding clubs that were the size of trees and maces with steel spikes that might shatter his scales...

But Talentaran saw Drovanius there, and stopped them, recognizing him now as an ally. And he said, "I see you have not been destroyed by the Law. Perhaps you were right long ago."

Drovanius said, "Destruction comes in many ilks, Talentaran. It has been long since I have come here... how goes your war?"

"I have dominated my brothers for many decades now, Drovanius, for your honoring of our agreement in the consignment of the ores of your land. For that I offer my gratitude."

"War has come to Sylveria, as I promised it would. But we have lost a great battle, and I seek a new weapon, something... devastating."

"We have fulfilled our end of the bargain, Drovanius. Do you now seek to renew it?"

"I do."

"What do you have to offer me? For you brought such an amount of ore to Nefaria before, that we are far from being in need of more."

"But will you not need more in a hundred years? Or a thousand? When the weapons of your forging have rusted away, you will be left defenseless in your pursuits, Talentaran. And what we brought you before is still but a small portion of what remains under the mountains, in the deep places of Sylveria."

"If you bring it here now, and we forge it, it too will decay. No, better that it remain in your world for now, unrefined. But I can offer you something in advance, on credit, and when I call upon you again, you must answer. You must bring to me that which is owed, whether it is a thousand years from now, or a hundred thousand. Will you agree to this?"

"I will, but what is it you can offer me? What weapon not given before can you grant me that will aid me in my own war?"

"Look around you, Drovanius. Do you see these giants that are four times taller than your own children, and ten times stronger? I will send to you from the shores of my land a hundred of these fierce and hardened warriors. They will sweep the lands of your enemies and crush them."

"There are Dragons amongst my enemies, and a hundred will not suffice, Talentaran. Perhaps a thousand will."

"A thousand? No. But I desire your victory—though still I do not claim to seek the destruction of Sylveria—and so I will lend to you a hundred of the Ogres, and a hundred of these Trolls. They will decimate the mightiest of your enemies. But when they have done your will, they must all return to me."

"That will help. But still I need something more."

"I have no more warriors I can spare to you, Drovanius. Is there anything more that I can offer?"

"There is one more thing. For I see that Imrakul shines its darkness here upon Nefaria, whereas it shines light upon Sylveria once it has returned from the Veil. And when it is here, at the Hour we call Highlight, a touch of the darkness seeps through and shines upon our lands, casting gloom upon the hearts of the people. Yet since the awakening of death in our lands, my people have been unaffected by it."

"You blither incoherent words, Dragon. Just tell me what you desire."

"I need a new weapon, one forged of a piece of Imrakul. A breastplate of steel fit for my own son, Norgrash'nar."

Talentaran considered this for a long moment before saying, "This is a request outside of my reach, Drovanius, for do you see wings upon my back? Do the Ogres and Trolls of Nefaria fly about in the airways? No! If you want a piece of Imrakul, fly there yourself and bring it to me, and then I will forge for you an insidious weapon, and armor for your son, and for his sons and daughters. But this is the end of our bargaining."

"Agreed," Drovanius said.

So it was that on that day Drovanius flew high into the sky, where the air grew so thin that it was difficult to breathe, and then landed upon Imrakul—for it was not so far above as most had thought—and in each of his claws he took a stone the size of a mountain top, and he took them down to Nefaria and laid them before the Drake.

He said, "Make me as much armor, and weapons, and devices as you can out of this, and I will give something to you more powerful than the magic of Sylveria and more useful to you than any ore. I will give you my soul."

"And what would I do with a soul?" Talentaran asked. "No, I have no desire to possess it, for if I were to take it from you, and if you were to betray me, then I would have little means of laying vengeance upon you, for it is your soul that makes you suffer, Dragon. No... keep your soul, Drovanius. I will make you the armor and weapons and devices of your desire, and they will be sent to your shores along with one hundred Ogres and one hundred Trolls on advance for the ore that I will one day need. Go now, for this is the end of our dealings, and in three days' time, you will have the means to destroy your enemies. When they touch upon the lands of your world, our agreement will be sealed."

And so Drovanius returned to Sylveria, where he continued to recover and grow stronger, and to wait for the gift he would receive from Nefaria.

THE BOOK OF

DISCORD

THE SKY CITY OF KETSELTET

Aranthia came across the Sea of Repose on the third day of
Wintermelt, soaring low over the waters so as to hopefully not be seen by
any of the Nescrai upon the Onilmar Plateau. Haldus'nar and Sarak'den
were upon his back; they were coming out of lands of Aranthia after their
own bittersweet victory on the lowlands to the east. Somewhere behind
them by a fair distance there were an estimated twenty ships carrying the
Haldusians who were coming to Verasian's domain to fight, who had come
off the Highlands. These were survivors from the battles there as well as
others who had gathered and volunteered to come and fight for their
brothers in the west.

The Crimson Dragon came to land upon Faigor Landing, which was a
raised landform high enough above the sea to resist the effects of Feltide,
but not so high as the Onilmar Plateau, which was to its south. Stone cliffs
fell to the sea, which would have to be mounted by the Haldusians when
they came, but Aranthia soared easily there to the Landing and Haldus'nar
and Sarak'den dismounted.

Here, the landing was nestled between the higher plateau to the south
and by Mount Hearin to the north. It was an unguarded area of the
coastline where they could sneak into Verasian's domain.

From the ground Haldus'nar and Sarak'den inspected the area, while
Aranthia circled overhead, all of them looking for signs that this might be
the way Drovanius and Norgrash'nar had come after fleeing Aranthia.
Here, however there was no sign of their passing and the Dragon came to
ground again.

"Do we wait for our people here?" Sarak'den asked.

"I don't know what is best right now," Aranthia said. "It will be at
least a full day before they arrive."

"We are safe here, and unseen," Haldus'nar said. "If we just wait we
can invade in force. Likely, the Norgrasharians have taken most of their
armies westward, toward Forthran."

"I do hope our brothers and sisters fare well," Sarak'den said
dejectedly.

"They will endure," Aranthia assured. "They have Alim'dar at their back, and the Adaasharians planned on marching northward. The enemy was not prepared for the people to be armed. So do we have rightness on our side."

"We do not have a force significant enough to trap them between us," Haldus'nar said. "I don't know what more we can do but to stay in Verasian and take the cities. Once Aranthia is secure, perhaps we can bring more of our people here to fight, and hope that the greatest force of the Norgrasharians are crushed in the west."

"Look!" Aranthia cried suddenly, pointing a giant claw to the west, between where they stood and the high cliffs of Onilmar. And there, coming into view was one of the Sky Cities of Kor'Magailin, drifting from the north. "It's Ketseltet. They will see us here!"

"And look," Sarak'den said. "Is that Drovanius circling the city?"

"I don't think so," Haldus'nar said. "He was wounded, barely able to fly. No, that must be Verasian."

"I still cannot believe what has come to the world," Sarak'den said, shaking her head. "How has such evil fallen on Sylveria? It doesn't seem so long ago that Verasian and Merobassi, and even Drovanius gamboled amongst us in the Valley of Naiad."

Haldus'nar and Aranthia reflected briefly on this, and the Dragon said, "Indeed the world has fallen. As soon as the door was opened, as soon as a seed of contempt was planted amongst the Dragons and the people of the world, evil began to grow. It was long held at bay as we tried to keep peace... but now it has been unleashed upon us all."

"We must crush this evil and restore Sylveria, somehow," Haldus'nar said.

"You must understand, children, that what you wish for is not even possible. For even if we defeat the Nescrai and Drovanius and his dark brothers, evil will remain. Even if Drovanius were to repent and to stop the war, evil would here exist, in the land, in all of us."

"We are not evil, Aranthia," Sarak'den said. "We fight for what is good and right."

"We do," the Dragon agreed. "But when the Law was broken, so too did we all become corrupted, not by our own actions, but by the choices of others. Look at how easily we brought ourselves to kill our brothers at Eswear'Nysin. Though it was necessary, it came too easily to us, I think... Now we fight, we bleed, we kill and we die. This is the consequence."

"So evil just wins?" Sarak'den said. "Then why even fight?"

"Evil will always be in us all now. But so will rightness. It is not just a battle for Sylveria we fight, but for our own souls. Since the assault on Eswear'Nysin we have been filled with contempt for our enemies, and rightly so, but these are not virtues of the righteous. We fight not to eradicate evil—for this is not even a possibility—but to reduce the suffering insomuch as we can."

"And to do this," Haldus'nar said. "We must end those who cause the suffering."

"Yes."

"Alright, then, what do we do now?"

"We fight," Aranthia said, turning his mighty head toward Ketseltet. "We have seen these cities used as weapons; let us try to take one for ourselves."

"I don't understand," Haldus'nar said. "What do you want us to do?"

"I will show you."

Aranthia then revealed to them a plan he had construed, and soon thereafter, Haldus'nar and Sarak'den agreed to it, for they had little other concept of what they might do here while waiting for the Haldusians to arrive by sea.

They had yet to be seen, so far as they could tell, even as Ketseltet drew nearer to Faigor Landing, and so once again upon Aranthia's back, they flew back toward the sea and around to the south of the Plateau of Onilmar, then up over, for this would grant them the greatest cover for the longest time as they came as close to the floating city as they could. And when they came off the plateau, they were right upon the city, and Verasian immediately saw them.

He roared out a warning to the Nescrai of the city. Aranthia soared as swiftly as his wings could carry him to the northern side of Ketseltet, opposite to where the Green Dragon soared, and he came to land upon an outer courtyard. Quickly, Haldus'nar and Sarak'den dismounted and there hid amongst the trees and bushes of a garden that was otherwise unoccupied. Then Aranthia took off again, and circled back to the south, where he would engage Verasian.

Husband and wife, hiding amongst the bushes of the garden, squatted in silence, waiting to make sure they were alone.

"We've never been into one of these cities," Haldus'nar whispered. "How will we even find our way?"

"I don't know. But this is our best chance at making a difference, at least for now. I hear nothing. I think the garden is clear." Cautiously then, they rose from their cover and looked around.

The garden spanned a distance of perhaps eight Breadths. Much of it was open terrain, with the shrubs and trees growing around the edges. Once, it had probably been well tended, but, as it was now winter, dead growth was littered upon the ground. There appeared to be but one entrance from the garden into the inner city, but there were also stone stairs that ran from that doorway up onto higher terraces, for the city was tall and shaped like a mountain, with towers jutting out at various places. Looking outward, they could see several of these towers, but only one of them had a window opening that faced them. Haldus'nar pointed to it and said, "If anyone looks through there, we will be seen."

"But from such a distance will they even know it is us?"

"Probably not. I will blend in well, but you may not. The Norgrasharians are likely in control of the city, otherwise why would it be here, with Verasian at its side? I doubt the Sylvai are freely moving about inside."

"Well, let's see what we can do about that..." this was not the voice of either Haldus'nar or Sarak'den, but another. For stepping into the garden by way of the entrance was a Nescraian man who was known to both of them.

"Aivus'nar..." Sarak'den said.

"Yes, and you should count it a blessing if only I saw you arrive."

"I scarcely believe my eyes," Haldus'nar said. "For of all those we might have encountered, why was it you?"

"Call it luck. Or circumstance. Or divine intervention. It doesn't matter."

"Luck?" Sarak'den said, her hand was on the hilt of her sword.

"Relax," Aivus'nar said. "I am on your side."

"The grandson of Norgrash'nar, and you would claim to defy him?"

"I would. Absolutely."

"It is true," Haldus'nar said. "Or at least it was, long ago. For Alak'kiin made mention of your encounter with him in Mar'Narush. You were... what? Leading a resistance?"

"I was trying to figure out what the original plans of these cities were... what exactly my grandfather intended."

"I recall now...." Sarak'den said.

"Yes. I didn't know what he was planning, I only knew it was bad. And Ketseltet is evidence of this, as are the rest of the Sky Cities. Where is Alak'kiin now?"

"I don't know. Last I saw he was at the Temple of Kronaggas."

Sarak'den turned to her husband and said, "Are we certain we can trust him?" Haldus'nar shrugged.

"For over two hundred years I have sought to stop the plans of Norgrash'nar, for I knew back then that he was all about deceit. And these cities have proven it. It was true what they all said, before this war, in years past, when these cities were first conceived... The Sylvai and Nescrai have lived together amongst the corridors and towers of Ketseltet ever since it rose from the plains. It should be no wonder that I am here, for this is my country. But the Sylvai are no longer free here in these places."

"They are prisoners?"

"Yes. Taken by surprise seasons ago. Though they shouldn't have been."

"What do you mean?"

"For years I have tried to stop the construction of these cities. I don't know how much Alak'kiin told you, but there were plans for them, drawn up more than two centuries ago. I saw them in my grandfather's chambers... I took one to study. Even then there were plans to imprison the Sylvai."

"How is that possible?" Haldus'nar wondered. "For all of us reviewed those schematics, and there was no indication of malicious intent in them. How could you know this?"

"There is not a lot of time right now to explain," Aivus'nar said, looking over his shoulder, toward the archway into the city. "There will be patrols passing by soon."

"Then let us move to the shadows," Sarak'den said, looking about, then pointing as she said, "There, behind those trees we will not be seen. Just speak in hushed voices."

"There are safer places to take you."

"I don't think we're ready to go with you just yet," Haldus'nar said. "You will have to forgive our suspicions, but Eswear'Nysin was just utterly decimated by your people and one of these Sky Cities."

"They are your people too, Haldus'nar. And do you side with the Nescrai? Of course not! Not every one of our kind has fallen to the Dark. Yes, most have. But not all. Still, I will go into the shadows with you, until you find comfort in my trust."

Once hidden behind the trees, Aivus'nar explained, "So the plans that were distributed all across Sylveria for the construction of Kor'Magailin... they were not the same as what I had in my possession long ago. They were modified so as not to seem suspicious. But who was it who installed the chamber doors and ballasts and fixtures of the cities?"

"How should we know?" Sarak'den said shortly.

"It was the Norgrasharians. No one would have suspected that such tasks could lead to such deception... but the chambers of the Sylvai have been made into prison cells, keeping them inside... and things worse..."

"And you knew this all along?"

"Yes. But what was I to do about it? I tried for years to rally my people to defend the Sylvai, to lessen their growing hatred. But they would have none of it. Their odium was too far infused within them. I tried to get work details that would lead me to those who might listen, but I couldn't."

"You are Norgrash'nar's grandson," Sarak'den said. "How could you not go wherever you wanted?"

"Grandmother—Kalenen—never was fond of me, and she suspected me of subterfuge when she heard a report that I was aiding in a small segment of the population of Mar'Narush that was trying to undermine their rule. Norgrash'nar never thought it was true, but it was enough to keep me here in Verasian's domain."

"So what is going on here in Ketseltet?" Haldus'nar asked.

"Ketseltet is here only to guard the plains, to watch for invaders from the west, should they break through the Norgrasharians that have gone there. But the Sylvai who live here are imprisoned in their quarters. They are being killed, slowly... executed only for the boost it gives to the morale of the people... who have become depraved beyond belief."

Sarak'den and Haldus'nar were beginning to believe his words, for he spoke with condemnation of the Nescrai. Still, they had more questions.

"How did you find us here so quickly?" Sarak'den asked.

"I understand your hesitation to trust me. I am Nescrai, of the direct line of Norgrash'nar. But I have heard of what happened in Aranthia, with Vainus. It is a tragedy. I can only assure you that I am not your enemy. Would I not have sounded an alarm if I wanted you found?"

"Perhaps you have... But you have not answered my question."

"Look, I cannot make you trust me. I saw you only by mere chance. I don't know if others have spotted you, but it is not safe right here. You can follow me and hope that I speak truly, or you can kill me, stay here, and be found. But I can take you to safety so that together we might make a difference this day."

They looked to one another and both nodded, silently agreeing that they had little choice but to trust Aivus'nar. "All right," Sarak'den said. "If you are being honest, if you are on the side of right, then let us make a difference together. But we have lost too many of our children to be forgiving if you deceive us. We will cut you down for treachery."

His dark eyes squinted, and he looked distant for a moment as he said, "I can only imagine what you have seen... Death is not something I have yet witnessed personally... I could not bear to watch the execution of the Sylvai."

"Before this day is over you will see death," Haldus'nar promised. "One way or another. Now, what do we do?"

"First, Sarak'den needs a disguise. No Sylvai freely walks amongst us." He raised a hand toward her face, then hesitated. "May I?"

She cocked her head, then nodded reluctantly. Aivus'nar incited his will, and he lightly pressed his hand upon her golden skin. She felt nothing but a faint warmth, but an instant later she looked not the same, for the skin of her face had become azure, like the Nescrai, and her features were changed. And it was not just upon her face, for the magic spread all over her body, and even her arms and hands turned blue. "Haldus'nar, remember this face, so that you will not be confused."

Haldus'nar stared at his wife for a long moment, committing to his mind the appearance she now carried. They did not want that he would forget, in the heat of battle, that she now appeared as one of their own. He nodded then and asked, "What kind of magic is this?"

"The same as all Naiadic magic," Aivus'nar said. "The power of the will. It was my grandfather who first created it, or harnessed it, believe it or not. He called it *transmutation*, used it to entertain in the courts of Mar'Narush, at first. Then later to move unnoticed amongst his own people to seek out dissension."

"Seems deceptive," Sarak'den said. "But useful to us now."

"Indeed. We should be able to move about freely now. One more thing before we go," Aivus'nar said. "What exactly were your plans when you had the Dragon bring you here to Ketseltet?"

Sarak'den, in her disguise, looked to her husband, then said, "To be honest, we hadn't really thought that far ahead. But we are not without magical abilities. We thought that while the Nescrai were distracted by the battle between the Dragons we might come inside and create disorder."

"Well then it is good I found you," Aivus'nar said with a sly smile. "Because that is exactly what I intend for us to do."

As they stepped into the interior of Ketseltet, the screeches and squawks and raging roars of combating Dragons could be heard off in the distance as Aranthia sparred with his brother Verasian.

"How have you made it so long—over two hundred years—without being found a dissentient?"

"I am family, Haldus'nar. I lived with all of you in Naiad, for a time. I have been with Norgrash'nar my entire life. He looks not so closely at close relatives. He assumes we all are aligned with his methods."

"How long have you disagreed with him?" Sarak'den asked. "How long have you deceived him?"

"Longer than I can remember. It was after we left Naiad, after we had come to Verasian's domain. I suppose it was when he started preaching to us and our children that the Sylvai were less than we, and that the Haldusians and the Darians were tainted blood. I never understood it... we were all family there, in Naiad. We all loved and laughed and played and grew together. I just never understood..."

"We should keep moving," Sarak'den said. "What do you have in mind for us, Aivus'nar?"

"The prisoners, the Sylvai... we release them, then we shut down this city and bring it to its destruction, right after we tell all of the other Sky Cities how to do the same."

"Is *that* all?"

Aivus'nar grinned, "Don't worry, these are all attainable. Remember, I have been studying the schematics of these cities for a long time. If enough of the engines fail all at once, the city cannot stay in the air."

"And for that we need help, right?"

"Yes. The prisoners. Come," Aivus'nar said. "This way." He led them down a corridor, walking casually but quickly, while Haldus'nar and Sarak'den tried to keep to the shadows of the lit hallway. Aivus'nar scowled, saying, "That's not the way to blend in. Look natural. Keep your hood over your head, Haldus'nar, and none are likely to recognize you. And you will not be at all known, Sarak'den."

They continued up the corridor, Aivus'nar in the lead. "Where are the prisoners kept?" Haldus'nar asked.

"In their own chambers. On the high levels of the city."

"Their own chambers? Can they not free themselves?"

"That depends on who they are. Those who are older have stronger magic, because they are stronger willed. But most of the people who came to the Sky Cities of Kor'Magailin were the younger couples, the newlyweds who thought it would be fanciful to live in the higher realms. Even with their own magic they cannot undo the locks, for they are sealed with the magic of the elders of the Nescrai."

"And this is why you need us…" Sarak'den said.

"Yes. It is why I count myself very fortunate to have found you this day. I could never free them all by myself. But with three of us, we might have a chance."

"And what do we do when we encounter guards?"

"We do to them what they have been doing to the more unruly of the Sylvaian prisoners."

"Keep them under close watch?"

"No. We kill them all."

As the three rose to the higher levels of the citadel, they passed by several of the patrols which were making rounds throughout the corridors of Ketseltet. They listened closely to the words of the guardsmen, searching for any information that might be useful, but mostly the Nescrai seemed more engaged in talk about the battle between the Dragons that was raging outside, and they paid little attention to other Nescrai who were going through the halls. For the Nescrai, all places in the city were unrestricted, as they all shared a common goal, and so they seemed not at all out of place.

The upper levels of the city had all been reserved for the Sylvai and in the first seasons of the raising of the Sky Cities they had been told that these were the chambers with the best view of the world below, which had enticed many Sylvai to move into them. But like most aspects of Kor'Magailin this had been a deception, for there in those quarters they would be more confined and easier to keep cut off from the essential workings of the populace and the mechanics of the cities.

"How many are imprisoned here?" Haldus'nar asked as they approached their destination.

"Two thousand, about."

"How are we supposed to open two thousand doors without being noticed?"

"We won't have to. These are the chambers of whole families who shared their domiciles. There are maybe three hundred of them."

Shortly, Sarak'den said, "Alright, then how are we supposed to open three hundred doors without being noticed?"

Aivus'nar patiently said, "To start with, we split up. There should be minimal guards. They know the Sylvai cannot release themselves and they don't expect that anyone has come to free their prisoners."

But his words were cut off as a sudden tremor rattled through Ketseltet. Outside, through one of the many windows that helped illuminate the interior, they could see a great burst of fire not far away; the heat pushed through, though by then the flame had mostly dissipated.

"What is happening?"

"I don't know. But it is best that we hurry."

They took the final flight of stairs that would take them to the halls of the Sylvaian chambers. There, the hallway split in three directions—two outer corridors encircled the whole of the top of the city, while the third went straight ahead. There, to the left and right ways, they could see small gatherings of the Nescrai, who peered out of casements that were between the rows of locked chambers, likely trying to see what had caused the disruption to the normally smooth movement of the city through the air.

"Remember," Aivus'nar whispered. "They do not know who you are. Take them out without mercy. Remember what they did to your people in Aranthia."

And with that, Haldus'nar took the right passage, Sarak'den the left, and Aivus'nar the middle. As each of them moved along they willed their own magic to over-power the seals upon the doors, so that the Sylvai could escape. But at first, they wanted not to alert the prisoners that they could walk free, not until all of them had been opened. And as they came to the guards at each of the apertures, they engaged them first with magic, for they were elders of the Naiad and possessed binding spells that could not in most cases be broken. And when the guards were bound, they remembered the slaughter at Eswear'Nysin, and hesitated not to pierce the Nescraian hearts with steel. As they killed their enemies, Sarak'den and Haldus'nar were both reminded of Aranthia's previous words, when he had told them of how evil had pervaded all of the people of Sylveria, including themselves. And they could find no fault in his reasoning, for now they were themselves executioners.

When they each came to the end of their respective halls, they had circled back around to the far end, which Aivus'nar had already reached. His sword too was bloodied. Though dark of skin, he seemed pale, for he had taken his first lives.

"Alright, now we are looking for a man named Maralor."

"Why?" Sarak'den asked. "Who is he?"

"He is Nescrai, imprisoned here for treason. He can take care of getting word out to the other cities. We have worked out how to take them down, to the ground, where they never may rise again. I will find him. Go stand guard at the stairs. Kill anyone who comes up here. There are no other friends to the Sylvai in this city."

"If he is a traitor, why haven't they already executed him?"

"Because it would be a blow to the morale of the people to see one of their own killed like this. Now, we must hurry and find Maralor."

"And we will release the people then?"

"Yes, as soon as I find him, I will tell them to take whatever they can find as weapons and to flood the halls of the city."

He started to go, but Haldus'nar stopped him, asking, "If we bring the city down, it will be a forceful impact, will it not? How many of us here will die or be wounded?"

"I won't lie… there will be casualties. But with any luck it won't be bad. We will not disable all of the engines. Only enough to lower us to the ground. Maybe slowly. Everyone will have to fight to escape the city. There are villages to the north that are more sympathetic to the Sylvai, if they can make it there they might live."

"I don't like it," Sarak'den said. "Too many lives at risk…"

"If we don't do this, they all will die. The Nescrai are executing them. Not all of these rooms are still occupied."

She nodded, and along with her husband went to stand guard at the stairs. Aivus'nar then began searching the rooms one at a time until he found the man he was looking for, who was named Maralor. He released him from his cell and hushed him, explaining in whispers only what the plan was. They came to us, and then Aivus'nar shouted throughout the halls all that he said he would, directing the Sylvai to take up arms and to swarm the city of Ketseltet.

Everything thus far that Aivus'nar had told them was true, and they believed now that his intentions were nothing but for the good of the Sylvai; despite his close relation to Norgrash'nar, he seemed a man of honor.

Maralor was a Garonite man who had come to live in the city of Ketseltet three years before. Having learned all there was of his own people's technology, he went first to Mar'Narush where he hoped to learn more of the advancements in knowledge. When the opportunity came for him to go to the Sky City, he seized it. Skilled as a technologist, he began working in the communications room of the citadel, where he learned new things that at first seemed to him like magic.

"How do the Sky Cities communicate with each other?" Haldus'nar asked as they moved through the halls, following Maralor. "I've never known of magic capable of communicating over distance, not as you describe."

"It's not magic. I used to think it must be. But it has nothing to do with willpower. Sound moves through the air in waves that carry on forever. You simply have to know how to direct it to where you want it to go, and how to listen for it."

"And you figured this out?" Sarak'den asked.

"No, the Norgrasharians did, long before I got here. I was fortunate enough to get to operate their implements. I saw how useful this was and I was thrilled with the opportunity. Then I began hearing of all that was being done to the Sylvai in the other cities, in the seasons before this war began. Abuse. Maltreatment. Even torture. And that was when I decided I would not be a part of it. I went to Lavanar, who was then lord of this city, and told him what was happening. I was naïve and thought he would care. I couldn't imagine that the son of Norgrash'nar would be so cruel. He had us fooled, thinking that he was a good man. Now he has gone off to war in the west."

"And he is *not* a good man," Aivus'nar added. "And Lavanar is *my* father."

Maralor nodded and said, "They instead threw me in prison, amongst the Sylvai, whom they said I could live with and die with since I was so enamored with them."

"When I heard of this, I came to him in his prison. No one suspected me; they never have. Only for this do we have a chance."

"So what will you do?" Haldus'nar asked.

"While the two of you disable the engines, we will be infiltrating the communications room and telling the other cities how to do the same."

"But it will be the Nescrai who hear the messages," Sarak'den pointed out.

"Probably," Aivus'nar said. "But we don't know what might be happening elsewhere."

"If the Nescrai receive such messages, they will tighten their security all around the engines, so that any who might try whatever we are going to try will be detained."

"That is exactly what we are counting on."

"I don't understand," Sarak'den said. "You want the Sylvai to get the messages."

"We want all of them to get it, and they will. Receivers are commonplace in Kor'Magailin. Many have them in their residences. But these were not to receive all commands given by the Nescrai, but rather other communications…"

"So there is more than one channel through which words can be sent?"

"Yes," Maralor said. "We call them frequencies. And in this case, we don't care who receives what we send."

"How does this help?"

"Who built the Sky Cities, Sarak'den?"

"I don't—everyone. Nescrai and Sylvai."

"Yes, and it was the task of the Sylvai to run wires and cables from the solar collectors outside of the city through the stone and into the lower cavities, where the engines operate. So the message we send will make the Nescrai put guards around the engine rooms when we tell the Sylvai to disable them. And while they do, hopefully some of them will have escaped, and will receive the message, and will instead go to the higher places to cut the cables. Without the power of the suns and moon, the cities cannot stay afloat."

"This all seems unlikely, Aivus'nar. Not that what you say is untrue… just that it is a longshot."

"You are not wrong, Haldus'nar. It is a longshot. But it is the best chance at destroying these cities. I am confident it will work here, and I have hope that it will elsewhere too. But if the Sylvai don't receive any encouragement, they may not even think to try."

"You said before that the cities would be sunken to the ground, if this works, never to rise again. Can't they fix them, repair the cables, and bring the cities back?"

"Not if we win the war," Aivus'nar said. "Not if we can eradicate the evil of my fathers and drive them from this land."

Reinforcements Arrive

As the moments passed the city of Ketseltet was rattled with increasing frequency. Through windows the occupants watched on as Aranthia the Crimson battled with Verasian the Green. Aranthia's lightning struck out, trying to disable Verasian, while the Green Dragon cast spells of conjuration to pierce the Crimson Dragon with stone and sword and spear. But as was often the case, when Dragons sparred, the result was a physical clash between them.

This is how the battle was progressing when Ashysin the Gold arrived, and it was fortunate for Aranthia that he did, as Verasian—not having yet fought one of his brothers—was at his peak and had suffered no previous injuries. Aranthia, however, had already faced off against Drovanius and had not fully recovered.

Neither had Ashysin yet fought against another in the war, for when the Noranites had cried out and the Metallic Dragons had their fire awakened, he had gone to their rescue, but Sharuseth, claiming that Mara was his domain, told him that he would save the Noranites. So Ashysin had gone northward, through the entire length of the Valley of Tears, and come into the Valley of Naiad. There he encountered a massive force of the Norgrasharians going down the Westward Slopes—fifty thousand strong and led by Relanar, second born son of Norgrash'nar—who were marching to the west to crush the Noranites before going on toward Whitestone.

But Ashysin would not allow this, and he had rained his fire down upon them when they came out of Naiad and upon the Plains of Kronaggas. His fire fell, the full wrath of his newfound power, down upon the Norgrasharians, devastating their numbers, but coming still far from expunging them. When his fire was expelled, he could do no more, for he was exhausted.

By the time he had recovered, at least to some measure, the survivors of the attack had spread out across the plains so that they would not suffer another aerial assault so concentrated. He would not, for now, be able to destroy the whole of the Norgrasharian forces. But he had weakened them considerably, and now there was a greater chance for the Noranites and the Darians in the west.

And so Ashysin, having no people of his own to defend, turned to the east, intending to destroy any other forces that might march across Verasian's domain, once his fire was rejuvinated. There, along the northeastern realm, he had seen the arrival of his brother, Aranthia, and had come to aid in this battle.

Inside the Sky City, the other men separated from Haldus'nar and Sarak'den, each of the pairs going about to bring their plan to fruition. While Aivus'nar and Maralor went through the passages of Ketseltet, there was no resistance, for the battle of the Dragons outside had intensified, and most of the residents were drawn to the windows to observe, for none of them had ever seen something so spectacular as the clashing of these titans. Additionally, there were thousands of the now released Sylvai surging throughout the city, trying to overtake their captors. So it was with relative ease that these two dissenters were able to walk directly into the communications room.

Maralor had worked in this room and thus he was well acquainted with the other four men who were here operating the devices that sent and received messages. But Aivus'nar had by this time cast a spell of transmutation upon his friend and the Nescrai therein did not recognize him as the traitor.

The four men were at work, seated before a panel that was covered in knobs, buttons and levers. Choppy voices could be heard, voices not of those here present, as these were communications coming in from elsewhere. From the distance at which the two intruders entered, the words were indistinct, but as they drew upon the men from behind, swords in hand, they could hear one voice coming through and it said, *"Naivar is failing! The Darians have taken it!"* And in this Aivus'nar and Maralor were encouraged, for Naivar was another of the Sky Cities. If one of the cities could be taken by the Darians, then it was entirely possible that they all could be brought to ruin.

Distracted as they were, the four operators had not a chance to react before the two insurgents ended their lives. The way now clear, Aivus'nar and Maralor were able to send out the message to all of the other cities at once, telling the Sylvai who were upon them how to shut down the engines of their respective Sky Cities. Now, all they could do was focus on bringing down Ketseltet, leaving the other cities to their own fates.

Haldus'nar and Sarak'den had never visited one of the Sky Cities before this day, yet the directions that were given to them by Aivus'nar and Maralor were concise enough that they had little trouble locating one of the hidden panels that was located on one of the upper levels of the city. This panel opened up into narrow corridors that ran behind the living quarters of the Sylvai. These were maintenance tunnels, and all along the walls were wires and cables that ran throughout the entirety of the city.

Although neither of them was proficient in the mechanical workings of the cities, they were able to recognize that there might be a problem with the plan outlined by the others. For they could see that wires branched off all along the corridor, passing through small holes that went into the stone walls and into the living quarters. These likely were the lines through which ran the signals from the communication rooms to the living quarters. The plan was to get message out to all of the people of the cities through these channels. They had hoped the Sylvai living in those cities would be able to receive this message so that they would know how to disable the engines.

But here, the wires had been broken, probably cutting off the previously imprisoned residents from hearing through the devices. If this had been done in all of the cities, the Sylvai might never receive the message.

"There's not much we can do about that," Haldus'nar said.

"But then Aivus'nar and Maralor are risking themselves for nothing," Sarak'den said.

"They have to try. If nothing else it will cause greater confusion amongst the cities when they realize that Ketseltet has been infiltrated."

"You're right. And it doesn't change what we have to do."

"It is our task to stop the engines. Nothing more. At least if we are successful Ketseltet will be incapacitated."

So together they continued through the passage, then up several flights of narrow steel framed stairs and onto the highest level of the city; for it was there that the solar collectors that gave power to the engines all routed the gathered energy, which was then transferred through large cables down into the core of the city and to the engine rooms.

Their allies had said that the cables would be unmistakable, as there would be thousands of wires running into a large capacitor or metal box. From there, the power of the suns would be directed through a massive cable. Either destroying the capacitor or severing the cable would result in the loss of power to the city.

When they found it, Haldus'nar said, "There's no way we're cutting through that cable. It's too thick."

"Look there, though, all of those wires going into the box... those must be what brings the power from the panels outside. The more of those we cut, the more power will be lost, right?"

"I suppose from what Aivus'nar said... Let's cut them all."

And so with their blades in hand they climbed up onto platforms that were there placed so that the builders of the city might access them for repairs. Without regard for anything other than bringing Ketseltet to the ground, they cut through them, hundreds at a time, with their swords and daggers. Yet when they had severed them all, there seemed not to be any change, for the city still seemed stable, save for the occasional collision with the warring Dragons outside.

"Are these the wrong cables?" Haldus'nar said.

"I don't know. This has to be them. We did exactly what he said."

Then they heard voices coming from the way they had come before. Metal armor clattered as a half dozen of the Nescraian guards came into view, scowling and yelling as they saw the intruders. Seeing them, the two took their blades in hand and prepared for the confrontation.

But there was not the opportunity to fight them, for at that moment, the entirety of Ketseltet began declining as the engines failed. The city shifted to its side, throwing the approaching Nescrai against the passage wall, and casting Haldus'nar and Sarak'den off the platform.

Now, outside of Ketseltet, both Ashysin and Aranthia—even weakened as they were—were at last able to bring Verasian to the ground, just as the

Sky City itself was seized from within and began its decline toward the grasslands below. It was not a gentle fall, and though it had hovered perhaps just a Span above the ground, it struck hard and its foundations were cracked when it hit, just west of where it had hovered.

Verasian, defeated, was able to slink off to the south. Too battered and worn themselves, Aranthia and Ashysin could not pursue him. Ketseltet was in ruins, smoking, fires blazing, people screaming. But many did escape, for the city had not collided with any structure as Vainus had at Eswear'Nysin. The Nescrai who escaped scampered to the south, back toward their cities of comfort. The Sylvai who survived came out of the city, carrying their wounded and coming to the plains just west of Faigor Landing.

Aranthia and Ashysin went to them, hoping to help in any way possible, for the injuries and deaths that had occurred were significant.

Haldus'nar and Sarak'den, as well as Aivus'nar, survived as well; Maralor had died during the collision with the ground, though not before he had successfully sent out a message to the other Sky Cities. Sarak'den was injured severely, from where her head had struck the stone upon impact, but she would recover. Haldus'nar was battered, but able to care for her, and for the other wounded Sylvai.

It was the third day of Wintermelt when Ketseltet fell, and upon Faigor Landing the survivors rested and waited for the Haldusians to arrive by way of ship.

The seafaring Haldusians arrived at Firstlight on the fourth of Wintermelt, and to the relief of Haldus'nar and Sarak'den, they had rallied four times the number of ships and soldiers from amongst their people than expected. And so this invading force was comprised of nearly ten thousand men and women, and two Dragons, all of them so swiftly hardened by a war that had thus far lasted only four days. While devising the plans of what they would do next, they took time to recover from their wounds, so that as many lives would be saved, and so that their force would be as strong as possible.

On the sixth day of Wintermelt, scouts reported seeing a Dragon that was moving northward to the west, between the Vaingar River and Kathor Mountain. Its color could not be discerned, and they knew not if it was Verasian or one of the others; but it was assumed that it was neither Sharuseth nor Merilinder, for why would they be so far away from their own people? Ashysin promised that after a few more days of rest, he would be ready to go and investigate.

Their recovery was slow, but they committed to taking as much time as was needed to raise the strength of their army, for it was a long march across the north, through Forthran, Naiad and into Mara. By the eighth day of the season, they considered themselves fit to march, and they hoped that they would find others along the northern route that would join them, for Aivus'nar was convinced that there were villages there which were more sympathetic to the Sylvai and their cause.

And that morning, at the Hour of Awakening, I joined with my brothers and sisters, there on Faigor Landing, south of Mount Hearin, and I was not alone.

It had been the third of Wintermelt when Ashysin, Merilinder and Sharuseth had been compelled to shed their misgivings about breaking their vows and had left me alone at the southern end of the Valley of Tears. If I had known that I would be left there alone, while the rest of Sylveria was engulfed in war, I would not likely have gone with them to the valley where I would be stranded with only a long journey by land ahead.

I was disheartened at first, for four of us had gone into the valley there in mourning, as each of us had taken a vow that would keep us from acting during the war. Yet I was the only one who had upheld my vow.

Still, I had heard the echoing screams that had driven the Dragons to break their vow, and I was not complacent in understanding why; but my oath had been to the Numen and not to the Law—which was a force or entity that I had never really known and didn't fully understand. As I stood there under the shadow of the Temple of Diras'Vorma, I wondered what consequences there would be for the Dragons' actions. Drovanius had broken the Law—not only his vow to it, but the Law of Balance itself; presumably, Verasian and Merobassi had as well. I regarded Aranthia the same as Ashysin, Merilinder and Sharuseth, and knew not what their fates would be for the breaking of their own vows.

Regardless, I was stranded in the Valley of Tears and had no idea what to do, so I decided after much consideration that there was little to do but to go home to the Valley of Naiad. I began my journey through the whole of the long valley, following along on the western bank of the Steel River, which was also called *Enar'udik*.

I was distraught during those hours; my people, the Naiad were beginning a war that I could not stop. I mourned for the dead and the dying, the Dragons and the whole of Sylveria—the innocent creatures who would also suffer for it. How had the world come to this? In five hundred years we had gone from a perfect world, a paradise, to a place that was on the brink of its own destruction. Evil had come into the world—an evil, supposedly of necessity, according to the Law. For in my time away from Sylveria, in whatever celestial realm the Numen dwelt, I had seen that the Dark arose because of Freewill.

I understood that without it—without Freewill—there might not have to be evil, but so too would there not be the ability to appreciate creation, to love, to create things of our own, to behold the beauty of the world. And although I also understood the need of the Metallic Dragons and the Sylvai and the mix-blooded Naiad to fight for their world, I did not regret the vow I had made.

Always had I been set apart from the others. I had been the last remaining when all of my brothers and sisters and cousins had married; I was the Thirteenth Naiad, and my fate was not to be the same as theirs.

So I determined that I would hold to my oath to the Numen, and I would not fight—at least not as the others fought—but rather I would do all in my power to become a beacon of the Light for the people of Sylveria—a disciple of the Numen, for surely that was what he had intended when I was called away in the depths of Kronaggas Mountain, when I had been shown many things.

My way through the Valley of Tears was slow, for the high hills of it were sluggish to pass and my mind, bent upon otherworldly things, slowed my progress as I tried to come to an understanding of exactly what I was to do, what it meant to be a servant of the Light. But as with all matters of the Light things such as these must be revealed in their own time.

As the days passed, I knew the war was underway. Not for any physical signs, but for a hollow tenor that encased the world, the air, the land, and my spirit. Evil truly was now amongst us, and Sylveria would never be the same again. It would suffer, and there was little that could be done for it.

Yet soon I learned that nature would not remain idle in times such as these. Sylveria had been a world of light, life, love and peace, and when such things were threatened, it would fight back. And as I contemplated many things upon my slow procession through the vacant valley, I began to notice things that were most unexpected.

It began with the Insects and the small mammals of this region—they came near to me in small numbers at first, but with increasing frequency as the Courses flowed. Birds soared in formation overhead, and Fish swam upstream through the river. Then larger animals came—Badgers and Buzzards, Tamarins and Tapirs, Foxes and fauna of every kind that lived here in the valley. I was reminded of when the animals of Vindras Vale had been driven out by the mining of the Garonites onto the Southern Plains. Yet now it was different, for they were not running from something; instead, they were going toward some destination, perhaps even following me toward some end.

For several days I moved slowly, just to see what would come next, and on the second day of Wintermelt the creatures of Mara that could scale the mountains arrived—Goats and Gorillas, Wolves and Wombats, Boars and Black Bears and other creatures of various kinds, all drawn to me by a force unknown, even from across the mountains. Then, on the third day of the Season, the Cats of Vindras Vale arrived, the Mountain Leopards, likely both fleeing from war in their region, and coming toward the light of life that was gathering in the Valley of Tears. And soon the creatures of the east came as well, from across the Grasslands of Verasian, through the mountain passes, where they joined with the multitude that was forming around me. These were Horned Antelope, Snakes, Bobcats, Cougars, Wonkans, Hyenas, Warthogs and Wildebeests, coming through the easier passes from Verasian's domain.

It was clear that they were coming to me, compelled by some inner working that I could not comprehend. Like a magnet they were drawn to me, for wherever I was they came to follow. Whether through common sense or through some mystical understanding, I knew that there was intent behind their actions, and that it was somehow for the benefit of the world that we shared.

Now I knew that I could both keep my vow and serve a purpose in the world, for these creatures had not come to lift my spirits, to flee the war, or even to mourn the destruction that was coming upon Sylveria—they were here to fight for it.

And so I led this army all the way to the northern end of the valley and when I came to a halt, not knowing which way to take them, they began to lead, eastward across Din'Algor Pass, into the domain of Verasian. As we passed through the farming settlements and towns of the Nescrai, the people raised not a weapon against us, for they had never seen such a procession and wondered what the cause of such a migration was.

Eastward we went until far across toward Mount Hearin we saw the encampment of the Haldusians, as well as Ashysin and Aranthia. It was the eighth day of Wintermelt, and we now had an army that I believed could handle whatever was ahead.

Yet I knew not the enemy that was soon to land upon Sylveria.

THE SCOURGE OF NEFARIA

When I, led by the company of beasts, came to Faigor Landing, where the Haldusians were breaking camp, they turned northward, now following only the lead of their instincts. I was there reunited with my sister, Sarak'den, Haldus'nar, their people, and Ashysin and Aranthia.

"I have never seen so many animals all at once!" Sarak'den said. "What is this menagerie of creatures you bring?"

"I didn't bring them. They followed me here, out of the Valley of Gold."

"But why?"

"I think the best answer to that question lies wherever they are now going. They do not follow me anymore, but take their own path."

"Where could they be going?" Ashysin wondered.

"The Dragon that went that way—probably Drovanius...." Aranthia said, considering. "He is surely up to something. It is there we should go. We should follow the beasts."

"We need to get to the west, through Naiad," Haldus'nar said. "The Norgrasharians march there, to annihilate the Noranites and Darians. We must go to their aid."

"But if there is a threat to the north we need to know," I said. "Or it might follow after us on our way west. And there is clearly something drawing the animals there."

"Let me go ahead, to the north, so that we can see what awaits, Ashysin said. "If Drovanius is there, it cannot be for anything good."

"Agreed," Haldus'nar said. "Then we will decide."

"I will ride with you," I said.

"And I," Sarak'den said.

"I will stay here and prepare the soldiers for the march," Haldus'nar said. "We need to get moving as soon as possible. We have lost much time."

So my sister and I mounted the Gold Dragon and by air we followed the succession of all the animals of the various kinds.

We flew west around Mount Hearin, and followed over the Guidetrain rail to the north. This was the track that Norgrash'nar had taken me upon long ago on the Guidetrain, and it was still active, though the train was nowhere to be seen. It was along this path that the animals remained, moving northward toward a goal unknown, and around the village of Dorias.

Countless animals had come, gathering still as the multitude moved along, but of animals powerful enough to make a real difference if there was a battle ahead, there were perhaps ten thousand. But even those that seemed not strong or large enough to fight had come, for it remained that this was their world as well.

We approached the eastern shores of the Felheim Sea at the Hour of Meeting and soared over the Nescraian city of Malis. Still northward we flew across the hill-covered lands of the north. A short time later we reached Svengard, which was the center of trade for this region, and just past that was the Svenmar Table. This was a small region where the plains that came before it from the south dipped down on both sides of a raised landform that jutted out to the north, overlooking lower lands below. It was there that the succession of Sylveria's creatures ended, for they gathered there, upon the table, and around to the east and west of it. Here they stopped, but still there was no sign as to why they had come here.

"Continue on, Ashysin," I said. "Let us see what is to the north." The Dragon nodded and flew on.

To the northwest was the Felheim Forest, and to the north and east the Sea of Repose. And there along the coastline we saw it... First there was Drovanius, perched upon the beach near the Kailin Shipyard, but he looked different somehow—paler, his once shiny scales were now dull, and his features seemed fierce but somehow demoralized.

"What happened to him?" I asked Sarak'den.

"Drovanius? I don't know. He was injured in the battle for Aranthia, but nothing we did should have caused this."

He looked not sickly, despite the missing scales and torn wings, but rather he was assailed by something else... then I realized what it was; Drovanius had been touched by the Dark, was tainted by it, wholly corrupted.

As we drew nearer, circling around to the west, I could see that the Black Dragon's enormous body had before concealed something there at the docks—a great vessel larger than any I had ever seen, a barge of cargo unknown—until just thereafter when I saw the first of the Nefarians charge off of the ship. It was soon followed by another, and then many more— these were the Giants of the dark lands, seen never before in Sylveria, and only by me for the visions given when I was away in the Temple of Kronaggas.

Then, in those dark dreams, I had seen them in Nefaria, as they were, just wicked textures upon the dark landscape; but here they seemed worse, more terrifying, for they were creatures of the purest evil and they showed darkly upon the colorful scenery of Sylveria. And then I fully understood what had befallen Drovanius—he had been mired by the Dark, and he would never be the same. He had gone there once again and brought back a small legion of these Giants, so bent on the destruction of his enemies was he.

"What... are those?" Sarak'den asked, wide-eyed and horrified, for though they were still small in comparison to the Dragon, they would tower over any of the Naiad, for they stood four heights tall, and viciousness was apparent in their demeanor and their nature.

"Those are the Trolls and Ogres..." I said, myself filled with anxious trepidation. "I cannot believe he would do it, Sarak'den... but he brought them from Nefaria."

The Ogres were alike to a man, with arms and legs bulging with muscles hardened by many centuries of warfare. Their faces were swollen and burned with lesions that leaked blood and pus, their teeth broken and rotted, and their eyes were filled with a lust for destruction. The Trolls stood as tall as the Ogres, but were covered in matted and tangled green and black hair, and their features were hideous, for they looked not dissimilar to the Ogres, but with long pointed ears, crooked noses, eyes as black as the Midnight sky, and terrible claws upon their fingers. Two hundred of them there were, split evenly between the two kinds, and this was an enemy that I did not know how to defeat.

Ashysin flew closer still, unable to believe his eyes, for he had never seen such monstrosities, and he called out to his brother, "What horror have you brought into our world, Drovanius?"

The Black Dragon turned, for until then we had gone somehow unnoticed, and he snarled, a vicious display that shocked me, and I knew that the full measure of Drovanius' corruption had come upon him.

And I noticed then, as he turned away, back to the Ogres and Trolls, that there was a man mounted upon the back of the Dragon, who wore plated armor that was as black as his own soul: Norgrash'nar.

Drovanius commanded the Giants, saying to them, "Go westward! Destroy the Naiad! Destroy Mara! Destroy all in your path!"

And with horrible roars and wails they charged, trampling the fields and shaking the very ground with their thunderous steps. Drovanius leaped into the air and took flight as well, to the west, ahead of the monstrosities.

"I will rain fire down upon these abominations!" Ashysin promised.

"What good would it do? There are too many...." Sarak'den said. "No... go back to Faigor. We must get the others."

As Ashysin turned back to the south and soared toward the Svenmar Table, we saw as the creatures of Sylveria were charging down the slopes, galloping, running, screaming their own cries of vengeance against the anathemas that had invaded their world.

"They will be slaughtered," Sarak'den cried, tearful and dispirited. "The animals do not deserve what we've brought on them."

"We didn't do this, child," Ashysin said, as sorrowful as she. "They did. Drovanius and Norgrash'nar."

When we returned to Faigor Landing, the company was prepared to move. Their plan was to go northwest, across the Vaingar River, between the Felheim Sea and Kathor Mountain and on to the Felheim Fields. From there we were to go down into the Lowlands of Forthran and up through Yor'Kavon Pass. We were invaders in this land; there were small cities and villages and farms all through this region, all of them Nescrai, and we did not know how we would be received. Aivus'nar had said that the people of the north were more sympathetic to the Sylvai, but he was unsure how they would take an army of the mixed Haldusians passing through their land. Nevertheless, this was the plan set in place while we were gone.

"What about the Ogres and Trolls?" I said. "We have to do something about them."

"You want to try to stop them?" Aivus'nar asked.

"We must at some point. Either here or in the west. Drovanius ordered them to march on Mara."

"If they're truly as big as you say," Haldus'nar said. "It will be no easy task to take them out."

"And they are strong too," Sarak'den said. "They wield clubs like the Felheim trees; with their brawn they could crush us with one blow. And the Trolls, they are just... hideous."

"We don't know what's happening in Mara," I said. "They may have defeated the Norgrasharians. Ashysin decimated their soldiers."

"I did," the Gold Dragon said. "But my breath was expired before I could finish them. Many survived and they grew smarter, spreading out over the Plains."

"They will not fight so well in the woodlands as the Noranites," Haldus'nar said. "They are not accustomed to it."

"If the Ogres make it to Mara," I said. "They will tear the trees out by their roots."

"Are they really that strong? Enough to tear a Baobab tree out by the roots?"

"I don't know. Maybe. The smaller trees at least. My point is that no one will be a match for them there."

"And we will?" Aivus'nar said.

"We have two Dragons with us," I said. "Aranthia, Ashysin, can you fight?"

"I can," Ashysin said.

"Of course, and I think we need to face them now, before they join with the Norgrasharians in the west. Then they will only be a stronger force."

"Then we march on Felheim! We must rid our world of this scourge," Haldus'nar said, then he began rallying the people so that they would begin moving along the path they had first intended, and hoping to cut off the Ogres and Trolls north of the Felheim Sea.

Unions of War

At the same time that the Haldusians were beginning their march to face the Nefarians in the east, on the eighth day of Wintermelt, 552, the differing armies of the west were uniting together as well.

For the Garonites, having been defeated in Southern Mara and forced to flee across the Varin'soth River, abandoning their gear and armor just to survive, came then onto the Plains of Kronaggas, where the Norgrasharians had been scattered after the attack by fire of Ashysin the Gold. They were there united together into one force, and the Garonites took up the armor of their fallen brothers and sisters, and as a whole they came to the South Umonar River, which was the western border with Mara.

And so too had the Adaasharians moved westward, past the High Hills of Imara, and into the burned forests of Southern Mara, then to the north, across the Southern Divide which had now become a wasteland with the ruins of the Sky City of Dian. From there they joined with the Noranites who had moved northward themselves, fleeing the wreckage. This meeting happened at the Cusp of Ayron, which was a crescent-shaped hill that served as a wall between them and Lake Abai.

Now, as the Adaasharians had moved across Southern Mara, there had been in the sky the city of Mishran, floating northward over the Hilly Lands. But from a distance, they saw as the citadel crashed to the ground there in Mara. It had been taken down, likely by the Sylvai who there lived. Likewise, on that same day, did the Noranites witness as yet another of the flying cities—this one Sartal, which was north of the Cusp—disappeared in decline to the northeast. They presumed that it too had been taken down by their people.

When the Adaasharians and the Noranites united, so too were Adaashar and Sveraden, and Norandar and Alunen brought into company with one another. Amongst them was only Sharuseth, for Ashysin and Aranthia were in the east at this time, and Merilinder, having come out of the mountains with the Adaasharians, had fallen ill from the smoky remnants near Aisper Hill and was not yet recovered enough to have rejoined the efforts, and he went west of Ayron to rest. This was on the ninth day of Wintermelt.

"Our scouts have reported that the Nescrai have united in the east," Alunen said to the others. "They are waiting at the eastern line, five Marches from here. Drovanius is with them, and possibly Norgrash'nar."

"How great are their numbers?" Adaashar asked.

"Forty thousand, maybe more."

"Then we are outmatched."

"Only for now," Norandar said. "We are still waiting for the Darians."

"Are you sure they're coming?" Sveraden asked. "This war has been on for nearly a season and they have not arrived yet."

"We don't know what might be going on in the north. Perhaps they were seized upon. For now, we must strategize as if they are not coming."

Alunen said, "I don't think the Nescrai will be too pleased to enter the forests. They are accustomed to moving unhindered on the plains. Our people have lived here most of their lives."

"Then this gives us an advantage," Adaashar said.

"Not if they use our own tactics against us. Set the forests on fire, driving us further to the west, then marching through the ashes. The Garonites would crave such revenge."

Sharuseth was present amongst this council and he said, "The snows are melting. It would take great heat to ignite the woods—a Dragon's fire—and it is only Ashysin, Merilinder and I who possess this. The others do not."

"Where did this power of fire come from?" Adaashar asked, "For we saw Merilinder unleash it upon the Garonites in the mountains, when so many of our people were buried."

"It is our magic now... no more can spells come to us so easily as before, for we have been cut off by the breaking of our vow to the Law. Fire is the greatest essence of our powers... Now we must defend what is left with it. Position all of your archers at the trees near the river. When they try to cross, or bring Drovanius against us, unleash your arrows. I will go there as well, and if they try to cross, I will unleash upon them."

"Alright," Norandar said. "Let us leave the people here to rest. The archers and us will go to the east and keep a close eye upon the Nescrai."

They left that morning to go eastward upon the ground; Sharuseth too crept through the forest, inasmuch as a Dragon can creep, so that they might not give away their approach to the Nescrai.

They arrived during the Hour of Darkening, and hidden in the trees they looked out over the western Plains of Kronaggas and saw the vastness of the enemy. Drovanius was amongst them, but the other Dragons, Merobassi and Verasian, were not. While most of the Nescrai had set up tents as though they would be there remaining for a long while, others seemed to be constructing something along the eastern bank of the wide Umonar River.

"What are they building?" Sveraden asked.

"A bridge perhaps?" Adaashar suggested.

"If they want to cross, why not just go to the south at Crossbridge Crossing or north to Tearway?"

"Perhaps we should go and burn it before they get this idea," Alunen said.

"Crossbridge is made of wood, and we could burn it, but what if we need to get across?" Norandar said. "If we trap them to the east, we will be trapped here in the west."

"They know that I am amongst you," Sharuseth said. "If they cross there, they know I will destroy it. And they know that Tearway is too narrow, and that we would pick them off with arrows. No, they are building here a stone bridge that my fire cannot melt."

"Then we must focus the archers here," Alunen said. "And keep the scouts watching to the north and south, to make sure."

"We can't let them build that bridge," Adaashar said. "Their numbers are greater than ours, and if they come across, they may lose some of their fighters to our arrows, but they will overwhelm us."

"We still have the power of fire on our side," Alunen said. "If the Nescrai come across in small numbers, the archers will take them. If they cross in force, Sharuseth will scorch them. There is no easy way across that will not cost them, and give us the advantage."

"You are right, Alunen," Sharuseth said. "But remember, my fire can only burn so long."

Both armies rested that day, neither prepared to cross. While the Sylvai were contented enough to wait in hopes that Alim'dar would arrive soon, the Nescrai were occupied with their own ventures, and when Firstlight came on the tenth day of Wintermelt, they saw why, for as the bridge of stone was being built, so too had massive, mobile walls been raised and positioned in front of the bridge. These were walls of wood and steel, which would burn in part, but which would grant the Nescrai safer passage across the bridge, even burning. They had raised twenty of them, intended to serve as shields and absorb whatever Dragonfire might come at them. Placing them at the forefront of the construction of their bridge, they were protected so as to make quick progress across the waters of the river.

This discouraged the First Awakened and Sharuseth, for they understood that by the time the walls would have burned, the Nescrai would have already crossed into Mara, and though many of them would fall to the archers, so too would many more make it into the cover of the trees and they would be forced into melee.

The stone bridge was completed at Midlight, but still the Nescrai waited, positioning their men and women and walls in what was clearly the last preparations before marching.

They waited until Highlight, when Aros would be mostly to their backs and where the Sylvai would be most prone to distraction by the sun. And they began marching.

The Sylvai had yet to devise a better plan other than to simply pick off as many of the Nescrai as they could with arrows, burn as many as possible until Sharuseth's fire was once again depleted, and then to retreat to the west to rejoin with their own army.

Two waves of the Nescrai crossed, guarded by walls, and both fell to the Dragon's fire. Those soldiers who made it across were slain by arrow. A third approached more slowly, and it too burned.

"They are testing us," Norandar said. "To see what we are capable of, how far our reach is."

And indeed, the fourth wall that came stopped further back than the others, and Sharuseth's breath would not reach it. A Course later it started moving again and now there was a large unit of soldiers positioned behind, advancing along with it. Sharuseth prepared to unleash his breath, but then something came upon him, upon all of them. Some of the Archers faltered and fell from the trees; others made it safely to the ground before collapsing. Alunen, Norandar, Sveraden, and Adaashar also felt it—a wave of some disturbance that swept over them from the east, across the bridge, and they could not act in those moments.

"What... is happening?" Sveraden cried.

"This is... like the Shadows of Dragonswake..." Norandar stammered. "But its time has passed and we cannot even see to the north... the Hour of Highlight is behind us."

"It has never been this strong... but this is the same... despondence... we are without hope," Alunen said, shielding her face with her hands as though it might stop it. "We must retreat!"

"To where? Whatever this wretchedness is, we cannot lead it back to the others," Adaashar said.

"Look, if you can," Sharuseth said. "The bridge... They have dropped the wall... but I cannot unleash..."

"Norgrash'nar is there!"

And indeed, now in the middle of the bridge, unhindered by the wooden wall, strode Norgrash'nar and an elite troop of men and women, all of them dressed in identical black armor. Upon the breastplate of each was a mounted green stone, and when Sharuseth and the Sylvai looked upon it, they had no doubt that this was the source of the hopeless dread that had befallen them. And as they came, the archers began to flee westward, away from the scene. The others resisted for now.

"What is that?"

"It is something wicked..." Sharuseth said. "We must stop it..."

"How?"

The Dragon had no answer, himself taken by the dark power that was emanating from the approaching company, led by their greatest enemy. Behind the armored soldiers was the bulk of the Nescraian army, and amongst them strode Drovanius the Black, now grinning wickedly, for he knew that his plan was working.

"We must get away..." Alunen cried. "Warn the others. Signal a retreat from Ayron, to the north, away from this... What can we do against such a power?"

They left then, Dragon and Sylvai, for there was nothing they could do but flee the scene, so great was the power of the Moonstone Armor that had been made for Drovanius by Talentaran the Drake as part of their dark dealings.

But the Nescrai would not bring the whole of their army into the forests, for there they might not be a match for the Noranites. Instead, they only came enough in force to drive the Sylvai northward, so that they could not again flee to the south.

Nirvisa'nen's Plight

On the eleventh day of Winterfel, when Kronaggas had left his temple for the last time, he had left explicit directions for his children. I had gone with the Dragon, and Alim'dar was there present with his wife Nirvisa'nen, his sisters Alunen, Sarak'den, and Sveraden, his brothers Norandar and Adaashar, and his cousin, Haldus'nar.

They had been instructed to wait five days, until the fourth of Wintertide, and at the Hour of Elation to strike the magic imbued tablet with the hammer which Norandar now wielded. They had known that Kronaggas was leaving this world, that they would never see him again, for death was soon to be upon Sylveria. And they knew that war was coming.

"Go back to your lands, if you wish, to prepare your people," Alunen said. "We will wait here, Norandar and I, and we will crush the tablet as Kronaggas commanded. We are already near to Mara, whereas you all have a long journey ahead. Go to your lands to prepare your people."

"We were all of us instructed to do this," Sveraden said. "And once it is done, we need to take a fragment back to Nysin'Sumuni, as commanded."

"Our people are already preparing," Adaashar said. "We will stay with you."

Haldus'nar said, "We will stay as well, and deliver a piece of the stone to Diras'Vorma on our way back to Aranthia."

"This is a task for us all," Sarak'den said. "Our people have been preparing now for some time. We will be ready for whatever the Nescrai bring against us."

"We can only hope we all will," Alim'dar said. "We cannot know how far they have gone, how deep their corruption. Not yet. My people too have been preparing, but I wish we had more time, for there is still much work to do. The forges are operating continually to supply weapons for the Noranites and the Adaasharians. There are still strategies to plan and men and women to train. If you all must stay here, then I hope you can forgive us if Nirvisa'nen and I depart early. For we trust that you will do as

Kronaggas has asked."

"I think we all understand," Sarak'den said, and the others agreed.

"You will be sending your shipments by Etakos soon?" Adaashar asked.

"Yes. Five hundred barrels, guided by trained oarsmen. Expect them before the war begins."

"We don't know what this war will bring," Sveraden said. "But I pray we will see you again, soon, Brother." She went to Alim'dar and embraced him.

Holding on to his most beloved sister, he said, "We will march from Whitestone as soon as possible. I've no doubt that the Norgrasharians will come from the east to try to destroy us all, and the Garonites from the mountains."

"We will do what we can about the Garonites," Adaashar promised.

"I only wish that we could be here on the mainland with you," Sarak'den said.

"I have a feeling that you will be kept busy in your own lands," Alim'dar said. "Make no mistake, Drovanius will seek avengeance against Aranthia, and your people. There have been none more hated than the Haldusians."

"When we have defeated them in our own lands, we will come to yours," Haldus'nar promised.

"You will always be welcomed, Brother." Although in times past, the Nescrai had been considered more of cousins to the Sylvai, and though Haldus'nar and Nirvisa'nen were Nescrai, it had now become a matter of respect and bonding that Haldus'nar was considered our brother, and Nirvisa'nen our sister.

"We will take our leave then," Nirvisa'nen said. "May the light of this world remain upon us all."

The Father and Mother of the Darians then left Kronaggas Mountain and began the journey back to their own lands, to Whitestone.

On the first day of Wintertide, a full season before the war began, Alim'dar and Nirvisa'nen had arrived back in Nirvisa'Iinid. There Alim'dar saw after the preparations for war, aiding in every possible way: he forged weapons, assembled armor, tended the horses that would carry his men and women into battle, and prepared rations for the long days ahead.

He rallied twenty thousand soldiers who were well trained in combat, and four thousand horses. His cavalry was likely the largest there would be on the battlefields. He made for both himself and Nirvisa'nen armor of the highest quality, as it would be the two of them who led the Darians in war. He laid traps along the southern borders of his lands, so that if retreat were necessary, they would be prepared. But most of all, Alim'dar made time in those last days to be with his wife, for they did not know what the coming seasons would bring.

Nirvisa'nen was in her garden on the third day of Wintertide and though it was cold and her flowers and herbs had yet to begin their new cycle she was content with the removal of the old growth, for soon Springrise would come and their life would be renewed. The cold didn't bother her; like all of her kind she had more of a tolerance for it, which had made living in Whitestone even better for her. Though she was happy in the moment, as she always was while tending her garden, her thoughts were distant and there was disquietude in her soul.

She had been trained to fight alongside her husband, and she would be on the battlefield with him when the time came, and this filled her with angst, for at this time she had not even seen death and did not fully grasp what it meant. She could not fathom what it meant to die: what did it mean to simply no longer *be*? Worse still, she worried that Alim'dar might be killed in the coming war, and she live... and how could she ever be happy if he were gone and she remained? Further still, how many of their children would perish, their descendants that had been increasing for over five hundred years?

The world was going to be far different after this war than it had been before, and Nirvisa'nen was not happy about it. And so it was that while she tended her garden it occurred to her that maybe she could stop it.

It was, after all, possibly her fault that Norgrash'nar had fallen so far. If she had chosen instead to marry him, so long ago, would he have remained true to the Light? Would the world remain at peace if he had not been drawn to the Dark? Or would Alim'dar instead have grown bitter, taking Norgrash'nar's place? She had no answers to these questions, only ideas...

"Perhaps if I go to him," she thought. *"I could convince him to stop."*

But as it turned out, there was no need for her to go to him, for on that very day, as she was alone in the garden, Norgrash'nar came to her, as he had once before, long ago. She didn't see him at first, only felt his gaze upon her, and this was enough for her to sense his presence.

Her hands had been moving, pulling dead growth from the frozen ground, but now she stopped and said, "I know you are there, in this garden. Like a snake you slink into my presence, watching me, not afraid to speak, but only waiting to see if I will notice you there."

"Nirvisa... my love cannot be tamed." He stepped out of the shadows from behind a tree.

"Call me by my proper name, Norgrash'nar."

"You must listen to me, Nirvisa...nen. The time has come. You must take me up on all I have offered you."

"You know that I cannot. That I *will* not."

"Alim'dar does *not* love you. Not the right way. Not the way you deserve."

"Do you even know what love is? Look at what you have done to the world. We are on the brink of war. You are touched by the Darkness, just like Drovanius."

"We are the darkness, Nirvisa. We are Nescrai—you are Nescrai and you belong with your own. You belong with *me!*"

"I am right where I am supposed to be. Where I *want* to be."

Norgrash'nar fumed, but still he persisted. "I demand that you listen to me!"

"You demand? I have entertained your infatuation for too long, Norgrash'nar. I can but call out and a dozen Darians will be upon you before you can escape…"

"But you haven't done so already," he smirked. "You do not want me to leave, Nirvisa. You know the truth."

"I know that what you think is truth is lies. You're jealous in your boastfulness. You think too much of yourself."

"And yet it is not I who will betray you."

"You already have. You have betrayed us all. You have betrayed this world. End this madness now, before it begins. I beg you."

"I have done only what I know to be right, Nirvisa. Can your beloved Alim'dar say the same?"

"What are you talking about?"

"You know of what I speak."

"I do *not*."

"Who does he serve, Nirvisa? Who does Alim'dar bow down before?"

"He bows to no one, nor should he. He is a child of the Light."

"And yet he will betray you… because he does not love you like I do, like you deserve." Then, Norgrash'nar fell down on his knees, bowing before Nirvisa'nen, and said, "I will never betray you."

"Stand up, you mooncalf!" She said harshly, but he remained.

"This is my final plea to you, Nirvisa."

"And what if I were to take you up on this offer?" she asked. "Would you call off this war? Would you squelch the malice that has seeped into all of your people toward my children, and into the Garonites, and Drovanius and Merobassi and Verasian? Don't you remember a time when we all lived in peace, when we all loved one another, not as lovers, but as family? The world was so simple then, Norgrash'nar. Would you lead us all back to that, if I were to agree to come with you?"

Norgrash'nar did not immediately speak, but he stood up and began pacing around the garden. To her, the look in his eyes was madness, but to him he surely thought that he was of sound mind as he considered it. Finally he said, "I would." Another long pause followed. "If I could, Nirvisa. You know I have always loved you, and only you."

"You have a wife, Norgrash'nar. Love her. She deserves it, does she not?"

"I don't want to love Kalenen!" he hissed. "Only you..."

"It *cannot* be. Alim'dar is the man I love, and you have to get past this. You cannot destroy the peace of this world just for your own selfish wants. Fate has given me to him. And I tell you this, Alim'dar will *not* betray."

"You will see, Nirvisa. I will ask you one final time to come with me. Once more is all..."

"You have my answer, Norgrash'nar. Leave this city, or I will call the guards, and they will take you."

"Once more... is all..." he repeated, but made no move to depart. Then, he stepped up to her, and reached out a hand toward her face, but he hesitated, for his eyes had caught a glimpse of something else. And his hand fell down then, and grasped the amulet that hung from her neck, which had been there since first given to her by Alim'dar. This was the amulet containing the mysterious pink stone that I had brought from Haldus'nar. Then, still holding the amulet in his hand, still staring at it, he said, "Let me touch you, Nirvisa... Let me touch your face one last time, so that I will not forget you."

"No," she said curtly, stepping back, pulling the amulet free, and crying out as loudly as she could for the guards who would be just a short way out from the garden. His eyes filled with rage, and she said to him, "I will not be beguiled, Norgrash'nar. You want the truth? I always loved Alim'dar. Always. And had it not been him, I would have chosen Alak'kiin before you!"

He said nothing, only glared with a fierceness in his eyes that caused Nirvisa'nen to step back toward the stone entrance into the garden where the guards could now be heard coming. And then they were there, a dozen armed Darians, wielding sword and axe and bow, nocked and ready, waiting only for the command of Nirvisa'nen. Still Norgrash'nar glared, but made no move. He said, "I will destroy this entire world for you, Nirvisa..."

"Do it!" Nirvisa'nen commanded, and the bowmen fired, directly at the lord of the Nescrai. But the arrows pierced only a cloud of dust that materialized in his place, then struck the stone wall behind. Norgrash'nar had vanished—a kind of magic, it seemed, that was not supposed to be possible.

"Mother, are you alright?" One of the guards asked.

"Yes. Alert the entire city. He must be here still. He can't have just teleported away!"

All but two of the guards charged away; the others remained with her. One of them said, "Come inside, Mother. We must make sure you're safe, and alert Alim'dar."

"I will tell him," she said. "He needs to hear it from me."

In the central castle of Nirvisa'Iinid, Nirvisa'nen nervously awaited the arrival of her husband. The guards remained with her. She knew she had to tell him about Norgrash'nar's visitation—not only this one, but about the time before when he had come to her garden many years before. She hated that she had kept it from him, but until more recent times it had not seemed important, as this was the first visit he had made to her in over two hundred years. The more time that had passed, the more she felt it unnecessary, for she had increasingly thought that he must have gotten over her. Of course, when the rumors of war began, she could not help but wonder if the degeneration of the Nescrai, at his command, was because of it.

When Alim'dar arrived back in their chamber, where the guards had taken her, she ran to him and embraced him tightly, saying, "Let us not go to war. Let us find some way to end this."

He took her by the shoulders and gently pushed her away, keeping her at arm's length, and said, "What happened? They said Norgrash'nar was here in the city."

She nodded. "In my garden, while I was there."

"Did he harm you?"

"No... not physically... He only talked about his love for me."

"His love for you? Surely not! Has he never gotten over you?"

"Apparently not."

"That is madness... he and Kalenen used to come here, to our banquets, long ago. We were like brothers."

"It was all an act. He came here once before too, secretly..."

"What are you talking about?"

"A long time ago, before this war was even conceived of. He came here secretly, just like today, to my garden..."

"Why? Why didn't you tell me?"

"It didn't matter, Alim. I cast him off then as I did today. I did not encourage his affections."

"Are you sure? Are you certain that you did not entertain him?"

"Of course not! You know I have only ever loved you."

"I know, Nirvisa," Alim'dar said, pulling her close again. "That is not what I meant. I have never mistrusted you. I only mean... is there any way that he might have misconstrued your words to make him think that you held on to some kind of longing for him?"

"I don't think so."

"How long was he in the garden with you today, before you called the guards?"

"I... I don't know. A while."

"This has always been the problem, Nirvisa. How long did you take to finally agree to wed me? All because you could not stand the thought of hurting him. This was always your weakness."

Tears came to Nirvisa'nen's eyes and she buried her face in his chest, weeping, and said, "I know... I am so sorry, Alim... I love you."

"I know, my love. I have never doubted that. Do not be sorry for your weakness. A weakness that makes you care for others is not really weakness. It is this compassion in your heart that has kept you from following the other Nescrai into darkness. It is that compassion that I have always loved in you."

"Still... I love you, Alim... I am so scared."

"And I love you, more than anything. If he is in the city, the guards will find him, and he will never bother you again. His crimes are many. If he has fled then he will be undone in this coming war. This I promise you, Nirvisa."

Alim'dar's Verdict

By that night, no sign of Norgrash'nar was found anywhere in Nirvisa'Iinid, and though the search continued, it was thought that most likely he had left. Nirvisa'nen went to sleep at Lastlight, with four guards in the castle's bedchamber, directly behind the dining halls, which had of late been turned into more of a war room.

Alim'dar was there alone, standing over the large dining table that had been transformed into a miniature model of the lands of western Sylveria, from Whitestone to the Southern Reaches. Small carved stone figures represented the armies that he expected to be at play in the coming war.

For some time now Alim'dar had known his tactics, for he had determined, with his sons and daughters, all of the possible outcomes. The only aspects of the coming battles that was unknown, was the exact size of the enemy armies. By way of people groups, the Sylvai should have the advantage, because amongst them were the Noranites, Adaasharians, Haldusians and the Darians, whereas the enemy was made up only of the Garonites and the Norgrasharians. To Alim'dar, the problem was that everyone was scattered about the world, and it was well known that the children of Norgrash'nar and Garonar had multiplied rapidly. Additionally, they had been training under the guidance of the dark

Nefarians for far longer than had his own people or the Haldusians.

Nevertheless, there in his war room, now alone, Alim'dar still considered all the possibilities and outcomes of the war, and he could not see any way, despite the numbers, that his people could lose this war. This was irrespective of superior numbers on the part of the enemy, the influence of the Sky Cities of Kor'Magailin, or the fact that the Nescrai had three Dragons willing to fight with them, whereas they only had one; for in this season, he did not yet know that Ashysin, Merilinder and Sharuseth would soon join the war.

Alim'dar, though, considered all things. In most likely instances, the enemy would be fighting on foreign ground, in the realms of the Sylvai, and in Aranthia. Even if they were stronger forces, this should be outweighed by the fact that his people were fighting for their own survival, and in Alim'dar's mind, that was a more powerful motivator than the Nescrai could possibly possess. So too did he have faith in the training of his people and the Haldusians, who had supplied the Noranites and the Adaasharians with great quantities of weapons that had been sent out. Even if the enemy was better trained they would surely not outmatch in the number of armed soldiers. Most of all though, Alim'dar regarded the Light as a stronger force than the Dark; they had rightness on their side. All of these things he was sure would be enough, regardless of whatever unknowns might arise.

Now, as Alim'dar studied his war table for perhaps the thousandth time, an intruder materialized within his chamber, in a dark corner. But Alim'dar was not oblivious, and he immediately recognized the presence of the enemy.

"Come out of the Shadows, Norgrash'nar," he said. He would have immediately called for his own guard, but he was certain that the enemy would simply dematerialize again, as he had done in the garden. Alim'dar did not fear a confrontation with his cousin; he did in fact welcome it.

The Nescraian Lord stepped forth. Alim'dar turned to face him, his hand on his sword. "You will not need that, Alim'dar," Norgrash'nar said. "I am here to offer you peace."

"The instigator of all atrocities would offer me peace?"

"I would. I do not want this war. I do not want to see my people die."

"Then you should not have started it."

"I have made mistakes," Norgrash'nar said without a hint of regret in his tone. "I have come to offer you a choice, so that you might save your people."

"And what would you have me do for peace? Help you eliminate the Sylvai, or the Haldusians? Do you really think me foolish enough to align with you?"

"It is not a matter of foolishness. It is a matter of trying to save your own people. I ask you to do nothing. Keep your people here, and we will not cross over into Whitestone when we come. You will survive, as will your children and all of their descendants. Just stay out of the war."

"This is not going to happen," Alim'dar said firmly. "But now I have an offer for you... Face me now, without your steel and magic, and let the war be decided by the victor."

"Do not think that I have come to fight you, Alim'dar. My magic is greater than yours, but your sword is mightier. I have come to offer peace. The cost of this is small... If you will not stay out of the war, then let us avoid it altogether. I make a second offer to you: give me Nirvisa'nen, realize that she belongs to me and always has, and forget about her."

"Do you think me so foolish?"

"I will leave Whitestone with her and never return. I will call off the cities of Kor'Magailin and put my people to contentment in their own lands, and I will repress the anger of the Garonites. Even Drovanius will bow down and cease in his lust for war."

"Do not think, Norgrash'nar, that there is the slightest temptation, even if I believed you. For to remain true to the Light—as I will—there is no compromising rightness. Would I hand over my beloved wife to torment? Would my people be content with this, to sacrifice their mother to save their own lives? I will fall upon my own sword before I hand her over to you."

"I knew you would resist," Norgrash'nar said. "I considered it only a matter of honor to give you the option. And I tell you this... Nirvisa'nen has always belonged to me. If I cannot have her, then neither will you. I will have my war, and she will be taken from you."

"Enough!" Alim'dar lashed out, slamming his fist down upon his war table and scattering the pieces. "You will *not* take her. You will not keep the Darians out of this war. And you will not win, Norgrash'nar. Be gone from my city. If you remain, my men will find you, and they have already been ordered to finish you. Then, if you can survive so long, we will settle this upon the battlefield."

"I will. I will leave your city now, but keep a close watch upon your wife, Alim'dar, during the war. For she is vulnerable. This is my advice to you."

And then, in an instant, Norgrash'nar was gone again. That night, Alim'dar doubled the number of his children searching the city for Norgrash'nar, yet still he was not found, and they hoped that he was gone for good.

Discord in Nirvisa'Iinid

The search for Norgrash'nar continued all throughout the next day, which was the fourth day of Wintertide. Still nothing; the enemy was seemingly gone.

Now, this was the day of tragedy, for it was at the Hour of Elation when Norandar shattered the Tablet of Kronaggas, and the great White Dragon met his end. Though Alim'dar was not present for either of these events, he knew well what had happened. All of the Darians, and all of the Sylvai, began their mourning, for now death had truly entered the world.

As the days continued on, the preparations continued. Even more weapons were forged, more arrows fletched, more people armed for combat as the day of war drew nearer. The plan was to march into Mara at the first sign of the commencement of the war. They would aid their brothers and sisters, the Noranites, and pray for the Adaasharians as they marched through the Mountains of Ashysin; with any amount of luck, their southern allies would overwhelm the Garonites and eliminate them from the battle that was surely to come upon Mara. Haldus'nar had assured him that his people could handle whatever threat came upon Aranthia, for they had the help of the Dragon. After that, the Haldusians planned to march across Verasian's domain and to trap the Norgrasharians between themselves and the Noranites and Darians. It was a sound plan, so far as Alim'dar was concerned. But he had not accounted for the discord that came upon his own nation during those days...

For Norgrash'nar had not in fact left the city. He had remained in hiding, though not as one might think. Instead, he had used a magic of his own design to deceive the Darians. In this he had only to lay a hand upon one of the brown-skinned men, and his own face was transmuted into the appearance of the other. He could change his own appearance at any time, and this was a magic that the Darians could never have prepared for. And so he moved freely amongst the people of Nirvisa'Iinid with a face not his own.

Being the deceiver that he was, he found it not difficult to blend in, to act as though he were the man whom he impersonated, and to interact amongst that man's friends and family. And he began the rumor amongst them, that the dark lord of the Nescrai had been seen entering into Alim'dar's castle one night. When Alim'dar was asked about this, he did not deny it. But this was enough to give the slightest credence to the discord that was beginning, for so too did Norgrash'nar implant the idea amongst the people that Alim'dar was going to betray the Noranites, and betray Nirvisa'nen, their beloved mother.

These rumors passed through the city quickly, and though few believed, it was enough to plant seeds of dissent amongst them. And as the days of mourning passed, so too did the discord heighten, and the effectiveness of the Darians' preparation was diminished. Once that had begun there was little reason for Norgrash'nar to remain and he left Nirvisa'Iinid to return to Mar'Narush for his own preparations.

By the first day of Wintermelt, when the war began in the south, and when Alim'dar had planned on marching his army into Mara, the contention had grown so great within Nirvisa'Iinid that the army could not be effectively mustered. Half of the Darians now seemed to believe, or at least consider, that Alim'dar was no longer to be trusted, that he was working in alignment with Norgrash'nar. This stemmed from the love that the people had for their mother, Nirvisa'nen, for it was well known amongst all Darians that she had always been the one of their parents who had truly made the decisions for the people, who had led them to Whitestone—which they regarded as paradise—and who had tamed the eccentric passions of Alim'dar.

All of these things were true, at least to some measure, though both Nirvisa'nen and her husband considered them to be the attributes that made their people strong. Alim'dar had no issue with the people knowing the strength of their mother. But it was this intemperate love for her that had allowed for such discord to now arise in the city. Norgrash'nar had known exactly what he was doing.

Not all of the Darians subscribed to the rumors, and there was much verbal infighting during those days: it was this that was making the people ineffectual and not at all ready to march while their brothers in the south were being killed.

At last, Alim'dar, on the first day of Wintermelt—when word reached them that the war had officially begun—called together all of his people to address them in hopes of uniting them once again into an efficacious force that could achieve the much needed end of destroying the Nescrai.

His words inspired, once again, the determination of the Darians to rid the world of the enemy. But still, the seeds of discord had been sown.

At last the Darians were rallied, and at the Hour of Concession on the third day of Wintermelt, the Darians began their march from Nirvisa'Iinid toward Mara. They were a slow-moving army, for all of their men and women were clad in heavy armor, and the horse-drawn wagons and ballistas were slow to progress. But these were necessities for the strategies of Alim'dar to be employed.

On the fourth day of Wintermelt, the Darian army—twenty thousand strong—crossed into the far western region of Mara, near the Valley of Sloths, for there was the Sky City of Naivar, which they fully expected to displace.

THE TAKING OF NAIVAR

If the Darian infantry was considered effective in physical combat, so too were their archers masters of projectiles. The Toxophilites were the name given to both the archers and the operators of the ballistas of Whitestone. The wielders of sword and axe and spear and mace were well trained, but this training had only begun when Aranthia had brought to them the knowledge of warfare. But the Toxophilites had been training for hundreds of years—not for the sake of combat or war, but for shows of skill amongst the archers and for the moving of great stones in the construction of Nirvisa'Iinid. For the method employed by the Darians of the moving of the monolithic stones was to cut from the mountains the shape of the stones needed, and then to launch into them the great barbed projectiles that would then be affixed to great chains and ropes. Then upon logs the stones could be rolled into place further to the south.

But these ballistas had been adapted now for the sake of warfare, and with them the Darians planned to take down the Sky City.

There, upon the Western Plains, east of the Valley of Sloths, the army of Alim'dar moved, and as it did, so too did Naivar attempt to follow along. As instructed beforehand, the entire army continually positioned itself beneath the city, so that whatever weaponry it might unleash upon them would be obscured by its own bottom.

And when the Sailplanes were guided upon the backs of the Nescrai to come down upon the Darians, the archers easily took them to their deaths. Not one Nescrai landed upon the field alive or uninjured.

The Nescrai of Naivar then made the attempt of dropping great stones and burning oil down upon the Darians, all with only moderate effect. But all the while they only were revealing their tactics, and Alim'dar was positioning the ballistas. When the time was right, a hundred of the massive arrows were launched in unison, striking the lower stone levels of Naivar and embedding them in the rock. And attached to these bolts were long ladders of ropes that spanned the distance from ground to city, and the soldiers of Alim'dar mounted the lower levels.

When the Nescrai realized what was happening, they began raising the city higher into the air, so that fewer of the Darians might storm the city; once the ladders were raised from the ground, no more could ascend. Then, they released their arrows from above. But not many found their marks, as the ladders swayed in winds caused by the turbine engines of the city, and they were made into difficult moving targets.

When the Darians scaled the ladders and came unto Naivar, a battle there arose. Not nearly as many of his men and women made it into the city as Alim'dar would have liked, but to their benefit, it so happened that at the same time, a revolt was taking place there inside of the city, amongst the Sylvai who had been imprisoned.

Naivar was taken that day and the Sylvai and the Darians held control over it. They thought to keep it, to try to use it to their advantage to lord over the enemy, but Alim'dar rejected this idea, as he said, "If we keep it, the Nescrai might take it back, then use it further against us. But if we bring it down, we show all of the Naiad that these cities are not invulnerable. It will be a blow to the morale of the Nescrai, and will embolden our allies. No, today we take down Naivar."

And so the city was set upon a course to come closer again to the ground, and then was evacuated entirely. Once this was done, the Darians launched their ballista bolts into the spinning blades of the turbines, entangling them in rope and chain, and each of the engines failed. Soon, Naivar drifted over the Etakos Mountains, where it fell into the sea, in the bay of Iilan, never to rise again.

And the Darians, now reinforced with several thousand Sylvai who had come from Naivar, marched eastward, where they would join with the Noranites.

It was a slow march for the Darians across northern Mara as the melting snows of the season made the ground soft and muddy, and dragging their ballistas along with them was a challenging task.

They came at last unto the region of Central Mara late in the day on the tenth day of Wintermelt. Scouts reported that the Noranites and the Adaasharians were encamped at the Cusp of Ayron, and that the entirety of the Nescrai armies had come onto the western edge of the Plains of Kronaggas. So Alim'dar moved his men and women and instruments of war further east, to come to the border of the Plains, along the Eastward River. And at the Hour of Mourning, he sounded his horn of war, so that their allies would know that at last they had arrived and were in position, and so that their enemies would be discouraged, for reinforcements had arrived.

Battle for Felheim

In the east we went along the western shore of the Felheim Sea on the ninth day of Wintermelt, leading the Haldusians in an attempt to get ahead of the Nefarians, so that their way to Naiad would be blocked. Trepidation was with us, for the task ahead seemed insurmountable; even with our small army of ten thousand I wondered if we could win.

We came to the city of Torance, at the westernmost point of the Sea; we entered cautiously, for this was a Nescraian town and we knew not how we would be received. But the city was nearly abandoned and those who remained were common citizens and they seemed to hold no ill will toward us. I engaged one of the women whom I saw on the streets...

"Where is everyone?"

"They have gone to Shilton, to make a stand. There is a terrible enemy unleashed there."

"What are you talking about? The Giants?"

"Yes! Men—or monsters—bigger than any I have ever seen!"

"You were there?"

"Yes. I brought my children here this morning. They are killing everyone!"

Suspecting what was now happening, we moved onward to the east, toward the town of Shilton, which also was upon the shores of the Felheim Sea. At the Hour of Devotion we arrived, and had our presentiments confirmed.

For there in Shilton two dozen Ogres were killing everything in sight, distinguishing naught between the Nescrai who lived there and the Sylvai whom they had been brought here to kill, crushing the people with their clubs, demolishing the stone and thatch homes and structures of the city. These vicious creatures cared not for anything but destruction and I wondered if this was even what Drovanius had intended—for it was thought beforehand that the Nescrai of this northern realm were inclined toward less hatred of the Sylvai.

Haldus'nar led the charge into the city to come against the Ogres. Aranthia and Ashysin flew into the fray, the Crimson Dragon grabbing one of the Ogres by its shoulders and lifting it high into the air even as he pierced its flesh with his claws. But the Ogre was undeterred, and still grasping the tree that was his weapon, he swung it upward, striking the Dragon upon his head. Aranthia shrieked and lost his grip on the monster, and it fell back to the ground, crushing a troop of city soldiers who were fighting another of the terrible Giants.

Another Ogre made wide sweeps with its club and all of those who stood against it were struck down in a single blow. Another still was stuck by a hundred arrows from the archers of Shilton, and not one of them phased it, so thick was their skin with filth.

"How can we defeat them!" Sarak'den cried out. "They cannot be faced directly!"

"We have no instruments of war," Haldus'nar said anxiously. "No ballistas, no heavy weaponry. Only sword and spear. We will be crushed!"

"We have to retreat!" Aivus'nar yelled out over the cries of the citizens of Shilton and the fuming roars of the Ogres.

"We can't just leave the people to die!" I retorted. "There must be a way."

"*You* won't even fight, Alak'kiin," he said. He was right... I was dictating what the others should do yet not raising a hand against the enemy.

"Surround them, surround the city!" Haldus'nar cried out to his soldiers. "Form a circle!" The Haldusians began to move.

Ashysin, joining the battle, poured fire down upon one of the Ogres, charring the Giant, but accomplishing little other than to enrage it, for the burns and boils would not stop it. Yet the Dragon's claws that soon followed tore at it viciously, rending flesh from bone and bringing the monster to its knees, where it was dispatched by the soldiers that came for it. But another of the Ogres, seeing its comrade killed, struck the Dragon a mighty blow when it threw its steel spiked club through the air which shattered a scale of Ashysin and penetrated deep into tissue. The Gold Dragon wailed, and filled with his fiery rage, poured fire once more upon this enemy.

Aranthia, now injured, but not out of the contest, summoned his magic and a bolt of lightning cut the sky and struck the club of one of the Ogres. It split in its hand and burned the foul flesh of the Giant. Aranthia followed this with another spell, this one a burst of energy that knocked the Ogre to the ground, stunned. City soldiers took this opportunity to plunge their blades into the monstrous flesh, but few found their places deep enough to do real harm. Arriving soon thereafter, several of the Haldusians drove their spears into the eyes of the disabled Giant, so that at least it would be hindered.

On the adjacent side of the town square, a hundred of the Haldusians came against an Ogre, breaking from the circle that they had been directed to form. Fifteen of them fell to a single swipe of the giant club, but the others swarmed the legs of the Giant and cut a hundred gashes into its legs, cutting through muscle and tendon to the bone. The monster fell, crushing several of the soldiers who had not moved out of the way swiftly enough. Then, the remainder of the soldiers mounted its back, driving their blades into flesh. Still the Ogre was not killed, and though it could not walk, it still could fight, grabbing the men and women off of it and crushing their bodies in its mighty fists. Before it finally died of blood loss, it had taken nearly all of the one hundred Haldusians to their deaths.

Aranthia engaged another, this time coming from behind and taking the entirety of the Giant's head in his great jaws and tearing it from its shoulders with his mighty teeth. So foul was the taste of the Giant that the Dragon then vomited out the remains of his previous meal along with the remnants of the Ogre's brain.

Ashysin's fire was expelled again and he was weakened. Still, too many of the Nefarians remained...

Two more Ogres were felled by the Haldusians, but at the cost of the lives of hundreds. Still, nearly twenty of the Giants remained, and to kill them all would cost too many lives, for behind these monsters, to the east, were still the majority of the Nefarians. There was little hope of defeating them, and Haldus'nar signaled a retreat, back to the west. The city of Shilton was decimated, the battle lost, and we knew that we must find another way.

But showing no sign of tiring, the Ogres pursued us as we fled, and their great legs carried them farther, faster than we could move the army. This was a battle that was going to cost us incredibly, one we could not escape...

Just to the west of Shilton, we were forced to stop, to fight for our lives. I prayed to the Numen that something would break in our favor, for the odds were greatly against us. But no help came that day. Although between the brutal method of killing the Ogres that Aranthia had devised, and the desperate fighting of the Haldusians, we did fell all of the Giants that pursued us. But it was not without great cost, for half of the Haldusians and those who fought with them were killed, and the rest were exhausted or severely injured. We could not engage another troop of this enemy, or we would all be destroyed and the remaining Nefarians would continue their rampage across the land.

After the battle, as we recovered and as wounds were tended, I sat down to catch my breath along with Aivus'nar, Haldus'nar and Sarak'den.

"Sellos lies to the west," Aivus'nar said. "Beyond that, there are just small villages, farms and homesteads. They're scattered. But the Ogres will destroy them all."

"We have to find a way to stop those who remain," Sarak'den said.

"We took out only an eighth of their forces at best," Aivus'nar argued. "And we've lost over half of our own. There is no way to stop them!"

"There must be...."

"He's right. We can do nothing," Haldus'nar said dejectedly. "We cannot sacrifice any more lives for this."

"How many more will die in the west if we do nothing?" I asked.

"At least there will be greater numbers there, amongst the Sylvai. Maybe they can do more to stop them. Perhaps our allies there are faring better than we."

"They cannot be," Ashysin said, having listened to us from a distance, where he and Aranthia rested. "There were so many of the Norgrasharians going out of Naiad. I could not destroy them all. And we know not if the Garonites have joined them."

"Yet I agree with Haldus'nar," Aranthia said. "It grieves me to say it, but there is nothing we can do when more of these monsters come through here. We cannot stop them. Not all of them."

"So what do we do?" Sarak'den asked.

"We hide in the hills," I said, conceding that they were right. "Out of their path, and we wait for them to pass. Then, maybe, we can live to fight again."

And so we moved the wounded and the healthy to the north by a distance of a quarter March, and we waited.

It wasn't until Midnight on the tenth day of Wintermelt when more of the Ogres came. From the east they tirelessly charged, having likely destroyed everything across northern Felheim. I counted perhaps fifty of them as their dark shadows surged past our encampment. Twenty-five had fallen in our first battle, and here twice that had passed. So far we had not seen the Trolls... And so a hundred and seventy five of these horrors still remained, and I had no idea how we would defeat them.

Then, at Firstlight, we were greeted by an unexpected but welcomed visitor, for Verasian the Green soared into our camp from the south, from over the Felheim Sea, and he cried out to us, "These monsters are killing my children!"

"They have killed our people as well, Verasian," Haldus'nar said fiercely.

"Yes... I have seen the wasted city of Shilton... where did these things come from?"

"Drovanius brought them here," I said. "Your brother, your compatriot in this sickening war has brought this upon your children, and our peoples."

"I will not endure the sacrifice of my people so that he may win his war, and he will answer for this." Verasian was scorned by what he perceived to be a betrayal, for even the reverence he held for the Black Dragon was not enough to compensate for the destruction of his children. "These people were not even a part of the war," he hissed. "They refused to arm themselves, to participate, even against my urging. They did not deserve this."

"No one deserved this war, Verasian," I said fiercely now.

Seeming dejected, the Dragon said, "I will help you. I will help you fight these savages, these brutes."

"Even still, though we welcome your help in this, you have crimes to atone for, Verasian."

"We will worry about that later," the Dragon said. "For now, we must fight."

"It still will not be enough," Aranthia said. "It took the deaths of five thousand of my people and we destroyed only a fraction of these invaders.

What would you have us do?"

"The beasts of the earth are coming," Verasian said. "They attacked the monstrosities—the ones with nappy hair—in the east. Some were killed. Those animals that survived have been routed westward. They come within the hour."

I stood up, looking eastward, though not expecting to see the legion. "How many of them remain?"

"Thousands, Alak'kiin. The smaller beasts have now fled, but the Cats and the Apes and Bears and Boars are coming, and many others."

These were amongst the largest of the creatures who had followed me across the grasslands, but still I doubted that they could finish off the monsters. But then I had an idea... "Verasian, they are coming here... ahead of the enemy?"

"Yes, but not by far."

"Why?" Ashysin asked.

"I would break my vow this day if it would serve the greater good," I said. "And perhaps I can fight alongside you and slay these monsters without penalty for these are not creatures of our world. But I think I can do a greater service. Verasian, go to them, guide them here to us, to me."

The Green Dragon snarled and glared at me, for having grown in his pride over the many years, he thought little of taking orders from one of my kind, even though we had once regarded one another with the utmost rapport. Nevertheless, he took flight, back to the east.

When he returned, there was remaining a fair assembly of the beasts of Sylveria who had followed me. But as he came, Verasian screeched, "Alak'kiin! The Trolls come close behind!"

I stood on the fields and waited, and as I expected the beasts came to me, surrounding me, seeming even to look to me for guidance. I gave them much more.

As I moved swiftly amongst them, they bowed their great heads down before me, and I placed my hands upon each of them, two by two. But this was not just a touch of comfort and encouragement, for with each laying on of hands, I willed my magic upon them. These were spells of quickening, strength, and agility... everything that would empower them to fight at their best. And now I believed that we might stand a chance, for the number of these beasts far exceeded the remaining Nefarians.

The Trolls came into view soon thereafter, thirty of them, moving not so fast as the Ogres. They trudged across the landscape, dragging their weapons, which were alike to the clubs of the Ogres, but covered in moss and hair and the blood of their enemies who had fallen before them. They saw the legion of beasts, and the Haldusians before them, and they quickened their pace. Lustful for destruction, they saw another mass of victims, and they considered not any strategy, for they were beings bent only on ruination.

"Wait," I said to the beasts, who snarled and snorted, growled and grumbled at the sight of the abominations. Now empowered, they were ready for the fight.

Those Haldusians who were capable of fighting lined up nervously behind the animals; they were not ready to see another slaughter. Aranthia and Ashysin were as prepared as they could be, flanking the two sides of our forces, while Verasian—probably the most recovered of his injuries, rose into the air.

When the Trolls drew closer, the beasts stirred; when they came within three spans, they would be held back no longer and they charged the massive Nefarians. But Verasian was just ahead of them, and he poured out his indignation over the slaughter of so many of his children onto the Trolls in the form of spell after spell of conjurations, just as he had against Ashysin. Massive objects appeared out of nowhere—blades and stone and spear—to pierce and crush the flesh of the soulless monstrosities. Several fell immediately, and the beasts charged those that remained.

The great Black Bears tore at the legs of the Trolls, ripping flesh and tendon, bringing them to the ground. The boars pierced them with their mighty tusks when they were fallen. The cats climbed the matted hair of the malicious monstrosities, tearing into the torsos, arms, legs, heads and faces of them, tearing flesh and hair from the bone, bringing even more of them to the ground. And the great Apes crushed their skulls with huge boulders that their enhanced strength allowed them to wield.

Aranthia and Ashysin joined in, unleashing the last little bit of their magic of flame upon the trolls, and the Haldusians, seeing that the monsters were not faring well, charged in to make what impact they could.

In an Hour's time, the Trolls had fallen. The animals regrouped—what was left of them, for they had suffered great losses amongst themselves. Everyone—man, woman, creature and Dragon, was covered in the filth of the battle. Most of the Haldusians remained and had not been slain. Though it was a victory, it had exhausted the whole of them, and they were certain they could not, even with the Dragons and animals, win another.

"There were two hundred of them," I said to Haldus'nar and the others. "We have defeated but maybe fifty. Fifty others have gone to the west. There must remain another hundred. We cannot defeat them."

"We won't have to, alone," Verasian said. "I will go to the west, and I will find Drovanius and hold him accountable. And I will find Merobassi and bring them here, to finish off these terrible things. Do what you will now...." And he said nothing more, but took flight to the west.

"Let us go with him," Ashysin said to Aranthia. "We can do no more here. I can only fly... I am depleted."

"As am I," the Crimson Dragon agreed. To Haldus'nar and Sarak'den he said, "If they come, the remnants of the Ogres and Trolls, take cover. Hide in the hills and the mountains. Everyone is too weak to engage them again."

Then, the two diminished Dragons took their leave of us, and went off to the west after Verasian, to see if they could unite the other Dragons to destroy this terrible enemy that was killing all of the Naiad in the east.

"Let us hope they are successful," Sarak'den said. "If he brings Drovanius and Merobassi, they will not be there in the west to fight our brothers and sisters."

"Then let them worry about the remnants of the Nefarians," I said, fatigued. Though I had not wielded a sword or any other weapon, inspiring the beasts of Sylveria had taken its toll. "We should rest, then move westward, through Naiad. We will only be slaughtered here. Gather with us all of the civilians we can find along the way, to clear a path, for their own safety."

And so when we had rested we moved across the Felheim Fields, through Forthran, and climbed to the top of Yor'Kavon; we arrived there at the end of the tenth day of Wintermelt. But all of the animals had remained behind, still ready to fight the invaders, and there was nothing we could do to save their lives.

We had slain only a quarter of the Nefarian forces at great cost to our own numbers, and we felt not even the slightest bit victorious.

ALLIANCE OF DRAGONS

When Verasian found Drovanius on the western edge of the Plains of Kronaggas, Merobassi had already joined with him, and with the Nescrai. Having at last recovered from his wounds in Vindras Vale, he had flown northward to find the Garonites, who had now joined with the Norgrasharians, there on the plains.

Now, this reunion was not long after Norgrash'nar and his elite, Moonstone Armor-clad soldiers had made their first pass over their bridge into Mara, causing the others to flee. This was naught but an endeavor to determine the effectiveness, and to strike fear in the enemy. Once Sharuseth and those with him had retreated westward, so too did Norgrash'nar withdraw, for they had final preparations to make for the battle, and they were pleased that they had held off...

For at the Hour of Mourning on that day, which was the tenth of Wintermelt, 552, they heard the sounding of a horn of war that was not their own, but rather of the Darians, who had arrived to the northwest.

Scouts were sent out and by Lastlight they reported that there were twenty thousand of the northerners there, waiting to join the battle.

At that Hour, Verasian joined with them, and he spoke harshly to Drovanius and Merobassi, saying, "What are these murderous things you have brought into my lands, Drovanius?"

"What are you speaking of, *wurm?* For your tongue is bitter and your tone offensive."

"These Giants—Ogres and Trolls—they come...."

"Yes, that is the intention. They will weaken our enemy so that we may finish them."

"They will finish us all, clodpate! They have ravaged my lands in Felheim! They have killed our own!"

"The traitors who would not rally to our cause?"

"The Nescrai, our children, whom we swore to protect!"

"It cannot be undone, now, Verasian," Drovanius said. "Let them come, and we will open a way for them to cross into the west."

"Behold! Fifty Ogres come this way and will arrive by morning! Do you not see that our armies stand between them and the enemy?"

The Black Dragon considered this, then said to Norgrash'nar, who was present, "Divide your forces. Send half to the north to stand against the Darians if they come. Send the others to the south. Make way for the Ogres."

"If we divide our forces, we will show weakness to the Sylvai," Norgrash'nar said.

"It will only be perceived as weakness. When they see the Ogres, they will scatter. Send six of your Elite with the southern division, and keep the others with you, in the north. Spread them out amongst the Garonites and your people. None will stand against them and if they come, they will be driven back. Their forces will divide and the Ogres will reign over them."

Reluctantly Norgrash'nar agreed. "When we see the Ogres coming, then we will divide. Not before."

Then there was a ruckus coming from amongst the Nescraian soldiers to the east and word quickly reached their ears that there were other Dragons approaching. And when they looked they saw that Aranthia and Ashysin faltered through the air on a path low over the plains, coming from the east."

"They are not our enemy in this battle against the Ogres, Drovanius," Verasian said. "They helped to save our children in Felheim. Let them speak."

And indeed, when the two wounded Dragons came closer, they landed upon the plains and bowed their heads weakly, in a sign of truce. Drovanius, Merobassi and Verasian, along with Norgrash'nar, went to them.

"The enemy is not far behind," Aranthia said. "You must help us stop them."

"We will do no such thing," Drovanius said slyly.

"Drovanius, this plan will not work," Verasian said. "You have not seen these brutes upon the battlefields. They rampage across the land. They do not care who they kill."

"That is why we will get out of their way."

"Drovanius," Norgrash'nar said. "I think we ought to trust Verasian. How many of these Ogres are there?"

"Fifty come upon us now," Ashysin said. "And there are many more in the east, Trolls amongst them. They tear through your people and leave none alive. We must finish these who arrive now, and go to Felheim, or they will destroy everything."

"We must finish this war," Drovanius said.

"You desire war, Dragon, as do I," Norgrash'nar said. "But my people die far away and you would just abandon them?"

Drovanius, always prone to the admonishment of Norgrash'nar, said nothing, only considered all that he was hearing.

"We can only defeat them if we are together," Aranthia said. "Fire and magic... all of us must fight. Where are the others, Merilinder and Sharuseth?"

"To the west, I would assume," Merobassi said. "Merilinder left Vindras Vale before I. He would seek out his people, and they are there with the Noranites."

"I will not leave this war," Drovanius then said. "I will not fly with those who have betrayed us all."

"Your pride is your undoing!" Aranthia growled. "You would let the innocent of your own perish for your vainglory?"

He was silent again. Norgrash'nar said. "Drovanius, you know we are unstoppable, for the gift of Nefaria you have given us. Destroy this enemy in Felheim. We will follow your plans here. We will handle these Ogres that come."

The Black Dragon seemed unconvinced, but for the deference he held for his son, Norgrash'nar, he consented to follow. He nodded then, still reluctant. "Gather the others, if you must—Sharuseth and Merilinder—and we will fly as one to Felheim."

Aranthia flew to the west, into Mara and told Sharuseth and Merilinder of all that was happening. They were, like Drovanius, reluctant to leave the battle. But the Adaasharians and Noranites had heard the horns of Alim'dar, and knew that they now had the needed reinforcements. So upon the acquiescence of Adaashar, Sveraden, Norandar and Alunen, the two Dragons agreed to fly with the others, for Aranthia had explained that it was the innocent of Felheim who had not joined the war against them who were being obliterated.

And so the seven Dragons flew eastward, over the Plains of Kronaggas, toward Felheim, and as they approached the mountain of their father Kronaggas, they left the Ogres that were charging westward to their own intentions; for the Chromatic Dragons were convinced that they would be used against the Sylvai, and the Metallic Dragons and Aranthia believed they would first encounter the Nescrai, distinguishing not one from the other.

So too did they soar past the remnants of the Haldusians who were at that time resting upon the top of Yor'Kavon.

Thus, when the true battle for Sylveria began in the west on the eleventh day of Wintermelt, the Dragons were occupied far to the east.

WARCRAFT

ENUMERATIONS OF WAR

All matters of the war thus far were soon to culminate along the South Umonar River, which divided the Plains of Kronaggas from Mara. For this it was later called the Battle of Umonar. When the Dragons, both Metallic and Chromatic had left for the east to fight the Nefarians, the people were left upon the fields of war to devise their own strategies. The following are the numbers of the soldiers and instruments of war that comprised each division.

Of the Darians who had come out of Whitestone and camped along the northern line of the Falcalor River, which ran from the Umonar River into the Darian Sea, there were a total of twenty thousand. Sixteen thousand of these were infantrymen, nearly four thousand were mounted cavalry, and the remainder were the Toxophilites, who were the operators of the one hundred ballistas that the Darians counted as assets. All of them were armored in chain and plate armor, and wielded steel weapons. Alim'dar, Nirvisa'nen and all of their children were amongst them. So too were there amongst them those Sylvai who had come out of the Sky City of Naivar and who were ready to fight alongside their liberators. They numbered around two thousand.

Of the Noranites who soon came to camp west of the Umonar River, a range away from the riverbank, there were a total of ten thousand. Eight thousand of these were moderately skilled fighters, while the remaining two thousand were archers. They were armored in thick cloth and bark armor that had been woven and affixed with thick pieces of tree bark that could absorb blows. Their weapons were mixed of steel and wood. They were split equally in half and spread along the forest edge to the north and south. Norandar and Alunen were amongst them.

Of the Adaasharians, who had come from the Southern Reaches, through the mountains and Hest'Vortal, there were twenty-five thousand infantrymen remaining. All of their mounts, which had been the Druugal, had been slain in the collapse of the mountains of the Tybor River Valley, and so those who remained would have to fight on foot. Many of them were armored in chain, while others wore a thick hide armor derived from the thick shed skins of the Plains Serpents. They wielded staves and clubs, as well as steel blades that they had received from Alim'dar. They were spread across the north to south length of the Umonar River, ready to engage the enemy. Adaashar and Sveraden were amongst them.

The remnants of the Haldusians numbered only four thousand and they were footmen who were still far to the east of the battle, at Yor'Kavon. I, Alak'kiin, was amongst them.

Thus, the total number of men and women who would fight in this battle on the side of the Sylvai was sixty-one thousand.

Of the Garonites, who had been the first of their people coming out of the mountains to start the war in Mara, there were fifteen thousand foot soldiers, armed with spear and sword, mace and chain, and armored in steel and laced iron plate which had been given to them from the half of the Norgrasharians who had fallen to Ashysin the Gold's fire, when they came out of Naiad. Their forces were spread across the eastern bank of the Umonar River, amongst their brothers, the Norgrasharians. Garonar and Kuranen were not amongst them, for they had been killed by Adaashar and Sveraden in Hest'Vortal.

Of the Norgrasharians who had yet to engage any of their enemies in battle since they had marched through the Valley of Naiad, there remained twenty-five thousand. They were armored in steel plate and wielded steel weapons and great iron bows with arrows designed to carry great distances; and were also spread across the eastern side of the Umonar River, waiting for their leader to command them. Amongst them were twelve men and women, including Norgrash'nar, who were clad in Moonstone Armor, which was derived from the evil of Nefaria and which caused all of those who were near it to flee, if they were of good and noble heart. These were the generals of this army. Kalenen had not come to this battle and was safe in Mar'Narush.

So, of the Nescrai who were here to fight there was a total number of forty thousand, which was considerably less than the Sylvai possessed. But the Nescrai were better trained in combat, for they had many years to prepare themselves for this day. To no one throughout the armies was it certain who would win this battle.

There also remained the undetermined effect that the fifty Ogres of

Nefaria, who were charging westward across the Plains of Kronaggas, would have upon the battle.

The Dragons numbered seven still, and they were on their way to Felheim when the battle in the west began.

Here it should be noted that these enumerations are not to be understood as the entirety of any of the people groups who existed in those days. For in all instances, the youth of the cultures had not been allowed to fight. So too were there many adults who had remained behind in their own cities, towns and villages who were armed or ready to stand as a last defense should their own armies be defeated and the enemy come to their regions. The numbers of people not engaged directly in the war was great, for there had been over five hundred years of procreation beforehand; the total populations were unknowable, for the lands of Sylveria were full in the days before the war.

Likewise, it should be understood that in the days and seasons following the consummation of the war, there were uncountable small battles fought between the Sylvai (who were aligned with the Darians and Haldusians) and the Nescrai. But these were not the struggles that determined the conclusive outcome of the war.

THE OGRES COME

Now, Norgrash'nar had agreed to the plan of Drovanius, and at the Hour of Firstlight, when the Nescrai saw the Ogres coming, he ordered that their forces split; half moved northward, and half moved southward, so that the Nefarians would have a way through to the west, across the stone bridge they had constructed.

The monsters thundered across the Western Plains; the terrain was sundered by their passing. The tireless Giants held tight to their clubs and their ferocity as they prepared themselves, for when the Nescraian army came into their sight, their lust for blood was ignited once again. And as in Felheim, these brutes cared not for who or what they killed, and though they had been commanded to go west by Drovanius, they nevertheless deviated.

Rather, they were drawn to the Nescrai, who to them were fleeing in the movement of their armies, and they were like predators drawn to their prey. So too were they drawn by what they must have perceived was a fragment of their homeland, and the Moonstone Armor, derived from

Nefaria's moon, was as a beacon to the brutes, and they split off in two directions, each of them heading for one of the Nescraian armies.

Norgrash'nar had half expected this, and when he saw that twenty-five Ogres charged for his northern line of troops, he commanded that they scatter. Those who were his generals, clad in Moonstone Armor, spread out as well, so that not too many of the brutes would come upon any one. This served an effective purpose, for the archers of the Norgrasharians were able to equally apply their shots across the whole of the advancing Ogres.

When they came within range, Norgrash'nar and each of his generals gave the command to unleash a stream of their great arrows to the southeast, into the approaching horde of Giants. The arrows found their marks, many more struck than missed, but none of the Ogres were felled with ease or by anything short of a hundred of the oversized arrows, nor did they come to their end without taking many of the enemy with them, for as soon as the first round of arrows pierced the monsters' thick flesh they tore into the ranks of the Nescrai, their clubs swiping at the soldiers, sending many of them to their immediate deaths.

The Nescrai responded with swiftness, driving their blades into the legs of the Giants until they too met their end. Ogres fell, and swarms of the soldiers came down upon them. They were far from an undefeatable foe, yet not one of them fell without a considerable cost.

Although the brutes were being drawn to the bearers of the Moonstone Armor, five hundred men and women of the Nescrai stood between them and each of the generals; even more surrounded Norgrash'nar. When two of the Giants came for the lord of the Nescrai, Norgrash'nar proudly stood his ground, safely behind a thousand of his loyal followers.

The lord cast his spells to enhance the strength of his soldiers, as many as he could, yet still the Ogres seemed to have their rage heightened the closer they came to their targets, and by the dozens the Nescrai fell with each swat of the Ogres' clubs. Upon a hill beside the Falcalor River did Norgrash'nar wait for his own demise, and he raged inside because if he died here today, his vengeance would never be complete.

But as one of the Ogres finally fell to the swords of the Nescrai, and the other drew ever nearer their lord, there came help from across Falcalor; for there Alim'dar and the Darians had taken their positions, and had now drawn forth their ballistas to the very banks of the river, and seeing an opportunity to strike their enemy down, began launching the massive bolts into the fray.

Their targets were neither the Ogre nor any particular Nescrai, but rather, the Darians considered that any of the enemy there felled would be less that had to be slain later. But to Norgrash'nar's benefit, one of the bolts struck into the heart of the Ogre who was coming upon him, and his life was spared.

When the last of the northern branch of the Ogres died, so too had the number of those who would come against the Sylvai been decreased by three thousand.

As half of the Ogres had turned northward to come against Norgrash'nar and the Garonites, so too had the others gone southward, for amongst them were half of the generals clad in the Moonstone Armor, which was drawing them onward.

Now amongst these generals were Rekasen, Kalniisin and Dugazsin, who were the three daughters of Norgrash'nar. Although they were loyal to their father, the three sisters became fearful of the Ogres when they saw them charging, and not wanting to be the targets of such terrible things coming at them, each of them removed their armor and cast it to the ground, so that they might blend in with the others.

The three other generals who had retained their armor, each became the center of the Ogres' assault when the Nefarians plowed through into the lines of terrified Nescrai, driving forward, seeking first those who held the power of Nefaria—the bearers of the Moonstone Armor. Here too were arrows launched, but without the leadership of their lord, their apprehension was their weakness, and most missed their marks when shot from a distance; when shot at close range, only a few did anything but enrage the Ogres further.

The brutes trampled through the ranks, nearly oblivious to the slashes and jabs made by the Nescrai, heading only toward their targets. And when they reached them, they were of course unaffected by the power of the armor, and they reached out and crushed those few who still held on to the power of the Moonstone Armor. With mighty blows and swipes of their clubs, and trampling over the soldiers, they killed or disabled eight thousand of the Nescrai that day, before they too were finally cut down. The three daughters of Norgrash'nar had survived because of their fear.

So the Nescrai had their numbers reduced that morning by eleven thousand, in the north and the south. And, watching from a distance, the Sylvai gained in their morale, for they had seen darkness fall upon darkness, and the number of their enemy reduced. So too was the morale of the Nescrai diminished, for over a fourth their forces were demolished by a weapon brought to them by Drovanius the Black, their own father.

THE DIVIDED ENEMY

When Alunen and Norandar, who were leading the southern half of the Sylvaian armies, saw that the Nescrai had divided, and that the monstrous Ogres were tearing into the enemy, they determined that this was a time of opportunity, for their enemy would be distracted. So they ordered their units to charge across the stone bridge that Norgrash'nar had built and to attack the southern division of the Nescrai, just as the Ogres were being finished.

It had been decided beforehand, amongst the Sylvai, that Adaashar and Sveraden would remain to the west of the river, so that if the battle were to turn against them, they would have reinforcements still.

And so two battles were to come, one in the north and one in the south, both upon the Plains of Kronaggas.

At the Hour of Elation the Ogres had come upon the Nescrai; now, at the Hour of Midlight, Alunen and Norandar brought seventeen thousand of the Sylvaian soldiers into the southwestern region of the Plains to stand against a lesser number of the Nescrai. The enemy here had not the benefit of the Moonstone Armor, for it had been either cast to the ground by the daughters of Norgrash'nar, or trampled into the soft and thawing soil; all of it was now buried somewhere beneath the battlefield. But although it was not worn upon any of the Nescrai, the Moonstones held their dark influence over the Sylvai, and wherever they were buried, the Sylvai could not come near.

Swords clashed, skulls were crushed, flesh was torn from bodies as the two warring peoples unleashed the rage of the war of the past season. The Nescrai fought with skill, the Sylvai with passion, and neither seemed a superior force. Here in this battle, both Alunen and Norandar drew their first blood of the war, and they were sickened by what had become of their world—what they had become; for in drawing the blood of their enemies, they had lost their innocence. However, though they did not yet realize it, this was to their benefit, for as their inculpability diminished, so too did the power of the Moonstones lessen just a bit, for they had become children of war, and war was not of the pure righteousness that they had beforehand been a part of.

Battleworn and quickly exhausting, the Sylvai fought on, because this was a battle that had to be won. And when it was finished, a full hour had passed. Bodies laid strewn across the region, both Sylvai and Nescrai. The three daughters of Norgrash'nar still survived, but they were severely wounded. Hundreds of other Nescrai survived as well, some with deep lacerations, broken bones, pierced flesh and organs, and others who had surrendered with barely a scratch when they saw the overpowering fierceness of the Sylvai.

Both Norandar and Alunen survived as well, but their people had not fared so well. In all, more than three quarters of both armies had been slain by one another when at last the Nescrai surrendered. An hour of rest followed, until at the Hour of Meeting, Norandar took the majority of the Sylvai who remained and began marching northward now, to aid in whatever was transpiring in the north. Alunen remained behind, for she had sustained a substantial wound to her leg. Those who could not march remained as guards to the surviving prisoners of the Nescrai, who were bound upon the ground amongst the bloody filth of the battle.

As Norandar and his now smaller force went northward, they were then joined by the remains of the Adaasharians and Noranites who had waited, for seeing that the numbers had dwindled, Adaashar and Sveraden had thought it best to strengthen this army and close in on Norgrash'nar in the north, hopefully trapping the Nescrai between themselves and the Darians.

At the same time that Norandar and Alunen had led their army to the south, Alim'dar and Nirvisa'nen saw that the Nescrai just to their south were disorganized by the assault of the Ogres, and seizing upon the occasion, they sent their cavalry across the Falcalor River, to take advantage of the chaos. So distracted was Norgrash'nar and his generals that they failed to consider an attack from the enemy so soon. Regardless of this unexpected assault, the Nescrai recovered quickly once the Ogres were defeated; being trained well, many of them from their childhood, to be warriors, they were ready now to fight against the Darians, whom Norgrash'nar had specifically longed to engage. And at the Hour of Awakening, he had his opportunity.

While the Nescrai in the south had been disorganized and demoralized by the Ogres, here amongst their lord, Norgrash'nar, they fought with much more exacting approach and quickly moved into formations that would grant them the greatest strength.

The Darian Cavalry led the charge now, four thousand strong they tore across the plains, slashing their enemies down from above. Followed swiftly by sixteen thousand footmen, the Nescrai seemed overpowered, regardless of their superior training in warfare. Then, when signaled by the blast of a horn, the Nescrai fell back from the battle lines and surrounded their generals as closely as possible.

The Darians thought, at first, that the battle was won, but as they tried to charge in they found themselves no longer of the capacity, for the influence of the Moonstone Armor fell upon them. They called their archers forward, to take down the enemy from range, but even they could not get close enough, so powerful was the effect of the Moonstones, here enhanced by the dark magic of Norgrash'nar, here undiminished even by the loss of the innocence of the Darians.

Norgrash'nar and his generals, encapsulated by their soldiers, now made an apparent retreat, moving northeastward toward the Darian Sea. Unknown what this strategy was, Alim'dar and Nirvisa'nen ordered the pursuit of the Nescrai. At the Hour of Eventide, the Darians surrounded the Nescrai upon three sides, there not far from the mouth of the Falcalor River. The sea was to the backs of Norgrash'nar and his followers, yet none of the Darians could get close enough to assault them. Their ballistas had been left behind, on the western banks of the river, as they could not easily be brought across. And so the battle came to a standstill.

Then, when the day had passed, at the Hour of Last Light, the Darians were joined by Adaashar, Sveraden, Norandar and all of their remaining soldiers. The Nescrai were completely surrounded with their backs to the sea, yet still they did not concede the war.

THE WHITE FLAG OF NORGRASH'NAR

Throughout the night the soldiers of both armies rested. At Firstlight, Norgrash'nar came out from his ranks, alone, still clad in his Moonstone armor. In his hand he held a white flag that to them signified a request for negotiation. Together, Alim'dar, Norandar, Sveraden and Adaashar went out to him. Nirvisa'nen remained behind, because neither she nor Alim'dar wanted her near to Norgrash'nar.

The four stood firmly, weapons still in hand, for they did not trust that Norgrash'nar desired truce. Alim'dar held fast to twin blades, Adaashar to a spear ended staff, Sveraden to a longsword and shield, and Norandar to the hammer he had wielded ever since he crushed the Tablet of Kronaggas. This had become his weapon of choice.

Norgrash'nar came armed as well, though his blades were sheathed. But as he drew near, the influence of the Moonstones fell upon the Sylvai, and all were filled with the ominous sense of doom that accompanied. The closer he came, the more terrifying it seemed. Only Norandar had the will to overcome.

"How do you resist it?" Adaashar asked.

"I don't know. For upon the southern plains we all found the power of the Moonstones to be overwhelming at first, but as the battle raged on, it weakened. Now, though I feel it's dark power, I can resist."

Fidgeting in her discomfort, Sveraden said, "How do you overcome such despair?"

"How did you defeat the children of Norgrash'nar, who wore such armor?" Alim'dar asked.

"The Ogres did much of it. They trampled the generals, the stones of the armor were crushed—" Norandar cut off his own words, realizing the answer to the question. The Armors had, in the southern battle, been crushed, probably broken, and thus its power was diminished. This, he surmised, was how they had been allotted their victory. Yet he could not understand why he now could resist an unbroken stone. He said, "If I can resist, I will remain here to talk with Norgrash'nar. The rest of you must retreat."

Still, Alim'dar, Adaashar and Sveraden were determined to stand with their brother; but as Norgrash'nar drew even nearer, they could not bring themselves to remain, and Sveraden said, "Norandar, come with us, away from this madness. He will kill you."

"No. Someone must face him now. Perhaps he offers his surrender." And even when the others had no choice but to retreat from the approaching Nescraian lord, Norandar stood firm, hammer in hand.

Norgrash'nar approached. "The others flee while you stand alone, Cousin?" he said, eyes burning with the malicious evil that had consumed him.

"Have you come to offer your surrender?"

"No. I have come to demand yours."

"You are outnumbered, Norgrash'nar, and you are trapped with only a sea behind you. We can camp here, surrounding you for as long as it takes. We can bring in supplies. You are cut off and cannot win."

"We will see, Norandar. But I offer you this one last chance... take your people to the south, all of them. Your soldiers, the Darians, all of the people of your lands... Take them to the Southern Reaches and keep them there for all time. Then you may have peace."

"Now you would offer peace? Now that so many of our brothers and sisters and cousins have been slain?"

"This was always an option for you and your people, from the very start of this war you could have left. But you chose to resist, to fight. The blood of many is upon your own consciences, not mine."

"You speak foolishness, Norgrash'nar. There is no victory to be found. When the Dragons return, they will rain their fire down upon you, if you do not surrender. Your armies will be burned to extinction."

"That might be true," Norgrash'nar said. "If it were so that what you see here, upon the shores of the sea, were all that remained." Then he pulled from a sheath upon his armor a strange horn upon which were magical carvings, the likes of which Norandar had never seen, and he raised it to his mouth and blew...

And beyond the field where they met, to the north, beyond even the armies of the Nescraians, and out over the sea, a veil was lifted. For what had seemed a vacant sea beyond, now revealed a hundred Nescraian ships that lined the coast, behind Norgrash'nar's army, concealed beforehand by a magical cloak, now broken by the sounding of the horn.

Fury erupted within Norandar, for he and all of his people had been deceived and led here into a trap, for these ships were equipped with heavy weaponry, ballistas and catapults that now launched their projectiles over the Nescrai and into the surrounding Sylvai, so unexpectedly that the army was made to scatter. And as Norgrash'nar grinned in his deceit, he was momentarily distracted as he took great pleasure in the surprise that fell upon the Sylvai army. Thus, Norandar was afforded a single moment to act, and he seized upon it. Gripping his hammer tightly in hand, he swung with all of his might and struck the Moonstone that was embedded in Norgrash'nar's armor.

As the force of the blow shattered the stone, so too did it shatter Norandar's arm, and the hammer fell to the earth, just as Norgrash'nar was thrown four Reaches away. Norandar felt the power of the Moonstone pull away and vanish entirely, for its dark magic was sundered. But he too fell to the ground in pain, for the agony in his arm was now spreading throughout.

Norgrash'nar rose to his feet, anger flaring in his eyes, and he ran toward Norandar and buried his armored knee into his face. Bone shattered, and Norandar fell motionless to the ground.

Seeing this from a distance, Adaashar, Sveraden and Alim'dar rushed forward, now relieved of the influence of the Moonstone... but it was too late for Norandar, for Norgrash'nar followed his assault by plunging his sword into the heart of Norandar. Father of Mara then breathed his last breath.

His brothers and sister charged forward; seeing Norandar fall, they were consumed with sorrow and intense ire and they intended then to end Norgrash'nar. But amidst the chaos of the battle they had not seen that Miiganen, Norgrash'nar's fourth daughter, and general of the army had approached, wearing her armor embedded with the Moonstone, and the dark influence fell upon them once again, holding them back regardless of their rage.

"Come, Norgrash'nar," Alim'dar fumed. "Face me alone. This is our battle, our war."

Norgrash'nar smirked, "I will neither give you the pleasure of a quick death nor the glory of my defeat at your hand, Alim'dar. This battle is far from over." And then he and Miiganen withdrew, just as the barrage of bolts and stones from the ships continued to rain down upon the Sylvai.

"We must retreat!" Adaashar said. "Look, our people are scattered, the

Nescrai will march."

"Yes," Alim'dar said. "This battle is not over... Signal a retreat—to the northwest, lure them toward Whitestone. I have something waiting there for them."

And so together, despite the loss of their brother, Adaashar, Sveraden and Alim'dar went amongst the Darians, Adaasharians and Noranites and directed them to flee across the Falcalor River, through Eastern Mara, and toward Whitestone. As they passed by the River, they abandoned their ballistas, for they would be too slowed down to drag them across the plains.

The Ruination of Naiad

We came out of Yor'Kavon during the morning hours of the eleventh day of Wintermelt. Haldus'nar, Sarak'den, myself and four thousand men and women prepared to fight who were mixed of the Haldusians, the Sylvai who had come out of the Sky City of Ketseltet, and those survivors of Felheim, who were the Nescrai who had before refused to join the war, but who had seen the destruction of the Giants unleashed upon their homeland by Drovanius, and now agreed to fight with us.

The Valley of Naiad was in ruins, trampled by the armies of the Norgrasharians who had come this way upon their march to the west. So too had this been the path of the Ogres who had charged westward.

"This place looks not the same as it once did," Sarak'den said sadly.

"It is a wasteland," Haldus'nar agreed. "This was our..."

"Home," I said. Tears filled my eyes, my heart wrenched, not for the destruction before us—for I knew that with time the land could recover—but for the sorrowful thoughts that were creeping into my head.

"Norgrash'nar will answer for this," Haldus'nar promised. "For all of this."

"As will Drovanius," Sarak'den said.

I could say nothing all the while that we were descending from Yor'Kavon into Naiad. The evil that had come upon this once beautiful land was ineffable, the fear within me unimaginable in that moment....

"What has become of the..." I said, but could not finish.

Sarak'den knew why my heart was troubled so, and she put her arm around my shoulder as we moved on. Haldus'nar too stood close, breathing heavily in indignation, for though we had seen the destruction of this war, it had not struck us so deeply as to see our own paradise razed to ruin.

As we moved through the valley we came to Lake Iidin; once it had been a sight of beauty with glistening, magical waters. Now it was stained with filth, likely from where the Ogres had crossed. To the south were the Bison Fields, and there were not present any of the once great creatures that remained alive. They had been slain brutally, perhaps as food for the Giants, perhaps for sport. The carcasses of the animals were torn and shredded, bone exposed and there was the stench of death throughout.

"Let us stay to the south," Sarak'den said, seized with tears.

"No," I said. "I must know."

And so upon our way, we crossed to the north of the river, into the Hills of Nightrun, the place where we had once called home. And there for me was the most horrifying and heart-rending sight I had seen. For amongst the ruins of our ancient village were the corpses of the Dains, those great and loving creatures that had never done any wrong and who were the innocents of the world, now slain and mutilated as they had tried to fend off the advance of the Nefarians. These had been the first of all the creatures of Sylveria that I had encountered, even before I had first met my own kind. And Saxon...

He had been the best of friends to me, throughout all of my years. As I had been left alone without a wife amongst my own, Saxon had been my companion, the one to whom I could always return, the one creature in all of the world that I thought would always be there for me. And now, for the first time ever, as I walked through Nightrun, he was not there to greet me with his giant eyes, his loving licks and his playful demeanor. He was not there to jump upon me, pinning me to the ground, whining in joy as we were reunited.

Here now instead were the lifeless corpses of these wonderful creatures, and I was filled with a rage beyond reckoning. But my sorrow was even greater, and I collapsed to the ground, helpless and distraught, hopeless and without recourse, for without Saxon, what could ever be good in this world again? When I could stand, I ran amongst the bodies, searching for that of my dearest friend, but the Dains were too torn asunder to recognize any, and I collapsed again.

"Saxon!" I cried out, as much as my lungs could muster, praying that somehow he had survived this brutality and would show himself to me, come running to me when he heard my voice, as he always had before. But only death was carried on the winds. All of Naiad seemed dead...

Sarak'den and Haldus'nar tried to comfort me, but it could not be done. For me, the fullness of this war's depravity was seen here, and I was ready to be done with it—the war, and with life. No matter what happened, no matter the outcome of this war, the world could never be good again.

A full hour was lost upon me—time that would better have been spent marching to the west. Haldus'nar and Sarak'den had already sent the soldiers westward, promising that we would catch up. But if we waited too much longer, we would never reach them...

"I cannot go on," I said. My sorrow had entirely overtaken me. "Leave me behind. Go on with your people."

"We will not leave you, Alak'kiin," Sarak'den said.

"Yes you will. There are more lives at stake than mine. Go."

"Alak'kiin," Haldus'nar consoled. "We need you with us. We will not leave you."

"I will be of no use. Look at me... I am broken. This war has already claimed me."

Sarak'den fell to the ground beside me, her arms upon me, weeping, "We will not leave you, Brother. We must avenge all of this. We must make this world good again."

"It cannot be..." I cried, but could not finish.

"Please, Alak'kiin," Haldus'nar said, his voice cracking. "We cannot leave you, and we must go on."

Sobbing still, I said, "You have one another still. I have lost my greatest love, here in Nightrun. He was not like us, but he was more pure than us all. Keep together and don't let go... but leave me."

There would be no convincing me to leave Nightrun in those moments, or any soon to follow, and Haldus'nar recognized this. He said to his wife, "He is right, Sarak'den. We must move on."

"I will not leave my Brother!" She cried.

"You have to," I said. "You have to go on and win this war. I cannot..."

But Sarak'den held fast, and it took the forceful pulling of Haldus'nar to remove her grasp from me. She too was overcome with grief and now she clung to her husband as he walked away. But then Haldus'nar turned to me and said, "This is not the end for us, Brother. Do what you must here. Recover. Let your rage be the guide for whatever you do next. You are needed in this world, Alak'kiin. I will see you again."

And then they were gone, following after their people to the west, and I remained alone in Nightrun, amongst the bodies of the Dains. And though I wanted to seek vengeance upon the Dark, I could in those moments do nothing but cry for my grief.

That entire day was lost. When I was capable I would rise and search amongst the remains of the noble Dains, filled with sorrow for all of them, but searching mostly for one, so that I would know for certain, for still did my heart hope that somehow Saxon had made it out, had not entered into the carnage, and was still somewhere alive. But there simply was no telling one corpse from another, and the fact that he never came in greeting to me convinced my mind that the greatest part of creation, for me, was now gone forever.

I remained there in Nightrun throughout that night, and when I awoke, I was distraught again, for I had hoped the slaughter had been but a dream. But it had not, and now, facing what had occurred here, I was filled with a vehement rage that drove me onward. Although the Ogres who had caused this were now far to the west, I was certain they would be taken down by the armies there, and so I set my fury instead upon the east, knowing that there were even more of the monsters there, and though it would likely cost me my life, I would go there and do whatever I could to eradicate the foul abominations.

Victory in Felheim

When I went back across Yor'Kavon it was the Hour of Elation; when I had crossed the Lowlands of Forthran it was the Hour of Passions. And when I found the Ogres and Trolls, it was the Hour of Evenlight, on the twelfth day of Wintermelt. There upon the Felheim Fields did the Giants rampage, all of them, and amongst them fought the seven Dragons.

A dozen of the Giants had perhaps fallen, several more were burning under the wrath of the Metallic Dragons, and several more still were suffering under the magic spells of the Chromatics. But many remained, for a hundred had here come when the fifty crossed over to the west. And the Dragons themselves were battleworn, weakening in their strength if not their resolve.

Now from my many past travels across this region in years past, I knew the geography. West of Sellos were three other villages that were not built in the shadows of the mountains, but a March to the south, and there between them and the base of the mountains was the North Marshes, which were a land watered heavily by springs that fed into rivers that watered most of the Felheim Fields. These were lands uninhabitable to any creature who walked upon the ground, for even in places where it appeared solid, the ground sank to a depth of three Heights below the surface of the fields. I once had seen Verasian—in years long before this war—attempt to swim in its waters, only to be stuck, for the ground below the water was a thick mud and the Dragon had difficulty pulling himself out.

And this I knew was the answer to defeating the Nefarians, for if we could draw them into the marshes, perhaps they might become immobilized. The Dragons had been brazen enough to attempt a head-on confrontation with the Ogres, not considering enough how powerful this enemy was. Verasian, Ashysin and Aranthia should have known better, but like me, they had all been filled with such passionate rage as to think only of destroying this enemy. Now, though my grief was still present, I was set upon a new objective, for I had to relay my plan to the Dragons.

To go upon the fields amongst the warring Dragons and Giants would mean sacrificing myself, yet I counted it not as a price that I was unwilling to pay for the destruction of the Nefarians. My life now was inconsequential. I was exhausted by this war, distraught over all that had been lost, and did not have the determination to go on. And so I ran upon the field into the scrimmage.

Fire fell around me, lightning struck, clouds of gas erupted, clubs and giant boots crashed about me, yet I felt not a touch of these elements. So far I had gone unnoticed. "Ashysin! Verasian!" I yelled as loudly as I could when I had come to within earshot. Still fighting, only Verasian looked to me just as his giant claw crushed the head of a Troll.

"Get out of here, Alak'kiin!" the Dragon roared.

But so too had I drawn the attention of an Ogre, who came now stomping toward me. I held out the only weapon I had, which was a staff, as if it would guard me from being crushed by the Giant. Roaring victoriously, blood and drool pouring from its foul, rotten mouth, it raised its club high and began its descent... There was no way for me to move fast enough to avoid the blow, no Dragon unengaged to save me from my demise, and as the club fell, I closed my eyes, knowing that my final moment had arrived. Time slowed down for me then, as my thoughts had raced before, now they were calm; I accepted my end, and I whispered, "Saxon, I'm coming to you..."

Then there was a great crash, the air about me surged and shook, and the Ogre wailed. I opened my eyes... Still there were no others engaging the monster, yet now it was unarmed and clutching only the remnants of its weapon. All around me were shards of wood, the fragments of the club. And all about me, forming a dome, was some magical energy that was reminiscent of the light I had seen in the Temple of Kronaggas when I had gone into its depths and encountered the Numen... And I knew then what was happening.

For in the depths of the mountain I had said to the Numen, "*If you will give me understanding, I will make a vow before you, Numen, that never will I harm another creature of Sylveria, for I feel in your very essence that you are love, peace, and perfection.*"

And the Numen had responded, saying, *"Be careful of the vows you make, Alak'kiin. For you have not yet seen the tribulations ahead. But for your righteousness, I grant you protection, so long as you hold to your word. No harm can come upon you; you will not see death so long as you keep this covenant..."*

So it was that here on this day, amidst the foul Nefarians that could crush any man with a single blow, that I was invulnerable for the protection given to me by the Numen. For I had vowed to never harm a creature of Sylveria. But these Giants were not of our world—but of Nefaria, and they certainly fell not within the bounds of my vow.

Still, my magic was not strong enough to do much real harm to them, and I was skilled not with a weapon so much as my siblings had become, and though I might somehow find way to kill one of the Ogres, it would not be before at least some of the Dragons had been overwhelmed. And so I recalled my plan, and yelled to the Dragons, "To the north! The Marshes!"

Verasian again glanced at me, and I saw his eyes light up, and in that instant he understood what they needed to do. "Retreat to the air!" He commanded his brothers, and all listened to him, for he had become the leader amongst them in this battle. The Green Dragon thought to save me, to pull me from amongst them, for he was the only one who had even seen me there, so great was the disorder of blood and bone and torn flesh that littered the battlefield. But I waved him away, and he somehow knew that I was amongst them not to die that day, and he retreated into the air with the others.

High above, the Dragons conversed, breathing heavily, longing to return to the battle, though they knew they could not win without great loss amongst them. Then, Verasian, Merilinder, Sharuseth and Merobassi flew away, to the north, while Drovanius, Aranthia and Ashysin released a final burst of magic and fire down upon the Trolls and Ogres. Then, they too flew off, away to the north, hoping that the monsters would follow.

Alone on the battlefield with perhaps seventy of the Giants, I was relieved, for perhaps my plan would come to fruition. Those monsters who saw me remained, coming for me, while the others, enraged over this most recent outburst of fire charged off to the north, giving chase to the Dragons who had now come to fly low over the Fields of Felheim. Those who came against me were bewildered and furious at their inability to destroy me, for still the magical protection safeguarded me from all harm. At last, they gave up, and followed their kind to the north.

The Dragons came to land upon the mountains, along the Ledges of Aisorath, where the rails of the Guidetrain passed, and which overlooked the North Marshes. The first wave of the Ogres and Trolls, which was all but four—which were those who had remained behind to slay me—fell into the trap, and stumbling over one another, they became lodged within the muck of the marshes. Now, fire and magic could fall down upon them unhindered... yet this was not enough for the Dragons, and they instead sundered the stones of the ledges, causing them to crash down upon the Giants. Then, with the Nefarians trapped even moreso, they unleashed all of their remaining fire and spells and rage down upon them, and not one of the Ogres or Trolls remained alive.

Still, there were four of the Ogres who had not yet come to the Marshes, and when they saw the utter defeat of their kin, they roared in rage, and began retreating now back to the east.

Victory had at last come, all of the Nefarians were defeated, but it had come at a great cost, for tens of thousands had been slain in Felheim by the Ogres and Trolls, and now even the Dragons were depleted of their magic, fire and strength. It would take much time before they were recovered, and they each lay down there, south of the Marshes, to rest. I stayed with them, for without them, I knew there would be no way for me to get to the west before the entirety of the war had consummated, to whatever end.

The Vow of Ogres

Now, when the seven Dragons, including Drovanius, had come upon the Ogres and Trolls, they knew they had been betrayed, for it was the Black Dragon who had brought them here in his alliance with Talentaran, their Drake father. Enraged at this, they sought to destroy him, and all of those like him, before continuing their conquest of Sylveria. And when the last four Ogres saw that all of the others were perishing in the marshes, though they wanted to continue the fight, they thought instead to retreat, so that they might return to Nefaria and tell Talentaran of all that had happened.

So they ceased their warring and moved with swiftness back to the Kailin Shipyard, where they had arrived by way of the great barge. And they set it to move again upon the waters, which carried them far northward, between the lands of Merobassi and Drovanius, and then back to Nefaria.

And there they told Talentaran of all that had transpired. The Drake cursed the name of Drovanius the Black for his betrayal. It was then that the Ogres of Nefaria vowed revenge upon the Black Dragon, for he was a creature without honor.

The Battle of Diin'gar

The Adaasharians and the Noranites, led by the Darians and pursued by the Nescrai—now numbering nearly fifty thousand after the reinforcements from their ships had come ashore—arrived at their destination at the Hour of Attrition on the twelfth day of Wintermelt. Here, at Diin'gar bay, they made their camp for the night, for they had gained enough ground upon the enemy and now needed rest. Alim'dar was certain that the Nescrai would not come until morning.

As the soldiers of this last army made their preparations for rest, Alim'dar, Nirvisa'nen, Adaashar and Sveraden talked to make all plans ready for the next day.

"They will come in force," Adaashar said. "Outnumbering us, and by far outmatching us. What do you have planned?"

"I will not yet reveal to you what is to come," Alim'dar said. "Lest there be spies amongst us, ears listening from afar, for what comes is the last stand we make, the last chance we have at winning this war. You have but to follow my lead, and trust me."

"Of course we trust you, Brother," Sveraden said.

"When Firstlight comes, we break camp," Nirvisa'nen said. "And we make way for our home city."

"Nirvisa'Iinid is a mighty city, no doubt," Adaashar said. "But can its walls withstand the legion marching on it?"

"Just wait," Alim'dar said, and he seemed not too concerned. "Adaashar, Sveraden, you will lead the people toward Whitestone, until you see a sign. Then you will know what to do."

"What sign?"

"You will know it when you see it, dear Sister. And the enemy will know it as well. This battle will cost us greatly. But it must be fought."

"We will see it to its end," Adaashar said. "And if we are to join our brother, Norandar, in death upon the field of war, then so be it."

"So be it," Alim'dar agreed.

When Firstlight came, the Nescrai had moved close, travelling throughout at least part of the night. Adaashar and Sveraden began leading the people northward, around the bay of Diin'gar, toward Whitestone. Alim'dar and Nirvisa'nen remained at the rear of the company, watching every move of the enemy.

Norgrash'nar and his army moved swiftly, preparing to take the prize that was victory on this day, the first of Springrise. But their numbers were not quite so great as he had wished, for upon the previous evening, scouts had brought to him news that there was a small army moving from the east across the plains, and he was forced to diminish his main army by sending out five thousand troops to face them, lest they be later taken by surprise.

These were the Haldusians and their company, led by Haldus'nar and Sarak'den, and though they would not make it to the greater battle, their arrival was well timed, for they had forced a weakening of the Nescraian army.

The battle began at Midlight, when the Nescrai overtook what they thought to be the fleeing enemy. The Sylvai were just to the southwest of the bay, and the majority of them were within the shadow of Hargid Cliff. Now, this cliff rose high over a small plain that was between its base and the Umonar River. Across the river there was a land bridge by which they could continue, but instead they stopped there below, for Alim'dar had held in suspense his own reinforcements. For coming down from the top of the cliff there was a slope that eased down along the coastline of the Bay of Diin'gar, and from there came the augmentation of his forces.

At the back of the company of the Sylvai, Alim'dar, Nirvisa'nen and the Darians engaged the first onslaught of the enemy, their remaining cavalrymen at their side. The armies there clashed, and many men were felled by sword and axe and arrow and weapons of all manners. But none were so fierce as that which the lord of Whitestone next unleashed...

Now, Norgrash'nar had held back his generals, for the Nescrai were trying to catch the enemy and not drive them further away, and so they were at the back of the army, and there was no hindrance by their Moonstones upon the great White Bears of Whitestone as they charged down into the masses of the Nescrai. These were the same bears that had long held association with the people of Nirvisa'Iinid, who had now been transformed into mounts loyal to the Darians, and ready to defend their country; for these Bears much loved the honey that was given to them by the people.

The Bears were massive creatures, though not so large as the Sloths, but could mount two soldiers easily upon their backs along with all the weaponry and gear necessary; for standing fourteen feet tall while on all fours, two men or women wielded both bows and swords, and from this height, many were felled by their arrows. The Bears tore through the Nescrai, claws cutting easily through armor, their fur so thick that blade could barely cut them. Only piercing seemed to harm them, and this served in most instances only to anger them.

Over a hundred of the Bears lunged down the slopes into the enemy, and while they did so, the Sylvai turned and charged back to the east, back into the battle against the Nescrai. Alim'dar and Nirvisa'nen led this charge, themselves on horseback, and the Nescrai were so taken by this unexpected assault that they tried to withdraw. But it was too late for the first of those people who came against the Bears, and they were torn to shreds upon the battlefield. The Darians pressed on, into the masses of terrified Nescrai.

"Take your division to the north!" Alim'dar said to his wife. "I will go to the south and we will circle around and trap them between ourselves and our brothers and sisters!"

Nirvisa'nen nodded and cried out to her followers, and they turned to the north to cut through the flanks of the enemy, for it was only a matter of time before the Nescrai became organized once more.

So the Darians were split between the north and the south, surrounding the Nescrai while the Sylvai and the White Bears cut through the center, and the Nescrai were scattered across the battlefield. But Norgrash'nar had, when his army had pursued his enemy to the west, taken with him many of the ballistas left behind by the Darians, and now, at the back of the lines, amongst his generals, and as the White Bears approached, he unleashed a barrage of bolts and stones upon the creatures. At such a close range, the bolts easily cut through their thick hides, the stones easily crushed their massive skulls, and many of them were felled.

Still, it seemed inevitable that the Sylvai and the Darians would win this battle, for too scattered and disarrayed was the enemy. Yet Norgrash'nar had one final stage of his plan to enact, one that he was certain would bring him victory, one way or another.

A Final Plea

All throughout the battle Norgrash'nar had kept his eye upon a certain prize, for he knew that Nirvisa'nen was here amongst the enemy. And when he saw that she led a division of the Darians across the northern coastline he set in motion his final plan that he was certain would turn the tide of the battle back in his favor. So, taking with him one of his generals, who was Lavanar, his third born son, and a sizable unit of soldiers, he cut to the north to engage the Darians.

Upon the battlefield the enemy moved to engage Norgrash'nar, but nearly two thousand mounted Darians fell into a trap, for they came under the influence of the Moonstone Armor of Lavanar, and they were there held back. But Nirvisa'nen, more attuned to the goal was not so affected and she pressed forward further, not yet realizing that she had made distance between herself and her soldiers.

And Norgrash'nar seized the opportunity, and he took a spear and hurled it with deadly accuracy and pierced the steed upon which Nirvisa'nen rode. The horse tumbled to the ground and the woman went plummeting off into the mud. With Lavanar not far away, the Darians were entirely cut off from their mother as Norgrash'nar approached her.

"Nirvisa," he said to her, approaching. "I told you I would ask you one more time... to come with me. This is it. Leave Whitestone and Alim'dar forever. Come with me, and I will withdraw my forces back to the east and will never trouble your people again."

Rising from the ground, gripping her sword tightly, Nirvisa'nen raised it toward him and said, "What a fool you have become, Norgrash'nar. Your army will not win this battle. You will be defeated. Kill me now if you must, but you will not win."

"Nirvisa..." Norgrash'nar then took the weapons that were sheathed at his sides and unstrapped them, cast them to the ground, and said softly, "Do not be afraid. I have not drawn you here to kill you, for if I did, would your people not be all the more inspired to crush mine? No, I have brought you here, alone on this battlefield, only to talk."

"You've said everything you need to say already," she hissed.

"Not everything... Please, Nirvisa, if you will not come with me..." he paused, as if he needed final confirmation, to which she only glared at him. He said, "Then I will let you go. This war has become too much... too many lives lost. My own people... My own children. And I am sorry for all that I've done."

Nirvisa'nen lowered the point of her sword, but only slightly, for despite the seeming sincerity of his words, she still could hold little trust in Norgrash'nar. "If you are truly sorry," she said. "Then call off your army now. Cease this bloodshed so that as many as is possible might not perish.

"I will... only let me touch you one last time."

"Norgrash'nar, you have cast your weapons away. If you offer your surrender, sound your horn to call off your soldiers, to end this war, and I will do the same. No more need to die this day."

Norgrash'nar pulled forth his horn and raised it to his mouth, and with a great blast he sent signal all throughout the field of war. "It is done," he said. "I surrender to you. Do with me as you will, Nirvisa... but allow me to touch your face one last time."

She squinted suspiciously at him, wondering at how he could remain so obsessed with her after so long. Still, Norgrash'nar had signaled surrender to his army. Looking over her shoulder she could see that those warring nearest to them were already disarming, giving themselves over to the Sylvai and Darians. Lavanar was removing his Moonstone Armor even. The battle was over and the enemy had surrendered. "What do you want from me, Norgrash'nar?" she asked.

"Nirvisa, I will spend the rest of my life detained by your people. I am too great a threat, too much an offender, to hope for forgiveness. One last time, let me touch your face... I beg you."

As always, Nirvisa'nen then had the slightest compassion on Norgrash'nar, and though she would not concede her heart to him, she would entertain his delusions, for it was what she had always done. But as she nodded, consenting now to this final request, she kept pointed at his heart the blade of her sword, which was at the indentation where the Moonstone had been before it was shattered by Norandar. Here the armor was weak, and they both knew that the sword would pierce it with ease.

Nirvisa'nen said, "Lay your hands and eyes upon me one last time, if you must, Norgrash'nar. It is the last time you will look upon me. If you make the slightest misstep, I will end you."

Norgrash'nar nodded and seemed to have unreserved surrender in his eyes. He reached forward and laid his hand upon her cheek, and closed his eyes. He muttered words indiscernible to her, which she took to be some silent prayer to whatever madness had overtaken him. His touch was soft and gentle, but Nirvisa'nen felt not the slightest draw to him, for in allowing this it was only her intention to retain the surrender of the Nescrai, so that no more might die. When his words were finished, he moved his hand away and sank to the ground.

Nirvisa'nen turned and yelled to the Darians, who were now beginning their approach toward them, now not so influenced by the darkness of the Moonstones. "Keep him here," she said when they arrived. "And give me a horse."

The Darians all offered to her their steed, and she chose one to mount. "I go to my husband now." And with a command to the horse, Nirvisa'nen rode off to the south to find Alim'dar.

As she rode, she was seized with a sudden warmth that flowed over her, something she had never before felt. But Nirvisa'nen perceived it was naught but the warmth of assuagement, for at last the war and bloodshed was drawing to an end. But unbeknownst to her, this all was part of the scheming of Norgrash'nar...

Just moments before Nirvisa'nen had mounted the horse and began riding to the south, Alim'dar, not far to the south, was watching as the Nescrai seemingly surrendered by the horn call of Norgrash'nar. He looked through his scope, to the north, looking to see if he could see his people and his wife. And there they were, amongst the Nescrai, taking captive all of those enemies who had resigned. But he saw something else, for set apart were two figures facing one another, not in combat, but in apparent closeness, and he was certain that one of them was Nirvisa'nen, and the other Norgrash'nar. Immediately he set his steed upon a straight path for them, terror filling him, for he knew not what was happening there.

He rode hard. His eyes were filled with sweat and blood, his vision unstable as the horse charged at full speed. Then he saw as one of them mounted a horse and set its destination directly for him. Still he rode, unsure who he was about to encounter—he prayed it was Nirvisa'nen, for the other had fallen to the ground and was now surrounded by others, and he feared that despite the surrender, Norgrash'nar might have slain Nirvisa'nen.

Alim'dar's men were close behind; upon horseback two thousand rode with him. To the west, the Darians and Sylvai pressed forward to the east with their now unarmed prisoners, to within sight of the two mounted soldiers charging toward one another.

Nirvisa'nen, filled still with the insoluble warmth, pressed on, eager now as the war was over to be with Alim'dar, for now she could see that he came toward her with great haste. And as she rode she thought of all things that had been. She thought of the first time she had seen this man, her husband, upon the shores of Lake Iidin, when all of the First Awakened had come together. She thought of the quick affections that he had shown to her, and of their marriage in the Mountain of Kronaggas. She thought of when they had together led their people from the Valley of Naiad to Whitestone, and when they had raised the city of Nirvisa'Iinid from the wilderness. Most of all, she thought of the endearing love that she held for Alim'dar, and how—now that this war was over—peace could return to the world, and perhaps it could be made to be good once more.

Nirvisa'nen brought her horse to a stop, and dismounted, for Alim'dar approached. He too stopped and alighted himself. But as she started for him, she realized that something was terribly wrong...

Alim'dar slowed his steed; for now he could see who approached. Rage filled him, for he now was certain that something terrible had happened to his beloved wife. Grief seized him as the rider dismounted, grief that quickly transformed into undying fury. He leaped from his horse, sword in hand, and started forward. For there before him stood the greatest of his enemies, he who had brought war to Sylveria, and who had probably slain Nirvisa'nen to the north... Norgrash'nar... Alim'dar did not hesitate; he did not care that surrender had been signaled. Norgrash'nar must this day die. And he saw not even that the one who approached was unarmed, nor that she was even who she appeared to be. And he lunged for her, not knowing who she was...

And Nirvisa'nen never even realized in her final moments that the wickedness of Norgrash'nar was here complete, for she had been deceived; a spell had been cast upon her by the enemy, one that was intended to deceive Alim'dar.

Indeed, Alim'dar was deceived, for before his eyes was an image of Norgrash'nar rather than the true vision of his wife. And mistaking her for him, he drove his sword into her heart without hesitation, not knowing what he was truly doing.

And Alim'dar, in that instant, thought it quite strange that with his dying breath, Norgrash'nar spoke the words, "Why? I always loved only you, Alim."

THE TIDES OF WAR

And so it was that because his bitterness over the woman he could never possess was so strong, Norgrash'nar had cast a dark spell upon Nirvisa'nen, making her appear to Alim'dar as if she were him—the Nescraian lord. And seeking her husband through the horrors of the war, Alim'dar mistook Nirvisa'nen for the enemy, and he slew her with sword.

Of all the children of Alim'dar who were there upon the fields, those who had been with Alim'dar were also deceived, while the others had not been blinded by the dark magic, and they saw only one thing—the killing of their mother by their father. And here the seeds of dissent that Norgrash'nar had planted amongst the Darians in seasons past came to fruition, and they perceived that Alim'dar had always been aligned with the dark. And the tide of the war shifted once again.

Those who had seen their father kill their mother turned then upon their father, and began aligning themselves with the Nescrai, for in all of the confusion, there must have been things occurring of which they were unaware. One-half of the Darians turned that day to fight with the Nescrai, who, knowing of the plot of Norgrash'nar, welcomed them. They released their Nescraian captives and gave back to them their weapons, and the battle resumed just as Norgrash'nar sounded his horn once more. Now, the battle was turned, and none of the Sylvai knew if the Darians fought with them or against them, for there was too much guile amongst them. Those Darians who had not seen what had happened were perplexed when some of their brothers and sisters began turning upon them.

Amidst the chaos, the Sylvai and those still loyal to Alim'dar became a weaker force, for they were crippled by confusion, and they began drawing back to the west and north.

Alim'dar himself was dragged away by his own soldiers, for after having slain Nirvisa'nen, the spell was broken, and before his eyes her true form had been revealed. In this he was rendered ineffectual in his remorse. He was taken westward, just as the Darians and Sylvai attempted to regroup.

Norgrash'nar delighted in the fruition of his scheme, for although the battle was not yet won, he had achieved a great victory—he had taken Nirvisa'nen away from Alim'dar, and his vengeance was complete. The day was only half passed, and he was certain that his enemy would be entirely eradicated by Lastlight. The Nescrai and the deceived Darians pushed westward, killing as they went, and once again evening the battlefield. Still amongst them were five of the generals clad in Moonstone armor, and the enemy fled before them. The White Bears had by this time been slain. And there was little hope—in Norgrash'nar's estimation—for the Sylvai and Darians to recover. The war was all but won. When these fighters were eliminated, his armies would sweep across the land and slay all of those who remained. The Sylvai would be enslaved, the Haldusians and the Darians exterminated at last. His heart grieved for the loss of Nirvisa'nen, but he had, upon the battlefield, resigned to knowing that she would never be his. Now, of the utmost importance was the victory that was at hand.

But Norgrash'nar had not considered the full effect of what would transpire as a result of his deception. For it was that when some time had passed that day, when Alim'dar and his people and the Sylvai were fleeing to the west, that he found within him the passion to not only carry on, but to envision the defeat of the Nescrai. With Adaashar and Sveraden at his side, he rose amongst his people, now—alike to the awakening of Ashysin, Merilinder and Sharuseth in the Valley of Tears—not a mere man, but one enflamed with intense ardor and intent upon victory. For in his loss, he became entirely determined to deliver complete defeat to the enemy, and none would stand in his way.

He rose first amongst the Darians who had remained loyal to him, and then amongst the Sylvai who remained, and his words of passion inspired them, promising them glory when the Nescrai and the traitors were eliminated. So fierce were his words that they were all of them aroused to such an intense desire for victory that when they followed Alim'dar back onto the battlefield, they fought not as one man or one woman, but with a precision in combat so exemplary that it was as though each of them was an entire unit unto themselves. This galvanized machine surged eastward, and not one of them perished without taking a half dozen others with them.

Alim'dar, amongst them, sought out first the generals, and now entirely unaffected by their armor, slew these children of Norgrash'nar without mercy, shattering the stones and trampling them underfoot. Then he sought out the lord of the Nescrai, to finish him for good, but Norgrash'nar was nowhere to be found. For in seeing the brilliant display of the Light, enacted here by Alim'dar's passion, he had transported himself away, seeing that the battle now was certainly lost. He would, he determined, live to fight another day, and he abandoned those who remained of his kind there on the battlefield.

With such passion displayed, the Darians who had turned upon their father surrendered; the Nescrai fled. Eastward they went with swiftness, abandoning their weapons and armor in hopes of escape. For this they gained greatly upon them as Alim'dar marched forward in force; intent on not letting them escape, he would hunt them all the way back to their homeland if necessary. He would kill every last one of them, so that perhaps the world might recover from the evil that had consumed it.

By Lastlight, the Nescrai had come unto the Plains of Kronaggas, and they could travel no more, for exhaustion had overcome them. Although Alim'dar himself could have continued on indefinitely, his army was fatigued, and so they too rested, just a March away from the enemy, a mere hour away from their final victory.

Then the tides turned once more in the favor of the Nescrai—not in the arrival of reinforcements or any matter of events that would give them victory—but in an encounter that would at least spare their lives; for if not for this, they would have been eliminated by the passionate hatred of Alim'dar.

In the morning, on the second day of Springrise, the Nescrai continued their flight. But there upon the Plains of Kronaggas they met with another force; for the Haldusians, guided by Sarak'den and Haldus'nar, had won their battle against the division of Nescrai sent to them, and their remnant came unto the Nescrai, who now were without leaders, for Norgrash'nar had since fled, and his remaining generals were slain.

The Nescrai said to the First Awakened, "Let us live! Let us flee back to our own land, for Alim'dar is murderous in his rage. He will wipe all of us from the face of this world, as Norgrash'nar intended for your people. He has led us to our end and made us into killers. But we have surrendered our weapons and our ambitions, and seek only to go home to our families. Let us pass through Naiad, and we will never return to the western realms of Sylveria."

Now, Sarak'den was of the mind to let the Nescrai retreat, but Haldus'nar was unsure, and he said to his wife, "If we let them live, might they return to conquer us again? And if we kill them for their atrocities, eliminating them for their evil, what retribution might we incur? For I have seen visions of things to come, and I do not know which course of action will lead to our own demise. This is the curse of premonition."

"Then we must do what our hearts tell us, what seems right, here and now," Sarak'den advised. "And my mind is set upon taking no more lives than are necessary. For look at the Nescrai... they are utterly defeated here. Let us do what we must according to our conscience. I say we must let them live."

For the compassion that was in their hearts, and for the weariness of war and of the bloodshed and death they had seen, Haldus'nar and Sarak'den listened to the pleas of the Nescrai. So many had died, so many had suffered, and the last thing they longed for was more death. And they accepted the surrender of the Nescrai that day, and sealed an agreement with them, that never would the Nescrai return to the west, or set foot upon the lands of Aranthia. They would remain within the borders of Verasian's Domain, and would abandon any claim the Garonites held upon the

Mountains of Ashysin.

Then Alim'dar and his pursuing army came to the Haldusians, and Alim'dar said, "What have you done? Have you allowed the enemy to retreat, to live even?"

"There has been enough loss of life, Brother," Sarak'den said. "The war is won. The Dark has been driven away."

"The Dark will remain so long as they breathe!"

"We cannot eliminate evil by becoming butchers," Haldus'nar said. "For they have offered their surrender and will no more return to the western regions of Sylveria."

"And you can be sure of this, somehow?"

"We can never be sure of anything. But what will you do, Brother? March the remnants of our people into Verasian's realm and slaughter all of those who fought, as well as all of those who remain? Look, there are some Nescrai who have joined us, from Felheim. Their corruption is not complete. Would you eradicate the Norgrasharians and the Garonites completely, as they once vowed to wipe our children from existence?"

Rage filled him still, for too much had he lost, and he said vehemently, "*I would.*"

"Brother, let us bring our rage into submission. We are not like the enemy. We are not killers who seek the destruction of any people. We are of the Light, Alim'dar, and we must behave accordingly."

Alim'dar fumed. In his heart he understood the truth of Haldus'nar and Sarak'den's words, but for his grief and sorrow of losing Nirvisa'nen, he could not agree with it. And he considered then leading his people onward, and storming through the towns and cities of the Nescrai, and eliminating every last one of them.

But despite his anguish, there remained within him enough of the Light that he submitted to the will of his sister, Sarak'den, and Haldus'nar, saying only, "I will end my rage, for your words, for I know you speak true, though I feel not right about it, nor do I consider it wise. I pray you are right, that this war is over. But know that if it is not, if the Nescrai return in a day or a season or a year, that every life they take is upon your shoulders."

"We understand, Alim'dar," Haldus'nar said. "We—my people—will see to the return of the Nescrai to their own lands. Peace is upon us at last. The war is over. Let us gather our dead and try to rebuild this world."

EPILOGUE

THE CONSUMMATION OF THE FIRST DRAGONWAR

After the victory of the Dragons over the Nefarians in Felheim, I returned to the west to gather with my people. As I traversed the Valley of Naiad, my heart still glum and filled with sorrow, I passed by the defeated Nescraian army that was returning to Verasian. My soul was filled with rage over all that they had done, all of the darkness that they had let into the world. Yet I saw them as a humbled enemy, now relinquished of their warlust, and knowing that this bode well, my anger was stilled, and my rancor was tamed.

Then on the Plains of Kronaggas, I met with my brethren and together we wept over the loss of so many lives.

Peace returned to the lands of Sylveria, though it was a bittersweet victory, for too many of the people's sons and daughters, mothers and fathers, and sisters and brothers had been lost in this conflict.

The Darians carried their dead back into Whitestone and buried them in graves marked with carved stones. So too did Alim'dar take the pierced body of Nirvisa'nen and return it to Nirvisa'Iinid, and sorrow filled his heart.

I was with him when he gathered her remains; my sorrow stung my eyes, for once I had loved this same woman, but my own heartache could not, I knew, compete with that of my brother. As he lifted her body I saw as an amulet fell from her chest. Indeed, it was the very amulet that I had brought to Alim'dar many years ago, a crafted item forged by Haldus'nar and intended as a gift for Nirvisa'nen. Adorned with a mysterious pink stone encased in intricately designed metal, she had worn it all these years. Now, it would be left behind, weathered into the dirt, and forgotten. I had not the heart to retrieve it, even for the sake of my brother.

The Noranites gathered and buried their dead amongst the Trees of Mara along with their father, Norandar, who had been killed by his assault upon Norgrash'nar. His hammer was taken and kept amongst his sons and daughters as a relic of the war, a symbol of the bravery of their father. Alunen had survived the war, and she would continue to serve as the much-beloved leader of her people, though only for a time.

The Adaasharians burned their dead, there in Mara, before returning home. Adaashar and Sveraden had survived the war, though all of their firstborn children had not. It was with great mourning that they then led the remnants of their soldiers back to the south, through the mountains and back to the Southern Reaches.

The Dragons recovered from their fatigue in Felheim. Ashysin, Merilinder, and Sharuseth flew into Mara, to aid their people as best as they could in the rebuilding of their lives. Aranthia too returned with Haldus'nar and Sarak'den to their lands and there began the reconstruction of their country.

Drovanius, Merobassi and Verasian returned not unto their people, for each of them had realized, to varying degrees, that they had been responsible for so much of the destruction of their world. For Verasian and Merobassi, shame was their penalty, and they retreated into the hidden places of their domains where they vowed they would never align themselves with the people again, for too much corruption was in the world.

And I, amongst my people, before they departed again for their own lands, wept over all that had been lost, all of those we loved who had perished, and for the loss of the innocents of the world. None of us were pure any longer, for we had all been touched by the darkness of war.

Yes, peace returned to Sylveria, but it was short-lived…

For when six seasons had passed, when the world turned into Autumn, the Sylvai discovered a terrible truth—that the pact the Nescrai had made was forged entirely out of deceit, and was meant only to give them time to regroup. Norgrash'nar had learned from all of his mistakes of the war, and on all fronts had strengthened his abilities. And as it was, the Norgrasharians had far more people ready to serve destruction to the Sylvai who had not before fought in the war. They raised up new armies, new machines of warfare, and new revulsions toward their enemies, for there would always be enmity between the Nescrai and the rest of the people of the world; they had declined so far in their moralities that they no longer could see others as anything but worthy of destruction.

There was little warning to the Sylvai; the Nescrai came in the night, through every crack and crevice of the mountains into Mara and the Southern Reaches, across the sea into Aranthia. But they came not near to Whitestone, for they feared the wrath of the Darians.

When the assault began, a call went out to Alim'dar, telling him that he and his fierce fighters were needed again, for the Nescrai had returned. But embittered as he was, now in a state of eternal mourning, Alim'dar refused their call. Even the Metallic Dragons went to him, pleading, urging him to take his place of leadership once again, promising that this time he could do as he pleased to the wicked Nescrai. But Alim'dar rebuffed them, telling them, "I told them that the blood of their people would be upon their own hands if they allowed the enemy to live. But they listened not to me, and now they can suffer for their own foolishness."

Without the passion of Alim'dar, the Sylvai were a far weaker force, and within a matter of a single season, the last battles came.

In the Southern Reaches, Adaashar and Sveraden led their people in a final desperate attack on the Nescrai. Ashysin and Merilinder were there with them, yet they had become so diminished by the war that they were useless in saving their children and they were forced to retreat. The Adaasharians fell that day, and their mother and father fled their own deaths and hid in the mountains.

Upon the Plains of Kronaggas the remnants of the Noranites stood with the last of the Haldusians and with Aranthia and Sharuseth. Although all of the Sky Cities of Kor'Magailin had fallen in the previous war, the Nescrai had devised great methods to combat the Dragons, and as Aranthia perched upon the high places of Kronaggas Mountain, raining down the last of his magic upon the overwhelming enemy, and as Sharuseth poured out the last of his fire, great ballistas larger than any used in the previous war launched giant bolts with chains attached, and Aranthia became entangled within them. As he fought against the restraints, the force of his struggle cracked the very stone of the mountain, and it collapsed with a thunderous crash that shook all of the plains, the curved peak of Kronaggas' Temple Mount was sundered, and it fell upon the plains below, crushing both Sylvai and Nescrai. So too was Aranthia pulled by the mighty machines to the ground. Sharuseth escaped, for once his fire was expelled, he could do nothing more and his injuries were too great.

Led by Norgrash'nar, across the Plains of Kronaggas, and into the Valley of Naiad, the Nescrai dragged the flailing Aranthia, for he was in bonds now too strong for even a Dragon to withstand. And they brought him onto the Hills of Nightrun, next to the Lake of Iidin, and there performed the most vicious act that had ever been seen upon Sylveria. They tightened the chains upon the Dragon, so that he could no longer move. Then, with spear and lance and all weapons they could find, the fallen Nescrai pried from his body the scales, and pierced him a hundred thousand times—once for each of their brothers and sisters who had died in the war. And while the Dragon still breathed, they tore out his innards with great machine-drawn forks that hollowed out the great Aranthia. Then at last, mercy came to the Dragon; he cried out a final triumphant roar—though he had lost this struggle—and he breathed his last breath. All of this had been done at the command of Norgrash'nar, whose evil had far surpassed that of his fathers. When he later heard about the brutality done to Aranthia the Crimson in the Valley of Naiad, even Drovanius the

Black cringed at the ruthless savagery that had consumed his children.

The Hills of Nightrun and the Lake of Iidin were forever stained with the blood of the great and noble Dragon. The power of Aranthia's blood remained for a long time thereafter, and it was later whispered amongst those few who survived this war that his blood would always live within the earth of the Valley of Naiad and that his sacrifice was an eternal symbol of salvation.

When the Nescrai were through with Aranthia, there was naught left of him, for every scale had been removed and taken as a trophy, every bone broken or harvested, and even his claws were cut off to be used as implements of war.

After these final battles, the few Sylvai and Haldusians who remained alive were taken captive by the Nescrai, for this war was over, and the evil was victorious because of Alim'dar's refusal to fight. As it was, Norgrash'nar deemed that he would not take the Darians—for in truth he had come to fear the might of his cousin.

Sarak'den's Curse

For my divine protection, I had survived this final war. So too had the remainder of my siblings—Adaashar, Sveraden, Alunen, and Sarak'den. Haldus'nar remained alive, but he had been taken captive by the Nescrai amongst the final remnants of the Haldusians. There remained but one safe haven for the rest of us, and that was within the realm of Whitestone.

We gathered there upon the plains south of Nirvisa'Iinid on the last day of Autumntide, in the year 553. There the Darians found us and they took us into the castle of Alim'dar to stand before their lord.

"You have caused all of this, Alim'dar!" Sarak'den spat at her brother. "If you would have heeded our call, we might have held back the enemy!"

He glared furiously at her, and to me he seemed not the same man he had once been, so devastated had he become over the loss of Nirvisa'nen. There was not in his eyes a semblance of repentance as he said, "What were we commanded to do, at the beginning of this war, by Kronaggas himself? Yes, we were told to show no mercy to the enemy. Yet you failed in this. I told you, Sarak'den, their blood would be upon *your* hands. It was you and Haldus'nar who let them go. Had you listened to me, we would have torn through the east and slain every last one of them! You must now suffer for your foolishness."

"How can you be so cold, Alim'dar?" Sarak'den said; tears filled her eyes. Her sisters, Alunen and Sveraden, tried to comfort her, but they too were so torn by the absolute devastation of their people that they could do little more than cry themselves. So too were Adaashar and I rendered speechless by the cold-hearted indifference of Alim'dar that we could only watch the exchange in silence.

"This war has made me cold, Sarak'den. Do not think that you are the only one who has suffered loss. Do you not know of what has become of Nirvisa'nen?"

"Of course I know! But do you think that somehow justifies your allowance of our destruction? Do you find pleasure in knowing that we have lost our families as well?"

"I find pleasure... in nothing...." Alim'dar said coldly. "The life that was worth living died on the battlefield upon the Plains of Valor... for me. You know it's true, Sarak'den... this world is lost. It does not matter that our children or our husbands or our wives have perished. Everything is lost... and I long only for death."

As dark as his words were, I could deeply relate to them, for through the destruction of these wars, too much had been lost, and even I saw no path that could bring Sylveria back into the Light, no way that the once peaceful lives we led in the Valley of Naiad could ever be restored. Too much evil had fallen upon it. All was lost...

Sarak'den's rage matched Alim'dar's sorrow, and she said, "You want death, Brother? You think you have earned such peace?" He only stared at her, emotionless, lost in his madness. "You will not have it. My curse falls upon you, Brother, and it is this: *your bitterness will forever grow and your lands will become as cold as your righteousness, and neither you nor your loyal people will find rest in the cover of death until the repentance of Drovanius, which may never be in coming!*"

Then, there before us all, Sarak'den clutched her sword and turned it, and fell upon her own blade, sealing her final words with the malice that was in her heart. Pierced through the heart, she died there upon the floor of Alim'dar's chamber, and all except him wept yet another casualty of this war.

THE END OF THE AGE

And so the 1st Age of Sylveria ended with the Sylvai and Haldusians enslaved to the Nescrai. The Metallic Dragons were so weakened by the war that they could do naught but retreat into the mountains, vowing that they would someday rise again to get vengeance upon their enemies and free their children from the bonds of slavery.

Of the First Awakened Sylvai, only five of us survived. Three of them were Alunen, Sveraden and Adaashar. Now, after having seen their people slain and taken into captivity, and after witnessing the death of Sarak'den by her own hand in the placing of the curse upon Alim'dar, they fled Whitestone and traveled in secrecy back to Kronaggas Mountain. There, they burrowed deep through the ruins and found a passage that led into the Temple below. None but I knew that they had gone there, and though they wanted me to come with them, I refused, feeling still that despite all that had happened, there was more I was intended to do. They sealed the entrance into the mountain then, with them inside, and they vowed to one another that they would guard the piece of the stone tablet that there remained encased in an altar as Kronaggas had commanded them, until the time when the prophecies spoken at the start of the war were to be fulfilled. This was all they had left.

Also, Alim'dar survived to the end of the age, but his heart remained filled with such bitterness that the Nescrai had come to fear him, and he was allowed to remain in his isolated and now cursed land.

Of the Awakened Nescrai, the survivors were Norgrash'nar, Haldus'nar—who was imprisoned by the Nescrai—and Kalenen. But shortly after the end of the war, Kalenen took her own life, for even in death she knew that her husband still loved Nirvisa'nen.

All of the other Awakened Naiad, save for myself, were dead by the end of the 1st Age.

And I—Alak'kiin—returned to the place from where I first awakened, in the cave along the northern mountains in the Valley of Naiad, for I was depleted. There, in the darkness, I prayed for death, for absolute misery was upon me. There was no hope for the world; all was lost. Our paradise had been corrupted, and there was nothing left for me, or for any of us. The Dark had won its war upon the Light, here in Sylveria.

But I was not granted death that day; I slept for a long time, then, while the Nescrai dominated the world of Sylveria, keeping the good people who remained under harsh oppression, forcing them to do their labors, treating them as objects of their desires, and abusing them in the most vile of ways. These were shown to me in scattered visions as I slept; horrid nightmares troubled nearly every moment of my sleep. At first, in my unconscious state, I reeled at these obscene visions, but with time, I knew they were for a reason; I knew that they were to prepare me for what was to come.

And whilst these scenes were meant to trouble me, to bring me to a greater understanding, I was given occasional relief, for so too was I given visions of a small pack of animals trotting through the hills and plains north of the mountains of the Valley of Naiad, in a region untouched by war, a place called Kaliim. These were the surviving Dains of Naiad, and frolicking amongst them was one whom I knew very well.

All of these were the things that happened during the 1st Age of Sylveria, in the Shadows of Dragonswake.

Saxon

Septemper 7th, 2014 -- January 27th, 2022

There is Power in Words!

Power-in-Words.net

www.ingramcontent.com/pod-product-compliance
Lightning Source LLC
Chambersburg PA
CBHW071156250626
47159CB00001B/112